Mad Wife Crisis

by

Jemma Forte

Printed in the United Kingdom

Second Edition

Praise for Mad Wife Crisis

"This witty, inventive novel will intrigue every woman who has thought about the men in her past and wondered, 'what if?'" - ***Sarah Pekkanen,*** *bestselling author of* ***Things You Won't Say*** *and* ***The Opposite of Me***

"A witty account of rollercoaster events that will get you thinking about the "what ifs" in your own life" - ***Heat***

"Forte's setup is clever, and the results are by turns hilarious and poignant. Anyone who has ever daydreamed about roads not taken will enjoy the journey." - ***Booklist***

"An easy reading story that bristles with warmth and humour" - ***Hello***

"A must read for all women" - ***Digital Spy***

"*Mad Wife Crisis* addresses some pretty heavy questions with a light, humorous touch, providing a perfectly balanced look at love and marriage and how relationships change over time. Forte tackles love, sex, and infidelity as well as friendship and parenthood...Filled with likable characters, *Mad Wife Crisis* is lively and engaging without becoming too heavy or dramatic." - ***Chicago Book Review***

"Anyone who's ever wondered what could have been if they'd settled down with someone else will enjoy this book. With its unusual structure (told in alternating flashbacks from 1994 until the day before the accident), and it's unexpected ending, this is not run-of-the-mill chick lit. Using a lot of humour, and a few surprisingly deep moments, Forte analyses the nature of happiness, the exhaustion of parenting, the struggle of a midlife crisis and the tricky balance of love and friendship" - ***Shelf Awareness***

Acknowledgements

This book originally came out under a different title and it was Madeleine Milburn who saw to it that it was published. She's an amazing lady and I'm ever grateful to her. Special thanks to my top team, Lucy Townsend and Imogen Forte. Between the two of you my books are looking exactly the way I've always wanted them to.

Writing this book coincided with a pretty turbulent time in my life, my own mid-life crisis if you like. Thank you to my unbelievably wonderful family for seeing me through it.

Mum, Mauro, Dad, Sally, Jessica, Jim, Isabel, Paddy, Imogen, Harry, Georgie, Louie and Alfie, I love you all. Thanks for putting up with me, not that you have an enormous amount of choice.

Thank you to my wonderful friends, you know who you are and to those of you who have supported me by buying my books, writing reviews and engaging on social media. It means so much.

And to Lily and Freddie – love you both to pieces and look forward to slightly embarrassing you for the rest of my life.

PROLOGUE | *Friday May 18th*

Jennifer Wright slammed the door and ran down the road as fast as her ill-fitting footwear would allow her to, tears blurring her vision. She didn't have a plan. All she was conscious of was her need to get away from her husband and his ability to hurt her. Not that he was letting her get away that easily.

'Jen?' Max yelled down the road, clearly in no mood to consider what the neighbours might be thinking. 'What the hell do you think you're doing? Come back. For goodness sake, you've made your point.'

Jennifer ignored him. If anything, she picked up the pace. She'd always loved living in the suburbs of South West London partly because everybody looked out for everybody else. Today however, it would have suited her far better if she'd lived in a place, where people didn't give a damn about their neighbours. That way she could have wailed like a banshee and charged down the road without worrying she'd provided the man walking on the other side of the street, (the dull husband of the quite nice woman at number forty-two) with a juicy bit of gossip.

She'd caught his look of alarm as he'd taken in her tear stained face and heavy coat, which was far too warm for this unusually hot May evening. Not that there was any way she was taking it off, for what Jennifer knew, but the man from number forty-two didn't, was that all she had on underneath was a lace bra, a G-string, suspenders and stockings. The killer heels she'd originally teamed the whole ensemble with had been kicked off mid argument, replaced by a pair of Crocs that happened to be nearest the front door and were usually reserved for gardening purposes. Her stockinged feet were slopping about inside them.

Panting with exertion, Jennifer finally came to the end of the street. Briefly she turned round to see what Max was doing. She could just about still make him out, hanging out of their front door, obviously in two minds about what to do given that their children were sleeping inside.

Screw him.

Karen.

That's who she needed.

Fumbling in her pocket with shaky hands, Jennifer found her mobile which she'd had the sense to grab on her way out.

Half walking, half running now, she rounded the corner onto the busy main road and scrolled through her phone looking for her best friend's number. Wiping her face with the back of her hand she managed to rub away some tears but was surprised by how persistently they kept on coming. Briefly she acknowledged the huge possibility she was having a nervous breakdown.

As she headed for the zebra crossing she listened to Karen's phone ringing and prayed she'd pick up. She did.

'Oh, Karen,' Jennifer managed, speaking loudly against the traffic, choking on tears again.

'Oh my god, what is it? What's wrong?'

The concern in her voice almost floored Jennifer for a second. Thank god Karen's house was only ten minutes away. She couldn't get there soon enough. If only she'd chosen a less-hot coat.

'Oh Karen, it's all gone wrong and I just don't think I can do this anymore....,' Jennifer broke off, half stumbling over an uneven bit of pavement. Wretched Crocs. Then a bus whizzed past just as Karen was answering. It completely drowned out her response.

'Come again Karen, I couldn't hear you.'

'I said where are you? Do you want to come round?'

'Yes please,' Jennifer wailed, putting one foot out onto the road.

'Good,' said Karen 'Well just come straight away and I'll open a...'

But Jennifer never got to hear what her friend was going to open, (though forced to guess she would have gone with a textbook bottle of dry white wine), because at this point her phone was flying high up into the air and she was staring at it aghast, wondering why everything had suddenly gone into slow motion. At the same time, although she didn't exactly feel it, she was also aware of the most enormous impact, of a sickening crunching sound and of the metallic taste of fear, dread and regret coursing through her body which was now being flung skywards having been hit very hard by a car. For a brief moment, just as gravity was about to take command and begin Jennifer's brutal descent toward the hard ground and the bonnet of a Ford Fiesta, she was filled with an illogical, yet undeniable sense of embarrassment. For the thought entering her brain at that precise moment was that, if she was going to be hit by a car, there was a strong chance that whomever was driving and/or an ambulance team were about to discover her very slutty underwear.

And that was the last conscious thought she was to have for a very long time...

1 | FRIDAY
One Week Earlier

Jennifer Wright hadn't been entirely sure for a while now if she really liked her husband anymore. As a result, she'd been suffering from a sort of creeping, low lying anxiety for months. The thought of living out the remainder of her days in the suburbs with him, terrified her and she'd lost count of how many times she'd been struck by one solitary thought recently: *Is this it?*

To some degree, it was less a thought, more a feeling. She was only thirty-eight but felt like she was hurtling in slow motion toward middle- age and decrepitude, while swept up in an unstoppable snowball of routine, malaise and domestic servitude. Lately, she could be in the middle of any number of mundane tasks, when from nowhere she'd be practically knocked over by a violent urge to run barefoot through long grass, dance till dawn (preferably on some form of narcotic), sleep in a yurt, or, failing that, to have the sort of passionate, filthy sex with a stranger that would leave her panting and covered in a film of sweat.

But Jennifer was a married mother of two, with a part time job, and was fully aware, not only of how wildly inappropriate these yearnings were, but also how... impractical. There'd be consequences, ones she didn't have the heart to deal with, and besides, these days, if she danced till dawn it would take her at least a week to recover and having to organise the childcare would be exhausting and very expensive.

'Is this it?' whispered her subconscious, again. The thought it might be freaked her out to say the least. However, at a loss to know what to do about any of it, she'd decided simply to wait things out, to try and remain positive, keep taking the Prozac and not jump out of a window, for the time being.

Until one Friday evening in May, when Jennifer decided it was time to take the matter of her marriage into her own hands.

All relationships went through patches she thought determinedly, clipping on her suspender belt and adjusting her newly bought, black and red bra whilst manhandling her boobs into it. She owed it to the children to try and make things better, and after nine years of togetherness at least she still *loved* Max. It was just a shame it was such a familiar, unexciting version of love which occasionally had the tendency to veer off into violent hatred territory. The fact they hadn't had sex for five months certainly wasn't helping matters.

Feeling surprisingly nervous Jennifer pulled open her wardrobe door so she could appraise herself in the full length mirror that hung behind it.

Wow. She hadn't looked this tarty in a long time. The evening sunlight poured through her bedroom window, bathing the entire room in a golden glow, highlighting the fact that they desperately needed a new carpet.

At first Jennifer felt incredibly self-conscious, standing there, trussed up in broad daylight. Eventually however, she grudgingly admitted that she kind of got away with it. She'd always had an hourglass figure and these days it was probably covered by less flesh than it ever had been even pre children. In her twenties she'd taken her figure for granted. Post-partum however, not only had she been hit with the realisation that actually she wasn't immortal, but had also worked out that she was stood at a fairly major crossroads. One way led to elasticated waists, one piece swimsuits and never being able to reveal her upper arms again, the other to still being able to look good in the odd bit from Top Shop, skinny jeans and the vaguely hateful yet better than frumpy 'yummy mummy' moniker. Jennifer had jogged determinedly in one direction, started doing boot camp religiously at the park twice a week, stopped eating cake and started getting stressed about her marriage, which all did wonders for her figure.

She peered at her face, wondering vaguely how old a complete stranger would guess she was. There was no denying she was in the midst of her fourth decade and yet it was hard to pin point exactly what it was that was different about her face now to how it had been in her twenties. Yet that difference was undeniable. She still had friendly, warm brown eyes but nowadays when she applied eye-shadow much of it disappeared into a crease she was pretty sure hadn't been there before. She had good cheekbones and her thighs looked good, yet she had to make sure she didn't lose *too* much weight or her face was in danger of starting to look gaunt. She had faint crow's feet round her eyes and a bit of a frown line which had deepened visibly around the time her babies had become toddlers at which point there had suddenly been more to frown about.

Don't eat the snail! Don't bash your sister! Don't poo in the bath! Etcetera etcetera.

Turning round so she could glance back over her shoulder and examine what her bottom looked like in her new very uncomfortable G-string, she decided that if she squinted she didn't look *that* far off the girl she'd been when she'd first met Max. Screw it, she thought; fired up by a growing sense of confidence. She was old and wise enough by now to know he wouldn't care anyway. Rather than scrutinising her for imperfections he'd only be seeing the naughty underwear, the effort she was making and the invitation.

She drew the curtains. Better. Now, she just *felt* like a completely different person. Across the room her phone was vibrating. She tottered over to it in her heels. The display showed it was her best friend, Karen, phoning to check up on her.

'I feel like a right old scrubber.'

'Good,' said Karen 'You're supposed to. You're about to seduce your husband.'

'Oh god,' groaned Jennifer, returning to the mirror to examine herself from all angles again. 'I'm not sure I can do this. I'm not sure I *want* to do it truth be told. I've still got this week's episode of The Apprentice to watch.'

'You have to,' Karen said frankly. 'Not see The Apprentice, though at some point do, it's hilarious, but have sex first. If you don't, you run the risk of him going elsewhere.'

Jennifer wasn't so sure. Karen had been flabbergasted when she'd admitted how long their dry spell had been and was clearly working on the proviso that no man could live without sex, but then again, Karen was married to a man who woke her up most mornings with something hard jabbing into her back. Whereas these days, Max seemed to have lost his sex drive completely.

'Still on for a drink next Tuesday?' Jennifer said, changing the subject. It felt weird making small talk while dressed as a sex worker.

'Definitely. I'll try and leave work a bit early and I think Lucy's coming but Esther still hasn't got a babysitter.'

Just then Jennifer heard the sound of Max's key in the lock. 'He's back. I'll call you tomorrow,' she said, cutting off Karen and racing over to the bed where she got herself into position. As she did, it suddenly occurred to her that instead of being consumed by lust, Max might find the sight of her trying to seduce him wildly funny. *Oh my god, what if he laughs at me?*

Quickly, she swerved her mind back round to the task ahead, acknowledging along the way that it was probably as much her fault as it was her husband's that they hadn't done it for so long. She was usually exhausted by the time he got home, busy trying to get the kids to bed and looking forward to nothing wilder than a glass of wine and some telly watching. Tonight however, with the girls at a rare sleepover at their grandparents, there was no excuse. They *would* have sex. She felt quite militant about it.

Downstairs she could hear Max taking his shoes off. She waited for him to call up the stairs, but instead it sounded like he was heading straight for the kitchen. Still, he'd come looking for her soon enough.

Minutes passed. There was no sign of him. Then she heard him leave the kitchen and go into the lounge. Damn. This wasn't the plan. He was supposed to come looking for her, find her leaning back across the bed like a wanton sex goddess. Then, filled with raging desire caused by the fact she was wearing a bra that wasn't flesh coloured and pants that weren't large and from a Marks and Spencer pack of three, he was supposed to leap on her and ravish his way back into an intimate relationship.

Still nothing. She had no choice other than to heave herself back up and reach for the house phone, the suspender belt disappearing rather depressingly into the crevice of her belly. She rang his mobile.

'Hello?'

'What are you doing?' she asked, making a monumental effort to sound less irritated than she felt.

'Nothing. Got myself a beer and I'm watching a bit of sport. Why, what are you doing? What are we having for dinner?'

As Jennifer was treated to a crystal clear image in her head, of her husband in his usual position, lying on the sofa caressing his nuts, 'relaxing' with a bit of sport on, while waiting for dinner to magically appear in front of him, any vague urge she might have had to sleep with him evaporated. She was a woman on a mission though. The bra alone had cost forty pounds. She wasn't giving up that easily.

'Come upstairs.'

'Do I have to? Can't you come here?'

'Please?' begged Jennifer, feeling the last vestiges of sex goddess slip away from her, like smoke.

'Ooof,' exclaimed Max down the phone 'Great goal.'

Jennifer quietly put the phone down and stared into the middle distance for a while before slowly peeling off and unclipping her temptress outfit. Once she had, she shoved it all into the back of her drawer, and replaced the prohibitively expensive underwear with a pair of pyjamas before heading downstairs to cook lamb chops, baked potatoes and green beans, served on a bed of deep resentment.

Later, as she and Max sat masticating their overcooked chops in front of The Apprentice, Jennifer wondered if a man would ever desire or appreciate her body again, or whether that was it until she died. She loved her children, wouldn't swap them for anything in the world and certainly wasn't planning on rocking their status quo by jeopardising what they had as a family. Yet neither could she bear for things to continue as they were, with her feeling so physically frustrated and mentally unfulfilled. Both her ego and her soul were starving, desperate for scraps of anything to fill them up again. Not for the first time she found herself questioning how the decisions she'd made in life, had led to this particularly disappointing moment in time. Then she began plundering the reserves of her memory, something else she'd been doing a lot of lately, searching for feelings she longed to relive, for there was enormous comfort to be taken from the fact that of course, things hadn't always been this way...

2 THE PAST

Aidan, summer of 1994

The alarm beeped, penetrating the deepest of sleeps.

'Jen, wake up. It's already 9 o clock. We've got to get ready and if you want a shower you need to hurry. I said I'd meet Mark at *The Pink Flamingo*.'

'Five minutes,' Jennifer answered drowsily, idly scratching a mosquito bite on her leg. The whirring of the ceiling fan was in danger of lulling her back to sleep again though so she forced herself to open one eye. Despite her groggy state she was already enjoying the gurgle of anticipation building in her tummy.

They'd only arrived on the island of Kos five nights ago after a fortnight of taking it relatively easy on the quieter Greek island of Santorini. Before that they'd been to Mykonos and Rhodes. There had been the odd moment of tension, but generally speaking, she and her friends had managed five weeks of travelling with no major disagreements and were having the time of their lives. They'd originally planned on visiting a few more islands before heading home but Jennifer had a strong feeling that they'd probably spend the remainder of their trip here, until either their money ran out or their livers packed up. Whichever came first. Kos had simply proved too fun to leave, what with Bar Street (self-explanatory), the outdoor clubs that stayed open till the sun was starting to rise in the sky, the sandy beaches and the biggest appeal of all, tonnes of gorgeous men.

They'd all slept with someone, though if she were being totally honest, Jennifer rather regretted her liaison at the beach with a handsome Greek guy on their second night. She knew she'd lived up to the reputation English girls seemed to have, of being easy. By the same token, she'd decided not to lose any sleep over it. She wasn't proud of how little it had meant, but still didn't see why girls should feel any worse than guys did, about what amounted to nothing more than a consensual exchange of bodily fluids. The only thing that had been slightly awkward was bumping into him from time to time. Neither of them could be bothered to keep up the pretence of interest now the act had been done.

Can I borrow your red dress Jen?' asked Esther, emerging from the bathroom in a towel, strawberry blonde hair hanging in damp tendrils around her face.

Since arriving on Kos the four of them had eased into a routine which consisted of sleeping until midday, at which point they'd force themselves to get up, no matter how much their heads were splitting, for tanning purposes. Then, after an afternoon of roasting themselves at the beach, they'd return to the apartment, shower, slather themselves in more after- sun than was probably necessary and have a sleep. Making sure first of course that they'd set the alarm so there was no danger of missing out on another night of partying.

Now, without waiting for a response Esther bent down to extract the dress, which was rolled in a ball and stuffed in Jennifer's rucksack. Only the minute she did, the red dress became exactly what Jennifer wanted to wear that night. Esther borrowing her clothes was starting to get on her nerves, partly because with her long freckled limbs, she looked totally amazing in all of them.

Esther was the rare sort of girl who actually looked better with no make- up on at all. She wasn't overtly sexy and yet was probably the most naturally pretty of the group. Back home, in

London it was usually Jennifer's more obvious sex appeal or Karen's big boobs which guys noticed. However, whilst it might have taken their fellow students at College a few glances before they finally worked out how just how attractive Esther really was, on holiday, her tall physique and bare faced beauty made her the instant star of the beach.

'Um, sorry babe I think I'm going to wear it,' Jennifer said sleepily.

Esther tutted 'Shit, what am I going to wear then?'

'Don't know, but hurry up,' said Karen, drawing deeply on one of the two hundred Merit cigarettes she'd bought at Kos airport, before adjusting her dress straps in order to heave her considerable cleavage up as much as possible. 'I am so up for it tonight.'

'Makes a change,' teased Jennifer.

'Shut up,' said Karen, grinning, teeth white against her brown face.

Not for the first time Jennifer visibly balked at the sight of Karen's hair. When they'd first arrived in Greece Karen had announced her intentions to go blonde with the help of a bottle of Sun- In. Typically, she'd ignored all her friend's protestations completely, despite the fact Sun- In was never designed to be used on dark hair.

As a result, instead of the sun kissed highlights Karen had been imagining, her reward for being so pig headed was patches of dodgy orange hair which looked like straw and was brittle and coarse to the touch. It had looked horrendous when she'd first done it but at least then she'd been pale. Now she was so deeply tanned, it looked even worse.

Luckily for Karen however, what she had in her favour was her attitude. She'd always had incredibly thick skin meaning it would take more than orange hair to ruin her holiday. Whereas, had the same thing 'happened' to Jennifer, it would have been a complete game changer. And as for Lucy, who'd always been self- conscious about her looks, partly because she'd never had brilliant skin and suffered from a bit of acne, if she'd had to deal with the Sun In disaster, she probably wouldn't have left the apartment ever again. Whereas Karen pretty had a 'fuck it' approach to most things, which would get her far in life, occasionally into trouble and lots of male attention.

Tonight, she'd tried to mitigate the disaster by gelling her hair back off her face. It looked seriously bizarre but as ever Karen preferred to concentrate on the positive so was reeking of confidence due to how good her boobs looked in her mini dress. Jennifer admired her for it.

As Jennifer looked at her friends, her best friends, getting ready for their night out, she was filled with the sense that this was a carefree time to be treasured. When they got home, A level results would be waiting for them and the next stage of education would begin. After that, who knew what lay ahead for them? But for now they didn't have to worry about anything except having fun and working on their tans, a task they'd applied themselves to earnestly and with far more zeal than they probably had to their recently taken exams. Only Lucy with her pale, almost translucent skin and mousy blond hair was still roughly the same colour she'd started out, though not for want of trying. She almost seemed proud of the fact her back was burnt and resembled streaky bacon though, for she was currently slipping on a backless halter neck top.

'Do I look alright?' she asked now.

'You look lovely,' said Jennifer sincerely, lazily stretching one leg out over the white sheet she was still entwined in. 'Those polka dot shorts are really cool.'

'Come on,' nagged Karen, who was dying to meet up with her Mark. She'd met him four nights ago. He was twenty four, from Wigan and a policeman which was a constant source of amusement given how horrendously they were all behaving.

'Right,' said Jennifer, heading for the shower.

***

Two hours, a quick pizza (they ate as cheaply as they could every night, preferring to save their money for drinks) and one bar later, they were in the best club on the island. ***Club Kaluha***. The club was huge, and outrageously expensive to get into unless you struck it lucky and got a pass from one of the PR's who scouted Bar Street looking for girls to entice in. Jennifer and her friends hadn't paid to get in once so far, but poor Mark and his mates had had to stump up every night, much to their chagrin.

There was an inside section of the club but the majority of it was outside and in the middle was a massive pirate ship surrounded by palm trees. Walking in, having greeted the bouncers who by now they were on first name terms with, they were met by a wall of house music and what felt almost like an electrical charge of energy in the air, palpable anticipation. Then again, everything was always going to feel magical when there was a warm breeze, everyone was in holiday mode and people's biggest concern was who fancied them.

'You alright,' said Lucy to Jennifer, coming to join her on one of the outside seating areas where she had a good view of the ship and the main bar. She'd been sitting there for a while now, on her own, enjoying the music and watching the world go by.

'Yeah, well happy. You?'

'Good. Bit sad though. I don't want this to end.'

'I know,' said Jennifer 'It's been amazing. Still, I reckon uni's going to be a right laugh.'

Lucy nodded. 'Wish we were all going to the same one. You and Karen are so lucky.'

'Look at Esther,' interrupted Jennifer, nudging Lucy hard and laughing.

The two girls chuckled as they watched Mark's mate, who for some inexplicable reason was called 'Bonehead,' trying desperately to chat Esther up. Esther looked decidedly unimpressed as Bonehead advanced ever closer to her, shouting in her ear against the music. At the same time she was backing away, partly because he had a terrible lisp so was literally spraying her with his enthusiasm.

'Mark's nice but his mates are well annoying,' said Lucy.

'I know,' agreed Jennifer 'I feel like we've slightly lost Karen to Mark too which is a bit of a shame. She's obsessed.'

And then, at exactly the same time, they saw him.

'Oh my god,' mouthed Lucy. 'Are you looking where I am?'

Jennifer certainly was. He was absolutely gorgeous. Without even realising she was doing it, she suddenly found herself sitting up and angling her entire body in his direction.

He was standing by the bar, to the left of the ship, and was nodding his head in time to the music, watching a group of girls who were dancing next to him, enjoying their buzz. He completely stood out from the crowd. He was wearing a t shirt and combat trousers but his body was that of a demi-god and to Jennifer he seemed to ooze testosterone, sex appeal and something more dangerous. His arms were muscular yet lean and brown. He put Mark and his mates in the shade. They were mere boys compared to this specimen of manhood.

Just then he turned and caught Jennifer's eye and as he did, a number of things happened. Firstly, Lucy realised in a nanosecond she was out of the running. Secondly, Jennifer suddenly sensed that the next few days were going to be very interesting, and thirdly he gave her such a confident grin she suspected he was thinking along the same kind of lines as she was. It was as if he liked what he saw but more thrillingly, clearly knew he could have it.

'He's coming over,' squealed Lucy all flustered.

'Oh my god,' panicked Jennifer, realising her friend was right. 'I shouldn't have had that slice with pepperoni on it. Quick Luce, smell my breath.'

'Fuck off weirdo,' complained Lucy, shoving her away. 'And no, you're fine anyway.'

Jennifer stopped breathing on Lucy, pulled her skirt down and rearranged her legs to look as slim as possible. As he continued his approach, she flicked her long, brown hair over one shoulder, realising as she did how obvious she was being. She flicked it back again but then worried in case she looked like she was having some kind of attack.

'Alright girls,' he said, finally coming to a stop directly in front of Jennifer. His accent was broad and northern.

'Alright,' said Jennifer looking him straight in the eye, acknowledging the instant flicker of attraction that she'd felt between them. This was going to be so much fun.

She frowned at Lucy who was making a silly face at her as if to say *I see you flirting Missy.*

'Drink?'

Jennifer nodded, her eyes never leaving his. Nerves dissipating, she concentrated on letting him know she was more than a match for him and felt her stomach flip as he grinned again and looked her up and down in a way that could only be described as filthy. Every nerve ending fizzing, Jennifer watched as he returned to the bar where the queue for drinks was three people deep, while Lucy elbowed her excitedly in the ribs.

'Oh my god, oh my god, oh my god,' squealed Jennifer, eyes still glued to him.

Unsurprisingly, the barmaid noticed him at once and served him straightaway. She obviously knew him and the easy way in which he bantered with her, made Jennifer briefly wonder what she was getting herself into.

A minute later he returned carrying three lethal looking cocktails. Jennifer was pleased he'd got one for Lucy.

'Here you go. B52's'

'Thanks,' said Jennifer, tossing her hair again and shoving her breasts out as far as she could, until that is, she realised Lucy was laughing at her at which point she returned them to their normal vantage point.

'You're gorgeous,' he said, matter-of-factly.

'Not so bad yourself,' she shot back, thrilled by his flirting.

'Thanks for the drink,' said Lucy, giving her friend a large wink and slinking off to leave them to it and find some fun of her own.

Half an hour later, Jennifer had found out that his name was Aidan, that he'd been on Kos all summer and that he was the most exciting person she'd ever met. He didn't seem to conform to any rules. He'd left home, was travelling the world, his only real plan being to permanently escape his home town of Carlisle and to end up living in Australia. They'd already kissed and it was so charged with sexual excitement it had practically blown her head off. Now he was sliding his hand gently up and down her thigh, which tickled a bit, in a gloriously shivery kind of way.

'Do you want one?' he said suddenly, pulling a little bag of white pills out of his pocket. He took one out and offered it to her. It had a picture of a dove on it.

'Not sure,' said Jennifer, truthfully.

'Your mates can have one too, I've got plenty and they're very clean.'

Jennifer shrugged, determined not to display how much her mind was racing while she worked out what to do. She'd not had ecstasy before but everyone she knew who had, like Karen, said it was amazing.

'If Karen's up for it I will,' she said, leaving Aidan behind to go and get her friend who was inside on the dance floor.

Once she knew she was out of his line of vision, Jennifer stopped trying to walk sexily and started practically galloping toward her friend, gesturing to Karen to meet her half way. 'See the guy over there, Aidan, he's got some e's,' she shouted into her friend's ear over the deafeningly loud music. 'Shall we have one?'

'Oh my god, so not only have you pulled the hottest person on the island, he's got pills as well?' she shouted back, out of breath from dancing, eyes shining. 'You are such a bitch. Why didn't you say earlier? Make sure he gives one to Mark too.'

Jennifer nodded and turned on her heel, thoughts racing. She quickly came to a decision. With regard to the pill, she should probably just go with the flow. Her dad had always told her that in life it was better to regret something you'd done than something you hadn't which sounded like good advice to her, even if he probably hadn't had class A drugs in mind when he'd said it......

One hour later and Jennifer was standing in the middle of the club, with her hands in the air, feeling happier than she ever had in her entire life. 'Rhythm is a Dancer' by Snap was playing, a tune they'd heard an average of at least three times a day recently only at this precise moment it sounded more amazing than it ever had before.

Jennifer scraped her hands through her hair and exhaled noisily; letting the rushes she was experiencing travel up her body. Right now there was not one place on earth she'd rather be.

Suddenly she felt Aidan's hands on her shoulders, massaging her, kneading her. His touch was so firm and felt so good that she staggered a little bit, almost losing her balance. She turned round.

'Alright,' he grinned, chewing gum, his eyes wide and pupils really black.

'Yeah,' was all Jennifer could manage to utter, but she grinned back at him and it didn't seem to matter in the slightest that she'd lost the power of speech. She literally couldn't care less. All that did matter was that she was with her best friends, and with Aidan, who happened to be the most beautiful man she'd ever seen in her life, listening to music that was literally transporting her to another dimension. She looked over at Karen who was dancing at a hundred miles per hour as if someone had told her all human life depended on it, Mark watching adoringly from the side, a daft grin on his face. Meanwhile, Esther and Lucy had kicked their shoes off and were having a chat on the cushions, stopping now and again only to give each other a big hug. God she loved them all.

'Good isn't it?' said Aidan.

But Jennifer was too fucked now to reply. Her jaw was trembling a bit and she could feel her eyes rolling slightly in the back of her head but she wasn't remotely bothered. Quite the opposite in fact. Instead she was relishing every minute of the warm, soupy sensations that had taken over her limbs and merely wanted to enjoy them flooding over her.

'Hey you, you ok? Come and sit down,' instructed Aidan.

Stumbling slightly but happy to do as she was told, Jennifer let herself be led to the cushions where her mates were sitting.

'Jen,' they said delightedly as if they hadn't seen her for a week, eyes huge and shining. 'Come here babe. Love you.'

'Love you too,' she said softly before lying down on the cushions. She was overcome by a desire to writhe around on them but something told her it was probably best not to.

Maybe she'd run that thought past the girls.

'Don't you feel like rolling around on the cushions?'

'What?' said Esther, whose jaw was also quivering slightly.

'I said,' repeated Jennifer, suddenly desperate for some water 'Don't you feel like rolling around on the cushions?'

Lucy nodded. 'I do, I feel like stuffing them up my top too and pretending I'm up the duff.'

This struck Jennifer as not only funny but wise.

'And I feel like sticking one down my pants so I've got a massive butt,' added Esther.

'And I feel like....' Jennifer tried to join in but was defeated once again by ever increasing sensations that were flooding her system. After a long pause, she uttered 'sticking one up my arse.' Only by then, the thread had been rather lost so it came out as a totally random statement. However, rather than feel embarrassed, she was amused by how ludicrous it all was. Besides, what anybody thought just didn't seem to be a problem.

'Stick what up your arse?' enquired Aidan, looking confused.

'Nothing,' muttered Jennifer, the notion of trying to explain her thought process far too daunting.

'You girls are funny,' said Aidan, head bouncing in time to the beat, and as they bathed in his compliment, it was like they'd known him for years.

'Where did you all meet?'

'School,' said Esther looking really out of it and clearly loving the next tune that had just come on 'Everybody's Free' by Rozalla.

Karen came whooping over 'Come on you lot. Tune! Come and dance Jen, on your feet now.'

'Too wasted,' she managed.

'But happy?' checked Aidan.

'Oh yeah,' she said, flopping back onto the cushions.

Everybody's free to feel good.

She waved her hands around, playing air piano.

'Hey, you girls are great,' said Aidan, continuing on the same theme, chewing gum frenetically.

'We sure are,' concurred Lucy, trying to pull her friends in for a hug, but Jennifer was too wasted. She just wanted to sit in peace in her own space without being manhandled.

'Love you girls.'

'Love you too,' agreed Jennifer, hardly able to open her eyes, she was rushing so intensely.

'Even Bonehead's alright,' said Esther, looking over to where he was busy stacking boxes.

'I may have let Bonehead have a cheeky half, whereas this lunatic told me she definitely wasn't coming up so she's had a whole one,' Aidan said, gesturing to Jennifer.

'Have you?' said Esther and Lucy in unison, slack jawed.

'Yup,' said Jennifer, collapsing into the cushions again. 'Oh my god this tune is amazing.'

'Nutter,' said Esther.

'Can I have another one?' asked Jennifer.

'No you cannot,' said Aidan, stroking her leg as her friends looked on, not knowing whether to be impressed or worried by how well Jennifer had taken to the drug. 'I can see I'm going to have my work cut out with you, you little minx.'

And that was it. From that sentence forward, continuing in the vein of giving everything little or no real deliberation, choosing instead to be steered only by instinct and desire, as you do when you're young, Jennifer and Aidan were an item.

3 Present Day

Everything was very, very quiet, apart from the dull and monotonous yet ominous thudding in her head. There was stuff going on around her, commotion, chaos even, but she could only very vaguely decipher what any of it was. It seemed far away and she wasn't sure she had the inclination to tune in properly anyway, for instinct told her that if she were to, that suddenly everything would really hurt.

Instead she let herself drift further toward a state of mental limbo, refusing to choose the path of either resistance or acceptance. Something terrible had happened. That was a certainty. Her entire body was like a piece of lead, and she had precisely no control over it.

Then, a scream pierced the warm, dense fog she was in. It was a guttural, horrifying sound.

'Jen,' yelled the same voice, their tone desperate and distressed.

Karen.

It was Karen.

And then came another voice, one she didn't recognise, telling Karen to stay back. Not to touch.

She knew she should probably be feeling more than she was. Doing something perhaps, and yet doing anything was a complete and utter impossibility. It never occurred to her to open her eyes. She didn't think she could, anyway, and yet still she managed to be dimly aware of flashing lights and at one point of someone pulling her eyelids and asking her things. She wished they'd all go away and let the soupy haziness which was shrouding her, envelope her completely. That would be easier.

4 Saturday

While Max went to collect the children from his parents, Jennifer raced round the house trying to get it into a vaguely fit state. Friends were coming for lunch and she was running behind. If she was honest she wasn't feeling a huge amount of joy about the fact they were coming. Lately they'd had a lot of people over and while it was nice to socialise, Saturdays were starting to feel as structured and routined as the rest of the week, what with the cooking, cleaning and never- ending washing-up and putting away. Still, in reality, if it was Karen and Pete who were coming over, she'd be looking forward to it a whole lot more. Apart from anything else, Karen wouldn't care if the house was a tip, or if she served up a bit of old spaghetti.

Whereas with Judith and Henry Gallagher, she felt obliged to achieve that 'I've thrown this magnificent feast together effortlessly, a la Nigella, wearing an unstained, silk dressing gown and simultaneously raising two angelic children in a house liberally festooned with fairy lights,' look, that actually requires *tonnes* of effort, perspiration, lots of shouting at the children and some swearing. But then, when it came to Judith and Henry, 'friends' was probably rather a loose term and therein lay the problem.

Judith was a work colleague of Max's who was alright...ish, but she talked about work incessantly, in a way which usually made Jennifer feel totally excluded from proceedings. With Judith always hogging Max, Jennifer was left feeling obliged to entertain Henry, who frankly was hard work. A quiet, uninspiring, pretty humourless bloke, Henry was one of those people who liked to exist under an umbrella of shyness, as if by labelling himself thus, he was excused from having to make any effort on the conversation front. As far as Jennifer was concerned however, once past the age of twenty-one, no matter how 'shy' anyone was, they should still at least pepper a chat with the odd question, thus making it a two-way thing. As it was, whenever Jennifer was doing her bit by talking to Henry she felt like she was interviewing him.

To add to the already non enticing prospect of lunch with the Gallagher's, this was the third time in two years she and Max had invited them over for a meal and they'd never returned the invitation. Max insisted it was a good idea for him to 'keep in' with Judith, for work reasons. But Jennifer was starting to think it was probably Judith's turn to spend hundreds of pounds in the supermarket on feeding *their* faces, and that furthermore, perhaps she didn't give a shit if they 'kept in' with her or not.

Having finally finished tidying downstairs, even going so far as to squirt a bit of polish on the coffee table so at least the room *smelled* clean, she started on the children's bedrooms. By the time she'd got to her and Max's room though she'd lost the will, and was suddenly overwhelmed by the prospect of still having to produce a meal for four adults, three children and a baby. So, after she'd stuffed everything that was on the floor into the laundry basket, she stopped for a second and sunk onto the bed, taking advantage of the unusual silence. For a few minutes she reflected on how easily she'd given up on her mission to seduce Max. As she did, the disappointment from the previous evening washed over her once more, and she found herself wondering idly when and indeed *if* she should try donning her new underwear again. After all, Max wasn't psychic, so to be fair to him how could he have known what she'd had in mind? If she'd been really serious about having her wicked way with him, she probably should have gone downstairs and shown him what she was wearing because if he'd had the visual stimulation maybe he would have gone for it. So why hadn't she done that?

She sighed. Marriage. It was such bloody hard work sometimes. Make an effort was all anybody said and it *was* an effort. That was the problem. She missed the days when being with each other wasn't any effort at all. The days when *not* being together were the ones which felt like the effort.

Eventually Jennifer willed herself to get up and continue her attack on the house but it wasn't happening because her thoughts had turned to a subject which had been occupying her mind a lot lately. Sex. Or rather, lack of it. As soon as she allowed the thought in, she felt a lurch of possibility in her nether regions.

The next thing she knew, despite the fact the potatoes desperately needed peeling if lunch had any hope at all of being served for one o clock, her hand had slid into her knickers. Right, she needed to be quick so who should she think about? Aware that time wasn't on her side she turned to an old favourite, if you like, a golden oldie, though part of her detested the fact she was still dining out on sex she'd had nearly twenty years ago. However, when it came to fantasy, Aidan was still guaranteed to get her going. And fast.

Once again Jennifer returned to a hot, airless room, which had a bed with a squeaky mattress and a ceiling fan, and replayed the best sex she'd ever had in her entire life. Images of brown limbs entwined and his strong hard body pressing into hers, manoeuvring her into positions she hadn't even known existed, swam into her head. An enjoyable three minutes later, and her very old flame was just on the brink of giving her an almighty orgasm when she became dimly aware of the key turning in the door downstairs. She couldn't believe it...

'We're back,' called Max up the stairs.

'Muuuuummy,' two little voices yelled in unison, feet charging up the stairs.

'Shit,' gasped Jennifer, withdrawing her hand, and springing into an upright position, utterly frustrated. Thirty seconds more and she'd definitely have been there. 'Hello -ooo,' she called back, slightly screechily. 'Have you had a lovely, lovely time kids?'

As she leapt up from the bed she experienced a bit of a head rush. Quickly she patted her hair down and did her jeans up, legs slightly wobbly.

The children barrelled in. 'Mummy.'

'Hello my little loves, how are you?' she warbled 'I've missed you. Were you good for Grandma?'

'Yes,' said Eadie.

'What about you Pol'?'

'Yes,' her youngest agreed, though she seemed more interested in trying to get her t-shirt off.

'What are you doing?'

'I need a wee.'

'Ok, well you don't need to take your top off to have a wee do you? Come here.'

Just then Max called up the stairs. 'Jen, what the hell have you been doing? You haven't peeled the bloody potatoes. They're going to be here soon and nothing's ready. You haven't even laid the table.'

Jennifer rolled her eyes so vigorously they actually hurt a little bit. 'Well... feel free to go for it.'

'Alright, there's no need to be sarcastic about it, it's just you said you'd get things under control while I got the girls and nothing's done.'

'Alright,' said Jennifer testily, stomping onto the landing and into the bathroom so she could plonk Polly on the toilet before heading downstairs.

She found Max in the kitchen, peeling potatoes angrily. Whole chunks were coming out.

'I'll do that,' she said, trying to grab the peeler off him.

'No, it's fine, I'm doing it.'

'What are you so grumpy about anyway? Is it that much of a big deal that little wifey hasn't done everything by the time you've got back?'

'Little wifey hasn't done anything, let alone everything,' muttered Max.

'Oh rubbish,' disagreed Jennifer. 'The house was a complete state if you must know, and besides, I'm getting a bit sick of having people over every single weekend when we don't even enjoy it.'

'Yes we do,' said Max, shooting her a look of real disdain.

'No we don't,' she replied petulantly, simultaneously acknowledging that now they were sounding like their children.

'We do,' said Max, oblivious.

'Oh yeah, we're having a great time preparing for the arrival of smug-arse, 'high powered' Judith and dullard Henry. And it goes without saying I can't wait to spend the rest of the day washing up after them while you bum- lick her,' huffed Jennifer.

Max wrinkled his nose at her choice of words, which actually made Jennifer giggle for a second and broke the tension.

'Muuuuuuuuuuuum,' yelled Polly from upstairs. 'I've got wee wee on my sock.'

'Yours,' said Max.

Jennifer turned on her heel, faintly wondering if she'd get away with quickly locking herself in the spare room, so she could finish what she'd started earlier. Hmm... probably not.

***

Half an hour later the doorbell rang meaning the people she couldn't be bothered to see, let alone entertain, had arrived.

Taking a deep breath and summoning up a smile she opened the door.

'Hello everybody, come in, come in,' said Jennifer, ushering them all into the house and down the hallway. 'It's so lovely to see you all. Oh my, look at James, hasn't he grown and doesn't he look *so* like you Henry?'

'He's a chip off the old block alright,' agreed Judith, immaculate as ever in tasteful navy, which she'd offset with funky 'weekend' jewellery and ballet pumps. 'No questioning who his dad is.'

Jennifer agreed totally. James really did look exactly like Henry, only given he was ten years old, looking like a gone to seed, middle- aged man wasn't necessarily a good thing. 'So how was your journey?' Jennifer enquired brightly, snapping out of her reverie before anyone noticed her staring.

'Fine,' said Judith, kissing her on both cheeks and handing her a bottle of wine. 'Sorry we're a bit late. Work's been so manic I simply had to have a bit of a chill out this morning! I bet Max did too, we've literally been working like Trojans this week.'

'I can imagine,' said Jennifer, quite wanting to punch her.

An hour and a half later than planned, lunch was finally on the verge of being served up. The children were all starving despite having been fed various 'just to keep you going' snacks and were getting fractious. Judith and Henry had polished off two entire bags of kettle chips and had already had an argument about who was driving home. Oscar, their eighteen-month old baby, was having a sleep upstairs and they were well into a third bottle of wine. Meanwhile, Max was sucking up to Judith so much it was making Jennifer's skin crawl. She herself was worryingly pissed given that she still had to get lunch on the table.

As Judith roared with laughter at yet another dull work anecdote of Max's, Jennifer flinched. The way Max was giving her his undivided attention was grounds for jealousy quite frankly, only she couldn't be bothered to make a fuss. Instead she just felt saddened that every time she tried to join in with a vaguely witty remark he barely looked in her direction. Perhaps she should get her tits out she thought wryly. Run round the kitchen with them jiggling about.

With little enthusiasm Jennifer replenished the crisp bowl, (this time with Frazzles and Pom Bears instead of posh Kettle Chips – it was all she had left). As she did so she smiled weakly at dull Henry who was sat on a stool by the island like a fat useless turd. She was just about to ask him yet another question about how his work was going when she realised she didn't care and couldn't be bothered. So instead she turned her back on him, and bent down to open the oven to investigate what might be happening in there. As boiling hot air blasted her in the face, she realised she was one hundred percent, definitely, without a shadow of a doubt, drunk.

She was also glad and a little bit smug, that for once, she'd cut corners by picking up (on Karen's recommendation) some small stuffed chickens from the local deli. Not having to cook a meat dish of some description meant all she'd had to do in theory was make the roast potatoes and cobble together a salad. So why did it all feel as stressful as though she'd been preparing a banquet for eighty under the same conditions as the Masterchef final?

Seconds later she emerged from the oven once more, red in the face, sweating, and clutching the ludicrously heavy tray in an oven glove only to realise that the island needed clearing before she could put it down.

'Max,' she called over to where he was deep in conversation with Judith about something tedious.

'Max!'

'Hey, there's no need to yell. What is it?' he said, trying to sound like he wasn't snapping when in fact that was exactly what he was doing.

'Sorry,' she said, hands practically on fire. 'Clear a space for this. It's very heavy,' she grimaced.

'Oh right,' he said, finally realising her plight.

Finally dumped on the side, one by one, Jennifer lifted the little chickens out of the roasting tray and onto the chopping board. They were less chickens really, more parcels of poussin, tied up with string and stuffed with pork and herbs. Jennifer immediately decided that she wouldn't bother fobbing the meaty creations off as her own. After all, she'd never boned a piece of meat in her life (fnarr fnarr) and had certainly never been arsed to tie up anything you could eat with string.

'Ooh, those look wonderful Jennifer,' said Judith, gliding over to have a look at what she was about to stuff her self- satisfied face with. 'Aren't you lucky Max? That's what comes of having a wife at home who's got time to actually create things like this.

Poor Henry is lucky if I remember to buy him a ready meal aren't you?'

'I do work,' said Jennifer, defensive.

'Do you?' said Judith, looking first surprised and then apologetic, as if she'd just realised her error. 'Oh god of course you do, and it goes without saying that looking after children is probably the hardest job of all. I certainly wouldn't have had another if I'd had to stay at home and look after them,' she honked, loudly enough for her offspring to hear and therefore quite possibly need therapy in the future.

'No, I mean, I do *work*. I have a job,' explained Jennifer '*And* I look after the kids. I work at an estate- agents on the high street three days a week.'

'Oh god brilliant,' said Judith lamely 'that must be really fun.'

Jennifer picked up the carvers and tried not to look menacing. God she really did feel quite arseholed. She needed to eat.

'Those look good,' said Henry, ambling over.

'Right, well, why don't you all sit down?' ordered Jennifer with meaning, wanting them to give her some space while she plated up. 'Judith, get the kids sat down. We'll do their plates first.'

'Oh right,' she said, looking startled at having been asked to do anything.

Jennifer didn't care though. She was too busy trying to figure out if the chickens were definitely cooked through. To her alarm they looked a bit pinky inside and a bit...well.... unappetising really.

'So, what's that then?' Max asked, also looking alarmed by the colour of the meat.

'Oh, that's just the pork they're stuffed with. Don't worry, it's supposed to look like that,' Jennifer assured him, secretly wondering if a night on the toilet lay ahead for them all.

'They don't carve very well, do they?' Max added, in a muted whisper.

Jennifer gazed hopelessly at the chickens which had sort of collapsed in on themselves and were looking less and less appealing by the second. Sort of like grey and pink mush.

'Just get it on the plates,' she muttered, feeling deeply stressed now and too pissed and hot to handle the situation. She was pretty certain it was just the pork stuffing that was lending them that strange hue so they were just going to have to go with it. Frankly she was past caring, though she did add as an aside 'But make sure you give the kids the bits from around the outside.'

Once the children had all been given their plates of food (which they unanimously declared they didn't like before having even tried it) and their drinks, (one beaker of juice being knocked over immediately as tradition required), the adults got on with helping themselves to lots of salad and potatoes.

'You didn't make these yourself did you?' Judith asked Jennifer, looking slightly worried as she surveyed her plate of unidentifiable meat.

And here it was, crunch time, time for Jennifer to explain that no, of course she hadn't made them and that yes, they did look a bit weird didn't they? And yet, for some reason known only to the inner machinations of her befuddled brain, that isn't what came out.

Instead, the normal Jen, the one who was usually pretty down to earth about stuff, was punched in the head, literally knocked out flat by the other part of her that was dominant at that precise moment. That is to say, the part that was exhausted by the daily grind, that was strung out, drunk, in need of a holiday and some rampant sex, and who was also suffering from a monumental mid- life crisis and had been prescribed anti -depressants only a few weeks earlier. That Jennifer took over and said, after an unnaturally long pause 'Yes I did... I did make them'

At the other end of the table Max looked confused and frowned at his plate.

'Wow,' said Judith tentatively. 'They look really... complicated. How did you go about it?'

'Well.....' Jennifer said gingerly, feeling suddenly drowned by her own lie 'I... er..... bought them, boned them...and then stuffed them with pork and herbs before... kind of, tying them up.'

'Right,' said Judith and in that moment Jennifer knew that Judith knew that she was talking absolute bollocks.

'Mum,' piped up Eadie, looking miserable.

'Yes darling,' said Jennifer, teeth gritted. 'What is it?'

'I don't like my beef. It tastes like cat poo. Can I have some toast?'

'It's chicken not beef and it's *please may I have* some toast?' replied Jennifer.

'Please may I have some toast?'

'Yes,' sighed Jennifer faintly 'Anyone else?'

For a second Max looked sorely tempted but soon readjusted his expression when Jennifer glowered at him on her way to the toaster.

The rest of the meal was pretty torturous. Only Henry seemed blissfully unaware that he was eating something which resembled road-kill. Everyone else performed a sort of cutlery ballet- dance around their plate, consuming lots of potatoes and salad, and expertly leaving a pile of pinky grey mush to one side, with either their knife and fork, or a napkin, placed cunningly over the top.

After the meal Jennifer cleared away, scraping tonnes of discarded meat into the food recycling bin. As she did so, she wondered at what point she'd become so sad and pathetic that she couldn't have admitted that she hadn't made the disgusting food herself and that probably none of them should have touched it, in case they all got the chronic shits. When had she become the sort of person who cared what people like Judith and Henry thought anyway? When had she transformed into such a middle class stereotype, desperately trying to impress? When had she turned into her mother?

Much later that night as she climbed gratefully between the sheets, head thumping with a same day hangover, she said to Max who was already half asleep 'Chicken was a bit weird wasn't it?'

'It was alright,' he said, his eyes shut and his body turned away from her. 'It just looked a bit like cat food. Why did you say you'd made it?'

'Don't know,' she replied truthfully, staring at the ceiling, hot with embarrassment just thinking about it.

'You did yourself a disservice anyway,' he added. 'Your cooking's far nicer and Judith doesn't cook much so it's not like you needed to compete. She works too hard to ever get round to doing any domestic stuff.'

'Oh, so now you're having a go at me for not making something are you?' Jen retorted defensively.

'No,' he sighed, clearly wishing she'd shut up and go to sleep. 'I'm giving you a compliment on your cooking really but I'm also saying I think they knew you hadn't made it anyway.'

'Really?' she said, despite the fact she'd figured this out on her own, having it confirmed was mortifying, to the point where *another* bad night's sleep was probably on the cards. 'Why?'

'Because you went weird and replied really slowly, so it was obvious.'

'Oh god I'm so strange,' she whimpered. 'The thing is I'm feeling a bit down at the moment you know.'

'I know,' he said, and with that he fell fast asleep, as he had an annoying habit of doing when he was tired, leaving his wife to ponder in the darkness the fact that lying hadn't really achieved anything. In fact, it was clear to her that the only thing she'd stuffed by doing so (and it certainly wasn't the chickens) was herself.

Perhaps the whole debacle was a sign that she needed to be more honest about a whole load of things.

Two hours later, bored of her insomnia, head whirring, Jennifer slipped out of bed and crept into the spare room. Able to spread out she tried to relax. Half an hour later, still awake, she decided to finish what she'd started earlier in the day in the hope that a good healthy orgasm might help her get to sleep. And so it was that she returned to that hot summer back in 1994 when, unlike now, whether they cooked or not was of little or no consequence to her or her friends; they'd had far more interesting things to think about.

5 THE PAST

Aidan, summer of 1994

'Come with me,' said Aidan, the green eyes she'd got so used to, bore into her, pleading with her. 'I know we've only known each other five minutes but what we've got doesn't come along every day. I'm telling you.'

'How can I come with you?' repeated Jennifer, who inside was in complete turmoil. Something was pulling her, like a magnet, telling her to throw caution to the wind, to follow her heart, or possibly more accurately, her loins. They'd barely come up for air since they'd met and Jennifer had never known anything remotely like it. She knew she was relatively inexperienced on the sex front, having only slept with three people in total (actually four; she kept forgetting Greek bloke on beach), but Aidan had made her feel things she hadn't dreamed were possible. They fitted. In bed they made total sense and as far as she could tell he was also an exciting person, someone who was creating his own path in life to tread, one not constrained by parental pressure or some traditional idea of how things should be played out. And that was the problem in a way. Jennifer had always *liked* knowing how things should map out. It had never occurred to her to stray even remotely from the plan which she and her parents were in agreement was the right one for her. The right one for most people.

School, college, travelling. Next on the list was university, followed by career, marriage, babies. That was life. Wasn't it?

And yet here was someone asking her to go completely off-piste. And she was tempted. Sorely tempted. She was pretty sure she loved him, or was definitely on her way to falling in love with him and knew if she let him go she might regret it forever. The thought of never sleeping with him again and therefore not experiencing that unbelievably exquisite pleasure was unbearable too. She licked her lips and stared down at her green flip flops. Her feet were pleasingly brown. It was *so* hot.

'Look,' said Aidan 'I'm not going to beg. That's not my style. And if you say no I guess I'll understand, though I think you'd be making a massive mistake. Like I said, what we've got is special. I know it is, and besides, what's the worst that could happen? I'm asking you to come away with me, but I wouldn't be kidnapping you. If it didn't work out you could just get on a plane home.'

'But my university place...?' questioned Jennifer, wondering if she could really deny herself the opportunity to be with him when he'd turned her entire world upside down in a matter of days. Maybe it was time she was more adventurous? And he was right, she could always change her mind, couldn't she? But as this thought trailed away it was replaced by the feeling of absolute certainty that her parents would be beyond livid with her for being so irresponsible and for not consulting them. Then again, it *was* her life.

'Look, the boat leaves in half an hour. I'm going to be on it,' said Aidan. 'If you're coming with me, you need to say goodbye to the girls and get your stuff. What's it to be?'

'Oh god,' said Jennifer. 'I don't know.' And for precisely ten more minutes she still didn't.

And then she had a chat with Karen who looked at her with such horror that she was even contemplating the idea of going off with someone she'd known for a total of seventeen days that something took over. Something irritatingly sensible.
And so it was that the boat sailed off with a hurt and more devastated than he'd imagined he might have been Aidan, taking him off for adventure and ultimately Australia.

She may have made what she thought was the 'right' decision but that didn't prevent Jennifer from feeling utterly desolate and distraught. She wailed as that boat sailed off into the distance and at one point even contemplated throwing herself off the jetty and swimming after it. Anything to have just one more feel of those arms around her.

What had she done? Would she regret this for the rest of her life?

6 Present Day

'Stay with us Jennifer, come on love, you can do this. Hang in there.'

Why was everyone yelling? She was so tired. All she wanted to do was sleep. She was so close to being able to just slip away yet simply wasn't being *allowed* to. She felt very muddled about this and slightly bullied.

'Patient's suffering agonal respirations and has a C02 of eleven. Likely in anaphylactic shock. Let's commence CPR.'

'Jen, please hang in there, I'm so *so* sorry. I love you.'

'Sorry Mr Wright, can you please just stay out of the way. It's very important.'

What was Max doing here, she wondered. For a second she was tempted to open her eyes to have a look but she wasn't able to because suddenly a burning sensation swept through her so violently she would have done anything to make it stop. It was pain on a level she wouldn't ever have thought possible. Every cell in her body was on fire, doused in hot, white agony. Then, as quickly as it showed itself it subsided, and once again she reverted to her numb state of nothingness.

Then, someone was applying pressure to her which hurt in a different way. She craved peace and all at once sensed a way in which she could achieve it, for there was definitely a direction she could go that would remove all this pain, plus any further possibility of it.

She reflected for a second, suspended in time and space, floating almost. In all honesty she wasn't totally sure she wanted to go that way either. She wasn't ready, which meant there was only one option left available to her. So once more she submitted to the grey fog of nothing. And as she sunk back into it, more cries of panic sounded around her.

Meanwhile, as the paramedics went about their frenzied business of trying to save her life, the strangest things were happening in Jennifer's bruised brain.

None of us can really comprehend what the human brain is capable of doing, in the same way that Jennifer had no clue as to the true capabilities of her laptop. All she tended to use her PC for was to write e mails, do a bit of shopping or social networking, meaning its dual core processor was never fully taken advantage of. She was always stunned when Max, who was far more tech savvy than her, did some simple task on her computer, in a way that made her realise she was only ever utilising around ten percent of what it could probably do, if only she knew how to operate it properly.

It's the same with the human brain, only on a far grander and more mysterious scale, its true power being so tricky to un-tap. Most of its work and activity happens at a deeply sub conscious level and yet, even beyond that, there are areas of it which we never unearth even when dreaming.

Right at that second, within Jennifer's skull, a series of lightning fast connections were being made, ones which she never usually would have been privy to if her head hadn't made contact with the hard ground quite as brutally as it had, thus flinging her software into disarray. Something extraordinary was happening.

As her synapses furiously connected and fused, three tunnels of white light suddenly showed themselves to her. There was one to the left, one straight ahead and one to the right. Not for the first time that day Jennifer wondered if she was dying. Was this what death looked like? Instinct told her it was something different though and suddenly she knew, without needing to be told, that rather than leading her to the afterlife, these tunnels represented different lives she could so easily have led, like parallel universes. Ones which were usually buried and hidden, deep in the core of the brain.

What she was being given here was a gift. The gift of being able to see what life would have been like had she chosen the *other* route, or made a different decision, at three different points in her life. And so it was that Jennifer let herself fall into a deep and very informative coma. As her own private miracle started, she began to glide toward the first tunnel, the one to the left which was swirling with clouds of light at its entrance. This was the one marked Aidan. The first of three parallel lives she could so easily have lived.

7 TUNNEL NUMBER ONE

Aidan: what could have been

Jennifer slipped out of bed and padded across the room to pull the curtain back. Sunlight immediately poured in and though it was still early she could feel the heat of the day penetrating the glass. She gazed out at the view, loving the way the sea glinted and twinkled through the gaps in the rooftops. Their little one-bedroom apartment in the bay-side suburbs of Brisbane was very basic, very compact, but it was also only a twenty-minute walk from the beach.

She opened the window a fraction and breathed in deeply. Then she tipped her face back and let the already strong rays bathe her skin with warmth.

It was strange getting up every day knowing it was going to be hot and that the sky would almost definitely be blue. She'd always considered herself a total sun worshipper but having been away for so long now, the sense of urgency to get out there and work on her tan had started to fade. Sometimes, if she were being totally honest, she found the constancy of the temperature relentless, a tad monotonous, to the point where recently she'd found herself secretly craving a bit of grey sky. This was ironic given that she was always the first to moan about the abysmal climate in England and yet what she missed about the British weather was the subtle change of seasons. Nothing beat a glorious, breezy, spring day, or that first sniff in the air which told you that autumn had arrived, when the light became more golden and the leaves were falling from the trees, crunchy and brown.

'Hey sexy.'

'Oh, you're awake,' she said, turning round to see Aidan grinning at her from the bed. He was so brown, toned and fit from all the hours of running on the beach he was doing most days. She still felt a lurch of desire every time she clapped eyes on him.

'Yeah funny that, given that you've pulled the curtains wide open. Now, seeing as you've woken me up, get your sexy bum over here,' he said, eyeing her greedily.

She was only wearing a small vest top and a pair of knickers.

'I know what you're after,' she grinned back at him, knowing full well he'd have a raging hard on. He woke up with one every morning. In that way he was a bit like the Queensland weather, predictable.

'Just shut up and come here,' he said, flinging back the sheets to reveal that her guess was indeed correct.

Not needing to be persuaded, Jennifer approached the bed and succumbed to half an hour of intense passion. Before Aidan, she hadn't been aware of ever having such a voracious sexual appetite but he'd definitely woken something up inside of her that she supposed must have been lying dormant before.

After what was, as ever, mind- blowing, energetic sex, they both lay flat on their backs panting, sated, sweating.

'You're amazing,' said Aidan, idly tweaking her left nipple.

'So are you,' she replied 'Seriously amazing.'

'Love you,' he said, hugging her tight. Jennifer marvelled at how safe he made her feel. The chemistry between them was something she doubted could ever be replicated with anyone else. Sometimes they were almost savagely passionate with one another. She didn't think there was anything she wouldn't be prepared to do with him physically and, as a result, she had never felt so confident in her own body or so empowered in terms of the effect she knew she was capable of having upon him.

'Are we going to the beach then?' said Aidan.

'Not the building site?'

'Nah, that can wait. It's too much of a scorcher. Maybe tomorrow?'

'Ok,' she agreed, flopping over to her side so she could get up and start getting the beach bag ready.

Just then the phone rang.

'Yours,' said Jennifer lazily, though a second later she regretted this when she remembered it would probably be the scheduled in phone call she'd arranged with her parents before they retired to bed on the other side of the world.

'Yup, here she is,' Aidan was saying, in a fed up, vaguely unfriendly tone which simply confirmed it was them.

Jennifer sat up and reached over for her vest top which she pulled back over her head before taking the phone from him. It was such a small apartment that there wasn't anywhere for her to go where she could talk without Aidan listening in, so rather than standing up in the tiny kitchen, where he'd be able to hear every word anyway, she just stayed where she was. Never having any privacy did get to her sometimes.

'Hi Mum, how are you?'

'Oh alright,' said the so familiar voice, made tinny from the sheer distance it was travelling.

Jennifer pictured her parents, sitting by the phone together, probably ready for bed in their dressing gowns, in the lounge with the radiators blasting.

'What have you been up to this week Jen?'

'Oh, this and that,' she replied 'Working, bit of beach action. You know? The usual really.'

'I thought you were going to that Surfers Paradise place.'

'Oh yeah, we were, but we didn't in the end,' said Jennifer, turning around so she had her back to Aidan. He was looking grumpy like he always did when she chatted to her parents. It was getting on her nerves.

Three months ago, at exactly the time her mum and dad had been expecting her to be landing at Gatwick back from her holiday with the girls to Kos, Jennifer had rung them from Athens to break the news that she'd essentially decided to throw caution to the wind and take an unplanned gap year. In Australia...

To say they'd been furious had been an understatement. Her dad had shouted, her mum had wept, though as it transpired, it was less the fact she wasn't coming home which enraged them so much, but more the fact she wasn't coming back because of a man they hadn't met.

Their reaction had been *so* bad that Jennifer had seriously considered giving up on her adventure altogether. Had even thought it might be best just to admit defeat and head home straightaway, tail between her legs. In fact, she'd just been about to tell them that she was sorry and that she would do exactly that, when her mother had interjected with 'One whiff of male attention and you go and lose your head Jennifer. It's pathetic when you think about it.'

And that one comment had changed everything. For at that point, Jennifer's mood had switched from apologetic and shamefaced to resolute and determined. She'd been utterly insulted by her mother's accusation and had said as much to Aidan when she'd got off the phone a few minutes later in order to have a think, on the proviso that she'd call them back with a decision.

She'd left him drinking a beer and smoking a cigarette in a dusty roadside cafe in a busy square and as she'd approached, it was obvious to her that despite desperately trying to appear nonchalant he was in fact really nervous, which was endearing.

As soon as she was in earshot he'd asked 'What happened?'

'They went bloody mad,' she'd replied, still a bit shell-shocked from the whole experience. She jumped as a moped whizzed past, almost knocking her off her feet.

Aidan motioned to her to come and join him properly and gathering her wits and checking left and right she eventually came to his table, mind whirling as she tried to comprehend what had just happened.

She'd always hated confrontation and miraculously had managed to avoid too many bust ups with her fairly conservative parents up until this point, which was partly why she was so livid with them now. How dare her mother have talked to her like that? Like she was some stupid, dozy tart who was so needy of male attention she'd do anything to get it. She'd never given them any cause for worry or upset in the past and yet now she was deviating off the path just a little bit, they didn't have the patience to at least try and understand her reasons. Yes, Aidan had been a massive part of the decision not to go home, but that was life. You met people and things happened and given that they hadn't even met him it seemed ridiculous for them to have formed an opinion of him already. It was so unfair. They gave her no credit whatsoever.

'So what's the score then?'

'I said I'd call back in ten minutes so we could all cool off,' she'd replied, avoiding both the question and his stare slightly.

'And?'

'Oh I don't know,' she'd replied truthfully, feeling unbelievably torn 'They're really mad at me Aidan and it was awful hearing them so pissed off. Plus, Mum's desperately worried that if I defer I might lose my place altogether.'

'Well she would say that wouldn't she,' suggested Aidan.

Jennifer shrugged, doubtful her mum was that manipulative. 'I'm so thirsty I almost feel faint, have you got enough money for me to get a beer?'

'Yeah, go for it,' said Aidan pulling some ancient Drachma notes out of his pocket and signalling to the waiter.

'So what's it to be then babe?' he enquired again a few minutes later once Jennifer had had the chance to drink some of her cold lager 'Sunshine, the land of opportunity and some hot romance with me? Or back to mummy and daddy and the rain?'

'I don't know,' Jennifer had replied feeling really conflicted. She also felt a bit stupid. She'd probably been deeply deluded thinking her parents would just accept her reasoning for ducking out. Their fury had really knocked her though.

Realising she needed time to think Aidan dropped the subject and so they sat in slightly tense silence, watching the world go by, until Jennifer got up. 'Right, there's no point sitting here putting it off. I'd better go and ring them back.'

As she marched back across the busy road to the centre of the square where the phone booth was, her head was spinning.

What should she do? She still had no idea so decided it would probably be best just to see how the conversation panned out.

Her dad had picked up the phone 'Right, now I hope you're phoning to tell us you've seen sense.'

This wasn't a good start in terms of making her feel like returning to the bosom of her family.

'I've phoned to discuss things like an adult,' she shot back.

'Well, that's a start,' he said 'So in that case, surely you can see that running off with some good for nothing beach bum, while ruining your life in the process is entirely the wrong thing to do.'

It was a shame he'd taken that approach. It was a shame he hadn't simply asked her how she was and how she was feeling because he might have got a very different response to the one he received and the conversation may have played out another way.

As it was, three days later Jennifer and Aidan boarded a plane to Australia and although she was experiencing an underlying sense of panic as to whether or not it was definitely what she really wanted, the fact she was proving a point to her parents was enough to prevent her from changing her mind.

If relations had been bad at that point they'd taken an even worse turn once she'd phoned them again from Sydney, where they'd stayed for the first few weeks before heading to Queensland, at which point her furious dad had demanded to speak to Aidan. At first he'd refused, which had made Jennifer feel very uneasy. Eventually however, sensing that if he didn't Jennifer was going to freak out, Aidan had acquiesced, albeit reluctantly, at which point her dad had given him very short shrift, venting all his frustrations and feelings of helplessness at the person he held responsible for his daughter's unfamiliar behaviour.

Aidan hadn't appreciated being shouted at though, and rather than taking the reprimanding on the chin, had retaliated with a few barbed insults of his own which hadn't helped matters in any way. Now, a few months on, things had calmed down a bit but no matter how much Jennifer tried to explain to her father that Aidan had only been sticking up for her, they wouldn't budge on their opinion of him. Meanwhile, Aidan refused to understand that perhaps her father had only been feeling over protective and was worried about his daughter.

So here she was having yet another awkward conversation with them while Aidan glowered and sulked next to her.

'So why didn't you go to Surfers Paradise then?' her mum asked now, in a way that sounded to Jennifer somehow accusatory.

'Because we decided to go another time,' she lied. In reality they hadn't been able to afford to hire a car but she wasn't going to tell them that.

'Hmm, well it seems a shame since you are there not to be doing anything, or seeing anything other than Brisbane,' remarked her mother pointedly.

Jennifer swallowed, determined not to have another row.

'How's dad?'

'He's right here, do you want a word?'

'Please.'

'Hello love,' said her dad and Jennifer blinked back a tear. She didn't half miss them.

'You'll never guess what happened to Martin at work the other day.'

It was true, she never would, so Jennifer let her dad witter away, filling her in on the day to day minutiae of his life in a way that made her feel closer to home.

Afterwards her mother came back on the phone 'I saw Karen's mum the other day.'

'Oh yeah,' said Jennifer, wishing Aidan would stop staring, stop listening, while simultaneously preparing herself for the next dig.

'Yes. Karen's loving university apparently. She's got loads of new friends and is really enjoying the course.'

'Good for Karen,' huffed Jennifer.

'Oh don't be like that Jen, I'm just saying, there's no need to be so defensive.'

'You're not just saying though are you? You're having another go at me for coming here, only I don't know how many times I have to tell you that I can go next year.'

'*If* they agree to you deferring your place. We've still not heard yet have we?'

'No, not yet,' she agreed.

Minutes later as she finally put down the phone, she swallowed hard.

'You ok?' said Aidan 'Don't let them make you feel like shit.'

But Jennifer's previous good mood had dissolved entirely. Every time she spoke to them it was the same. It stirred up so many mixed emotions; doubts, fear and anger at their handling of the situation.

'Listen, fuck 'em. Just forget about them, babe. Now let's get up and head to the beach.'

I don't know,' she said flatly, wishing it were that simple. 'Perhaps we shouldn't be going today you know. Perhaps it would be more sensible to head down to that building site to see if we can get you some work.'

Aidan rolled his eyes 'You're such a killjoy you are. Don't let your parents ruin *our* day. Just because they want to be miserable buggers doesn't mean we have to be. I mean, look how gorgeous it is out there and you want to sweat into town because some idiot from the cafe says there *might* be some work going. That's hardly making the best of the day is it?'

Jennifer despaired. 'I don't know to be honest. I mean, yeah, it is a beautiful day, just like it was yesterday and the day before and the day before that. But it would also be good to be able to tell mum and dad that between the pair of us we had a bit more money coming in. Besides, we're not in England now you know? We don't have to drop everything just because the sun's out. I suspect it will be a beautiful day tomorrow too, only by then, if there *is* any work going it will have gone.'

Decidedly grumpy now, in that second Jennifer wished heartily that it would start pouring down with rain. A bit of damp and drizzle might force Aidan into doing something useful and they could have a day off from feeling required to be on the beach. She only had a couple of shifts in a cafe every week and he was working as a bouncer every Friday but that was the sum of their income at the moment. They were totally skint and their lack of a 'plan' bothered her greatly, though every time she raised the subject, Aidan didn't seem to understand what her problem was. As far as he was concerned, they were living in hot sunshine, near a beach and having a lot of sex so there wasn't anything else to worry about. His needs were pretty basic.

'Look, I'll go tomorrow when you're at work. There's no point wasting a day when we could be together, hanging out,' he said.

'Alright,' she said, too hot and lethargic to protest. By now she was also keen to get out of the stifling apartment. She decided to make an effort to snap out of the mood which she knew had been caused by speaking to her parents. She just wished they'd be a bit more supportive. Aidan, who could see she was feeling tense and sad, came over and started to stroke her back in a way that instantly made her shiver with physical pleasure.

'Hey baby, it's ok,' he soothed.

'I know,' she said unconvincingly.

His hands carried on lightly travelling up her back and then around to her front where he gently rubbed her breasts. His touch was incredible and never failed to arouse her.

'Is that nice?'

'Mm,' she sighed, giving in to the sensations and reaching around to feel if he too was getting excited. He was.

'Wow, you feel hard. We only had sex five minutes ago.'

'That's what you do to me little baby,' he whispered in her ear before pulling her around and kissing her passionately and deeply.

They fell into bed and gradually her troubles faded away. There was no point stressing about anything too much she supposed. She was in Australia so should make the best of it and enjoy being with this amazing man who had the ability to frustrate and delight her in equal measure.

Had she done the right thing? Who knew? Ultimately, she guessed, only time would tell but for now she was lost in the moment, and he moment felt unbelievably good.

8 Present Day

She didn't exactly emerge from the tunnel. The sensation felt more like an expulsion, one which was sudden, brutal and delivered with no warning whatsoever. Jennifer was left feeling extremely unsteady, muddled and depleted. She knew her brain desperately needed time to rest and recover from what she'd just experienced. It was frustrating because there was so much she wanted to absorb, mull over and digest about what she'd just seen, but for now she was nowhere near capable. She needed to sleep. Before she surrendered to the grey ether however, she quickly glanced around and noted that the three tunnels all still existed, though the first was definitely shining ever so slightly less brightly.

She knew then that she would have another opportunity to visit each of them and was swamped with relief. She couldn't wait to find out more about how things would have gone with Aidan. She wished she were up to it now for this was the most fascinating, terrifying and yet privileged gift she could ever have been afforded. For now, though, it was time to regain some strength and with that final thought she allowed herself to slip away.

9 Sunday

'Polly and Eadie need to get out and burn off a bit of energy,' announced Jennifer.

'Take them to the park then,' said Max, finishing the last bit of his toasted bacon sandwich, and only narrowly saving himself from being swatted with a copy of the Sunday Times by winking, to make sure his wife knew he was joking. 'Come on then, let's take them to the swings now, and then perhaps we could go out for lunch, so you don't have to cook again?'

Jennifer acknowledged that this was a kind thought but wondered what was preventing him from making something.

'Or should I say, so you don't have to buy in any revolting stuffed chickens that don't actually look or taste anything like chickens.' Another wink.

'Ha bloody ha,' said Jennifer, laughing despite herself. 'Ok, that sounds good. And there's a pie in the fridge which we can all have for early dinner but not much more than that so hopefully it'll be quiet at work tomorrow, so I can do a shop in my lunch break. Otherwise I'll have to go later.'

'Good,' said Max, who didn't really care. Food was his wife's department as far as he was concerned. 'Right, Po -lly, Ea -die, come and get your shoes on, we're going to the park,' he yelled, getting up to put his plate in the sink.

'Let's aim to wear them out as much as possible,' said Jennifer.

'Definitely,' Max agreed 'Then we can plonk them in front of a DVD this afternoon totally guilt- free.'

'Sounds good to me,' said Jennifer, wondering hopefully if that meant that he was thinking they might be able to sneak some afternoon sex in.

'Because I hope you don't mind,' added Max, looking sheepish 'But there's a footy match on that I really want to watch this afternoon and I told Ted he could come round and watch it here. He still doesn't have Sky Sports at his.'

'Oh....right,' she said feeling crestfallen and bored already.

'You don't mind do you?'

'No,' she sighed unconvincingly.

Later that afternoon, despite having been run out in the park all morning, like dogs, Polly and Eadie were still full of energy and though they usually got on pretty well, today they were directing it all toward fighting, forcing Jennifer to act as both bouncer and mediator. When she wasn't stopping them from killing each other, over of all things a broken Barbie, she was putting on washing, taking it out or shoving it in the mountainous ironing pile. All in all not the most riveting of afternoons and as she took out load after load she thought wistfully of pre children days when Sundays meant lying in bed with a hangover, which would eventually be cured by a Bloody Mary and a roast dinner at the pub, followed perhaps by a movie and some lovely sex.

'Come on you two,' she said now, or rather yelled, because by this point both her daughters' whining had developed into full blown wailing. 'Eadie, bash your sister again and I'll bash you.'

Of course she would never bash her kids in a million years so the threat was rather empty which Eadie could tell.

Eadie regarded Jennifer briefly as if weighing up how much trouble she'd be in if she ignored her. Then, obviously having concluded she could handle whatever was flung at her, proceeded to whack Polly once more.

'Right,' growled Jennifer, who had now officially had enough 'That's it, up to your room.'

As Eadie burst into noisy sobs, Jennifer sighed heavily, sick to the back teeth of all the squabbling but partly blaming herself for it. Perhaps her children had picked up on her generally unenthusiastic mood? If she'd been perkier today and more inventive in finding ways to entertain them, no doubt they'd be behaving fine but frankly she just wanted to be able to leave them to their own devices for more than five minutes. She was tired and would like nothing more than to get into her pyjamas and zone out to a bit of crappy afternoon telly.

Max scampered into the kitchen.

'All alright in here?' he said, charging to the fridge to get a couple more beers. 'Did I hear wailing?'

'Yes you did,' snapped Jennifer 'They're behaving like a couple of deranged chimps. I've sent Eadie to her room for bashing Polly.'

'Yeah Daddy, she hit me really hard,' said Polly, rubbing her arm to demonstrate how much it hurt.

'Er, it was the other arm Pol',' said Jennifer wryly.

'How could you miss that you bloody idiot?' Ted yelled from the front room at which point Max literally ran back out of the kitchen, bottles of lager in both hands and one under his arm, skidding on the wooden floor of the hall in his socks. As he disappeared he yelled over his shoulder 'Be good for your mother.'

'Come on you, let's get some colouring stuff out,' said Jennifer to her youngest 'But hurry up because I need to go and make sure Eadie's ok. And don't think I'm massively happy with you either Madame,' she added, noting Polly's smug expression as she gloated over how much trouble her sister was in.

Later, after thirty minutes spent with Eadie in her bedroom, who by now had worked herself up into such a state she'd needed soothing and stroking, despite the fact it had been her who had been in the wrong, Jennifer decided to join the boys in the lounge. That way if the children wanted anything their father might be forced to do something.

'Hello,' Max said, looking distracted and surprised to see her standing in her own front room.

Max was on one sofa and Ted was on the other. Both were sitting wide legged on the edge, beers in hand.

'You alright? Second half's just started. Why don't you see if there's a nice movie on upstairs? Must be something new out.'

'Because Eadie's watching Tangled on our bed and as much as I actually quite enjoyed it the first time round I can probably live without seeing it again,' she replied, flopping onto the sofa that Ted was sitting on. He shuffled up, slightly reluctantly, to make a bit of room, his eyes never leaving the TV.

'Alright Ted?' she asked.

'Yeah, great thanks,' he said, reminding her of when Eadie's friends came round to play and answered her questions about school politely, with enough clues in their tone to suggest they'd rather not be talking to her at all.

'How's Ali? Is she well?' she continued, not really caring if Ted didn't want to talk. She did. She was bored.

'Not bad thanks. Bit stressed. Mark's been off school with tonsillitis but other than that ok.'

'Good,' she said, flicking through Style magazine.

'Hey, have you seen your ex's latest chart position in this year's Rich List?' said Max, throwing the supplement in her direction.

'Oh god,' Jennifer rolled her eyes. 'Go on then, let's feel sick for a second.'

'*reUNIon* floated this year,' Max informed Ted, almost proudly 'He's worth a billion now.'

'You are having a laugh,' said Jennifer, though soon she knew it to be true for there it was, in black and white, accompanied by a picture of him. Tim Purcell. The ex- boyfriend she'd put up with for two and a half years, now worth a billion quid. She scrutinised the picture of him. His blonde hair was slightly silvery around the edges, but only slightly. He was a little more jowly but on the whole looked remarkably similar to how he had done fifteen years ago. He was good looking in a Nordic sort of way and had always had incredibly good skin, though his blue eyes were flinty and rather deep set and his nose was a little too sharp. His face couldn't have been more different to the one she'd eventually married. Max's mop of brown hair and friendly face may not have been anywhere near as chiselled but it was one that overall she far preferred staring at.

She wondered what it would be like to see Tim now, after all these years. Would they get on? They'd had a strange relationship. She'd always felt as if more than anything she'd *amused* him. She'd known he'd found her funny and sweet but she'd never got the impression that he massively fancied her. Then again, for her, it hadn't necessarily been a relationship based on physical attraction either. She'd just been so terribly impressed by him, by his flair, and had liked being associated with someone who everyone on campus was aware of. If she ever met up with him again she'd love to ask him what he'd seen in her. Not that it was likely. They were hardly likely to bump into one another since they mixed in totally different circles. Plus they'd never kept in touch due to the fact that they'd broken up on such desperately bad terms, which ironically was the one time he'd demonstrated that actually she had got under his skin. Or had it just been his ego making him so angry and upset when she'd told him she wanted to split up?

'What I'd do with a billion quid,' mused Ted.

'Buy yourself a Sky Sports subscription?' quipped Jen, but both men ignored her, they were back to frowning at the game. 'Perhaps I should get in contact with Tim and ask for a paltry little thousand pounds that I could use to get the tumble dryer fixed, pay some bills and have a splurge on clothes, eh? It would be pocket money to him,' she joked.

'Oof, what was that ref?' Then 'Bet you wish you'd stuck with him eh Jen? Instead of hooking up with this here loser,' said Ted.

Jennifer smiled and shook her head 'Not at all Ted, Tim may be rich but he was a bit of a cold shit really.'

'Bloody clever though,' said Max 'I mean, who hasn't been on '*reUNIon* at some point or another? Apart from my parents, who are literally the only people I can think of.'

It always struck Jennifer as slightly strange when Max went on about how clever Tim was. It was almost as if he was proud of the fact she'd gone out with him. She'd have half preferred it if he was a little bit jealous. As it was she suspected he'd probably love to meet him, have dinner with him, be able to discuss his career with him. In fact, given the choice, these days it wouldn't surprise her if he chose going to dinner with him over dinner with her.

Her phone beeped. It was a text from Esther, saying she was round the corner at the park with Sophie and could she pop in for a cuppa.

Jennifer phoned straight away 'Please come round. Max and Ted are here watching footy and I would love to see you. Also, Sophie can sort my two out and give them something more interesting to do than killing each other.'

Bored rigid of the swings Esther was round in minutes.

'I am so glad to see you,' said Jennifer flinging her arms round her friend as soon as she'd opened the door. 'Hi Sophie, how are you sweetie?' she asked her goddaughter.

'Good,' said Sophie.

'Go on then, Eadie's upstairs and ah... here's Pol. Have you finished colouring?'

'Yes,' said Polly, looking delighted to have a playmate that wasn't Eadie.

As the girls scampered upstairs Jennifer ushered Esther into the kitchen.

'Am I glad to see you? What a dull weekend I've had, bloody hell.'

Esther giggled 'Why? What have you been up to?'

'Ugh,' groaned Jennifer 'Well, we didn't have the kids Friday night but we managed to totally waste that window of opportunity to have some fun by doing nothing. Then, on Saturday, we had Judith and boring Henry round for lunch.'

'Oh god,' said Esther, who had heard enough about them to imagine what that would have entailed.

'Exactly, although I did nearly give them food poisoning which added a very small frisson of excitement. Then today I thought we were going to have a nice family day but it's ended up being a day of sport watching and beer drinking with good old Ted.' This last bit she said in a hushed tone.

'All sounds joyous,' laughed Esther, slipping off her jacket. She looked great as ever, though today she did look tired. Under all those freckles she was pale, though as ever her naturally strawberry blonde hair was shiny and brushed and no matter how tired she'd always look attractive. She'd aged really well and dressed in a way which made other women want to know where her clothes were from. She always bothered to add accessories and put outfits together in a way that told you she hadn't just picked up whatever was on the floor and thrown it on. Today her printed scarf and Alex Monroe gold bumble bee necklace were the items Jennifer was coveting.

'Sounds like you need a good night out with the girls.'

'I do,' agreed Jennifer 'You know we're going out on Tuesday don't you? Only to the Hare and Hounds but perhaps then we can get our diaries out and arrange something proper. Something which involves cocktails and dancing. Love that scarf by the way.'

'Thanks, it's River Island and yeah, I do know about Tuesday, although I'm not a hundred percent sure I can come yet,' said Esther. 'I still need to get a sitter.'

Jennifer suspected at that point she definitely wouldn't be coming then. Such a shame and it grated ever so slightly that she wasn't making it a priority.

'Tea?'

'Yeah please.'

'Anyway, enough of my boring weekend, how's yours been?'

'Not bad actually,' said Esther, a sly grin lighting up her face.

'Go on,' said Jennifer getting mugs out of the cupboard, happy that her friend was round. Her proper friend. It had restored her equilibrium.

'Jason and I are pretty skint at the moment so we've been in loads, but on Friday my mum babysat and we went out and got hammered. I'm talking properly pissed and when we got home and mum had gone, we ended up having amazing sex. It started in the hall and ended up...' She paused briefly to snort with laughter at the memory '.......in the downstairs loo.'

'You are kidding me,' said Jennifer, full of mixed emotions. She was deeply impressed, terribly envious, strangely proud and very relieved to hear that people were still having wild sex with their husbands even if she wasn't.

'I'm not,' said Esther, giggling. 'It was hilarious. You know the type of sex you have where afterwards you're almost a bit embarrassed by how carried away you got.'

'Wish I could remember,' said Jennifer honestly, grabbing the milk out the fridge. 'By the way, they are brilliantly quiet up there aren't they? Thank you so much for coming round and saving our day.'

'Pleasure,' said Esther. 'Thanks for saving *me* from hours more of pushing Sophie on the swings.'

'No worries,' said Jennifer dolefully, her mind still on Esther's exploits 'Do you know the last time I can remember feeling faintly embarrassed after sex was probably with Tim.'

'Really? Why? What did you do?'

Jennifer grimaced 'You don't want to know.'

'Er, well that's where you're completely wrong.'

Jennifer wrinkled up her nose, embarrassed 'Let's just say he was quite kinky and leave it there shall we.'

'No way!' protested Esther 'I'm sorry but you have to spill the beans now Missy. If you don't I'll end up imagining all sorts of things that are probably far worse than the reality.'

Jennifer sighed, knowing she was beaten 'Ok, but tell anyone this and you're a dead woman.'

Esther pretended to pull a zip across her mouth.

'Ok, so basically, toward the end of our relationship Tim was only really up for it if I was... pretending to be someone else.'

Esther's eyes widened 'Do you mean he liked role play?'

Jennifer nodded and chewed a fingernail. Liked was an understatement.

Esther laughed heartily 'Oh god. I think I can vaguely remember you saying something about that at the time.'

'Hmm,' Jennifer said, wrinkling up her nose 'Anyway, maybe I should have just put up with his weird ways. Let me show you something,' she hurried into the front room and returned with the Rich List.

'Bloody hell,' said Esther, wide eyed once she'd been shown the relevant bit. 'That is a sick amount of money. God I can't tell you how much we could do with just a little bit of that. Things are really tight at the moment to the point where we're struggling some months to make the mortgage payments. Can you phone him and ask if we can have some?'

'I wish,' said Jennifer.

'That could have been you,' said Esther.

'Well, I don't know about that.'

'It could. Don't you remember how gutted he was when you broke it off? You could be that rich. Do you think you'd still have been friends with us now?'

'Course I would,' said Jennifer, insulted 'What do you take me for? Though having said that, I'm not sure Karen would have been popping round the mansion that often. She hated him didn't she?'

'She did,' confirmed Esther. 'I always thought he was ok though. He was so clever wasn't he? Had an answer for everything. Oh and I'll never forget that party he threw in your house that time. The one where Karen shagged Pete for the first time. It was awesome. Maybe even the best party I've ever been to. No one could ever accuse him of being tight with his cash.

'True,' agreed Jennifer. 'God that party was fun wasn't it? Or are we looking back through rose tinted glasses?'

As her mind returned to Tim, for once she allowed herself to be transported back to how life had been then, all those years ago. She always pretended she couldn't care less, but in truth, being permanently reminded by the business section of the papers that one of your exes was doing amazingly well in life was a little galling.

And deep down she knew it probably *could* have been her, enjoying the fruits of his labours, if she'd stuck with him. If she hadn't let her concerns that he didn't love her as maybe he should overwhelm her. Or, more to the point, if she hadn't decided that despite his protestations, he cared more about work than any living human being, and that that in itself was a problem she'd never be able to overcome.

Still, that was all firmly in the past and besides, she suspected that no amount of financial security would make up for the fact she'd spent much of their time together dressed as a police woman or a nun.

10 THE PAST

Tim, April 1997

Jennifer was just about to pour her powdered cup a soup into a mug when she made the mistake (or not as the case may be) of glancing inside the empty vessel, at which point she retched violently.

'Oh my god that is so disgusting,' she exclaimed, stomach heaving.

'What?' said Karen, coming to join her in the small kitchen, opening the fridge and peering hopefully into it.

'This mug's got mould growing in it. I think I'm going to puke.'

'Gross,' said Karen, closing the door again. Funnily enough a stick of limp celery or a Fray Bentos weren't really what she fancied.
'Shall we just get some chips before we get there?'

'Ok,' agreed Jennifer, unable to bear the surrounding debris a moment longer.

As a student you expected to live in a certain amount of squalor but their house veered dangerously into unsanitary territory.

From the outside it was amazing. A huge, grade- one listed, regency, terrace, located smack bang in the middle of a square just off the Brighton sea front. The paint may have been peeling, (not helped by the saltiness of the atmosphere) but when standing at the other side of the square, with your back to the sea, it still looked exceedingly grand and possessed the majesty of its era. Huge stone steps led up to a black, front door which was a struggle to open at times and had a huge brass knocker on it. Inside, the house had been adapted so it could be rented out with the student market in mind. On the ground floor there were three bedrooms and a bathroom, on the middle floor there was a vast communal lounge along with a further two bedrooms and a tiny kitchen. The third and final floor comprised of three more bedrooms and another bathroom.

Curiously, there was no dining table anywhere in the house, something which any parents who had visited at one time or another found baffling and always commented on, but which none of the students cared about one iota. Meals were usually consumed standing up or lying down.

Of course eight bedrooms meant eight housemates. Eight studenty, human beings, whose priorities didn't remotely involve anything like rubber gloves, cleaning fluid or tidying. As a result, the mess was unprecedented. Only two of the eight housemates were female and, while the girls probably did notice the mess more than the boys, on feminist grounds Jennifer and Karen resented being the only ones doing anything about it. After the first term, the girls had refused to do anything more about it, so then no one did anything to combat the mess and filth so the house permanently looked like it had just been burgled and the kitchen existed under a coating of grease. Washing up was done on a need-to-eat basis and everything generally felt a bit... *sticky* to the touch.

The only part of the house that wasn't completely grim to be in was Tim's room. His was on the top floor and was by far the largest in the house, a privilege he paid for - £20 more a week in rent to be exact. Stepping into Tim's room felt like entering another world. Not only was it the best room in terms of size and view; it was also the only room that was kept clean and tidy in startling contrast to the others in the house. Not that Tim was getting busy with the Marigolds; instead, he paid fellow student, Amber, £6 an hour for three hours every week, to come and clean his room and also to take away, wash and iron his clothes. For so many reasons this set him apart from his peers and yet Tim was a rare breed of student altogether. The most glaringly obvious thing that separated him from the rest of the student community was the fact that he always had a bit of cash. Not just the odd tenner, but wedges of the stuff which he kept folded in a money clip. He'd gone to a very expensive public school so undoubtedly had financial support from his family, but he also always had money making schemes on the go, ones which tended to actually be successful. This was reflected in his standard of living. Tim had his own fridge which was always pretty well stocked with lagers and nice food, ready meals like lasagne and curris and not just from Costco either but from Sainsbury's and sometimes even M&S. He had his own desktop computer complete with Windows 95, plus a two-seater sofa which was positioned against the window, meaning that when you lay on it you could fully appreciate the sea view. He also had his own hi fi and a kettle, making the room more like a self-contained studio apartment. Jennifer loved spending time in it. It certainly beat her tiny box room on the ground floor at the back of the house, with its own rather desultory view of a back yard which belonged to an unsavoury kebab restaurant.

To Jennifer, climbing into fresh clean sheets once a week also felt like a huge perk of going out with Tim. Unless of course, the night after Amber had been and cleaned it, coincided with one of Tim's 'work' nights, or as Karen referred to them, his 'I want to be alone' nights. Jennifer was used to Tim's ways though and in all honesty Karen constantly going on about how weird they were was sometimes more annoying than her boyfriend dictating when she could and couldn't stay in his room.

Now, as Karen and Jennifer gave up the futile task of looking for anything that might be worth eating they retreated to the lounge where Pete and Jim were playing FIFA on the PlayStation and listening to music. Empty McDonalds bags littered the table and with the curtains drawn, the only real light source other than a small side lamp came from the tropical fish tank which belonged to another of their housemates Darren. Jim was only wearing his pants, which wasn't a pleasant sight but one which the girls were used to enough that it didn't warrant a comment.

'So, Tim's not coming out tonight is he?' asked Karen, collapsing onto the sofa, her short skirt riding up her firm but chunky legs, her question sounding more like a hopeful statement, telling Jennifer everything she needed to know.

'Don't know,' she replied, immediately on edge. She wished Karen would just get over her dislike of Tim for once and for all. 'Why?'

'No nothing,' said Karen 'I don't mind either way, I just assumed it wouldn't be his bag. That is to say fun. Joking!'

'You going to that karaoke thing?' enquired Pete, his eyes not leaving the screen.

'Yeah,' said Karen.

'Do you want some draw?'

'Why not,' said Karen.

'Ok, you sort that out and I'll go and find out if Tim is coming or not,' said Jennifer, pointedly ignoring her friend's dig.

She thundered up the stairs to the third floor, taking them two at a time in her platform trainers which she was wearing with a miniscule top that showed off her flat belly and an A line short skirt.

'Are you coming out tonight or what?' panted Jennifer, having banged on Tim's door and received a *Come in.*

'I'm not my precious,' replied Tim, not looking up from his desk 'Sean's coming over to show me the code he's written. We're having a meeting.'

'Ooh,' she moaned. 'Please come?'

Tim finally turned and gave her an approving look followed by a lop- sided grin, so endearing it made her want to run over and kiss him. Not that she did.

Tim's demeanour was generally one which encouraged people to keep their distance. But while they didn't tend to go in much for spontaneous affection what they both did relish was sparring with one another verbally.

'Hmm, let me think about it, my options are: a/ stay here and see all my ambition and dreams come to fruition, or b/ go out in the rain to watch you and Karen murder what were perfectly decent songs to start off with in a shitty karaoke gay bar on the sea front. You're alright thanks.'

'Vicky's coming,' joked Jennifer, grabbing the life size cardboard cut- out of Posh Spice which Tim had pinched from Blockbuster Video the previous week when he was pissed.

Ms Adams was wearing the white mini- skirt and bra top which she'd worn for the Brits. Ginger Spice was downstairs in the lounge too, in her iconic union jack dress, casually leaning against the wall, only with an extra black moustache and glasses which someone had thoughtfully drawn on.

'Well that's a different story then,' said Tim 'If old lovely-legs is going.' But of course he didn't mean it, for his attentions were firmly back on his computer.

Jennifer tried not to feel put out. She'd been going out with him long enough to know he wouldn't change his mind and there was no point grumbling given that his drive, ambition and clever brain were the main things that had attracted her to him in the first place. Jennifer had always got the sense that Tim was destined for success. He just exuded utter confidence in the fact that he would make it.

Admittedly, half the time she didn't entirely follow what he was on about when it came to his plans to cash in on what he felt was going to be a huge surge in terms of internet usage but his passion for the subject was infectious. His latest idea was to create some kind of platform on the world wide web for people to find old university, college or school friends, that then allowed you to find out how they'd done, in terms of what jobs they'd gone on to, whether they were married or not and if they'd had children. It would be called '*reUNIon*' and was less a social networking experiment, and more a way for people to be utterly nosey. It would allow you to link up with people and then, once they'd given their permission, you'd be able to see their page which would be formatted almost like a CV. However, before you could see it, the site would ask you to predict what you thought those people were doing. In other words, if you had signed up to it you might receive an email from an old classmate asking if you wanted to see what they had predicted about you. Tim was convinced that people's natural desire to know what others thought of them would be the key to its success.

'So what's Sean bringing round?'

'You wouldn't understand,' said Tim, bluntly.

'Try me.'

'He's been developing some programs. That's all. I *told* you he's written some code'

'For '*reUNIon*'?'

'Yes,' Tim said, sounding a touch exasperated, which made Jennifer feel sad. She was just interested but as ever when Tim was focused he really had no energy left for anyone or anything else. Just then, Darren yelled up the stairs.

'Tim, someone here for you.'

'Great,' said Tim, bounding into action, brushing past her in his eagerness to get to Sean, practically flattening her as he did so. Jennifer gave up and sighed. She'd lost him so she might as well get on with her evening. Karen would be pleased anyway. With that she left the room and picked her way across the landing which had piles of dirty laundry strewn all over it.

Later that night, or rather, in the early hours of the next day, Jennifer and Karen staggered home. After five minutes (which felt more like an hour due to how desperate they both were for the loo) of taking it in turns to stab the front door with their keys they finally made it into the house. Giggling like schoolgirls, cross legged and clutching one another in an attempt not to piss themselves laughing, it took them an age to get up the stairs. Once they had though, they both raced to the loo to pee long and hard like horses, before reconvening in the lounge at which point they peeled their coats off and Karen got out all her skinning up paraphernalia.

'I'm just going to see if Tim's still up?' said Jennifer, who couldn't be bothered with pretending she wasn't dying to see him.

'Fine,' said Karen, only slightly huffily. 'No doubt he will be because he hasn't taken over the world yet.'
As Jennifer bounded up the stairs she decided it was probably time to have it out with Karen once and for all. She couldn't keep putting up with her jibes. They were getting on her nerves. It wasn't her fault Karen was single at the moment.

'Tim,' she said, banging on his door, having seen light coming from beneath it. There was no reply but there was music playing, Oasis by the sound of it. She barged in.

Tim and Sean barely looked up, so engrossed were they, huddled over the wretched computer.

'Er....yoohoo, hello, Earth calling my saddo geek boyfriend.'

'Oh hello you,' said Tim looking up. Despite having the pallor of someone who hadn't had any fresh air all day, his eyes were shining and he looked excited and thrilled. As he leaned back his shirt rode up exposing a glimpse of his lean hairless stomach.

'How's it going?' said Jennifer, suddenly feeling slightly queasy. Running up the stairs probably hadn't been the wisest of moves given that she had litres of various spirits swooshing around in her belly. She swayed across the room and sank thankfully down onto the bed. She reached down to pull off her trainers and once she'd manhandled them off, chucked them across the room. They made a huge thudding sound as they made contact with the wall.

'Amazing,' said Tim 'We're doing fucking amazing, thanks to Sean.'

Jennifer smiled weakly in Sean's direction. Sean who had the social skills of a jellyfish as far as she was concerned. Sean who, if she were being completely honest, she slightly hated because she was just a little bit jealous of him. Tim never looked this happy and satisfied after a night in with her that was for sure.

'Will you come downstairs and have a drink with me and Karen?' she said, trying not to sound petulant but not sure if she was succeeding due to being so drunk. Ugh, now that she wasn't filling her lungs with sea air, the alcohol was making its effect well and truly known.

'Um...'

Jennifer got up, rolling her eyes heaven ward as she braced herself for the inevitable no.
'...Yes my little drunkard, why not? I'd love to. And then you can tell me all about your evening.'

Jennifer smiled 'I'll re-enact it if you like.'

'Even better,' said Tim pulling a face 'Come on Sean, we should have a break.'

'Cool,' muttered Sean, not moving.

Tim got up and rubbed his face with both hands. Then he came over to where Jennifer was and regarded her with interest as she bent down to retrieve her clumpy shoes.

'I can see right up your skirt,' he said in a way that gave Jennifer an immediate thrill.

'Come here you,' he said, pulling her towards him and encircling her in his arms. He lightly stroked her belly with his hand in a way that was a mixture of quite nice yet also irritating.

'You are wrecked aren't you,' stated Tim, suddenly noticing how much Jennifer was frowning. Her brows were knitted together due to the amount of concentration required simply to stand up straight.

'I'm fine,' she said defensively.

'Good,' he said, running his hands all over her body.

It was the affection she'd been craving for a couple of days only right this second being touched was making her feel vaguely nauseous. She needed to eat something. She needed toast.

'Can I take some of your bread?' she said, pulling away and gesturing to his fridge, lumbering over to it before he'd even had the chance to answer.

'But of course,' said Tim. 'Eat an entire loaf if you like my sweet. And if '*reUNIon*' takes off like I think it's going to, I shall buy you your very own bakers.'

Jennifer wasn't really listening though. She was too intent on getting at the sliced white which she had confidence would restore her sugar levels and hopefully make her feel less pissed. She had planned on toasting it downstairs but in the end so desperate for some starchy carbohydrate was she that she just ripped one slice in two and shoved one of the halves into her mouth plain. As she chewed, it stuck to the roof of her mouth.

'Don't ever let anyone tell you you're not completely classy,' joked Tim.

'Come on, let's go and have a drink then,' she said, mouth full.

'Yes,' said Tim 'Because you look like you definitely need one.'

Jennifer tried hard to think of a witty response but it was far too much effort so she gave up and lurched toward the door. Tim followed her but seemingly when it really came to the crunch

Sean couldn't be torn away from his computer for neither love nor money nor vodka.

In the lounge Karen was reclining on the main sofa which was so threadbare and ancient it had pretty much collapsed in on itself a long time ago. When lying on it, it often felt more like one was lying on the floor. She was doing some impressive recreational multi- tasking by smoking a spliff, keeping one eye on the telly and also playing music. 'Don't Speak' by No Doubt was blasting.

'Evening, Karen,' said Tim, in a tone that suggested he was up for a bit of a wind up session.

Jennifer sighed inwardly as she realised she'd now be in charge of keeping the peace.

'Right... booze,' she said. 'Shall I make us all a vodka?'

'Yeah, said Karen. 'Where's the bag, we didn't leave it did we?'

'No, it's here by your feet,' said Jennifer, extracting the plastic bag which had a half bottle of vodka and some orange juice in it from where it was wedged down the back of the sofa.

Of course it went without saying that there were no clean glasses or mugs anywhere to be found in the kitchen so she went downstairs to her room to fetch some paper cups which she'd purchased only the other week precisely for times like this.

Due to being so utterly rat-arsed, the effort of now having charged downstairs at high speed left her swaying in the middle of the room for a few minutes while trying to remember what she'd come down for. Her mind had gone completely blank and she could hardly keep her eyes open. Still, finally it came back to her. Cups. Paper cups. Now she felt smug. Well done her. She was conscious of getting back to the lounge quickly though, so as soon as she'd retrieved them she raced back, leaving her door wide open in her haste. It wouldn't do to leave Tim and Karen alone for too long. They'd only end up sniping at each other.

It was too late, though, and as she approached the lounge her heart sank.

'But wanting to know what people 'do' is just blatant snobbery isn't it?' Karen was arguing, albeit from a lying down position which put Tim, who was sat upright, at an immediate advantage.

'Oh fuck off Karen, you should hear yourself. What's snobby about being curious? About being interested?'

'Because you're suggesting that what we 'do' defines us, like some middle aged fart at a drinks party saying 'And what do you do?' she said, in a voice like Maggie Thatcher.

'Here are your drinks,' said Jennifer brusquely, splashing liquid into the paper cups until they were pretty much two-parts vodka one-part juice.

Tim took his and slugged it back. As he did he winced. 'woah, that's strong?'

'Pussy,' said Karen unnecessarily, downing hers in one and then looking like she deeply regretted it.

'Anyhow,' said Tim 'The point is Karen that if you think *reUNIon* is such a shit idea you won't go on it, which is entirely your prerogative. And yet I'd bet good money that in five years' time, if you got an email telling you that Ed Fisher wanted to find out what you were up to, and not only that, that he'd predicted what he thought you were up to, you'd be intrigued. So don't try and tell me you wouldn't have a look at that point.'

This was a bit below the belt. Ed Fisher had been, up until five weeks ago, Karen's boyfriend. And then he'd dumped her, cruelly. Not only had he terminated their relationship he'd told her it was because he didn't really fancy her and because he saw her more as a friend, by text. She'd cried pretty much for a week.

'If that arsehole got in touch with me in five years' time, I'd be fucking livid,' she yelled.

Jennifer slugged back her drink nervously. 'You two,' she interjected. 'Can we talk about something else for once?'

'Like what?' said Tim, sarcastically 'What do you want to enlighten us with my angel?

Jennifer gulped and as she did so she became aware of a horrid metallic taste in her mouth. This was swiftly followed by an ominous lurching sensation in her stomach. Horrified, she brought her hand up to her mouth.

'You ok?' said Karen.

'Gonna puke,' she managed, before acing from the room as the cocktails she'd drunk earlier made an unscheduled reappearance.

'I am one hell of a lucky guy aren't I?' said Tim.

'Yes, you are actually,' replied Karen loftily, wishing Jennifer's vomiting sounds weren't quite so loud. They weren't really helping her case.

11 | Present Day

'What's happening, Doctor?' asked Max, sounding strung out. The scraping sound of the plastic chair against the floor, indicating he'd leapt to his feet the second the doctor had appeared through the door. 'Well, we're encouraged that she's made it through surgery. At one point we were extremely concerned about the build- up of blood around the skull but it appears to have eased off. Having said that, she's not completely out of the woods yet, although her vital signs have stabilised.'

A pause.

'Perhaps we should continue speaking in the corridor, Mr Wright.'

Good thought Jennifer. Good. She needed quiet and wanted to be left alone in sterile silence. She felt herself slipping a little further back toward oblivion, then suddenly she was hooked violently back to reality again for the second time that day. As brutally as though a giant fist had gripped her and purposefully yanked her back, purely so she could address a thought which had been loitering on the periphery of her consciousness, tapping her brain, desperate for her attention.

Polly and Eadie. As maternal instinct took over and penetrated everything, her daughters were flung into sharp reality. Her babies, her girls. The stab of emotion she encountered in that moment as she thought of them was gut wrenching, panic inducing. She didn't know if they were ok and during this rare moment of lucidity she fully understood that she was powerless to find out. She couldn't be like this. They needed her. What was happening? She was a prisoner in her own body, helpless, petrified. If Max was here, wherever 'here' was, then who was looking after them? Her mum? Karen? But as quickly as panic and fear welled up, it subsided again as confusion swamped her once more.

She battled in vain to stay attached to this awareness of her daughters, but it proved too difficult. As quickly as their images had formed, they slipped away again, until within seconds she couldn't remember anything. Instead, the overriding sense returned that she was detached from whatever was happening, that she was miles away from the very place she was in, and that she was being encouraged to drift away further and further from it. Perhaps she should? At first she'd been pleased to emerge from the fog but it was enticing her back again. And so she succumbed once more to the new murky world she now existed in.

As Jennifer drifted away she let the falling sensation overwhelm her once again, this time confident of what to expect. She wasn't disappointed. There they were, the tunnels of light, and it was with a sense of real anticipation that for the second time she headed toward the still-open portal on the left...

12 TUNNEL NUMBER ONE

Aidan: what could have been

Gasping, Jennifer jabbed Aidan in the ribs, signalling for him to roll off so she could lie back and enjoy that brief period of utter contentment which follows an epic orgasm.

'Wow.'

'Hmm,' agreed Aidan, reaching over for his rolling tobacco. She surveyed his back. Since he'd hurt his ankle he'd not been able to go swimming or running and he'd piled on the pounds.

He still had a lovely broad body though; even if it was remarkably pasty and carrying a lot more fat than it had done. Still, his physique would always err on the side of good for his frame was masculine, tall and well proportioned. She surveyed the tattoo which spanned the width of his lower back. He'd had it done six months after they'd arrived in Australia. Sun drenched, heady, exciting days when it had still seemed like anything was possible. It was a Celtic pattern with a large sun in the middle and recently Jennifer had started to hate the very sight of it. It represented the elusive sunshine which Aidan had spent the best part of nearly sixteen years hankering after, chasing, but which somehow always remained just out of their reach. Just then, the strong, very wet Carlisle rain started hammering against the window panes as if to illustrate her point.

'Typical,' muttered Aidan.

'Why, what are you up to? Are you going to fetch that paint for Nathan's room?' asked Jennifer hopefully.

'No, I'm supposed to be signing on at three and I'm probably not going to have time to do that and get the paint am I?'

'Guess not,' said Jennifer flatly, hoping he wasn't trying to wriggle out of it. The feeling of peace she'd had from their physical exertions short-lived as ever. She'd finished work very late last night, was exhausted and frankly, picking up the paint was the least he could do. She had absolutely no idea why he couldn't get round to it. It was as if he was deliberately not doing it to spite her and she was almost tempted to get the bus to Olly's now and collect it herself. That way they could make a start on Nathan's room like they'd been promising him they would since his birthday. Only, Aidan collecting the paint had become a point of principle.

She inhaled deeply through her nose, as she'd been taught to in yoga class, desperate to remain in a good frame of mind a while longer.

Aidan sucked deeply on his skinny cigarette.

'Did Olly say if he had any more decorating work?' she said, knowing he'd hate her asking but unable to help herself.

'He didn't,' he replied tersely.

'Alright, I'm only asking,' said Jennifer, getting up abruptly, knowing her mission to remain zen was futile, so infused with intense frustration was she. She grabbed her old, tatty dressing gown from the hook on the back of the door and wrapped it around her thin body. Between working in the restaurant, Aidan's insatiable sexual appetite and the stress of never having enough money, keeping the pounds off wasn't something she'd ever had to worry about.

'Well don't. You know I'll tell you when he's got something. Why would I not?'

Jennifer didn't reply. There was no point. There'd only be a row and she could do without one on her only day off. Instead she left the bedroom and went into the tiny kitchen to make a cup of tea.

'Do you want a brew?' she called, biting her lip in an attempt to quell the tears which were suddenly threatening to spill down her cheeks.

'Go on then,' called Aidan 'Seeing as I've got to go out in this rain I may as well.'

As Jennifer waited for the kettle to boil, she wished Aidan would go. Apart from anything else her new book on reflexology had arrived and she wanted to start reading it in peace. She was seriously considering applying to do a course. Emma, a friend of hers from yoga, who was already a qualified practitioner, had told her a lot about it. The subject completely fascinated her. Becoming a certified reflexologist would not only provide a way to earn some more money but she suspected would also be something she'd enjoy.

If only Aidan would find something to get enthused about. It would make life a lot easier. Suddenly she was unable to prevent one solitary tear from rolling down her cheek and onto the laminate worktop which due to how old it was never looked totally clean no matter how much she scrubbed it. She wiped the tear away impatiently, bored of feeling down. Bored of feeling bored.

She glanced at the cork notice-board which was covered in bills, all of which needed paying, takeaway menus, letters from Nath's school and in the middle, a photograph. A tatty, dog eared photo of her mum and dad, whom she hadn't seen for eighteen long years now. For what felt like the thousandth time her hand went to her dressing gown pocket to finger the letter she'd received from her mother only a week ago. It had come to her work address and she knew it pretty much off by heart.

Her mum wanted to see her. Her dad still hadn't come round but her mum had decided it was finally time to let bygones be bygones. The only decision that needed to be made was where and when. Possibly the most surprising thing of all to Jennifer, was that rather than questioning the decision to contact her mother in order to hold out an olive branch, all she did find herself debating was why she'd left it this long.

As she was stirring the teas Aidan appeared behind her and wrapped his arms around her.

'Alright gorgeous?'

'Yeah,' she said miserably, feeling anything but.

'You just rest up while I go out. Put your feet up,' he said, as if he was bestowing some massive favour upon her.

Too right she'd be putting her feet up. She had a double shift tomorrow, and one the day after that and besides, 'putting his feet up' was all Aidan seemed capable of doing these days, so why shouldn't she?

'Even go back to bed. I know you've been dying to start reading that book. Then perhaps me, you and Nath can have something from the chippy tonight?'

'Alright,' she agreed, slightly mollified 'Sounds good.'

'Eh, what's up?' he said, spinning her round to face him 'If you're still worried about my mobile bill don't be. Worst comes to the worse I'll get my old 'pay as you go' out but knowing you you'll rake the tips in tomorrow. I know my girl and not only are you my sexy little minx, you're a bloody good waitress too.'

In that instance Jennifer figured she should just tell him. After all, given everything she'd given up for him over the years, friends, family, an education, prospects, surely he wouldn't begrudge her the chance to rekindle relationships which had been put on hold for long enough now? There wasn't so much water under the bridge as opposed to an entire river.

'Mum wrote to me,' she said calmly, deciding to omit the fact that she'd been the one to get in contact first.

Aidan's face froze so, assuming he hadn't heard properly, she repeated what she'd said.

'Mum wrote me a letter. She wants to see me and I think I'm going to go.'

'Why?' he said, looking totally flummoxed.

'Honestly? You need to ask why?'

'Of course I need to ask why,' he exclaimed, looking thunderous. 'After all these years of being sanctimonious, judgemental arseholes, I hardly think I'm weird for thinking you should give them a wide berth. They treated you like shit.'

Jennifer shook her head. 'No. That's the thing. I don't think they did. Not really,' she said. 'In fact, the older I get the more I think I treated *them* like shit. I'm the one who disappeared off to the other side of the world. I'm the one who gave up going to university so I could disappear to Australia with a bloke they'd never even met. And I'm also the one who then had to break it to them that that particular pipe dream had been ruined due to you getting caught with drugs. I happen to think *most* parents would take a pretty dim view of that.'

'This again,' cried Aidan, outraged 'Are you ever going to get over it? It's not like I was dealing heroin or anything. A bit of pot it was. Where's the harm in that? I was bloody unlucky to get caught but I was hardly ruining lives.'

'Except you were,' Jennifer muttered, feeling on the brink of a very dangerous conversation.

'What's that supposed to mean?' he said, his face stony.

'Nothing,' she said rolling her eyes in frustration 'It's just that... well, you have to remember that the whole point of me not going home was because we decided we wanted to live in the sunshine, to build a life in Oz, in the sunshine. Only it didn't quite work out like that did it?'

'No, it didn't Jen, but then you forgetting to take your pill was hardly the plan either was it?'

Jennifer shrugged. The memory of finding out that on top of everything else she was pregnant at the age of twenty two was still more bitter than sweet.

'But I stood by you,' retorted Aidan, indignant and hurt. 'I stood by you when thousands of blokes might have left you to it, or forced you to have an abortion. I was a free spirit remember? Having a wife and kid wasn't exactly part of my master plan either but I'm glad we did it. I wouldn't be without Nath, would you?'

'Of course not,' said Jennifer sincerely 'Of course I wouldn't be, but I'm not so sure I should have had to go without having my mum and dad in my life for all this time either. And....... perhaps if I'd been less chippy with them, less defensive, maybe even a bit apologetic about how things had turned out I wouldn't have had to be.'

Finally she met his gaze. He looked defensive and huffy, knowing full well that her words were an accusation aimed firmly at him for he'd always encouraged her to be on the offensive with her parents.

'Look at us,' she said, gesturing around the small kitchen and flat. 'I'm thirty-bloody-eight, Aidan. Thirty-eight and living in a shithole. I work every hour god sends in a stinking restaurant which I'm starting to hate and for what? I've got no real friends here apart from Emma and she's flaky at the best of times, no family, except you and Nath of course, and I spend most of the time feeling....'

'Feeling what?' he said, stonily.

'Feeling... a bit... embarrassed about how things have turned out,' she admitted quietly, knowing that although it was a terrible thing to say it was also unutterably true.

'Well screw you,' Aidan said, and as he did, the lurch in Jennifer's stomach told her she may have said too much. There were some things you couldn't take back and as much as she resented him he was still her man and for all their problems he still held her tight, each and every night, which did much to soothe her troubled head. They were still intimate all the time and although things had hardly turned out like they did in the movies, the physical bond they shared, the child they'd made and the years they'd been together were a pretty efficient type of glue.

'I'm sorry,' she called after him.

'Whatever Jennifer, I don't want to hear it,' he said, going into the hall and pulling on his doc marten boots before storming out, presumably (hopefully) to go and sign on.

Jennifer flinched as the door slammed. She stood still for a while, soaking up the silence and wondering what to do. Eventually she decided upon nothing. He'd be back later and they could talk then. In the meantime, she'd got a few things off her chest which might be healthy and she was still determined to meet with her mother. So nothing had really changed.

13 | TUNNEL NUMBER ONE

Aidan: what could have been

'Someone here to see you, love,' said Lindsay, the manager of *Red Peppers*, the brasserie where Jennifer worked. The conspiratorial wink which accompanied this piece of information told Jennifer it was definitely Aidan. She confided in Lindsay a lot. The older lady was kind, always had time to listen and usually appreciated having a bit of gossip to think about other than what was happening at the restaurant. And so last night, when things had quietened down at around ten o clock Jennifer had told Lindsay how Aidan was sulking with her and had been ever since she'd announced her intention to see her mum. Her boss' advice had been concise and to the point: 'Tell him to bog off and to stop being such a baby.'

'Go on, you can have a quick ten minutes,' Lindsay said now, grabbing an apron 'I'll cover for you. Have table nine had their wine?'

'Not yet and the couple on two have asked for more bread. Thanks Linds',' said Jennifer gratefully.

She went to the front of the restaurant where Aidan was indeed stood waiting for her, incongruous in his huge woolly cardigan and combat trousers. For a while now his hair had been slightly dreaded and not for the first time Jennifer wished he'd smarten up his act a bit. If he stopped dressing like some kind of crusty perhaps there'd be a sliver of a chance he could get himself some work? It wasn't like there was a massive demand for middle aged, pot smoking surf dudes in Carlisle.

'Is Nath at home?' she asked, feeling exhausted to her very bones now that she'd stopped for a second.

'He's next door, getting a drink from the newsagents.'

On cue, Nathan appeared, clutching a can of Fanta.

'Alright, babe?' said Jennifer, pleased to see him. He was still in his uniform. 'Has your dad given you some tea?'

Nathan nodded.
'What did you have?'

'We had egg didn't we?' answered Aidan on his behalf.

'Shall I ask Lindsay if there's any spare banoffee?' said Jennifer, knowing it was his favourite and wishing she had more time to cook for her son. He was looking so tall. His body, which at one point had been quite scrawny, all arms and legs, was starting to fill out. He was sixteen and growing before her very eyes it seemed. Her beautiful boy was becoming a man.

'Banoffee would be ace if there is any,' Nathan said, still boyish enough to get excited about his favourite dessert.

Jennifer gestured to Aidan to head out to the back of the restaurant while she got Nathan settled at one of the only spare tables with a huge slab of creamy pie.

'There you go love, get that down you. Right, I'd better go and see what your Dad wants.'

'Ok…oh, hang on a minute, Mum, I've got something for you.' Jennifer watched as her son stood up briefly again so he could get into the pockets of his trousers. He fished out a crumpled ten pound note and five pound coins and placed them on the table.
'What's that for?' she asked, bemused.

'It's for you,' Nathan said, sitting down again and making a start on his dessert, eyes practically rolling to the back of his head as he enjoyed his first hit of thick cream and toffee.

'What's the money for Nath?' repeated Jennifer.

'I earned it the other night, didn't I? When I babysat. I want you to have it.'

'Don't be silly,' she said immediately.

'I'm not. You're always working in here and I know Dad hasn't done much lately, so I just want to help out a bit.'

Jennifer swallowed, touched by her son's gesture; yet despairing that her boy was learning to be a man, not from example but as a result of his father's glaring uselessness. 'Thank you,' she said, reaching out to accept the money as that was clearly what Nathan wanted but deeply saddened by the fact he'd picked up on how much they were struggling. She went to give him a hug across the table.

'Mum,' he protested, embarrassed by her public display of affection.

'Sorry,' she said grinning 'It's just I don't half love you, my precious, generous boy. And I don't want you worrying about money. We're fine.'

'Pack it in,' said Nathan, smiling.

'Right, I'd better go and see what Dad wants,' she said, wishing it was the end of the night so she could go home with them. It had been a busy lunchtime shift and the evening was shaping up to be the same which was great in terms of tips but not so good for her aching feet.

Round the back of the restaurant, in the small courtyard, Jennifer breathed deeply. The fresh May evening air was good for the soul. Occasionally, when she could afford it, she liked to go to a yoga class in the church hall round the corner from the flat. The teacher, Kerry, was amazing; fifty years old with a figure most thirty-year olds would be proud of. Lithe, toned and strong, there wasn't much physical evidence she'd been around for half a century. Kerry had once told Jennifer that everyone had a finite amount of breaths to take during their lives, hence why, if you could slow down your breathing and therefore your stress levels, you would live longer.

Whenever Jennifer remembered this and made the effort to become 'aware of her breath' she was often dismayed to discover how sharp and quick her intake was. It was always a depressing reminder of the pace she was going at and she worried that if she didn't slow down and her teacher's theory was correct, she might keel over any minute.

'You alright?' asked Aidan, looking sheepish as she approached and flicking away the ends of a roll up which he stamped out with his boot.

'Yeah, what did you want to talk about? Has this got anything to do with Nath? Because I'm worried about him you know. He's not stupid. He can tell when things aren't right between us.'
'Nath's fine. Come here you,' he said, drawing her tense body in for a hug.

Ordinarily she would have enjoyed the comforting sensation of being encircled in his arms only right now she was too in need of a shower to relax into it properly. *Red Peppers* was a lovely restaurant but she'd be quite happy never to see a piece of deep-fried camembert again as long as she lived. It was their most popular starter and the stench of fried cheese seemed to be ingrained into the fibres of every top she owned.

'So anyway, I came to say that if you really want to see your mum, it's fine by me.'

'That's good of you,' she said sarcastically.

'Look, there's no need for that, Jen. You have to remember that up until a week ago I thought we were on the same page as far as your parents were concerned, you know? I mean, you're the one who used to get so fed up with their attitude and with how judgemental they were.'

Jennifer shrugged. She couldn't agree or disagree because if she were being totally honest, she couldn't really remember how things had managed to get as bad as they had. She also wasn't sure she really cared any more either. All she did know was that she had a family, and that many moons ago she also used to have good, good friends, better ones than she'd ever made since. Only the other day she'd looked up Karen on *reUNIon*. It hadn't taken long to find her at which point she'd written her prediction of what she'd thought she'd be up to now. She'd written that she thought she'd be happy, married, possibly with a couple of kids and no doubt in some high powered impressive job, living the high life. She was still waiting to hear back though and if her old friend did ever make the effort to respond, she wasn't sure she'd be brave enough to read what Karen had predicted for her. After all this time she still missed her though. She missed all her old friends in fact but not as much as she missed the feeling of belonging. Furthermore, these days she was starting to think she might need, or maybe just want, more in her life than she had at the moment. Hence the reflexology course which was one of the ways in which she intended to improve things and make life more interesting. She'd given up a lot to be with Aidan and knew she was in danger of growing bitter if she didn't take charge of her own destiny a bit more because, if she was being honest to the point of being brutal, she wasn't totally sure he'd been worth it. All the sacrifice, all the tears and sadness that had gone hand in hand with the disintegration of her relationship with her parents.

It hadn't mattered how many times she'd tried to stick up for him, or had tried to explain that actually, dabbling with a bit of marijuana hardly made him an evil drug baron. It had been a pointless task because her parents were the kind of people who considered all drugs to be inherently dangerous and wrong. Full stop. Worse still, what they really couldn't get their heads around was why he would have taken such a risk when he was responsible for their only daughter.

At the time Jennifer simply hadn't been able to even consider that they may have had a point. If she had, she would have also been admitting to herself and everybody else that she'd made a mistake. A huge, life changing mistake.

She regarded Aidan now. Her man. He was so bloody useless and yet there was something about him which still, after all these years, she was drawn to. Something chemical no doubt. She stepped towards him and held his face in her hands, looking up at him as she had a thousand times before.
'It's fine, let's forget about it. I'm just pleased you're cool about me seeing her.'

They hugged and as they did Jennifer buried her face deep into Aidan's side. As ever she drew comfort from the physical sensation of being held and used it as a balm to soothe her sad, troubled soul. This felt normal to her, but what she didn't realise was that she'd forgotten what it was to feel truly happy.

14 | Monday

For three days a week Jennifer worked in Hayes and Ludlow, one of the many estate agents on the High Street. She was permanently amazed by how any of them managed to stay in business. So many shop fronts had changed in recent years, hit by the recession, but it seemed that in this enclave of South West London, if you were a hairdresser's, an Indian restaurant or an estate agent you could weather any financial shit storm.

Before having children Jennifer had worked in marketing, something she'd been able to use her degree for. She'd quite enjoyed it; she'd worn a suit and had often gone for after work drinks with her colleagues. And then she'd had children, at which point it hadn't made much financial sense for her to continue working. So the suits she could no longer fit into anymore had been put away, as had any shoes with a vague heel. Gradually she'd come to terms with the fact that the hours between five and seven were no longer nice ones to drink during, unless you counted a quick swig of wine gulped directly from the bottle in order to get through bath time, and she was happy with this arrangement. By the time she'd forked out for childcare there wouldn't have been a great deal of her wages left in her pocket, plus she hadn't banked on the emotional guilt she would feel when considering leaving her offspring in a nursery or with a child-minder when she didn't really have to. Max's wage was enough for them to survive on. Just about. Although their monthly expenditure certainly became something that had to be planned down to the last penny.

However, as soon as their youngest, Polly, had started school in September, working had become a sensible option again. The money couldn't be anything but extremely useful and it certainly beat feeling obliged to clean the bathroom on a day to day basis. Of course, having been out of the rat race for so long and with jobs so scarce, Jennifer had known she was unlikely to get anything even vaguely resembling her old career. So, although being an estate agent hadn't exactly been her burning ambition in life, when she was offered the job, she'd decided it was far, far better than nothing. She got to poke around people's houses, it got her out of her own house and into other people's and there was the added bonus that she got to chat to Lee all day.

Lee was lovely. Black, young and very handsome. He was really quiet, or at least he was until you got to know him. He had a kind face and a shaved head, usually two things that don't go hand in hand and yet possibly should, for as it turns out they're a remarkably good combination, and as he grew more comfortable around Jennifer, that is to say once he'd got the measure of her, his true personality unfurled, revealing charm, wit and a pretty sexy glint in his eye. A glint that Jennifer knew she was too old to reciprocate and yet couldn't pretend she hadn't noticed. Due to the fact she wasn't dead and that her womb was still intact and in good working order.

Every day, Lee travelled miles into work from his flat in Wood Green which was pretty much at the end of the Piccadilly line, meaning his commute consisted not only of a very long tube journey but also a bus ride from Hammersmith. How far he was prepared to travel to work amazed Jennifer, but then she had enough self- awareness to know she'd probably adopted her fellow neighbours' rather parochial attitude that unless something was happening within spitting distance of your front door it was all a mammoth effort. Take going out for instance. Many of the mums at school would speak of 'going into town' as if it were akin to trekking in the Himalayas in terms of adventure. Popping to nearby Kingston or to the Kew retail centre was considered pretty adventurous so hopping on a bus and then a tube to get anywhere was positively outlandish. Jennifer liked hearing about Lee's exploits, partly because they were varied, but mainly because they didn't involve anywhere local.

Right now he was filling her in on what he'd been up to at the weekend.

'So then where did you go?'

'So after that we ended up going on to this amazing club in Shoreditch. Have you heard of East Village?' he asked, at which point Jennifer decided she might quite passionately love him for assuming there might be even a vague possibility she'd know where the hell he was talking about.

'Um,' she turned her head to one side, in what she hoped was an attractive fashion 'I've definitely heard of it,' she lied 'But I don't think I've been there.'

'Oh right, well you should. It's brilliant. There was this one DJ who I'd definitely go and see again. He was amazing. He played, like, really, really good Dubstep mixed up with more commercial tunes. Like remixes of pop tunes, Adele and that.'

'Cool,' said Jennifer, wondering what Dubstep was and deciding to google it and find out the minute she could. God she'd love a night out clubbing. She hadn't had a proper dance since… well, probably New Year's Eve and that was in someone's kitchen surrounded by men who were wearing cords or chinos. When she was at university she'd loved raving, had discovered it with a vengeance and for the first two years had spent a lot of time getting wasted. Thinking about it, she'd spent a lot of the third year getting wasted as well, only with a bit of studying thrown in for good measure. Then, after university, once she'd got a job and had started working, she'd continued to go clubbing regularly at weekends, liking nothing more than getting sweaty in a room full of strangers who only had the music and the atmosphere in common, rendering small talk not just pointless but also impossible. Instead it had been enough simply to grin at one another like loons, and dance. All pretty tribal and primitive if you really thought about it, and yet perhaps more natural than endlessly discussing secondary education over Jamie Oliver recipes and never ending bottles of wine. Better for the waistline too.

She smiled ruefully now as it occurred to her that in those days she could have told Lee where all the best nights in London were, who played at them, plus could have sorted out the guest list to boot. Not anymore though.

'What did you get up to?' asked Lee.

'Oh...er, well the kids had a sleepover on Friday so we just had a night in,' she said, blushing as she did so, hating how that mere sentence sounded so full of innuendo. Wasted innuendo. Then, on Saturday, we had some mates round for lunch which was really fun,' she fibbed.

'Oh cool, that sounds nice,' he said politely.

'How old are you Lee?' she asked suddenly, changing the subject.

'Me?' said Lee, looking surprised.

'Well there's no one else in here right now.'

'Twenty-three.'

'Ooh lucky bastard,' she replied flatly.

He shrugged, conveying that of course there was nothing lucky about it at all. Twenty-three years was simply the amount of time he'd been on the planet.

'I'll be twenty-four in October,' he offered, almost apologetically. 'Why? How old are you then? You're not that old.'

'How old do you think I am?' she said, noting the word 'that' and not liking it. She knew full well asking him to guess was a horrible thing to do to him, but didn't care sufficiently to stop herself.

'Um...'

She could see Lee concentrating, desperate not to mess his answer up thus offending her. She knew then that whatever age he thought she was he would undoubtedly shave a few years off, just to be polite.

'Thirty, thirty-one?'

'Thirty-eight,' she said, surmising that in that case he must think she was about thirty-four, which wasn't bad at all. She'd take that.

To her immense pleasure Lee looked genuinely surprised. 'Oh right, well you definitely look younger than that. You're a proper....'

'What?' laughed Jennifer.

'Nothing,' blushed Lee, looking mortified 'I was about to say something really… Well, something which would have put you well within your rights to think I was an idiot.'

'Oh go on, you've got to say now,' urged Jennifer. This was more fun than she'd had in ages, only just then Patrick Ludlow, one of the partners, came in, putting paid to any more inappropriate, non -work based, flirtatious chat with a minor.

Reluctantly Jennifer picked up a set of keys on her desk and went to meet her two thirty viewing, the last one she'd do before picking up the children from school.

In that moment she hated herself slightly because deep down she'd been hoping that Lee had been about to call her a 'Milf'. A word which was tasteless at best, offensively sexist at worst and which would ordinarily have her feminist hackles up. Yet had Lee thought she was one, if she was being entirely honest, she would have felt pleased. Oh god, she was definitely going through some kind of rather worrying 'phase'. There was no doubt about it.

As she showed a couple around a rather pokey, over- priced, two-bedroom flat all she could think about was how despite his youth, Lee afforded her the respect of speaking to her on his level. He didn't treat her, or make her feel boring or 'Mumsy' but instead spoke to her as a friend and as a woman, reminding her along the way how good that felt. She liked having a younger friend and briefly wondered whether she should suggest joining him and his mates on a night out at some stage. Or would he balk at the idea of being seen out with someone who occasionally bought clothes from Marks and Spencer, albeit only from The Limited Collection (never from Autograph and *certainly* never from Per Una)?

She was pretty sure Max wouldn't mind if she said she was going clubbing with Lee. He'd probably take the piss out of her a bit but to be fair he was usually pretty cool about things like that, allowing her freedom, because he trusted her implicitly. So maybe she should stop being so wet and just do it?

Still, twenty-three. That had been a fairly devastating moment. She'd had him down as at least twenty- six. What had she been up to at twenty- three she wondered once she'd said goodbye to the by now disillusioned and thoroughly depressed couple who'd just realised they probably couldn't ever afford to get on the housing ladder unless they bought a skip and lived in that.

At twenty-three she'd been in her last year at university and was going out with Tim of course. Tim who was busy planning the empire he was going to build, rule and dominate. God, it all felt like a million years ago in some ways.

That night Jennifer cooked an especially nice dinner for herself and Max, insisting that they ate it at the table over a bottle of wine.

'So, how was your day?' asked Jennifer.

'Good thanks, Judith and I had to give a presentation this morning which went really well. She certainly knows how to communicate that one. I'll give her that for nothing.'

'Did she ever 'communicate' anything about last weekend by the way? Like for instance, did she have chronic diarrhoea on Sunday night or was she ok?'

Max grinned 'I think she was fine, although I had to come clean about the chickens.'

'What do you mean?' said Jennifer, frozen in horror.

'It's not a big deal, I just told her they were from a deli and that we'd been a bit worried that we might have poisoned everyone.'

'Oh god,' cringed Jennifer, wishing he hadn't and feeling inexplicably furious that he was always being so fucking chummy with ruddy Judith.

'She was fine,' added Max 'We laughed over it. We also laughed about the fact that Henry just shovelled it all in without even a second look, whereas we were all clearly quietly worrying for our guts.'

'So you were laughing at me basically,' mumbled Jennifer.

Max tutted 'No, we weren't. Funnily enough Judith and I don't spend our time being mean about you.'

'Oh, well what do you and Judith spend 'your time' doing then?' spluttered Jennifer, shaking parmesan unnecessarily vigorously over her spaghetti Bolognese.

Max sighed but said nothing.

'What?' snapped Jennifer.

'Nothing.'

'No seriously what? Don't just sigh like that. I'm not stupid. I can tell you've got something to say.'

'I'm just a bit fed up with you being so...angry all the time. I don't know what's got into you lately. You're so aggressive about everything.'

Jennifer put the cheese down and regarded her husband before exhaling hard. He had a point. Yet what she wanted to articulate but for some reason couldn't, was that she was only acting aggressively because lately the way he was being made her feel defensive. 'I know.... you're right. I don't know what's got into me lately either.'

'Well not me, that's for sure,' Max quipped, which did at least raise a smile, albeit a sad one.

'I just......'

'What is it?' he said and for the first time in a long time Jennifer felt like he really wanted to know.

'I don't know,' she said truthfully 'It's just lately I've been questioning everything you know?'

'Like what?'

'Like what the hell I'm doing with my life. I mean, I'm thirty-eight, I work three days a week in an estate agent, which is perfectly fine, only I earn pretty much less money than our weekly food bills. You and I seem to be in a bit of a rut. Plus, I seem to irritate you more than I used to, and I know we've got everything and that I should be bloody grateful for that... but I just feel so sad at the moment. And a bit... frustrated... And, if I'm being totally honest, I'm getting a bit fed up with hearing about flipping Judith every five seconds.'

Max looked at her for a while then shovelled some more spaghetti in his mouth, seemingly unmoved by her outburst.

'You,' he said, pointing at her with his fork 'are having an M-L-C'

'A what?' said Jennifer, irritated that he had already come up with some crap acronym for what she personally felt was a pretty life changing and difficult phase.

'An M-L-C,' he repeated. 'Mid. Life. Crisis. You've always been a bit impatient so instead of waiting to get to forty you're bringing it forward to thirty-eight.'

'I'm not sure it's as simple as that,' said Jennifer, feeling flustered. 'I mean, admittedly I'm sure there is a bit of that in the mix. I hate being our age sometimes. I hate the fact we never go out dancing and that a lot of people my age wear boot-cut jeans but it's more than that Max. I don't think they just hand out anti-depressants to anyone.'

'I know,' he said, not looking totally convinced 'And I know you've been down but you've got to remember that you're doing great. You're busy with the kids. You've got a job, which helps bring in a bit of spending money.'

'Patronising.'

'Sorry.'

'How about a holiday?' suggested Jennifer, suddenly desperate not to be anxious and confused all the time. 'I know we said we weren't going to have one this year but you know what? I think it might be just what we need, as a family and more to the point as a couple.'

'No,' said Max. 'You were the one who wanted to paint the front of the house last year, plus we don't know what's happening with my work so let's just stick to the plan. We can go to my parents in the holidays for a while.'

'Oh well that'll be a stress buster,' said Jennifer deeply sarcastically, before taking a deep breath and trying again. 'Ok, look, I know money's a bit tight but how about if I take on some extra days at the agency? Then I can pay for us to go away.'

'Er......where?' laughed Max, in a way that made her want to grab the grater and use it on his face.

'I don't know. Perhaps we could get a good deal somewhere last minute in Spain, or wherever. I just think I've been feeling so down lately and a change of scene might sort me out. Give me something to look forward to. I don't care if it's somewhere cheap and cheery.'

'Look, I just think it's a bad idea,' said Max 'I would rather not go anywhere than go somewhere shit and depressing just because it's the only thing we can afford. If my contract gets extended we'll go on holiday next year, but this year we're in the middle of a massive recession in case you hadn't noticed so we have to go without and that's that.

'Again. Patronising,' said Jennifer.

Later, as they sat in silence watching telly, Jennifer thought despairingly of their earlier exchange. She wasn't naive or stupid. She knew there was a bloody recession on but sometimes wished Max would be a little less cautious. Yes, they would have to scrimp a bit to go away but wouldn't it be worth it? Wasn't getting things back on track between them worth splurging on? After all, a divorce would be far more damaging to their finances than a holiday she thought bitterly, deciding against voicing this out loud.

For some reason her ex, Tim, popped into her head. There was no chance he'd be going without a holiday this year she thought wryly. His wife was probably permanently on one long holiday, like a leathered lizard bedecked in jewels. In fact, they probably owned a frigging island somewhere. Like Richard Branson.

'Do you want to watch another episode?' yawned Max.

'No, you're alright,' she said 'I think I might go and have a bath.'

Ten minutes later as she slid into water hot enough to cause serious problems with her veins, Max suddenly gave her a terrible shock by poking his head round the bathroom door on his way to bed.

'By the way,' he said 'If you start wearing mini- skirts with knee high boots we can definitely confirm the M.L.C.'

Jennifer summoned up her most sarcastic face possible and casually flicked him the bird before sliding into the water, thinking as she did so, and I can confirm that you are well and truly getting on my tits.

15 THE PAST

Tim, August 1997

Things hadn't been particularly great between Jennifer and Tim for a while now. Throughout their final year at Sussex, his obsession with *reUNIon* had over ridden everything, including his degree, meaning that instead of achieving the first he'd always been predicted he'd eventually come away with a 2:1. Jennifer had probably only truly realised the extent of his belief and zeal for *reUNIon* when he hadn't seemed too bothered. She may have given up trying to compete ages ago but that didn't mean she didn't feel jealous of the object of his obsession sometimes. If *reUNIon* were a woman she would merrily scratch her eyes out.

As for Jennifer herself, degree wise she came away with a third. She was pleased to have passed but deep down felt a gnawing anxiety, a worry that perhaps she may just have wasted a few years of her life which she'd never get back. She'd had a great time socially, could skin up with one hand and had built up a pretty impressive resistance to alcohol but other than that, what had she really got out of her years at university? On top of her rather non astounding academic achievement she was also concerned that, with regard to her and Tim, it was starting to feel like their student days may have been the glue holding them together.

She was in a huge amount of debt, was living back at home and for the time being was working in Miss Selfridge. Her mood was mainly despondent and she and Tim were ploughing on with their relationship yet didn't seem to be having much fun. Meanwhile, Tim had (typically) managed to rent a flat which was ridiculously luxurious for someone of his age, companies were beginning to take an interest in his software designs, plus he had lots of meetings lined up and a potential job at Apple. These days, just simply being around him was enough to make Jennifer feel like one big massive loser.

At the same time the pressure was on. She was only too aware that this summer was the very last bit of time she could get away with being directionless and without any kind of real career plan before people (her parents) started to lose patience. It was as if she could almost see the days disappearing like sand through a giant egg timer and she could hardly bear to think about the fact that despite the still clement weather there was a definite hint of autumn in the evening air. It was the last day of August, summer was officially drawing to a close and she was half expecting a claxon to go off, along with a tannoy announcement saying 'Jennifer, your time's up. You are now officially expected to get your shit together and be a responsible adult.'

Last night she and Tim had been out for drinks at a bar and had come back to his after, (always preferable to hiding up in her small room at home, her mum banging on the door every five minutes asking if they wanted a cup of tea when in fact what she was really checking was whether or not they were having sex).

'Shall we go out for breakfast?' asked Tim now, still bashing away at his computer. He'd been up for a while, had showered, got dressed and probably changed the world while Jennifer had been dozing and trying to figure out whether she wanted tea or coffee.

'I don't know,' she said unhelpfully, staring into the middle distance.

Tim lived in Notting Hill in the most beautiful flat Jennifer had ever been in. It had one spacious, light bedroom which had two huge windows, each of which was flanked by a tiny wrought iron balcony. When standing on them you could see right the way up and down the whole of Elgin Crescent and beyond, to the hustle and bustle of Portobello. Tim had furnished the bedroom sparsely. There was a huge bed with crisp white linen which got changed weekly by the cleaner. Naturally. Other than that there was just a huge white freestanding wardrobe and some shelves which housed his collection of biographies and huge tomes on computing. The bathroom was en suite and didn't actually include a bath. However, the powerful shower more than made up for the lack of one. The living room, which was where they were sitting now, had wooden floors, was spacious enough to include two large grey sofas and led onto an open plan kitchen diner which was small but perfectly formed. It boasted a stainless steel oven with no less than six gas rings on top of it. Jennifer stared in that direction now, appreciating as ever how the walls of the kitchen area had been painted a startling but gorgeous shade of bright sky blue, the perfect contrast to the pale wood units and stainless steel appliances. The living room was painted in some deeply tasteful shade of pale taupe and had two sets of floor to almost ceiling height glass doors on one side which were also framed by wrought iron Juliet balconies. The doors were open now and the morning breeze was blowing the calico curtains into the room.

'It's like a soft rock video in here,' she joked absent-mindedly but Tim didn't reply. Instead he finally shut down his computer and almost without taking a pause between activities, leapt over to where she was sitting and made what can only be described as a lunge for her. With a look of intent and a mischievous, somewhat off-putting, school boy grin on his face, he grabbed her, stuck his hand up her jumper and started massaging her left breast. He wasn't particularly tender about it though. If anything it was slightly painful. However, mistaking her gasp for one of passion he upped the ante, and before she knew it he was really going for it, tuning in her nipple like he was trying to get an FM frequency.

Still, it seemed to be working for him for his breath grew short and as he huffed and puffed in her ear Jennifer decided she ought really to try and get into it. She was still in her pyjamas so he had pretty easy access to everything. However, when he suddenly stopped and looked at her with a pleading expression she'd come to know only too well, her heart sunk.

'Estate agent?'

'Really?'

'Yes,' he said enthusiastically 'You should go out into the corridor and pretend you've arrived to do an evaluation.'

At this Jennifer felt full of irritation at which point she couldn't pretend anymore. 'Why can't I just be naked for once?'

What?'

'Plain old me is never enough is it? You always want me to be someone else these days. But to be honest I don't really feel like putting on a suit right now and acting like I'm terribly excited by your flat's potential.' Her frustration was a long time coming and finally, after a long time spent avoiding the issue, it now bubbled over, causing her to say 'Just for once it would be nice if you wanted to have sex with me, Jennifer. Not Trixie the masseuse, Suzy the police officer, Laura the teacher or now Jane the frigging estate agent.'

At this Tim pulled away, practically throwing her onto the other side of the sofa 'Oh well that's charming. Talk about know how to get rid of someone's erection for Christ's sake.'

'Well, I'm sorry,' said Jennifer primly 'But perhaps you need to take into consideration what I want for a change, which is not necessarily always having to remember my lines and be in fancy dress every time I want to have sex with my boyfriend.'

'No, all you want is to whinge at me,' he said, though Jennifer noticed that at least he'd had the decency to blush a pale pink.

'That's out of order,' she snapped. 'As if I nag?'

'It's true. Nag, nag, nag, that's all you do,' he said.

'That's rubbish,' she said, hurriedly pulling up her pyjama bottoms 'What on earth could you say I nag you about?'

'Ooh, well, let me see now.... my work, er.... seeing you, what I'm up to on a day to day basis, Sean, whether or not I'm coming out to whatever night of torture you and Karen have arranged.' He paused, letting his mean words sink in. He looked very defensive and Jennifer sensed he was only lashing out so much because he was still embarrassed about his ridiculous addiction to role play.

'Frankly, what you should be focused on,' he continued now, unable to look her in the eye 'is what you're doing with yourself and with your life.'

'Oh well, it's all coming out now,' said Jennifer, who by now was so angry that she'd started contemplating what to throw out of the window. On a braver day she'd have plumped for the computer but knew it would result in death and not just hers if it landed on a passer-by's head.

'I'm just saying that if you spent a little more energy deciding what it is you want to do, rather than worrying about how much time I spend with Sean, or how little time I spend with Pete and bloody Karen you might be better off.'

'Oh will you get over yourself,' shouted Jennifer. 'Honestly, if I hear you mention Karen in an argument one more time I'll lose it. What have you got against her? I mean, I know she can be prickly sometimes but now she's with Pete she's calmed right down, they're very happy and bring out the best in one another. She's been so much more tolerant. Why can't you be the same?'

'Tolerant?' spat Tim. 'If two people have to be tolerant of one another then I would suggest they shouldn't bother going to the effort full stop. Life's too short. And yes, the fact she's had a complete personality transplant since getting together with Pete hasn't escaped me but why I should be a slave to her ridiculously volatile state, which seems solely dependent on if she's getting any sex, is anyone's guess.'

'Well at least she's not permanently trying to remember which accent she's supposed to be putting on,' stormed Jennifer, livid beyond belief, springing up from the sofa and heading for the bedroom. Arguing while wearing pyjamas was making her feel weird. She needed jeans and a jumper for this.

She had been so happy when Karen had got together with Pete at the end of university (ironically at the farewell party that Tim had thrown at their house, which was probably the best party Brighton had ever seen, and that was saying something). Pete was a good person, a big bear of a man, bright, kind and handsome and of West Indian descent, he'd worked very hard to get to university and had ambitions to be a graphic designer. He and Tim had got on, to an extent, but you could tell Pete thought he was stuck up. And he was right. Anyway, Karen was at last happy, and although nobody could have predicted that after a whole two years of living under the same roof, barely noticing one another, that she and Pete would have finally found each other, (underneath a pile of coats in Darren's room to be precise) the minute they did, it seemed obvious they were a great match. 'At least Karen's got a personality unlike the almost mute freak that is Sean,' she yelled from the bedroom where she had already yanked on some knickers and jeans and was in the process of doing up her bra.

'And at least he's got a brain and knows what he wants out of life,' retorted Tim.

And in that instance Jennifer stopped feeling angry and went cold. And a fraction of a second later she decided that she might be finished. Because actually, deep, deep down she knew that what he'd said earlier was probably right. With Tim she *did* turn into a harridan, a nag, a banshee. His success made her feel inadequate and yet didn't inspire her to do anything about her own situation. Instead, it fed her permanent sense of insecurity. Did she love him? She didn't really know, so perhaps that answered that one. Did she like him? Sometimes. She loved the way he challenged and stimulated her intellectually. Did she admire him? Hugely. There was something about Tim that screamed 'I AM GOING PLACES.' But did she want to go with him? She was no longer entirely sure she had the energy or the desire to. If she really thought about it she might possibly love his flat more than him. It was a tricky one though, a dilemma. She knew only too well there would be plenty of girls lining up to take her place if it became up for grabs. And no doubt they'd happily dress up in a Minnie Mouse outfit if it made him happy. Was this something she'd regret further down the line? Would she ever meet anyone else as eligible? Was the fear of ending up alone enough to stick with a relationship that didn't really make her feel happy?

Pulling a sweater over her head she decided what to do and as her decision was made, she was flooded with an eerie sense of calm.

'Tim,' she said, wandering back into the sitting room.

'What?'

'I can't do this anymore. We don't really make one another happy so why are we bothering? I think we should call it a day.'

'What?' he repeated, completely thrown. He sunk down onto the nearest sofa.

'I just think we should admit defeat,' she added more gently 'You see, you're right, I do spend far too much time having a go at you, mainly because I get jealous of how much attention you pay your work all the time.'

There, she'd said it.

Tim sighed 'And I only get frustrated because I know how much potential you have and it irritates me to see you procrastinating all the time and never actually... actioning anything.'

'Which just goes to show how different we are as people and that we'd probably be better off without one another,' she said flatly, knowing she was right and just wishing she'd had the balls to say it about two years earlier.

Tim got up and paced the room 'You're wrong,' he said.

'Am I?' said Jennifer.

'Totally wrong,' he said firmly. 'You're right for me Drew. Opposites attract and I don't really mind your inertia. It's only you I worry about because I know not having any direction gets to *you*. Personally I wouldn't care if you never did anything because I'm more than happy to take care of you. You know I am. You know I'm an old fashioned bloke at heart and I have no problem with men taking care of the finances and women looking after the home.'

'We're not living in the dark ages,' she spluttered. 'I don't want looking after thank you. And I don't necessarily want to be a ruddy housewife either.' Jennifer was surprised by her use of the word 'necessarily'. It was as though she was hedging her bets and disappointingly meant Tim was probably right. She really didn't know what she wanted out of life.

'Oh well that's a load of crap if you don't mind me saying,' said Tim. 'Of course you do. I've been looking out for you ever since we met, but I'm saying that I don't mind. I like it.'

Now Jennifer was completely on the back foot. Was that really how he'd seen it all these years? As though she'd been some pathetic free loading sap he'd had to look out for. And anyway, what exactly had he done for her? Though even as this last thought was formulated she was already thinking back to university and of all the times Tim had bailed her out. Of all the times he'd 'taken care of' a phone bill she couldn't afford. Of how much food she used to squirrel out of his fridge, secretly acknowledging that she was saving herself a few quid each time. She hardly ever paid when they went out and when she did, she used to make a thing of it, making sure he got the message. Ultimately however, if she had occasionally taken advantage of his deep pockets it had only been because she knew he could more than afford it and because he never minded. She felt ashamed. It was time to get a back bone.

'I do mind you saying and I don't like it,' she said. 'I don't want to be taken care of and I wasn't really aware that I had been or that you'd noticed. I mean, you've always been very generous but I wasn't aware I was riding on some Tim Purcell gravy train.'

'Oh come on Drew,' he said 'Don't give me that bullshit. And don't make some big issue out of it. Like I said, I have no problem looking after you. I like that you're a bit scatty, that you're quirky. I need that. It's a good foil for me. You're funny, you're sweet. I like your little eccentricities.'

Jennifer gulped and felt really, really sad that in two and a half years this was the first time he'd been able to articulate what it was he liked about her. She'd always wondered.

'You make me sound a bit.... simple.'

'Well, I have to say Drew, at times I do wonder.

Tim's attempt at a joke wasn't appreciated though.

'My name's Jennifer,' she said firmly. 'Not Drew. Just Jennifer. I am not a public school boy.' At this point she seriously considered adding '*which is why when you asked me to dress up as 'matron' I was particularly disturbed'* but thought against it because Tim was looking hurt enough as it was. 'Listen, we've had a good run, and yes, you are generous and perhaps I have taken that for granted, so I'm sorry for that. And I'm not saying I don't take the blame for my own lack of direction. But it's not just that. We don't do anything together anymore. We don't have fun together, go out together. I don't feel like we're together, haven't for ages. All you do is work.'

'I'm building a future.'

Jennifer nodded. 'I know and you'll be hugely successful, you already are. But, whilst I may be a bit dreamy and useless by comparison, I want to enjoy the present, and I'm not sure you'll ever know how to do that, no matter how much you achieve.'

His face was grim, his eyes flinty and confused. She could practically see his mind racing, so desperate was he to regain control of the situation. For a split second she felt really angry with him because actually he was quite controlling in a passive aggressive kind of way and perhaps if he hadn't put her down as much as he had she might have a bit more confidence in herself.

'So what are you saying? Do you want a break?'

'No,' she said quietly 'I'm saying that I think we should split up. I'm saying that while we've had some great times, we've forgotten how to have fun and that we're only young so that's not on. I'm saying that we don't necessarily bring out the best in each other and that I don't want to compete with *reUNIon* anymore. I'm really sorry.'

Tim gazed at her in shock from across the room and if she'd had any small lingering doubts as to whether or not she was doing the right thing they now all disappeared, because there wasn't just a physical distance between them but a whole aching chasm of wrongness. If she ended up lonely and depressed for the rest of her life so be it. It was surely better to be single than in a vaguely dysfunctional relationship. Even as she thought this though, she was overwhelmed with a sense of panic which she determinedly ignored.

She waited patiently, expecting Tim to digest what she had said, to think logically about it, before analysing the facts and then to interpret and manage them dispassionately. To her surprise though, instead he did something very out of character and that she never would have expected. He wept.

'Don't do this Jen,' he pleaded, his blue eyes suddenly brimming with surprised desperation and tears.

For a while she didn't reply. She was simply too surprised by his.... surprise.

'I just don't think we bring out the best in each other,' she repeated, now feeling a definite and very welcome sense of relief about having formed her decision. It was only then that she realised just how many doubts she must have been having for some time now. 'I'm sorry.'

'I can't believe you're being such a bitch,' said Tim.

'Don't get nasty,' she warned.

'Seriously though, I have done nothing but love you,' he ranted 'And this is how you repay me. How could you?'

She sighed and not wanting to continue the scene went to get her stuff from the bedroom. Though she'd probably leave the police woman outfit where it was.

'Just think about it for a few days Drew...um... Jen. Just don't do this on a whim, you'll regret it.'

'I'm sorry,' she repeated 'I've made up my mind.'

She gathered all her stuff into her hold all and switched on her phone. How odd. She had eight new text messages and the voicemail symbol was flashing. The first message she read simply said 'have you seen the news?'

'Weird,' said Jennifer.

'What?' said Tim, looking fairly pitiful. His tears were terribly disconcerting. So out of character.

'Switch on the telly a moment,' she instructed, and when he ignored her she went back into the lounge and did it herself.

Within seconds the reason she had so many messages, five of which were from her devastated mother, became clear. Princess Diana had died.

For the next three hours what had just passed between them suddenly became irrelevant, unimportant and completely secondary to the story which was unfolding on the news. Tim and Jennifer sat gazing at the footage in shock, feeling desperately sad. Jennifer was in floods and Tim was pretty choked, which was unexpected given that he was completely anti-royalist. A long while was spent wondering how it was that things could change so irrevocably on the turn of a sixpence before Jennifer finally felt able to wrench herself away from the telly to make her journey back to her mum and dad's. As she said goodbye she suspected it was the last time she would see Tim, because deep down she doubted they'd remain friends.

She was partially right. It was the last time Jennifer would see Tim in the flesh and yet a mere twelve months later there was no escaping his face and she saw him practically every day. When *reUNIon* finally, possibly inevitably, took off, it was everywhere, and so therefore so was Tim - including on one occasion, The Ten 'O'clock News.

16 | TUESDAY

'How did it go?' mouthed Karen, as Jennifer barrelled toward her friends in the pub, looking flustered.

'Fine,' she said dismissively, not wanting to discuss the disaster that had been last Friday night and her failure to lure her own husband into bed.

'You alright? You look stressed.'

'It's Max,' she said 'He knew I wanted to get out tonight and promised he'd get back early but of course ended up *having* to stay later at work. He's being really weird at the moment.'

'Well it's not his fault if he has to work late, I guess,' said Karen mildly, holding her handbag on her lap, like the queen. Having come straight from work she was wearing a rather staid black skirt suit and shirt and looked quite matronly. She didn't really resemble the feisty, big-boobed sex bomb she'd been in her youth but Karen had always been happy in her own skin and didn't care. She hated exercise and loved food and drink.

By contrast, Lucy was in firm control of her appearance. She was gym and yoga honed, spent a considerable part of her wages on good haircuts and highlights and had worked out that what she suited most was slim fitting clothes in shades which complimented rather than battled with her English complexion. After years of not feeling attractive in her youth, she had finally found her style mojo and grown into it.

'Anyway, enough of all that,' said Jennifer, not wanting to sound unreasonable but also unable to quash an uneasy niggle she'd had for ages that all was not right with her husband. 'How are you both and where's Esther?'

'Couldn't get a sitter,' said Lucy 'Or...wouldn't get a sitter, not sure which. I think money's a bit tight for them at the moment.'

'Ah, fair enough,' said Jennifer, thinking what a shame it was that these days it was seemingly impossible for their foursome to be precisely that. It was so difficult to find a time when they could all simultaneously abandon the responsibilities of work or childcare for a few paltry hours. 'I'm going to the bar. Are you both on wine? I'll get a bottle?'

Karen and Lucy nodded. As soon as she was out of earshot, Karen, pulled a face 'She's not happy, is she?'

'She's alright I think? Not her usual bubbly self admittedly, but she seems ok,' said Lucy.

When Jennifer returned from the bar though, Karen was determined to get to the bottom of things. 'Come on Jen, you're obviously fed up. Why don't you tell us what's really wrong? It can't just be Max getting home late. Surely that's not such a big deal?'

'Oh I don't know,' replied Jennifer, smiling wryly at how well Karen knew her. 'It's no biggie really. I'm just feeling a bit down. Things aren't that brilliant between me and Max at the moment, which he keeps blaming squarely on the fact that I'm having some sort of mid- life crisis, which to be fair I probably am.'

'Aren't we all,' laughed Lucy.

'Probably,' agreed Jennifer. 'It's a weird stage of life I think. I mean, on the one hand I'm permanently trying to remind myself that I've 'got it all', that I've got two lovely children, a husband, a roof over my head etc., yet on the other, if you'd told me when I was twenty-one that by thirty-eight I'd be permanently exhausted, that I'd be working part time in an estate agents and my relationship would be really stale, I'd have been horrified. Maybe I've always had a rose-tinted view of how life should be and I'm just a bit disappointed by the reality.'

'I know what you mean,' agreed Karen vehemently 'Take last week I got told by my bitch boss that I can't have a pay rise *yet again*, then five minutes later found out my male equivalent is earning ten grand more a year than me, so believe me when I say I know that 'how did it come to this' feeling.'

'That's awful!' said Jennifer. 'Total sex discrimination. Surely you can do them for that? Have you spoken to HR?'

'I'm working out what to do,' said Karen gloomily. 'To be honest, it's all me and Pete have talked about lately, so it's nice to think about other things tonight.' She laughed 'So let's get back to your problems.'

Jennifer shook her head in sympathy for her friend. 'Well, I'm so sorry to hear that and you know where I am if you want to talk about it. And, if it's schadenfreude you're after, at least you have a career. At this stage, there's not much chance of me ever resurrecting mine, which is probably why I focus so much on the shortcomings of my marriage.'

'But you and Max are solid as a rock,' protested Lucy, which Jennifer thought was a bit weird. It was her relationship after all. She was the only one of them actually in it so probably had a better idea of the shape it was in.

'Christ, if you two are in trouble what hope is there for the rest of us?'

Jennifer shrugged, uncomfortable about being held up as an example of the perfect couple all the time, a symptom of having married someone who got on well with all her friends. 'Well,' she answered eventually, thinking it was probably time to inject some positivity into the conversation before they got the urge to smash their wine glasses in unison and communally fling themselves on the floor, wailing. 'I think there probably is hope actually, and it comes in the form of Esther and Jim because, although they've been together since the dawn of time, I don't think *they* have any problems in terms of staleness. I know they've got their problems financially but the other day she told me that after a recent night out they ended up doing it in their downstairs loo. I couldn't believe it.'

'You're kidding me,' gasped Lucy 'They're like rabbits those two. How do they manage to keep things so fresh? I'd genuinely love to know.'

'Why? Aren't you and Dave getting on?' asked Jennifer, curious to hear.

'Oh, we're alright,' Lucy said flatly 'You know, we're fine, although recently I've wanted to murder him on a pretty much daily basis, not helped by the fact I've got a terrible crush on someone. There's this guy who works in the Pret, round the corner from my work and I've developed a complete fantasy about him, probably because my sex life is so non -existent, but I've been going there fully made up most days. I'm spending half my wages on coffee and feel permanently wired.'

'I had no idea you and Dave didn't have a great sex life,' said Jennifer, genuinely shocked.

'Well, it's not really the sort of thing you broadcast is it?' shrugged Lucy 'And it goes without saying I'd appreciate it if you kept it under your hat please.'

'Of course,' said Karen, who was dying for a cigarette. Usually she'd have already gone outside to have one by now but she didn't want to miss any of the conversation. It was all coming out tonight.

'Oh Luce. Well if it's any comfort, I know how you feel,' said Jennifer, full of genuine sympathy *and* empathy 'I know Max still loves me, but he just doesn't pay me any attention whatsoever. In fact sometimes I feel like he hasn't looked at me properly for years. It sucks doesn't it?'

'It's awful,' agreed Lucy, leaning in suddenly and lowering her voice to ensure only her friends could hear what she was going to say next 'I mean, you know you've hit rock bottom when you go to the clinic for a vaginal probe, to check you haven't got fibroids...and you actually enjoy it.'

Karen recoiled, her face a shocked picture, turning this way and that to check no one anywhere near them had heard 'That's one of the funniest and yet also most disgusting things I've ever heard in my life,' she gasped.

'I know,' laughed Lucy 'Or the most depressing, I'm still not sure which. I even told Dave about it, to demonstrate how truly desperate I am for him to get his mojo back but he just grunted and called me a weirdo. Now come on Jen, Max can't be that bad.'

'Mm....well, you say that, but I can't remember the last time he told me he loved me, or made me feel wanted. Every time I try to reach out to him he's either too tired, or can't be bothered. He's so.......casual about me, so complacent that sometimes I just really wish.....' Jennifer stared down at her glass and for a worrying moment her friends thought she might be about to cry. '.....sometimes wish I could have that feeling again, you know the one you get when you first meet someone and everything's amazing and they're madly in love with you and can't keep their hands off you.' She stopped, needing to express herself fully but slightly embarrassed by the next bit. 'I suppose I want to be....grabbed. I want to be....desired, loved.'

'But Max *does* love you,' insisted Lucy, seemingly determined not to hear what she was saying. Possibly Jennifer's woes held a mirror up to her own marriage and it wasn't one she wanted to look at. 'Any fool can see that.'

'Oh I don't doubt he loves me, like he loves his slippers or his iPad, but I don't think he *fancies* me anymore. He never wants to throw me on the bed, or stroke my face or stare into my eyes.'

'Oh for god's sake,' giggled Karen despite herself. 'You've got two children, of course he doesn't. That sort of passion never lasts, but it doesn't mean he doesn't find you attractive anymore.'

Oh really? Well then how come we haven't had sex in months then.'

'How many months is months?' asked Lucy.

'Four........no, actually five now, nearly six.'

Already privy to this information Karen simply looked on, though her face demonstrated how dire she really thought this was,'

'I'm not kidding,' said Jennifer in case anyone thought she was.

'I don't think that's that bad,' said Lucy, looking miserable.

That shut them up, not that Jennifer took any satisfaction from it.

'You are joking?' said Karen. 'Why? How many have you gone without for?'

'Seven... ish?' she half whispered.

'That's awful Lucy,' stated Karen.

Jennifer agreed. Was there an actual complacency virus going about?

'Well, it's probably not *that* out of the ordinary,' said Lucy, defensive 'I mean we have got two children who never bloody sleep, and I Dave's just been so stressed ever since he lost his job he's lost all his confidence. Sex is the last thing on his mind right now.'

'Fair enough,' agreed Jennifer nodding. And it was. Dave's sense of self- worth had diminished before their very eyes ever since he'd been made redundant. 'And I suppose with me and Max, we were never the sort of people who liked doing it in the evening. We always used to like doing it at the weekends, you know, when you could be leisurely about it in the mornings, so when you have children there's just never really an opportunity.'

'Blimey,' said Karen, still looking like her friends were talking another language. 'No wonder you both seem a bit frustrated. I think Pete would prefer doing it in *front* of the children, no matter how scarred it would leave them, rather than go without.'

Jennifer sighed 'It's not just the sex I miss. It's excitement. Sometimes I find myself worrying that I could be on my death bed thinking 'why didn't you get your kicks when you could you silly woman? Before you were too old and ugly to do anything about it.' I found myself remembering the time we went to Kos the other day.'

Her friend's faces immediately lit up at the memory.

'Oh my god, what were we like?' grinned Karen. 'Do you remember that awful policeman I was seeing?'

'Mark,' said Lucy.

'Yeah Mark. Did I tell you he sent me a Facebook friend request?'

'No way,' said Lucy 'He remembered your name after all these years?'

'Sure did,' said Karen proudly 'Of course I'm on there with my maiden name I suppose....he sent me a prediction via *reUNIon* too. Sorry Jen.'

'Do you remember sexy Aidan?' asked Jennifer, ignoring the reference to *reUNIon*. She was used to it.

'God yes,' said Lucy 'I was so jealous of you. He was beautiful.'

'I know. I'd love to know what he was up to now.'

'Drug dealing in Australia?' suggested Karen drily.

'No,' tutted Jennifer 'I doubt it. I'm sure he probably is in Oz but I don't think he'd be doing that. Don't you remember he wanted to start up a scuba diving school? He's probably living the life of riley, on the beach, brown as a berry, healthy and happy.'

'Do you remember how close you came to going off with him?' asked Karen. 'I still get palpitations thinking about that now. I can remember standing on that jetty thinking, oh my god I'm going to have to explain to her mum when she comes to pick us up at the airport'Ah hello Mrs Drew, no Jennifer isn't with us. She's decided to stay with a sex god called Aidan and his nice big bag of white doves, which are the other thing she's taken quite a fancy to.'

They all laughed.

'I seriously considered going with him you know,' said Jennifer.

'I know you did,' said Karen indignantly. 'Don't you remember me crying about it?'

Jennifer nodded vaguely. She could remember only too clearly the details of that scorching hot afternoon. Only she'd hate her friends to know quite how often she'd found herself recalling them lately.

'You were always lucky on the man front. Do you remember Steve?' added Karen.

'Ah lovely Steve,' cooed Lucy, looking positively drippy. 'He was such a poppet wasn't he? I always had a bit of a soft spot for him, and in terms of someone adoring you, my god Jen, you literally couldn't have asked for anything more. He used to look at you like a puppy dog. Now there's an example of a man who would have walked on hot coals for you and was permanently complimenting you but, if you remember, it used to drive you mad,' she said, practically wagging her finger 'To the point where it was the precise fact that Max was a bit cooler with you that made you feel like you'd met your match. You loved the fact he wouldn't let you get away with stuff like Steve did.'

'True,' said Jennifer 'I did love Steve though. It wasn't that I didn't appreciate how lovely he was to me though. Finishing with him wasn't an easy decision by any stretch of the imagination. I got rid of a good man there and we all know they don't grow on trees don't we.'

'We do,' said Karen 'which is why you're so bloody lucky to have bagged another one. Babe I reckon you need to stop thinking there's something better for you out there. Stick with what you've got. It works, you've got a lovely house, two happy secure children and if you upended all of that who knows how difficult life would be.'

'Who said anything about upending anything?' spluttered Jennifer, who in truth was feeling a bit unnerved by Karen's ability to not only hit the nail on the head but to also smash it hard with a mallet in order to truly illustrate her point. She'd never been one to mince her words.

17 | Present Day

'How is she today? Any change? Sorry we're late, we would have been here earlier but I thought it important we check on the girls first.'

'I know,' said Max, before bursting into tears which surprised him more than it did anyone else. He had thought he was bearing up really well but the sight of Jennifer's parents looking so flooded with anxiety for their daughter was too much and brought home the severity of the situation once again.

'Oh you poor man,' said Lesley, his mother in law, drawing him in for a hug. It was the first time such a physical exchange had occurred between them during all the time they'd known each other but he went with it and was surprised by actually how comforting it was to be drawn into her ample, rather matronly bust.

'How are the kids?' managed Max eventually 'They don't know anything yet do they?'

'They're fine, don't you worry about them. They've still no idea which personally I think is for the best at this stage. Till we've got a better idea of what's going on. Anyway, we left them with Karen, happy as pie, making fairy cakes. She's been a star.'

'When's the doctor coming round?' asked Jen's dad, Nigel.

'I didn't know he was unconscious,' joked Max weakly.

Lesley and Nigel looked baffled, unsure if they'd heard correctly.

'Sorry,' said Max, quickly realising gags probably weren't really called for, especially not such bad ones. 'That wasn't even funny was it? In fact, it's the sort of feeble joke Jen would usually crack at a time like this,' he babbled 'Out of nerves. Completely inappropriate. I think I might be going a bit doolally. I haven't slept much…'

'It's alright, love,' said Lesley, eyeing him with such a mixture of concern and pity it seemed to confirm that she wholeheartedly agreed with his analysis of his own mental state. 'Do you remember when Uncle Ken died and Jennifer got the giggles at the funeral because the vicar's toupee was blowing around in the wind then half slipped off his head at the graveside?'

'Oh gosh yes,' said Max, smiling sadly at the memory, grateful to Lesley for bearing with him.

'Thinking about it now, it probably was quite a comical sight, but at the time I was furious with Jen for not having more decorum,' she added wistfully.

They all fell silent for a second, lost in memories. Max hated it. The atmosphere they were creating was too similar to how people reflected about the deceased, yet his wife was still alive, sort of.

'Anyway, thinking about it, the doctor should actually be here by now,' he said eventually, determined to change the mood despite the fact he was still pretty choked up and having to use every ounce of bravery in order to stay composed. 'The thing is, you don't like to make too much of a fuss because the staff have been amazing, but at the same time, they never come when they say they're going to.'

'Oh but you're right, you mustn't make a fuss,' agreed Lesley, horrified at the mere thought.

Inside Jennifer's bruised head, what her mum had just said was one of the few things to penetrate her consciousness.

It was a typical comment for her mum to make for she was the type of woman who would eat a dish she hadn't actually ordered in a restaurant and had been mistakenly given, even if she hated it, rather than 'make a fuss.' The familiarity of this personality trait was in itself a comfort. It was also a comfort to be aware of people's presence, ones she knew cared about her, only she was still very confused about why she required comfort. Something terrible had happened. But what?

Hearing her mum's voice made her desperate to find out whether or not she would have rekindled her relationship with her had she stayed with Aidan. She hoped they would have done. It wouldn't say much for them if they couldn't have found it within themselves to have salvaged something of it. The next thing she knew she was tumbling through space once more, a sensation she was starting to become accustomed to. She hovered outside the portal, suddenly reluctant to go down, *scared* to go down. It would be beyond devastating to discover that their relationship hadn't been able to survive one lousy decision. One stupid mistake. What should she do? She looked around, floating, like a fish suspended in a bowl. There were, after all, two other portals beckoning to her to go down them. She *had* to discover what would have happened between her and her parents but perhaps not right now. No, now she would go in another direction. It was time to explore the second portal. The one marked **Tim**.

18 TUNNEL NUMBER TWO

Tim: what could have been

'So you can't come?'

'I'm so sorry Karen, I would have loved to but I'm meeting Tim. He's taking me to some do.'

Jennifer could practically hear Karen's irritation crackling down the phone but there was no way she was going to cancel her plans just to placate her. She wasn't going to apologise either. She hadn't done anything wrong and was getting fed up of always being made to feel like she had.

'What's it tonight then?' asked Karen reluctantly and Jennifer could picture only too well how she'd be rolling her eyes with disdain.

'Tim's got tickets to the Serpentine party in Hyde Park. It's supposed to be pretty amazing. There'll be lots of people from the art world there but also loads of celebs and cocktails and canapés and all of that malarkey. Tickets are a few hundred quid a pop.' Jennifer winced. Had that sounded like she was showing off? She hadn't meant it to. She was simply trying to demonstrate to Karen that her plans weren't casual ones she could easily break.

'Oh well, having a curry with me and Pete can't compete with that,' said Karen.

Jennifer detected a more than slightly sarcastic tinge to her voice. She despaired and not for the first time wished she'd never told Karen about the argument she'd had with Tim the day Princess Diana had died. It was nearly a year ago now but ever since she'd mentioned that, for an insecure moment, she'd briefly considered finishing it with him, Karen had acted like she had carte blanche to be as scathing as she liked about their relationship.

Now Jennifer constantly felt an urge to justify herself to Karen and to defend her decision to stay with him. Yet it didn't seem to matter how many times she explained over and over again, that ultimately she'd decided not to dump him because he had so much to offer, in so many different ways, it was like her friend refused to listen.

Jennifer was sick of it. It was her life and it wound her up that Karen acted as though by comparison her and Pete's relationship was so perfect, to the point where the more she thought about it, the more she was starting to think that perhaps she might just be a tiny bit jealous. After all, Karen and Pete struggled to make ends meet most months whereas Tim had made it. He'd done what he had always set out to do. He'd invented something and it was all coming to fruition. He was rich. *ReUNIon* was taking off and that was entirely down to his hard work, vision, drive and dedication to making it happen. She was *proud* to be with him. He was so clever. A genius to some extent and yes, he may appear distracted much of the time but then of course he was. He had a growing company to manage. He had the attention of many major captains of industry, from politicians, the media, and not just in Britain but globally. He was manically busy but when they did have time together at least he compensated for the times they weren't by showing her the high life. They ate at amazing restaurants, got invited to incredible events where the drinks were free, the canapés were delicious and there was invariably a goody bag to take home at the end of the night. She was always meeting interesting people these days and had learned more through being with Tim than she ever had from anyone else. Ok, so perhaps he wasn't always the warmest and there were elements of their sex life she found unsatisfying but there was more to life than snogging. Like companionship and security, both of which he offered her in abundance. He was the cleverest person she knew. She wasn't going to do any better. She'd have been mad to ditch him only to end up lonely and full of regret.

'Ok, well, have a great time,' Karen said flatly.

'I will,' said Jennifer, feeling sad. Why did Karen always have to rain on her parade? She sighed and as ever, keen to keep the peace, attempted to make sure their conversation ended on good terms. 'Can I come round next week for a curry instead?'

'Course,' said Karen, who at her end was determinedly pulling herself together. She had enough self- awareness to know she was giving Jennifer a hard time but half the time couldn't help herself. Tim made her skin crawl, always had done. Physically he reminded her of Beavis from *Beavis and Butthead* which was how she and Pete referred to him in private. She found him repellent and arrogant and was convinced her friend could do better. She also suspected that Jennifer was only still with him for the money and the lifestyle being Tim Purcell's girlfriend provided. If Tim worked in a shop would she still be with him?

'Why don't you come round next Tuesday or Wednesday?'

'It's a date,' said Jennifer 'Though Tuesday probably works better for me and it's nearer so put it in the diary.' After they'd got off the phone Jennifer allowed herself five minutes just to sit on the bed and gaze dolefully at the wall, until she realised that unless she started getting ready she'd be horribly late.

Half an hour later and Jennifer was dressed and ready to go. Tim had bought her a beautiful Diane Von Furstenberg wrap dress from a very expensive shop in Notting Hill called The Cross. It was silk and beautifully made and the colours were vibrant, fiery oranges and reds. The style was slightly too conservative for Jennifer's taste but she appreciated how lucky she was to have it and wanted to please Tim by wearing it, even if she did think it would be better on a woman in her forties. He'd suggested she go to the hairdressers and have a blow-dry but being totally honest she preferred her hair more natural. All the moneyed women round Notting Hill looked like clones of one another as far as she was concerned with their coiffured, crash helmet, invariably blonde highlighted hairstyles.

Just as she was applying a final slick of lip gloss the doorbell rang, so she picked up her clutch bag and clacked to the door in her high heels.

Tim's driver was standing on the front step.

'Oh… hi Ray,' she said 'Is Tim not with you?'

'He got held up Jen but said to say he'll meet you there.'

Jennifer's smile slipped off her face slightly but there was no point saying anything to Ray. In fact, there was no point saying anything to anyone. Her boyfriend would be there when he could be and if she had to sit outside The Serpentine in the car for a while that's what she'd do. There was no way she was going into that party on her own.

Twenty minutes later Jennifer was idly day dreaming out of the window about nothing in particular when the car suddenly glided up to the pavement.

'Hang on a minute, we're not here yet are we?' asked Jennifer. 'Why were they stopping in Knightsbridge?'

Ray turned round from the front seat. 'Actually, Mr Purcell asked if we could make a quick pit stop here, if you don't mind.'

'Oh right... shall I wait in the car, then?'

'No Miss, if you would be so kind, there's someone waiting for you inside so you should come with me.'

Thoroughly confused Jennifer looked out of the window again.

They were outside The Mandarin Oriental Hotel and Ray was coming round to her side of the car to open her door.

Wondering what on earth was going on Jennifer got out, hoping this wasn't going to take too long. She'd be annoyed if Tim was still doing business. She hadn't seen him properly all week and he'd promised her that tonight he'd finish at a decent time so that they could enjoy the party. As she followed Ray up the steps of the hotel, she got the strangest sense that the hotel doormen were half expecting her. She decided she was being

paranoid. She probably just stuck out like a sore thumb in her bright dress.
'What's going on Ray? Where are we meeting Tim?'

'Don't you worry,' he said mysteriously and she knew then that she wasn't going to get any more information out of him.

'I'd best leave you to it Jen. I can't leave the car here I'm afraid, I'll get a ticket.'

'Oh...really...'she began but he'd already turned and gone, and was hurrying back to his waiting car.

Feeling rather self- conscious and a tad irritated she resigned herself to the fact that she now had no other choice but to go in to the hotel and find out what was going on. She let the incredibly enthusiastic doorman usher her through to the main reception where the first thing she noticed within the opulent surroundings was a uniformed member of the hotel staff standing clutching an enormous bouquet of white flowers. There were lilies, roses and huge white delphiniums so large they pretty much covered the woman's entire face. They were absolutely beautiful and Jennifer wondered who they were for. Perhaps some celebrity was about to turn up which would explain why the doormen were all on such red alert. Just as she was thinking this the legs beneath the flowers started walking towards her.

'These are for you Miss Drew,' said the woman, once she was only a few feet away, almost teetering underneath the weight of the blooms. She handed them over to Jennifer.

'Oh my gosh,' she gasped, overwhelmed and enjoying the incredible perfume that was coming from them 'They're amazing thank you so much. Are you sure they're for me? Are they from Tim?'

'Indeed they are Miss. Now, I'd like you to follow me, only perhaps let's leave the flowers with reception to look after and we can collect them again later. They're a bit too big to carry around aren't they?' she said smiling.

At this point all the irritation and confusion Jennifer had been experiencing dissolved completely and instead she started to get seriously excited. There had been so many times over the years when she'd had to put up with broken arrangements, or had to wait around for Tim for hours on end while he finished up his business but never had any of these times involved being handed a massive bouquet. She felt like Julia Roberts in Pretty Woman. Not like a prostitute, but in a 'being spoiled by a millionaire in a fairy-tale' type of way. It was obvious by now that Tim must have planned something amazing. A delicious dinner before the party maybe? She was touched. It had been a long time since he'd done anything romantic for her. He'd encouraged her to do a fair amount of shopping recently which was nice, but somehow giving his credit card a workout, although fun, didn't make her feel special like this did. For a brief second she wondered if he was going to propose but as quickly as the notion came to her she dismissed it again. No, he wouldn't. Not yet.

Once they'd disposed of the flowers she followed the woman through the hotel towards the lifts and they both got in. Jennifer watched as she pressed a button for one of the very top floors. As the lift made its ascent through the building the two of them stood in vaguely awkward silence, grinning inanely at one another. Jennifer was pleased to reach their destination. What on earth was going on? It was so exciting.

Coming out of the lift Jennifer found herself in a spacious corridor, decorated in decadent red.

'This way please,' the woman said with a polite smile. Jennifer followed; her stomach full of nerves. Together they walked right to the end of the plush, thickly carpeted corridor at which point the woman took a key card out of her pocket. As she inserted it, she stood aside to push the door open so that the room was revealed.

Jennifer gasped. The room, which must have been the hotel's most luxurious suite, was full to the brim with candles, carpeted with them if you like, save for a path through the middle which led to a terrified looking Tim.

'What's this?' squawked Jennifer 'What are you doing?' Not the most romantic or profound thing to say but she was terribly nervous by now.

'Well come in then,' said Tim, encouraging her to stop standing gormlessly in the doorway.

Doing as she was told, Jennifer started to make her way toward him, picking out a path for herself between the flickering candles. Once she'd reached him she watched incredulously and for a second it was as if life had gone into slow motion as Tim slowly got down onto one knee, simultaneously producing a duck egg blue box from his pocket and saying 'Jennifer Drew, I know I'm not perfect but I hope I'm perfect for you. Please will you marry me?'

Tears filled her eyes. She couldn't believe it. Couldn't believe she was being asked for starters but also couldn't believe how much effort Tim had gone to and that he had it in him to be so romantic. By now he'd opened the box and for a second the sight of the ring completely distracted her. The ring was amazing. Not the kind of ring she ever would have imagined a girl like her to wear. It was from Tiffany's for a start and was a ring for a rich person, a statement ring. The kind of ring that would need insuring and to be kept in a safe on holiday. The sort of ring you couldn't in all seriousness contemplate wearing if you planned on doing any washing up, gardening or swimming. The diamond was quite simply enormous, a proper rock, which glinted and twinkled in the candlelight, set on a very traditional platinum band.

Eventually she tore her gaze away in order to look at Tim. He looked nervous. Tim was never nervous. Her mind swirled this way and that. Did she want to be his wife? Did she want to spend the rest of her life with him?

She gulped. Of course she'd always known this moment could be a possibility and she wouldn't have stayed with him all this time if it wasn't ultimately what she'd always wanted. Would she have? Christ she was so flummoxed.

'Well?' said Tim, looking positively pained by now.

She laughed. Poor man. He was waiting. He was on one knee. She did love him. Of course she did. It had to be a yes.

'Yes.'

'Thank goodness for that,' exclaimed Tim 'And thank goodness I can get back up, my knee's killing me.' Getting to his feet he shook out his cramped leg then came towards her. They both smiled at one another, hardly able to digest what had just happened.

'So Mrs Purcell, are you happy?'

'Yes,' said Jennifer, eyes shining, wondering who to call first. Probably not Karen. She batted that decidedly depressing thought out of her head, determined not to give any headspace to anything as inappropriate as her friend's disapproval at this special time.

'I suppose I should probably kiss you then,' said Tim.

'Yes, you probably should,' agreed Jennifer, laughing at how deeply unspontaneous he was. God forbid he ever just grabbed her and kissed her because he was so overwhelmed by the desire to do so.

Tim came towards her and bending forward slightly, met her mouth with his. It was a tender kiss, a happy one, one that firmly sealed the deal.

So that was that then. She was going to marry Tim, her boyfriend of four years. She would be Mrs Tim Purcell, wife of the founder of *ReUNIon*. She could hardly believe it. Her mum would be ecstatic. Karen, maybe not so much...

19 | Present Day

Max tore through the hospital searching for a doctor, frantic in his pursuit. Eventually, after much helter-skeltering up and down slippery corridors, he finally spotted a nurse he recognised.

'Hello,' he panted, relieved beyond belief. It was so frustrating when you couldn't find but desperately needed a doctor. It made him feel so helpless. 'I'm sorry to bother you but I need you to come to Jennifer Wright's room right away please?'

'Everything ok, Mr Wright?' she enquired calmly.

'Yes, yes well at least I think so. I'm not sure really, or at least I don't know if it's a good or a bad thing but I'm pretty definite that unless I'm hallucinating, and I'm afraid there's a chance I could be because I can't remember the last time I had a proper night's sleep, I think my wife may have just smiled.'

'Ok...,' said the nurse looking grave but not as excited as Max thought she should be.

'Seriously her face definitely changed, which is amazing right, because surely that means she's thinking about something, or dreaming, or hearing, which in turn must mean that her brain is functioning on some level?'

'I'll see if I can find Mrs Wright's consultant for you Mr Wright and if he's here I'll ask him to come and see you in your wife's room. But please try to stay calm. I'm afraid that sometimes, when a patient is in a coma, their body can make involuntary reflex movements. It can be very distressing for relatives because of course this can give false hope.'

Max stared blankly at her. He didn't want to hear it. He knew his wife better than anyone and would stake his life on the fact that she had just smiled. Voluntarily. He was convinced of it.
'Hmm, well thank you, and if you could find someone that would be great please,' he said, suddenly realising he was on the verge of tears. Not just any tears either but violent sobbing which he was determined to hold back until he was alone. Smiling weakly he headed away from the nurse and traipsed back to Jennifer's room.

When he got there he closed the door behind him and allowed the inevitable tears of frustration to pour down his face. Then he collapsed into the chair which he'd spent an unreasonable amount of time sitting in lately and wept noisily until at least some of his grief and helplessness had worked its way out of his stressed out system.

When he'd finished, he felt calm. He also felt exhausted, drained and still very sad. He stared at his wife. His silent, slightly waxy looking, shell of a wife. Was she still in there? Could she hear him? Would there be a day when they'd be cuddled up in bed, feet entwined, talking about how lucky they were to have got through this nightmare and still be together? He'd give anything for that opportunity so that he could tell her how much he loved her, how much he missed her, how much he'd taken her for granted lately. He reached over for her hand. It was warm but disconcertingly limp. Why her? Why them?

Not wanting to go down that path which only led to more frustration he thought back instead to what had just happened. The smile which had brought with it such an incredibly soothing rush of hope it had almost bowled him over.

He'd been half dozing at the time and although the memory was a bit hazy now he was pretty sure it had been the slight rustling sound of a sheet which had made him look up. Rustling was probably too strong a word in fact, for it had been a minute sound, barely discernible but there none the less.

As he'd glanced up at Jennifer, instantly alert, it had seemed like her hand might have been in a slightly different position to the one it had been in before. And then, without question her face flickered. Her mouth definitely seemed to curl in an upward motion and it looked to Max, for all intents and purposes like his wife was smiling.

He hadn't stopped to think about it for very long and instead had been so alarmed and also so joyful, so hopeful, that his instant response had been to hurtle through the corridors searching for a member of staff.

As the weary consultant and even wearier Max discussed what he'd seen (or as the consultant preferred to put it 'what he *may* have seen' which really got Max's back up) deep inside Jennifer's psyche a different type of debate was going on.

She'd re- emerged from the portal marked Tim and was still mulling over the fact that if she'd stayed with him they would have ended up engaged. It was so funny and yet she wasn't altogether surprised. What had surprised her was how romantic he'd been. Who'd have thought it? She wondered what she should do now. Usually after a trip to one of her alternate universes she was so depleted she needed some time out in the grey ether to recover and recharge. However, now she felt fine. She was just totally intrigued, fascinated in fact to find out more. So she turned around and headed purposefully back down the tunnel again to discover how things would have gone. Would she have been blissfully content, living out many people's version of a fairy-tale? This certainly seemed like a possibility.

20 TUNNEL NUMBER TWO

Tim: what could have been

'You look nice, Mummy.'

'Thank you Hattie, come here, darling,' said Jennifer, beckoning to her youngest daughter to come for a hug.

Hattie padded across the room to where her mother was sitting at her dressing table, in her vast dressing room, putting the finishing touches to her make- up and spritzing her neck, wrists and hair with perfume. Eau d'Hadrien by Annik Goutal, the one she always wore. Years ago Tim had told her it was really attractive for a woman to have a signature scent, so she'd stuck with the one she'd had at the time and it had indeed become the smell her children would always associate with her.

She drew Hattie towards her. The little girl was already in her White Company gingham pyjamas and had obviously had her hair washed as it was still damp and drying into natural ringlets. 'Are you ok sweetheart, where's Elisa?'

Hattie shrugged, looking fed up 'Putting Jasper to bed, but I want *you* to read my story today.'

'I can't tonight. You know Daddy's got all his work people coming and Mummy's got to be there.'

'But you haven't read stories for ages.'

'Yes I have,' said Jennifer, refusing to be put on a guilt trip, something Hattie was very good at. 'Who read 'The Selfish Crocodile' to you yesterday?'

Hattie tried to continue looking hard done by but ruined the effect by allowing a small grin to escape. 'But before that you haven't.'

Jennifer paused. Her daughter's cut glass accent still took her by surprise sometimes. She was starting to sound more and more like the queen, or perhaps an Enid Blyton character, a result of the very expensive, Notting Hill Gate school she'd started at last September. Jennifer wasn't entirely sure it sat all that well with her. She worried that later on in life if her daughter sounded too posh she might be bullied. She wondered what she could do to combat the problem. Force her to watch box sets of Towie or Eastenders perhaps? Get her a job in a garage? Get Aunty Karen to give her anti-elocution lessons maybe?

'Look, it has been a busy time sweetie and I know Mummy's been out a lot but Daddy goes to Hong Kong next week and then I'll have loads of time again. So I promise I'll make up for it on the stories front then. But right now, I've got to get downstairs or otherwise the first guest will arrive and I won't be there, so go back to your floor and find Elisa will you?'

Knowing it was pointless to argue further Hattie turned round and padded out of the room, an air of weary resignation about her, which made her look even more adorable. It was her little shoulders which got to Jennifer somehow. She sighed, wishing she didn't have to go downstairs and play the corporate wife. Deep down she was only too aware that recently she seemed to be permanently telling all four of her offspring that she didn't have time for anything which mattered to them. Still, Tim had never been so busy, so she didn't have much choice. And as he liked to remind her, they wouldn't have all of 'this' if he didn't put in the hours that he did. It was interesting though, she often thought the kids would prefer to live in a house with less bathrooms in exchange for more time with their parents.
If only she could convey to Hattie that actually, reading stories to her would be a luxury and that given the chance she'd do anything rather than have to entertain the bunch of stiffs that were on their way right now. Gouge her eyeballs out with a spoon. Anything.

Forty minutes later and the evening was well underway. Nearly all of the twenty guests had arrived and were being plied with drinks and canapés. As ever Jennifer had done her homework so knew not only what everyone was called, but also what they 'did', what their other halves were called and how important to Tim they were in terms of business on a scale of one to ten. She would allocate time devoted to making sure they were being 'looked after' accordingly.

'Darling, will you make sure there's some more claret for Jeremy?' said Tim now, as an aside. He didn't even look her in the eye, just gave her elbow a discreet nudge before turning his attentions back to the man who had a redder nose than Rudolph. However, it appeared Jeremy's attention had been stolen away by a woman with an impressive cleavage which he was now practically dribbling into.

'And try to look a bit happier,' added Tim, seeing as he wasn't being listened to anymore 'You look like you're here under duress.'

Jennifer gave him a withering look. 'Ten out of ten for accuracy,' she shot back.

'Don't fuck this up for me, Jen,' he said resolutely, a fake smile plastered across his face. 'I need all of these people on side if there's going to be a merger. And if it's so much of a chore for you to be here, then try thinking of it as your job.'

'Alright,' she agreed between gritted teeth, nodding politely at someone who'd just arrived 'But stop lecturing me will you?' Tim looked at her with enormous disdain, only she couldn't take him seriously because she'd just spotted a tiny piece of lettuce on his nose.

'You've got canapé on your nose. It looks ridiculous.'

Tim looked immediately chastened and patted his suit jacket, searching for a hanky. 'You could have told me earlier,' he snapped.

'Terribly sorry, I didn't realise I was supposed to be monitoring your face,' added Jennifer primly, her face a mask of composure 'Though if I had been I would have told you that you've also got what looks like a piece of duck stuck between your teeth. I'll get that claret.'

Over the years Jennifer and Tim had got saying one thing while looking like they were saying another, down to a fine art. Anyone observing would probably have thought the couple had just shared an affectionate private joke as opposed to a couple of scathing put downs. But then, as the wife of someone as powerful as Tim, over the years Jennifer had learnt how to play the game and how to cope with tedious evenings spent entertaining his clients and associates. Not that it was exactly hard. All she had to do was look groomed, make polite conversation and give instructions.

Come to think of it that was pretty much what she did in a nutshell these days. Give instructions. She gave instructions to the chef about what everyone would eat and then, when it was served, everyone complimented her on how amazing the food had been, which always felt weird when she hadn't even shopped for it, let alone prepared it. She gave instructions to the agencies where she hired staff from, as and when they needed extra help, on top of the help they already had. On this occasion she'd 'instructed' that they needed an experienced cocktail maker to work behind the bar, plus three waiting staff who could pour drinks and serve dinner. This afternoon she'd instructed her hairdresser and her personal trainer on when she wanted her next lot of appointments to be and on Monday she would give instructions to their housekeeper who worked five days a week, the gardener and of course their two Filipino nannies who between them worked every day, meaning that Jennifer never had to 'do' anything. Just instruct.

A few weeks ago, on a rare night away with the girls she'd said as much but hadn't received much sympathy from Karen 'Oh my heart bleeds,' she'd said 'Well how about instructing them all to fuck off for the day and perhaps doing your own cooking and cleaning for a change? Or maybe, and call me crazy for suggesting it, even try looking after your own kids for a whole twenty-four hours? You never know, you might enjoy it. Give the staff the day off.'

Karen had been particularly brutal because she was drunk but Jennifer was glad she hadn't sugar coated what she really thought. It was just so difficult to explain to her friends that 'doing' everything herself actually sounded unbelievably appealing; liberating even, yet at the same time the mere idea of it frightened her half to death. Having so much help all the time had gradually made her feel superfluous to anyone's needs, especially when it came to the kids.

Tim had paid for maternity nurses to be there from day one. When their eldest, Edward, had been born she'd never forgotten the feeling of elation she'd had. She'd produced a human being, a breathing little person, her own flesh and blood and furthermore, despite having him at The Portland, had managed to buck the trend and have a natural delivery. It had been painful, brutal, bloody. She was a total hero! It was the first time in a long time she'd felt worthwhile, clever almost. And then the maternity nurse had arrived and taken her little bundle, who could so easily still have been inside her he was that tiny, away. Never had anything felt so utterly wrong.

Despite her protestations, Tim had insisted. She never need have an uninterrupted sleep he'd said. She could remain in the marital bed at night and by day concentrate on getting her figure back.

This 'luxury' was the saddest thing she'd ever experienced. To this day she was certain it had contributed towards her postnatal depression. Only the worse the depression got, the more it was deemed a good idea for her to have more 'help.'

Sometimes she couldn't believe that she and Tim had gone on to have a further three children. Or more accurately she couldn't really understand why they'd bothered. Edward was thirteen now and on his way to becoming a moody teenager, Tilly was ten, Hattie was six and Jasper was four. They were four children with enormously different personalities, interests and needs. She loved all of them, of course, yet there was no getting away from the fact that neither she nor Tim had played much of a role in actually raising them. In fact sometimes she felt that as far he was concerned they'd been churned out like status symbols. The only thing which made her feel vaguely better about her mothering skills was that no matter how shit they were, they were hundreds of times better than Tim's fathering ones. At least she'd changed the odd nappy herself. At least she'd tried. Plus, much of her time was spent torturing herself with maternal guilt whereas she was pretty sure that for Tim, the way he was as a parent wasn't something that ever pricked his conscience. He paid for everything, so in a very old fashioned sense he felt that was all that was required. He provided. It was like living in a Jane Austen novel at times.

She slipped away from the drawing room leaving her guests (not one of whom she considered to be a friend) to mingle, drink champagne and eat their canapés.

Frankly she was grateful for an excuse to leave for a minute. Prior to Tim's request/order she'd been struggling to make small-talk with the wife of his financial advisor. At one point things had got so desperate they'd discussed whether or not children should be allowed to give up the piano or not for *twenty-five minutes.*
Jennifer made her way through the corridors and into the spacious hallway, stopping only to check her appearance in a huge gilt edged mirror which hung on one wall.

She still looked immaculate. Her hair had been blow-dried that afternoon. It was big, slightly stiff but with a wave at the bottom. Very Kate Middleton. She was wearing a new silk shift by Stella McCartney which probably wasn't quite conservative enough for Tim's tastes but which she loved, with some gorgeous Marc Jacobs heels. Her skin was looking far younger than her thirty-eight years due mainly to some expertly injected Botox and aided by monthly facials. She looked rested, slim, toned and totally dead behind the eyes. Her phone vibrated in her pocket. It was a text, one which improved her mood beyond measure. It was the fix she needed and she responded quickly before continuing her way to the staircase which led down to her vast kitchen. So vast it actually took up the basement floor of the entire house and was larger than most people's flats.

Downstairs, their chef, Joe, and two of the waiting staff were milling around, engaged in one activity or another.

'Hello Jennifer, everything alright?' asked Joe, treating her to a big friendly grin. He'd been with the family for four and a half years now.

'Fabulous thanks. The quail's eggs are disappearing at a rate of knots as are those homemade cheese straws.'

'Oh good, that's what I like to hear.'

'Would you mind going to the cellar and grabbing another bottle of the Montrachet for Jeremy? You know Jeremy, the one who's got a face like a side of beef.'

'I do indeed,' laughed Joe.

'I can get it if you want,' offered one of the young waiters.

'No, don't you worry,' insisted Joe. 'The starter's all plated up so I'm fine to go. Besides, it's best to make sure we open the right one eh? Some of those bottles are worth more than you'll earn in a year young man.'

'Thanks Joe,' said Jennifer, leaving them all to it and clip clopping out of the kitchen and back upstairs.

Back in the hallway she hesitated for a fraction of a second, checking to make sure no one was around. Then, certain that she was alone, instead of making her way back to the party she turned left, heading with purpose toward the rear of the house and ultimately the largest of their three sitting rooms (or drawing rooms as Tim liked to call them. Sitting room was a compromise. When she really wanted to wind him up she went with lounge which admittedly didn't quite work as a description of a room that was so baroque it was more like a ballroom but she detested his snobby ways.) She closed the door quietly behind her and picked her way across the room to the French doors which led out onto the garden, one of the largest in London. The striped, immaculate lawns almost went on for as far as the eye could see and the rest of the garden had been designed as if it belonged to a stately home with lots of topiary and very neat beds which were completely colour co-ordinated. Despite having four children there wasn't a plastic slide in sight.

Jennifer ventured out onto the flagstones and tiptoed along the side of the house until she came to another door which was slightly ajar. As soon as she reached it a hand appeared and yanked her inside.

She immediately giggled and felt a lurch of happiness and desire as those same hands drew her in and started to explore her body.
'Oh my god you feel so good in this dress.'

'Do I?'

'Yeah, you look amazing in it too. Absolutely gorgeous.'

'Oh, I do love you,' she gasped, her heart full to the brim with love and wondering how it was possible to feel this turned on so quickly.

'I love you too gorgeous girl,' said Joe, his hands everywhere, his mouth in her hair, kissing her face, her neck. 'What's the situation later?'

'I don't know,' she said doubtfully. 'You know how he gets at these things, he'll probably be up till five am, talking utter shit, but if I can come and see you I will. I'll have to play it by ear.'

'Please try,' groaned Joe, pulling her into him 'I've missed you so much it's ridiculous. It's been far too long since I've had that lovely body lying next to me.'

'I know, you don't need to tell me,' grinned Jennifer, wide eyed 'I've been pining for you the whole time.'

'But if you can't get away, no worries my love, I don't want it to be a stress.'

'Ok, speaking of which, how long have I been?'

'Don't know,' said Joe, pulling away, but stroking her face so tenderly she experienced the most enormous pang for him. His expression was pained, par for the course these days. Their affair was getting harder the deeper they fell.

'I love you,' she said for the second time, meaning it passionately.

'I love you too little squidger,' said Joe, his Yorkshire accent such a contrast from Tim's clipped public school tones. Then again everything about him was.

'Don't forget the wine,' she whispered, tearing herself reluctantly away and back outside.

'I won't,' he said, disappearing back toward the cellar.

'Where've you been?' asked Tim five minutes later, having spotted her as soon as she'd reappeared in the drawing room. 'I asked you to get more wine, not drive to France and stamp on the grapes yourself.'

'Sorry,' she replied 'I was just making sure everything's under control for dinner. I think we should start thinking about getting everyone into the dining room. Otherwise we won't be eating till ten.'

'Right you are.'

As the evening progressed, Jennifer's mood took a serious nosedive.

She did her best to be engaging, to be the perfect host, but her heart wasn't in it. It wasn't even in the same room. It was languishing downstairs in the kitchens where Joe was of course. It was a joke. Despite the fact this whole event was taking place in her home, the evening felt like precisely nothing to do with her. She played with her food. Joe had cooked the most incredible rib of beef which he'd served with creamy artichoke mash, perfectly cooked vegetables and a fricassee of mushrooms that was out of this world. But she had no appetite. The latest anti- depressant she'd been prescribed made her feel permanently a bit wired and not for the first time she wondered if they were a waste of time. Was she actually clinically depressed? She was starting to doubt it gravely because she never felt even remotely miserable when she was alone with Joe. Quite the opposite. And yet for years doctors had told her she had depression when in fact there was a distinct possibility she'd just been sad and unfulfilled.

For what felt like the thousandth time that hour her thoughts returned to the man who had been her best friend for two years now and her lover for seven months; seven amazing, painful, confusing, sad, yet unbelievably golden months. Since having Joe in her life she'd reassessed everything. She'd also been permanently saturated in intense stress and guilt, not surprising given that she was committing adultery, and yet she also felt more *herself* than she had in years.

Joe, it seemed, was her soul-mate, her rightful other half, but while that bit was clear, the situation was so complicated. When the affair had first started she'd tried to convince herself it would be purely sexual and would serve to extinguish some of the sense of yearning she'd felt for so many years. She and Tim may have managed to conceive four children but to put it bluntly, it hadn't taken many 'go's' with any of them. Since their youngest, Jasper, had been born they'd barely had sex at all and Jennifer had eventually reached the point where the thought of having sex with her husband revolted her. When she'd married Tim, she'd had a few underlying worries that sexually they weren't hugely compatible but had genuinely believed it didn't matter. She'd thought that other things counted more, such as respect, admiration and intelligence. As it turns out however, a right good snog can count for a lot. Of course being with someone who had literally changed the world was a powerful aphrodisiac in itself but years down the line the respect aspect of their relationship had begun to wane. She had allowed him to manipulate her into the kind of wife he wanted her to be, a trophy wife, one who was entirely reliant on him. Furthermore, while Jennifer's confidence had gradually diminished, resentment toward her husband had grown until it had reached a point where she hardly recognised who she was or who *they* were. She no longer cared if he'd invented the sodding wheel.

Then Joe had entered her life and simply by being him, had thrown everything into perspective.

Joe was a good man, for whom sleeping with someone else's wife had never been the plan. He'd also fallen hard and given his strength of feeling was never going to be satisfied simply with being Jennifer's bit on the side. It wasn't long before the two of them were smitten, utterly and hopelessly in love to the point of obsession. Every meeting was tinged with tragedy, with worry about the future and with deep frustration. Whenever they had sex the strength of her feeling meant she always ended up in tears at the end because she was in a painful quandary. If she were to leave Tim she'd be breaking up her family, turning her back on a man who although was flawed had always stuck by her. She'd be doing the 'wrong' thing no matter how right it felt and would be losing everything familiar to her. If she stayed however, she'd lose Joe and that was too unbearable even to contemplate.

The situation was starting to make her ill. She was torn, confused and frankly terrified. She suspected she belonged with Joe, no matter what the consequences, but that didn't mean the consequences weren't huge. None of it was made any easier by the fact that Joe simply couldn't fathom why she was prepared to even contemplate staying with Tim when he talked to her the way he did. He could see first-hand what a snob he was, which as far as Joe was concerned was the worst thing a person could be.

But contemplating leaving the father of your children was daunting. She'd been with Tim since university and to this day people constantly told her how ridiculously lucky she was to have landed him. As if she was almost a booby prize by comparison. Then, of course, there was the lifestyle she enjoyed, the money. Tim had made her sign a pre- nup and she'd agreed happily, wanting to prove the point that she wasn't with him for his cash.

Now, as much as Joe told her there were more important things in life than money, she had her children to think of and was unable to comprehend how she would cope, having been dependent on Tim for so long. Was she mad for even considering leaving him? Look what she'd be giving up? She glanced around the opulent dining room, the work of an over enthusiastic interior designer desperate to justify his grotesque fee and the bunch of stuffy, rich dullards who were sat around the Louis XVII table.

On second thoughts....

'So tell me Jennifer, what are your plans for the summer?' asked Maurice Fellowes, one of the largest shareholders of *reUNIon* who Tim had cruelly placed her next to.

Maurice was quite literally the short straw from what was already an unbearably tedious crowd. In fairness, not all the entertaining they did was quite this bad. Sometimes they had uproarious dinner parties with clever, creative people. People who had helped make *reUNIon* what it was or others whom they simply knew for social reasons. However, these days *reUNIon* was only a fraction of the business which Tim was involved with and it seemed to Jennifer that the more money you accrued, the more you were obliged to socialise with people you wouldn't ordinarily give the time of day to if you were skint and didn't need to.

'Well, we're going to our place in the South of France as soon as the children break up and then, at the end of August, Tim and I leave them there and we go to the Earl of Bradwick's boat. You know Bradwick I'm sure?'

'Oh yes, frightfully nice chap.'

Jennifer smiled pleasantly, wishing she could think of a reason to go and see Joe in the kitchen. The thought of being separated from him for a whole summer was unbearable, physically painful almost and she wasn't sure how she was going to cope. In fact, she was already determined to concoct some story so she could return to the UK for at least a week. He'd asked her to come to Yorkshire with him and there was nothing on earth she would rather do than spend time holed away in a little cottage with him. It would be heaven. By contrast, the prospect of spending weeks in luxury with Tim was one that filled her with nothing but a sense of dread and foreboding.

She literally couldn't bear time away from Joe but if she said anything, it was his cue to look at her those warm eyes of his and say 'Well, you know what the answer to that is my little squidger. Leave him and be with me.'

She sighed heavily.

'So what are you and Margaret doing for the summer Maurice?' she asked politely, despite the fact she couldn't give even the smallest of shits.

'Well, we're braving Cornwall, and just praying it doesn't rain like it did last year.'

Oh how brave thought Jennifer wryly, fully aware that the house they owned there was more like a castle and was fully staffed.

She was pretty sure they'd survive.

'And then we'll be going on to Tuscany where we shall stay through until the end of September, which is always the nicest month there I find. Very good meat by the way. Wonderful food, you're a marvellous host Jennifer.'

'Thank you,' she said. Urgh, what she wouldn't give for a normal night out. With normal people. Thank god she still had Karen, Lucy and Esther in her life, although even with her old friends, having so much money still sometimes created problems, no matter how hard they all tried to pretend it didn't. Not for her. She couldn't care less about it and would gladly have given them all as much as they wanted. If paying for them all meant they got to do things together she was more than happy to facilitate that. But her friends had their pride, and how much generosity it was appropriate to accept was one of the things Karen found particularly tricky to handle. As a result, it was often them, as opposed to her, who were guilty of making an issue out of her wealth. Sometimes they didn't include her in stuff just because they assumed she'd turn her nose up at it, when actually she would have loved to have been invited. At other times, when she invited *them* to events or to come abroad with her and Tim, they couldn't necessarily afford the flights or the spending money that was required but didn't know how to tell her without it sounding like they wanted her to cover it. The one saving grace was that every April, without fail, they allowed her to pay for the four of them to go on a girls skiing trip. It was always the best week of her entire year.

Just then her phone vibrated in her pocket. Expertly she managed to slip it out and onto her lap, her gaze never leaving Maurice's rheumy eyes as he blathered on about restaurants in Tuscany and how much he loved peasant food.

As soon as she thought she could get away with it, her eyes flickered onto her lap. The text read:

> Hello sexy. Hope you're not bored rigid. Have put something special in Tim's dessert. Hopefully see you later xxx

21 | Wednesday

'Why does everything in life have to arrive ruddy flat packed?' swore Max, who was currently struggling to make sense of the instructions he was holding. Not surprising given he was staring at the section written in Swedish.

'It can't be that hard,' said Jennifer

.

'Eurgh,' said Max, which didn't mean much but was an expression of how hung-over he was feeling. Last night Ted had come round to keep him company (and to watch Sky Sports) while Jennifer was out with the girls, and between them they'd managed to get through more beer and red wine than was probably necessary.

Apart from a bit of a furry mouth he hadn't felt too bad at work, but the hangover had finally landed and now he was severely regretting his ill-advised decision to embark on a major bit of DIY. The fact that Jennifer had predicted that precisely this would happen only made matters worse.

Meanwhile, Polly and Eadie were watching agog, thrilled because they knew full well that whilst bedtime might be imminent it was also impossible due to the chaos in Polly's room. There were bits of wardrobe everywhere, plus the contents of Max's tool box all over the floor.

'Yeah, come on Daddy,' joined in Polly now. 'It can't be that hard.'

'When I need your opinion...' he said, frowning at her.

'Why haven't I got any furniture for my room?' grumbled Eadie, looking miffed.

'Because you don't need it,' said Jennifer. 'You've got a whacking great wardrobe in your room and poor old Pol' has had to make do with no hanging space at all until now.'

'Right,' said Max, still looking flummoxed. 'Can you just hold that a minute Jen, I think this screw needs to go in there.'

'Are you sure?'

'No, I'm not sure, but at this point I can't stare at these stupid indecipherable things anymore and you never know it just might be worth a go, so humour me.'

Jennifer rolled her eyes and bit her lip, trying not to laugh.

'What's so funny?' snapped Max.

'Ok,' said Jennifer, growing slightly tired of the grumpy tone of voice he was using with her 'Well firstly I'm wondering why you have to do this now when the girls need to get to bed, when it could easily wait until the weekend, and secondly I was just thinking how quickly Steve would have had these up,' she added conspiratorially, confident that her husband would find the reference to her ex amusing and hoping a private joke would cajole him out of his mood.

She couldn't have been more wrong. At first he just gave her a look and a faint smile but seconds later, once he'd had the chance to fully digest what she'd said, he retaliated in a way that seemed really uncalled for.

'As it happens, firstly I'd rather get it out of the way, as opposed to spending my day off on Saturday doing it, and with regard to Steve, we can't all be good at everything,' he said, looking decidedly pissed off. 'Just as you aren't a breadwinner like Judith for example, I'm not good at sodding DIY. Though if you would rather be with someone who is, perhaps you should look Steve up and tell him you're on the market. I'm sure he'd leap at the chance to meet up.'

'Alright,' said Jennifer, stung by his hurtful words. 'There's no need to jump down my throat. I was only joking. Usually you're always up for a laugh about Steve. And there's no need to bring up frigging Judith's name or to pit me against that silly witch. That's just nasty.'

'Oh get over yourself,' said Max.

Now Jennifer really was fuming.

'Stop arguing,' barked Eadie, fiercely.

'Sorry love,' said Max immediately 'we're not arguing, just having a debate.'

That was rich thought Jennifer, who was itching to say as much only didn't for the girl's sakes. At the moment it felt like she couldn't say anything right and she couldn't even blame his mood on anything specific. Things were fine. They could do with more time for themselves but that just went hand in hand with being a parent. That was the norm. And besides, when the children had been tiny babies and life had been far more sleep deprived he'd managed to be pleasant towards her then, so what was his problem now? The thing she usually treasured most about their relationship was the fact that he was her best friend and that together, they usually saw the funny side in everything. She missed it.

'Right, come on then you two,' said Jennifer firmly. 'It's time for bed and your father clearly isn't going to be finished for hours so Polly will have to go in our bed and I'll move you later.'

'O-oh,' whined Eadie 'That's not fair.'

'Tough,' said Jennifer.
Later, once the girls were finally asleep in bed, Jennifer got the chance to tell her husband exactly what she thought of how he'd behaved.

'Just because you're incapable of having a night with Ted without getting totally rat arsed doesn't give you the excuse to come home the next day and infect us all with your misery,' she chastised.

'I know,' said Max 'And I'm sorry I got grumpy, but you know I hate DIY at the best of times.'

'Yeah, I do,' agreed Jennifer 'Which is precisely why I told you to leave it until the weekend in the first place, but what I'm more annoyed about is the fact that every chance you get you compare me to that bloody woman. Why do you do it?'

'I don't' said Max.

'You do,' said Jennifer, despairing 'You bring her name up all the time to the point where I even thought at one stage that you might be having an affair with her. Though actually, I've come to the conclusion that hopefully you'd be more discreet about it if you were. As it is you're permanently going on about her or comparing me to her. It's not bloody on.'

'You're being paranoid,' said Max, just a tad too defensively. Jennifer leapt on her instinct.

'What? What is it Max? What aren't you telling me? Do you have feelings for her or something?'

'No,' he said, outraged.

'Promise,' she said faintly, suddenly terrified in case she was about to discover something she didn't really want to confront as a result of her digging.

'Yes of course,' he said, more gently now and coming over to give her a hug.

'It's just you're being so snappy with me at the moment.'

'Oh god. Not this again. Will you stop going on and on about how I've changed. It's driving me mad.'

Jennifer sighed and wondered whether to press the issue further. After all he'd kind of just illustrated her point. Plus she still wasn't wholly convinced there wasn't something to get to the bottom of.

'Relax these shoulders,' said Max, kneading them with his hands. They were so rigid it hurt but in a pleasurable kind of way.

'Hmm,' muttered Jennifer, still not wholly placated.

'Come on, I can feel how stressed you are.'

'That's nice,' she said, closing her eyes and finally giving in to the sensation completely.

'Good,' said Max 'You should book in for a massage somewhere, my treat.'

'That would be nice.' A solitary tear ran down her cheek. She quickly wiped it away.

'Or perhaps ring Steve and ask him to do it seeing as he was so brilliant with his hands.'

Jennifer pulled away, ready to retaliate but to her relief she could see immediately that Max was only joking.

'Idiot,' she said softly, playfully hitting him on the chest.

'Aah Steve,' mused Max, a smug grin on his face 'Do you remember the party?'

'Course I do,' said Jennifer.

How could she forget? It was the day she'd met her future husband and the day poor old Steve had suddenly realised he had major competition. She still felt mildly guilty even now after all these years. Steve had been nothing but lovely to her and if Max hadn't turned up she'd probably still be with him. But Max *had* turned up and ultimately she'd gone for it because she'd recognised a twinkle of something in his eye that she'd suspected Steve would never quite be able to muster up.

She sighed and snuggled closer into Max's shoulder. She hated the fact she'd had suspicions and doubts about her husband. She'd always trusted him but lately it was almost as if she didn't trust herself. It wasn't that she'd ever do anything but she definitely felt at a bit of a crossroads in general. Recently she'd found herself thinking about the past all the time, about how things had turned out and how things might have been. Perhaps she was projecting her own rubbish onto Max? In which case she needed to stop because it simply wasn't fair. She sighed. When was she going to shake this miserable feeling of malcontent? It was making her the kind of person whom normally she'd like to grab by the shoulders and shake while telling them to get a grip. Not a good feeling.

22 THE PAST

Steve, January 2000

At long last Millennium New Year's Eve was out of the way. It was enormously comforting to know she'd never be required to suffer the question 'what are you doing for the millennium' ever again. Well, not unless she planned on living for another thousand years. And in the unlikely event she did, at least by that point she'd be perfectly within her rights to answer 'Nothing. I'm not doing anything. I don't get out much these days because by rights I should be *dead*.'

The pressure to do something 'amaaazing' had been intense. At work, what everyone was going to 'do' for the big night had been all anyone could talk about for months. Inevitably of course, a handful of smug people with far bigger pay packets than her, had been able to say things like 'We're off to the Pyrenees', or 'I'm going dolphin watching in San Diego' and even 'we're just going to a small bash for five thousand, in Paris, with fireworks'. It goes without saying that these people didn't just earn more than her but also must have been unbelievably organised. She and Karen hadn't even been able to find a local restaurant for them and their friends to go to, that wasn't either fully booked or extortionate. These 'experiences of a lifetime' events must have been booked when they were toddlers.

In the end, Pete and Karen had hosted the night at theirs and it was great. Dinner for twelve with lots of music, vigorous kitchen dancing and tonnes of booze.

Karen had invited Pete's cousin David to the dinner, purely so she could try and match- make him with Jennifer. David was relatively good looking but had been excruciatingly dull and the final nail in that possible date coffin had been delivered once and for all, hard and severely, when he had proceeded to talk at length about how *reUNIon* was such a great invention and how his sister had reunited with her now fiancée on it........

Jennifer was too tipsy to find it anything but funny at the time and threw herself into dancing and having fun with her friends. She spent a lot of the time being swung around by Pete and having a laugh with Karen and her work friends.

The next morning however, she woke up to the first day of the new millennium feeling horrendously hung-over and a bit panicky. It was the year 2000 and she was single. What if dumping Tim had been a huge mistake. She hadn't met anybody else even remotely worth seeing since and to make matters far worse, he was now a bloody, ruddy millionaire, a fact that permanently seemed to be rammed down her throat wherever she went. Every time she saw his face staring out at her from the newspapers made it harder for her to move on. Deep down she knew she'd done the 'right' thing because she didn't really miss him.

However, what she worried about was that if no one else came along she still might always regret leaving him. Ending up with a clever, multi- millionaire would have been far better than nothing. Wouldn't it?

On the upside, she had seen the millennium New Year in with laughter and people who felt like her tribe, plus now it was now over she'd never have to discuss what everybody's plans were for the most pressured night of the century and for that she was both grateful and relieved. So frankly, the greyness and general frugality of January was welcome, until Wednesday 7th January when her boiler broke down. And then it was just shit.

'Coming,' called Jennifer, rushing to answer the door, wishing she had slippers on, the floor tiles were so cold underfoot, even with tights on. Her tiny one bedroom flat in Tooting, which was hers and hers alone, and therefore a space she usually adored, was completely freezing. Last night she'd slept in a tracksuit and a coat but when she'd woken up, her nose, the only thing that hadn't been submerged under the covers, had been freezing, like a dog's. Unable to have a hot shower, her hair resembled a bird's nest and was far greasier than she'd normally ever allow it to be. Getting ready for work this morning she'd tried to solve this dilemma by scraping it all back into a ponytail and had compensated with extra make up, which on her pale, winter worn face, looked a bit like a drag queen. She was cold to the bone and simply couldn't warm up.

'Hi,' said the affable looking plumber, who was standing on her doorstep and who was hopefully going to be the answer to her prayers.

'Oh my gosh, thank you so much for coming. I'm literally desperate,' she said, pulling her coat even further around her. Underneath she was wearing a suit, ready for work. 'I don't suppose there's any chance you could have it fixed sooner rather than later, it's just I've actually got a massive day at work and should really be there right now but didn't think I could cope returning to this ice block again.'

'Er, well, give us a chance to at least have a look at what's happening and I'll let you know. But if I can, I shall get it sorted for you asap.'

He had an Essex accent.

'Oh gosh, I'm so sorry, you must think I'm insane. I think the cold may have actually frozen my brain.' said Jennifer, standing back to let him in, a good start in terms of him being able to fix anything. 'Then again I may have just got confused because I think it might actually be warmer outside than it is in here.'

'No worries,' said the plumber politely.

'Sorry, I'm Jennifer,' she said, starting again.

'Pleased to meet you, I'm Steve.'

Forty-five minutes later and the boiler had clunked into action, hot water was swooshing round the pipes and Jennifer was free to escape to work, unwashed, but confident that when she returned from work she wouldn't have to sleep in a coat.

'Thank you so much,' she gushed.

'No worries,' said Steve 'Glad I could get it sorted and thanks for the tea. It was nice to chat too.'

She grinned at him and was struck by what a nice face he had. During all the time they'd been chatting away, he'd been on his knees half inside the cupboard where the boiler lived so all she'd really been able to examine so far had been his backside. Not necessarily a bad thing. It was a nice backside but it was rather heart- warming to discover that he had a face to match. It was an open face which wasn't dazzlingly good looking but was really pleasant. It was a kind face, friendly and he had a good even smile and blue eyes.

He smiled back at her 'So, you off to work now then, you said you're in marketing but what does that actually involve?'

'You mean what is marketing?' said Jennifer, vaguely disappointed that he didn't know something as basic as that. 'It's basically it's all about identifying who your customer is, then creating value for them, reaching them and making sure you keep them,' said Jennifer, aware that now she really did have to get going, so moving to get her bag so she could sort out payment and leave.

'Yeah I know that,' he said, rolling his eyes 'What do you take me for? What I mean is who do you do marketing for? Or, if you like, who's your market and what kind are you in charge of?'

'Oh right, sorry' she said. She grinned at him, feeling stupid, though as she did, her teeth almost chattered together she was still so cold. She honestly felt like she might never be warm again.
'Big questions,' she said, deflecting them, mainly because she was in a rush and her mind at this point was now fully focused on the meeting she desperately needed to get to.

'You got to go?' he said, taking the hint.

'I do I'm afraid,' she replied, rooting around in her bag, looking for her chequebook. 'How much is that then?'

'It's fine, I'll send you an invoice,' said Steve.

'O-k,' said Jennifer 'Do you mind letting me know how much it will be for?'

'One twenty plus VAT.'

'OK,' she said, trying to mask her disappointment. There was no way she'd be getting the shoes she'd wanted forever this month. She should have been a plumber.

'So anyway, I don't suppose, and I promise I never usually do this, but I don't suppose you might fancy going for a drink one night?' asked Steve suddenly and as Jennifer looked up to check she'd heard right his cheeks flamed red. 'Though I promise, no more dull questions about work.'

'Er...I don't know,' replied Jennifer, honestly.

'Ok, no worries, I shouldn't have put you on the spot,' said Steve immediately, turning away and bending back down to rummage in his tool bag, getting ready to go and obviously masking his embarrassment.

Jennifer regarded him. He seemed like a perfectly decent bloke and he had just fixed her boiler. Plus, who else did she think she had, lined up exactly? Pete's boring cousin David? Her last meaningful relationship had been with Tim and that had ended over two years ago. Since then she'd seen one guy called Jack for a while but it had only lasted a month, at which point they'd simply stopped ringing each other due to a massive lack of interest on both sides. She'd had a couple of terrible dates, thanks to being forced by Karen to give online dating a go, and a one-night stand which she could hardly bear to think about it had been so unbearably clunky.

So why would she now turn down a date with a man who had all his own teeth, was seemingly nice and who had just saved her, definitely from hypothermia, if not death by frostbite? Was she insane? 'Actually...I'd love to go for a drink,' she said shyly. 'Really?' he said, looking pleasingly delighted and flashing her a wide grin.

'Yeah,' she grinned back. His smile was infectious. He had lovely teeth.

'Great, that's really good then,' he said. 'Ok, well I've got your number, I'll give you a call and perhaps we could go for dinner after or something?'

'That would be very nice,' she said. And then they both stood there, still grinning but now also feeling mildly awkward.

'So....anyway...,' she said, reaching for the front door at the exact same time he did.

'Oh sorry,' he said.

'No, no, after you,' she said as he went to grab his bag, realising they were now going to have to cope with leaving the flat at the same time and therefore continuing the conversation even thought it was clearly time for it to end.

Feeling gauche they shuffled out of the door together.
'Ok, well I'll see you soon then,' said Steve once they were both outside and Jennifer had locked the door behind her. 'I'm just going this way, to the van.'

'Oh...er right,' said Jennifer, now wondering whether to pretend she was headed the other way but knowing it would just make her even more late 'Um....I'm going that way too actually, towards the tube.'

'Oh cool,' he said, his face colouring a little.

And so they ended up strolling down the road, together but not, both smiling manfully despite the awkwardness of the situation.

Eventually Jennifer decided to do them both a favour by starting up a conversation 'So where do you live then Steve?' she said at the precise moment he decided to say 'Well, this is me, my van's parked here.'

Their sentences collided awkwardly.

'Oh right... well... not to worry then,' said Jennifer, cringing and unbelievably self- conscious by this point yet also really hoping he would definitely ring her. There was something about him that appealed to her more and more by the second.

'At the moment I'm staying with a mate in Mitcham though.... by the way.'

'Oh great, not too far then I suppose,' she said. 'O-k... well.... see you. Give me a ring.'

'Will do,' he said watching her go up the street. And although he knew it hadn't been the smoothest of meetings and that he wasn't going to win any points for his chatting up technique, Steve drove away feeling really chuffed and had a little spring in his step for the rest of the day. You see, underneath all that make up and that huge coat he could tell that Jennifer Drew was cute. More than cute. She was gorgeous. His cup of tea. Strong and sweet.

23 | Present Day

'Jen, I don't know if you can hear me, but it's me Max… anyway, the doctor's think it's worth a go. Talking to you that is, so I'm going to sit and chat anyway, just in case.'

It was strange. She kind of understood what he was saying on the surface and yet at the same time it was as if he were speaking a foreign language. Her brain couldn't really cope with the task of listening and understanding at the same time. Instead the words were just noise really.

'We're all really missing you. It's very quiet at home without you. The girls are fine. They know that Mummy's having a long sleep and they say a little prayer for you every night. I'm keeping close tabs on them and the school have been brilliant actually, especially Miss Kelly who's really been keeping an eye on Pol. So that's all ok. Think they might be getting a bit fed up with my cooking though...'

Max's voice cracked and he stopped talking for a moment, though Jennifer had no clue that the pause was necessary so he could regain his composure. She still wasn't really with him. He cleared his throat.

'For that matter I am too. Anyway, I've bought a paper with me so I thought I might just read some of it out to you. You know, keep you in touch with what's going on in the...'

But Jennifer had slipped back to where she'd come from, almost with intent, for the last time she'd emerged from a portal she'd noticed that the one to the left, the one marked Aidan was growing faint. She'd had a strong inkling at the time that if she wanted to find out anything else from that parallel universe that she'd have to do it quickly, while it still existed. She'd even considered what might happen if it closed while she was inside. Would she be trapped? Would she remain Jennifer from that life forever? She hoped not. There was nothing about that life that made her feel proud or happy. Had she gone with Aidan it seemed she'd have had a forlorn existence compared to the one she enjoyed with Max. In her real life she'd got her education, stayed in touch with her friends and family and ultimately gone on to create a safe, secure and largely happy family unit of her own. In the world of Aidan, she felt sorry for Nathan. Sorry for her own son. The son she might have had...

She started the drop, by now suddenly desperate to know that there was some form of resolution, if not for her then for the boy.

He needed his extended family she decided. Not just a strung out, worn out mum and a lazy, workshy dad.

She arrived. The portal on the left was even weaker than before so without any further procrastination she marched determinedly down it, feeling more nervous than she ever had about anything ever before.

24 TUNNEL NUMBER ONE
Aidan: what could have been

Jennifer sat in the cafe drumming the fingers of one hand on the formica table while decimating yet another packet of sugar with the other. She wished she hadn't ordered coffee. She felt jittery enough as it was and the caffeine she'd consumed wasn't making life any easier.

Where was she? Why wasn't she here yet?

For the hundredth time she glanced at the black and white clock on the wall. Three thirty-two. Her mum was now officially two minutes late for their meeting. Still, it wasn't like she was coming from round the corner she supposed. She had a horribly long train journey from the suburbs of South West London right up to the very North of England and then a cab ride to contend with. The wait was unbearable though and now she needed the loo again. Blooming coffee.

Jennifer stood up and for the second time since she'd arrived, headed for the tiny toilet at the back of the cafe. Once she'd finished she checked her reflection in the cracked mirror above the small basin.

She didn't usually wear a great deal of make- up but today she'd taken extra care with her appearance. In the days leading up to this one she'd agonised about what to wear for hours. She didn't want to appear dowdy or plain in her standard jeans and same old tops that she wore day in day out. But she only had them or a couple of dresses she reserved for special occasions. She'd decided that what she needed was a happy medium, because as much as she wanted to look nice she also wanted to avoid looking unnatural or as though she'd tried too hard. In the end she'd splashed out on a new top from Oasis. It had been so long since she'd treated herself to anything, she'd decided the occasion merited it. Besides, it had been on the sale rail so had only cost her £28.00 as opposed to £42.00 yet it made her feel a million dollars. Well, maybe a thousand...

Anyway, the point was it was *new* which was thrilling.

She sighed at her reflection. She looked ok but knew that no matter how many layers of blusher she added, her mum would undoubtedly detect the tired aura that permanently existed around her. Would it also be noticeable that she dyed her own hair and that she looked a few years older than the thirty-eight she'd lived?

Suddenly it occurred to her that if her mum had arrived by now, she might think she hadn't turned up so, with a start, she hurried back out of the loo only to immediately spot her mother sitting at a table, looking as nervous and anxious as she felt.

She was so much older.

Of course this was always going to be the case, yet no matter how much common sense had told her to expect someone she hadn't seen for decades to have aged, it didn't stop it from being a shock. Her mum looked far more like a grandmother these days. It was the strangest thing. Tears immediately pricked her eyes. It was so ridiculously good to see her but perhaps it wasn't until this very second that she realised not only just how much she'd missed her but also how much she'd missed out *on*. Unsure how to behave, she felt like a bag of nerves as she approached the table.

'Mum,' she said, completely choked.

'Oh Jennifer,' said her mother, leaping to her feet, her nerves clearly frayed by the stress of the situation. 'You're here. I can't believe it.'

'Neither can I,' said Jennifer and the two women stared at one another, both too moved to speak.

'Oh come here,' her mum said eventually, gesturing to her daughter to give her a hug.

As they embraced Jennifer couldn't help it, she sobbed noisily into her mum's shoulder. Eighteen years was a long time to go without seeing your mum. She'd been a nineteen-year-old girl the last time she'd seen her in the flesh. In other words, she hadn't seen her for essentially half her life, making do instead with phone calls. Until that is they'd really fallen out, (when she'd fallen pregnant), after which they'd barely had any contact at all apart from the odd letter.

'I'm sorry,' she repeated. It was all she could manage for now.

'Me too,' said Lesley with meaning. Finally, she broke their embrace and motioned to Jennifer to sit down opposite her.

'Now,' she said briskly, determined not to let the emotion of the moment overwhelm proceedings. 'Come on, we'd better pull ourselves together or they'll be sending in the men in white coats for us. Shall we order some tea and cake?'

Jennifer nodded as she sat down, before grabbing a white paper napkin out of the stainless steel holder to blow her nose on. 'Oh gosh, I'm so sorry about weeping. I really didn't want to be like this.'

She looked up to see that her mum was staring at her and for a few seconds she stared back.

'Do I look awful?' asked Jennifer feebly.

'No love,' said her mother, her whole face suddenly crumpling 'you look absolutely wonderful, a sight for sore eyes.' And with that, despite all her best efforts not to, she burst into tears herself.

'Oh Mum,' said Jennifer, feeling stricken and standing up to reach across the table. 'Come here.'

Her mum gladly accepted a second hug and they stood like that for some time, in a very awkward position, one that neither of them wished to change this time. Suddenly what anyone else in the cafe might be thinking was unimportant.

Instead, giving in to their feelings, they let it be the hug they'd both been waiting for and had needed for a very long time. Finally, they let go again and as they both sat down Jennifer absorbed every detail of her mum's face. She was so lined, so grey. She'd put on weight and looked quite tubby around her middle. She also looked like home.

'So, have you been happy?' asked Lesley, getting straight to the heart of things.

Of all the questions her mum could have started with, Jennifer wished it hadn't been that.

'Um.... yes,' she replied hesitantly after a lengthy pause, which kind of said it all.
'And Aidan, has he been good to you?'

'Yeah mum, Aidan's fine. I know you have this idea that he's some kind of monster but he honestly isn't.'

'And Nathan?'

'He's amazing. It's just so sad you've never been able to find that out for yourself.'

'There's still time,' said Lesley, pulling a hanky from her handbag and gripping it so tightly that the blood drained from her knuckles. 'If he'd see me I'd love to take him out perhaps? I don't know, I mean what do you think?'

Jennifer's heart ached as she took in her mum's pained expression. How much time had they wasted? 'I'm sure he'd love that,' said Jennifer at once. 'He's a real sweetie. Tries to pretend he's all cool in front of his mates but it's all a front. Underneath he's soft as butter.'

'You've got a Northern accent you know.'

'No,' said Jennifer 'Have I?'

'Ooh definitely,' replied her mother.

'So what do you want to do now then? Shall I get you this tea and cake?' asked Jennifer after a time, not particularly relishing the idea of showing her the drab flat where she lived. Ideally she'd postpone that a while longer.

'Do you know what? I think I might have changed my mind. I'm not sure I could eat cake after all. Not like me...Shall we have a little walk instead?' suggested Lesley 'That train journey was a long time sitting down. It would be nice to stretch my legs.'

'Good idea,' agreed Jennifer, motioning to the waitress that she'd like to pay for her coffee.

Then they gathered their bags and left the warmth of the steamy cafe for the cooler streets of Carlisle.

'It's so good to see you Mum,' she said.
By way of reply her mother extended a hand out of the sleeve of her coat and reached for Jennifer's in order to give it a little squeeze. And in that small moment it appeared that things were going to be ok.

25 | Thursday

Jennifer left work at six o clock on the dot after what had been a relatively successful day. That afternoon she'd managed to secure a deal on a three-bedroom house which had been lingering on their books unsold for far too long. The manager had been so happy to get it off the market and therefore finally shot of it, that he'd been particularly complimentary to Jennifer about her selling skills which had felt good. Although, truthfully, deep down Jennifer wondered if anything she ever said when showing people round properties actually made the blindest bit of difference to whether or not they ended up deciding to buy them. When guiding people round she sometimes caught herself solemnly saying things like 'And this is the bathroom' as if she were enlightening them with knowledge they'd otherwise not have been able to figure out themselves. When in fact the bath and the toilet were pretty large giveaways to the fact they weren't standing in the kitchen. Still, she wasn't about to let her boss know that she'd been pretty superfluous to the buyer's decision making process and instead allowed him to believe that without her the agency would still be lumbered with a three bed that most people in their right minds would never want to purchase due to the fact the ground floor was so dark it felt more like a dungeon.

Feeling chirpier than she had in a while, as she wandered home, she contemplated the upcoming weekend. Tomorrow night, once the children were in bed she planned on reprising her original plan of putting on some slutty underwear and seducing her husband. And this time it *would* work and they *would* have sex and they would reconnect on lots of levels and all would be well. After all, there was a huge possibility that a lot of this angst she'd been experiencing lately was down to the fact that she simply needed a good shag.

Then, on Saturday, the girls both had parties to go to and she and Max were out in the evening for dinner with friends she actually liked, which would be nice.

Yes, she'd definitely been worrying far too much lately about stuff that in the grand scheme of things was probably all manageable and not too disastrous. No one was dying. Everyone had their health. She was a lucky girl and needed to keep reminding herself of this fact.

Nearly at the bottom of her road she realised her phone was vibrating away in her handbag.

Scrabbling around for it, she caught it just before it went to answer phone.

It was their nanny, Ivana.

'Hello,' she said, wondering what she wanted and betting they'd run out of something.

'Jennifer....'

Oh god thought Jennifer at once for Ivana sounded very distraught. Her heart skipped a beat and hundreds of thoughts flashed through her mind in a nanosecond before Ivana finally managed to utter 'I'm so sorry, I think Eadie's broken her arm.'

Oh. My. God.

Later, around the time Jennifer had originally been hoping to be sliding into a nice relaxing bath after a lovely dinner with her husband, she and Max were sitting at Kingston hospital, feeling traumatised and looking almost as white in the face as the cast that was now wrapped around their eldest daughter's arm.

Jennifer felt a shadow of her former self having experienced the most stressful few hours of her life. The image of Eadie's arm sticking out at such a bizarre angle seemed to be burned into her retinas and would undoubtedly never leave her.

Upon racing into the house she'd found her daughter in a state of shock, lying on the couch in a daze, white as a sheet with her arm at said disgusting angle which Jennifer had struggled with even being able to look at. She'd stroked her daughter's brow and told her everything would be alright, grateful that Eadie was so still and calm because being totally honest the arm thing was making her feel very nauseous. Thankfully Ivana had already called the ambulance but she was wracked with guilt and worry and was literally wringing her hands and pleading with Jennifer for forgiveness. Not that by the sound of it she could have done anything to have prevented the accident. Eadie had simply been bouncing on the trampoline in the garden just as she did most days after school when it wasn't raining. She'd slipped, had landed awkwardly and that had been that. Jennifer knew this was the case and despite maternal instinct wanting desperately to have someone or something to blame she knew this wouldn't be fair so kept her counsel.

The minute the ambulance arrived though, Jennifer burst into tears, simply at the relief of someone medically trained finally being in their presence.

'Is she going to be alright?' she wailed.

'Yes, she'll be fine, but let's get her to the hospital as soon as we can.'

By now the shock was starting to wear off, meaning Eadie was suddenly far more aware of the pain she was in. At this point she started really crying and repeatedly yelling 'Ow, ow, ow' until she'd wound herself up into a terrible state. She didn't want the ambulance men or anyone else for that matter to move her so getting her into the ambulance was a bit of an ordeal to say the least.

Jennifer hated seeing her daughter so distressed but knew she had to remain strong at least till Max could join them. Thankfully she'd got through to him on his mobile straightaway and between them they'd decided that the best plan would be to meet at the hospital while Ivana stayed at the house to look after Polly, who was the only one in the family who seemed perfectly oblivious to the drama going on around her.
Throughout the whole time they were trying to get a near hysterical Eadie into the ambulance, she sat calmly in front of the TV watching 'The Little Mermaid' casually picking her nose.
At one point she even yelled at Eadie to stop making so much noise because she couldn't hear the telly.
Still, eventually they were in the ambulance and on their way and the medics were able to administer some heavy duty pain relief to Eadie which they assured Jennifer would also slightly sedate her. Jennifer spent the rest of the journey wondering if it would shed her in a bad light if she were to ask if she could have some too.

Once they'd finally arrived, the hospital was really busy so they had to wait quite a while in A and E before anyone could attend to them properly. When Eadie was eventually wheeled into a room to have her arm x-rayed and set in a cast, Jennifer was still without her husband so had to continue being stoic while ignoring the desire to retch every time her gaze fell upon her little girl's bent arm. When Max eventually arrived at the hospital, having jogged all the way from the train station, he was a sweaty stressed mess and Jennifer realised she had never been so happy to see anyone in her life. He was waiting for them as they emerged from the treatment room, Eadie on a trolley, pale and whimpering, and he immediately gave his wife an enormous, reassuring hug before turning his attentions to their daughter.

'Are you ok, Eadie Beady,' he soothed, stroking his daughter's hair and kissing her puffy face so tenderly it nearly set Jennifer off.

'It still hurts,' Eadie moaned, holding her rigid plaster-casted arm out. Remembering what lay beneath and the process which had occurred in order to get it back into a normal position Jennifer's stomach turned yet again. She'd have made a truly lousy nurse. Doctors and nurses were saints as far as she was concerned.

'You are so brave,' Max said to his daughter 'And you know what brave people get?'

'Presents?' Eadie tried hopefully, her puffy, tear stained face looking something other than pained and distressed for the first time in hours.

'Too blooming right they do,' said Max. 'Sackfuls of them, maybe even a games console?'

'Yeah,' squealed Eadie, her face a picture of disbelief. Her parents had always said she couldn't have a games console for another two years.

Maybe it had been worth breaking her arm after all?

Seeing her little girl look vaguely comforted meant Jennifer didn't even get annoyed by Max's slightly dubious parental approach. Sod it, if Eadie wanted a games console, at this stage frankly she could have one. She was just grateful that Max was here. For the first time in a long while she recalled how much she loved him, why she'd married him and the security and comfort that doing so had brought into her life.

It's amazing how things can turn on a sixpence though. As soon as they'd got Eadie to the ward, off the trolley and settled into her bed Max suddenly turned to his wife and said 'Can I have a word?' which struck Jennifer as a bit odd. He was her husband. He could say what he liked. He hardly needed to make an appointment.

'Course you can. Eadie darling, you try and close your eyes now. Have a little rest.'

Eadie must have been completely exhausted because she didn't put up any resistance to her mother's suggestion at all and merely closed her eyes at which point Jennifer and Max pulled the curtain shut around her bed and tip toed out into the corridor.

'Who was keeping an eye on her when it happened?' Max demanded to know as soon as they were out of earshot.

'What do you mean?' said Jennifer who by now was so tired she could only think about getting home and to bed. 'You know who was. Ivana was.'

'Well, how could she allow this to happen? I know the kids like her but after this I think we have to ask ourselves if we can really entrust the care of our children to her.'

'Oh for goodness sakes, Max. It could so easily have been one of us. It was an accident. It's not like Ivana went up to her and snapped her arm in two.'

'I know that,' retaliated Max 'It's just that...well...it has happened on her watch and I know you've always raved about her but you do have a tendency to see only the nice in people. And she is nice, but is she responsible enough to be in charge of our kids? Given that we're standing in a hospital I'd suggest the answer might be no.'

'Why are you sounding annoyed with me?' seethed Jennifer 'What the hell have I done? Honestly, I totally resent what you're implying and think it's completely out of order. Do you really think I would be so dippy as to leave the girls with someone I wasn't really sure about just because I thought they were nice?'

Seeing how angry she was Max backed down 'Ok, well perhaps we'll talk about it another time.'

'There's nothing to talk about,' replied Jennifer stonily. 'And don't you dare make Ivana feel bad when we get back either, because if you do I will be absolutely livid. No one feels worse about what's happened than her right now and I do not want to have to find new childcare when the person we've already got is so good. She loves the girls to pieces and to be honest is probably more vigilant with them than we are. All my friends comment on how wonderful she is when they see her out and about with them. Now, before I lose it completely, what I'm really interested in is finding out when we can get out of here. Eadie's exhausted.'

'She's not the only one,' said Max sheepishly and Jennifer could tell then that not only did he know he'd been out of order but also that she was being over the top.

Suddenly she didn't feel quite so cross anymore, just tired. 'She's going to be fine you know,' she said more gently, calming down.

'Course she is,' agreed Max 'Even on the way here I was thinking how many times I was in and out of A and E as a kid but you still can't help panicking when it's your own.'

'I know and I'm sorry I snapped. We have to keep it in perspective. It is only a broken arm and it'll mend. What we should probably be more worried about is the fact that our youngest might be a psychopath. I've literally never seen anyone so unbothered by seeing someone in horrific pain as she was,' said Jennifer, motioning to her husband to come in for a hug which he did.

'Now that really is taking middle class fretting to another level,' chuckled Max, kissing her tenderly on the forehead. 'Right, I'm going to go and see if we can get out of here. I know they said we should wait to have the cast checked again but I'm almost tempted to do a runner. Or at least to say that we'll bring her back in the morning to get it checked then.'

'Ok,' agreed Jennifer, equally keen to get home. As Max went off in search of a doctor, Jennifer returned to Eadie and pulled back the curtain. She was fast asleep, worn out by her stressful experience.

When Max arrived back ten minutes later he gave her a thumbs up 'We can go, we just need to sign a form on the way out.'
'Great,' said Jennifer. 'Though it almost seems a shame we'll have to wake her up now.'

'Well when our cab's here I'll carry her, that way, with a bit of luck she might stay asleep. Then, when we get back, I might eBay that bloody trampoline you know.'

'Do it,' said Jennifer vehemently.

'And perhaps I'll take the day off work tomorrow,' he suggested. 'That way we can bring Eadie back here to get checked together. Plus we're both knackered so it would give us a chance to have a bit of a chill out.'

'Yeah, oh shit.'

'What?'

'I'm supposed to be seeing my therapist tomorrow. My appointment's at eleven. I'll have to cancel if Eadie's not at school.'

'You didn't tell me,' said Max regarding his wife quizzically.

'Well it's no big deal,' said Jennifer.

'Well, you shouldn't cancel. Doesn't she charge for missed appointments?'

'Yeah.'

'Well you go then and I can bring Eadie here on my own,' said Max, drawing her in for another hug.

'Ok, great, and then tomorrow night,' Jennifer said, her voice slightly muffled by his jumper 'We could perhaps, you know, have a bit of a romantic night in. If you know what I mean?'

'Sounds good to me,' said Max. 'And impressive that despite the strip lighting, smell of antiseptic and our bandaged child being only feet away you've still got sex on your brain whereas here I am thinking how I might finish that wardrobe off properly.'

'Yes, well it would be nice not to have it lying on the floor anymore,' Jennifer replied, faintly embarrassed.

'I'll get you lying on the floor,' said Max, pinching her bum.

'Maybe,' said Jennifer primly.

'And after your Steve 'jokes' the other day I'd better pull my finger out and show you that actually I can be quite useful to have around. Otherwise you might run off with another plumber.'

'I doubt it,' laughed Jennifer 'You saw the last plumber we had round. Mick with no front teeth.'

'True,' said Max 'He hardly lived up to sweet Steve's standards did he?'

Jennifer smiled and rolled her eyes but didn't reply. Steve had been sweet. Really sweet and there was no harm in that. He'd been her 'one before the one' who could have been 'the one' if fate hadn't stepped in and brought Max to her.

'Anyway, you sit down and I'll go and sign this form and then come back for you both.'

'Ok,' agreed Jennifer.

She sank into the plastic chair next to Eadie's bed and wondered how it would feel to deal with incidents like this as a single parent? Horrible no doubt. Terrifying in fact. At that precise moment she felt sincerely grateful and hopeful that she'd never have to find out. She was also delighted that Max had offered to take tomorrow off. With a bit of luck she wouldn't have to set foot in a hospital again until the cast needed taking off, which suited her fine.

26 THE PAST

Steve, January 2000

Jennifer had been looking forward to her date with Steve all day which was a good sign. First dates were usually horribly nerve- racking events but she wasn't dreading this one at all. They'd had a couple of fairly long chats on the phone already which helped. Both times the conversation had flowed easily and given her an indication that the date would be enjoyable as opposed to an ordeal. Steve seemed really nice, really sweet and quite funny. She was interested in getting to know him better.

She'd taken all the first date precautions of course. She'd washed her hair the night before, and when she'd got home from work to shower and change, she'd also shaved her armpits, sorted out her bikini line and legs and put on a sexy, matching bra and knickers. Just in case.

They'd agreed to meet at an Italian restaurant. She had googled it and could see it looked pretty casual so she was wearing boot- cut jeans (the only jeans anyone was wearing in 2000) with a top from Whistles and high heeled ankle boots. Despite feeling relatively confident she still had butterflies as she approached the restaurant at seven minutes past eight.

As soon as she walked in she spotted him. Good. She would have hated to have arrived first. She was quite taken aback by how good he looked. She'd remembered him as having a really nice face but actually, on second sighting, he was better looking than she remembered and had the sort of face most women would probably notice in a crowd. His eyes were really blue and you could tell that although he wore his hair so short it wasn't because he was going bald but because he had a lovely shaped head and simply suited him that way.

He waved at her as soon as he spotted her and got up from his seat which she thought was chivalrous. He'd obviously made a bit of an effort too. He was wearing a shirt and looked clean and smelled of some nice herby aftershave.

'Hi, you look nice,' he said, leaning in to give her a kiss on the cheek.

'Thanks,' she said shyly, sitting down in the chair he'd just pulled out for her. His manners were impeccable.

'Did you come straight from work?' he asked.

'No,' replied Jennifer 'I popped home actually as I tend to have to wear suits and stuff to work. You know, really 'officey' clothes.'

She didn't add '*Which also gave me a chance to sort my pubic sideburns out.*'

'Cool,' he said 'Do you want a drink?'

'Yeah definitely, I'll have a glass of white wine please.'

The waitress who had just come over scribbled this down 'And I'll have a coke please?' said Steve which Jennifer slightly cringed at.

Fizzy drink for dinner? Really?

'Are you not a big drinker then?' she asked, wondering what kind of a person it made her that she'd rather he was than wasn't. At university being able to drink huge amounts had almost been a badge of honour.
'Not really. I quite like lager,' said Steve 'But I'm not massively into wine if I'm honest.'

'Fair enough,' said Jennifer.

'So, tell me about yourself,' Steve started manfully 'How come a gorgeous girl like you is single?'

Pretty smooth thought Jennifer. She grinned, flattered 'Well, I was in quite a long term relationship at university. Two and a half years to be precise.'

'Ok, so what happened, if you don't mind me asking that is?'

'No, not at all. Um... well, I'm not sure really. I guess it wasn't so much a case of anything specific happening to end it but more realising we just weren't compatible. He was a really clever guy and interesting to hang out with but to be honest he was a bit of a cold fish at times. He was pretty much incapable of expressing his feelings so I spent the whole time wondering if he actually did fancy me or whether he was just with me for the sake of it.'

'Really?' said Steve 'If I was your boyfriend I wouldn't be able to stop telling you how pretty you are.'

Jennifer didn't know how to react. What a lovely thing to say. He sounded so sincere too. Not creepy or disingenuous at all. 'Thanks,' she managed in the end, once she'd got over the shock of being complimented. It had been a while. 'Um, anyway, I guess it just didn't feel like he loved me in the right way which probably sounds a bit weird but by the end, as far as I was concerned, it felt more like we were friends than boyfriend and girlfriend. I don't know.'

'Fizzled out?'

'Yeah,' said Jennifer a bit doubtfully. By now she was revealing slightly more than she had originally intended to but was unsure how to stop the snowball of information that was rolling out of her mouth 'Though to be fair it wasn't ever massively sizzling even at the beginning so there wasn't a great deal of sizzle to fizzle. Besides, he had a wife of sorts.'

'What do you mean?'

'He was married to his work,' said Jennifer, teetering on the verge of telling him about Tim, only half wondering if she should so early on. Still, she'd gone this far. Perhaps she'd just get it out of the way. 'Have you heard of *ReUNIon*?'

'Course yeah.'

'Ok, well he kind of invented it.'

'You're kidding? He isn't that Purcell bloke is he?'

Jennifer nodded.

'Wow,' said Steve, trying to recover from having been emasculated within the first few minutes of the date. 'Ok, so very clever bloke then, although if you don't mind me saying?'

'Go on,' encouraged Jennifer 'Say what you like.'

'I always think he comes across as a bit arrogant in interviews.'

'I agree.'

'And he can't be *that* intelligent if he let you slip through his fingers,' he added, going red as he did so.

Jennifer grinned. He'd already paid her more compliments than Tim had in the first year of being together. It was nice.

'Well that's very kind of you to say. And what about you? How long have you been single for? Not long I bet.' Jennifer cringed. She'd been trying to match his kindness by saying something nice herself but in the process had managed to make herself sound like a cheesy old lothario.

'Oh blimey, let's see now, about six months.'

'Ok and who was your last girlfriend?'

'Lauren,' replied Steve and as he said her name Jennifer could tell that Lauren had meant a great deal to him. 'We went out for about three years.'

'Right, so a long time then,' she said, slightly unsure as to why, or how they'd got on to the subject of their exes quite so swiftly. Surely this was more of a third or fourth date kind of chat? Oh well they were doing it now. 'Was it a difficult break up?'

'Yeah I guess.'

'So......what happened then?'

For the second time Steve's face coloured and he seemed distinctly unsure about replying.

'What?' said Jennifer, his reluctance to answer making her far keener to find out more details.

'Well, it'll probably sound a bit heavy and I don't want to scare you off. We haven't even ordered yet,' he joked, looking more than a little uncomfortable.

'I know,' grinned Jennifer 'I was thinking the same thing myself when I told you about Tim but you've *got* to tell me now and I promise I won't get scared,' she said, despite the fact she wasn't one hundred percent sure she meant it. If Lauren had found out he was a money launderer or had a penchant for gimp masks she could be leaving before her pizza had even gone in the oven.
'Thanks,' she said to the waitress who arrived back with their drinks.

Steve seemed grateful for the distraction and said that they'd like to order their food. So they did, though Jennifer wasn't letting him off the hook that easily.

'So,' she prompted as soon as the waitress had left 'what happened?'

'Ok, well before I say, just bear in mind that we were together for a pretty long time. So I guess you consider lots of things that don't even enter your brain when you first start going out with someone.'

'Good disclaimer. Now tell me,' she insisted.

'Right,' said Steve, finally accepting that he wasn't going to be able to wriggle out of an explanation. 'Basically, what happened was, I realised we weren't on the same page as far as what we both wanted out of life was concerned.'

'In what way?'

'She didn't want to have children. Ever.'
'Ah,' said Jennifer, feeling mildly relieved. That was a fair enough answer, one that didn't have her running for the hills.

'Ok, well fair enough then. I would say that's a pretty sensible reason to have ended things if you know you do definitely want them.'

'I do,' said Steve with feeling. 'I love kids. Ideally I'd like three I reckon. Not that I said that to Lauren. I mean if she'd agreed to trying just for one at some point I probably would have stayed with her but she point blank refused even to consider it.'

'Was she a real career girl then?'

'Er, no not massively,' said Steve, shaking his head 'She's a beautician. She just doesn't really like being around kids. It's weird. Her sister's got a couple you see and she kept saying that her sister had lost her life. That she was always tired, that she was fat and never had any money. Only whenever I went round there I always thought her sister looked fulfilled and like she wouldn't change her life for anything. Besides, I think not wanting to lose your figure is a pretty lame reason for not wanting to have a child.'
'Was she fat?'

'Hardly the point.'

Jennifer blushed. She was such a weirdo sometimes. Only the other day she'd heard a story on the news about a man who'd murdered his wife after cooking dinner for her and all she'd been able to think about, apart from how awful it was, was how much she wanted to know what he'd cooked. What had he deemed reasonable for a last supper? It was just the way her brain worked. The details seemed important.

'I know it's not the point,' she agreed now 'but, was she?'

'Um, yeah, a bit,' said Steve, rolling his eyes in mock disapproval but clearly amused.

Jennifer nodded, while considering everything he'd just said in the last few minutes. It was very endearing hearing a man speak in the way in which he had. In her experience women tended to be more vocal about their desire for motherhood and a lot of men just appeared to go along with it when the time was right. She tried to think if she and Tim had ever discussed if they'd want to have children one day but couldn't remember. She didn't think he'd have been against it but she couldn't remember him ever definitely stating that he would as a fact. Besides, being a dad would take some of his attention away from *ReUNIon* and that would never do.

'Have you seen *Chitty Chitty Bang Bang*?' she asked.

Steve nodded.

'Did she share the child-catcher's views on kids?'

'She did, though fortunately she was better looking,' said Steve amiably. 'Not such a big pointy nose.'

'And she didn't wear black tailcoats and carry a massive net around with her.'

'Not often.'

There followed a bit of an awkward silence, only because given what had just been said, Jennifer now felt vaguely obliged to announce her own views on procreation. After all, if she didn't want to have children one day there was almost no point her being there. No point in him treating her to a pizza. Steve was right of course. Only insane people would think about such things when they'd only just met someone and yet the stark reality was that once you ploughed deeper into your twenties, if you wanted a family then you only really embarked on a relationship if you thought it might end up leading somewhere. Otherwise what was the point?

'Well, for what it's worth then,' she said in a voice that she hoped sounded light hearted but actually sounded vaguely like Alan Partridge 'I'd like at least a couple of sprogs one day.'

'Ok,' said Steve, raising his glass of coke to her 'Well good for you and don't worry, I'm not planning on impregnating anyone in the near future.'

He smiled cheekily, acknowledging that he fully comprehended how crazy this conversation was given that they hadn't even slept together. Just at the thought of that her stomach flipped in a very good way. Suddenly coy she looked around the restaurant at nothing in particular.

'Anyway,' he continued 'that was a bit awkward wasn't it? Sorry about that. I honestly didn't mean to extract your personal views on whether or not you'd like to be a parent or not within the first ten minutes of the date.'

'It's ok,' laughed Jennifer, who actually thought he'd managed to break the ice quite successfully. At least he could take the piss out of himself. It was sweet.

'Right, so what shall we talk about now?' he said.

'Ooh why don't we just go straight for another contentious and deeply personal subject,' said Jennifer 'Maybe, who we'd vote for in the next election? Or, how much we earn? Something nice and delicate like that.'

'Good idea, or perhaps you could just tell me how your day's been. Might be less controversial?'

'Ok,' agreed Jennifer and from that point onward the evening veered into more standard first date territory only with the edge of nerves extinguished completely.

Later, after they'd had their meal, they left the restaurant and stood out on the pavement, both reluctant for the date to end but unsure as to whether the other person felt the same. In the end Steve broached the subject.

'Well, I've had a lovely time but if I'm honest I'd like the evening to continue a bit longer. It's only nine thirty after all. But if you're tired...'

'No,' said Jennifer 'I'm fine, why? What were you thinking?'

'We could go for a drink in a pub?' he suggested 'Or, and I hope you don't think this sounds forward, perhaps we could go back to yours for a cup of tea and just chill out for a bit or something?'

'Could do,' said Jennifer who quite fancied doing that. She really wanted to snog him. 'Or we could go to yours? Mitcham isn't far.'

'Ah,' said Steve 'Actually, I'm not based in Mitcham anymore.' 'Oh right,' said Jennifer wondering why he suddenly looked so sheepish. 'Where are you then?'

'I've er, moved back home, just for the short term,' he said, and Jennifer realised at this point that he blushed incredibly easily.

'You mean with your parents?'

'Just with my mum actually. My dad died a few years ago so mum's on her own. Well, strictly speaking that's not true. She's got a boyfriend called Derek only they don't live together.'

'So where's your mum's place then?'

'Leytonstone.'

'Leytonstone?' she exclaimed 'That's miles away isn't it?'

'It's not close,' he agreed 'But it's not that bad. When I'm working I drive a motorbike to get down to these parts and just leave the van parked somewhere overnight. I biked here tonight as it goes.'

'Right,' said Jennifer, trying not to feel so downcast about the fact he lived so far away. With his mother! He was twenty-eight years old for Christ's sakes.

Her expression must have given her away because Steve suddenly piped up with 'Like I said it's only temporary. It's just I was spending so much on rent it was getting really difficult to save. Living at home for a few months means I can put away a lot each month which I really need to do in order to be able to get a deposit for my own place. And besides, living with Mum isn't so bad. She's amazing my mum. We get on really well. Plus, I get a great dinner every night. She even does my ironing.'

'Ah, that's nice,' said Jennifer, though if she were being totally honest she would have been more impressed if he'd said he looked after his own washing. If he wasn't paying rent surely it was the least he could do? There was nothing sexy about imagining his mum washing his underpants for him.

'So, can we go to yours, or would you prefer the pub?'

'Let's go to mine,' said Jennifer, her mind racing as she tried to remember what sort of state she'd left the flat in. She prayed she'd put away the hair removal cream. Otherwise that disgusting fishy odour would be lingering in the air. She'd have to get him in the lounge so she could have a quick whizz round.

One hour later and Jennifer was on the verge of her first ever kiss with Steve. They'd had cliché cups of coffee and had sat on the sofa together chatting away about this and that, both keen to get to the point where they could go in for a snog, wondering who was going to instigate it. Finally, just as he had all evening, Steve took the lead and reached over gently and turned her cheek so she was facing him fully. Then, staring at her with real tenderness he pulled her towards him and kissed her gently on the lips in a way that made her feel beautiful. Slowly he opened his mouth until she could feel his tongue and kissed her more expertly than anyone had since Aidan all those years ago. It was absolutely amazing and when his hand started stroking her leg she almost melted with pleasure. It wasn't long before their breathing got heavier as they became more aroused and the kissing became more urgent. God she'd forgotten how much she loved snogging and it appeared he did too because instead of immediately trying to move things on he kissed her for ages, really taking his time over it and seemingly enjoying it as much as she was. It was incredible. So sexy and so sensual. By the time he did start touching her elsewhere she was desperate for him to and was hinting at him to do so by pushing herself against him. He knew exactly what he was doing though and seemed only too aware that in itself the wait was one of the horniest things about the whole experience. Jennifer was so taken aback by how good Steve was she was practically grinning as they kissed.

It was worth the wait too, because when it came his touch was incredible. Every time his hand made contact with any part of her it felt insanely good so when his hand slid to the top of her jeans she couldn't resist letting him undo the fly. He touched her through her knickers in the most sensual way imaginable. He stroked her gently yet firmly in a way that left her panting for more. However, eventually she pulled away, breathless and knowing that despite the fact he lived with his mum and drank fizzy drinks with his dinner she definitely wanted to see him again.

'Are you ok?' he whispered into her ear, his voice thick with desire.

'Yeah,' she said. 'You're an amazing kisser.'

'So are you,' he said 'I am so turned on.'

Her gaze went to his trousers where she could see for herself exactly how turned on he was. She clearly wasn't going to be disappointed in that department either.

'I think perhaps we should stop though,' she said 'I mean I don't want to, but it's probably for the best don't you reckon? It being our first date and everything.'

'Whatever you say beautiful.' It was the 'beautiful' that did it. It almost made her cry. She had longed for Tim to say nice things to her for years. Had yearned for a bit of attention to the point where at times she'd been reduced almost to begging for compliments sometimes, like a dog sniffing around a table for crumbs. After their break up, she'd been lost in the dating wilderness for years, lurching from one dissatisfying experience to another. Now here was Steve, who she hardly knew but who had been so lovely all evening, telling her she was beautiful and it was so nice to hear.

'Perhaps let's just do some more kissing,' she suggested.

Steve was more than happy to go along with that plan, although predictably, it didn't quite end there. Half an hour later, unable to resist, Jennifer ended up having sex with him. On her sofa. And it was bloody great.

27 | Present Day

What Jennifer couldn't have possibly known was that by now she had been in a coma for three weeks. Three long weeks during which her friends and family had had to come to terms with the fact that she may not return to them. No matter how many times they asked the consultant for his opinion he could only offer them vagaries. The fact was no one knew what was going to happen to Jennifer, whether she'd live, die, or remain in no man's land until someone else made the heart rending decision for her.

This was harder for them than it was for Jennifer who was oblivious, cocooned in her own little world. A grey, foggy world which she drifted around in, sometimes aware of her anchorless state, occasionally surfacing to hear snippets from the real world before descending back to the place she was far more able to handle.

Meanwhile, her body was doing its very best to recover from the shock it had endured and her brain was scrambling to repair itself, to reboot if you like. Currently she wasn't wired correctly which was why she was able to experience things which normally one couldn't ever be privy to.

Every time she'd travelled down a portal it had taken it out of her though. Once she'd returned out of it, her brain would shut down again for a while. Right now however her consciousness was buzzing, positively yearning to make another journey, desperate to find out more about how life could have been.

She started her descent.

It took a while but as she reached the tunnels she looked eagerly about her to see what was what.

Damn. As she'd suspected it would have, the first portal had disappeared completely. Instead of a grey swirling, cloudy mist, there was now a black seal in its place. Tunnel number one was most definitely shut for good so she would just have to accept that and be thankful for what she had learned from it. However, the second portal, the one marked Tim, was still very much available, though it was a few shades weaker than it had been before. The third, which she had yet to explore at all, was still as bright as anything.
Tim or Steve?

So far she'd learned that by staying with Tim she would have turned into the kind of woman she'd probably detest if she were to meet her at a party. Groomed, pampered and not really serving much purpose other than to be a wife. She also appeared to be miserable, unconfident and too hung up on her 'lifestyle' to do much about it.

There didn't seem any point checking out life with Steve yet. He could wait. She could visualise it so well anyway somehow. Whereas she couldn't even begin to guess what would happen to her in the second portal. Would she leave Tim? Would she break Joe's and indeed her own heart for the sake of her children, or out of fear?

Tim it was.

Without further ado, she took a deep breath and headed for tunnel two for the second time.

28 TUNNEL NUMBER TWO
Tim: what could have been

'But what I don't really understand is why you can't just fly Karen out here?' repeated Tim, regarding Jennifer in such a way that told her to tread extremely carefully.

He was perched on the edge of their enormous seven-foot bed which was still rumpled from where he'd had a nap earlier. Since then they'd had an enormous lunch which their housekeeper had prepared. Jacqueline lived locally in Antibes and brought their lunches and dinners to the villa every morning, normally on huge earthenware platters, or in beautiful, brightly painted dishes that were synonymous with the region, along with fresh baguettes and croissants for everybody to have for breakfast the next day. Life in France was one long blissful blur of eating, drinking, swimming, fending off cheese and rosé top ups and playing with the children. Anyone looking in would have thought her existence was privileged, luxurious and heavenly and yet Jennifer was existing in her own private hell.

She hated her husband and missed Joe so much it was a daily challenge just to keep going.
'Why on earth do you want to leave here when you could just as easily invite her to come and stay with us?'

Tim had just showered and changed into olive green linen trousers, a white shirt and Hermes dark -brown suede loafers with no socks. His helicopter was due to meet him at the helipad reasonably soon but he seemed reluctant to get going, preferring instead to watch his wife pack whilst trying to get to the bottom of what her last-minute trip to the UK was really all about.
Jennifer wished Tim would leave so she could have some space, stop being questioned and concentrate on what she needed to take. She was feverishly excited by the prospect of escape, nervous something would happen to prevent her from going, guilty as hell and aware that, no matter what, it was vital she appeared nonchalant and normal. She was being scrutinised. She could sense it. It was exhausting.

The large terracotta floor tiles were cool under her bare feet and she was wearing nothing but a bikini with a Melissa Odabash kaftan over the top yet still felt hot and flustered. It was thirty-six degrees outside and although they had a very sophisticated air conditioning system installed throughout the villa, in the daytime she preferred the windows to be open. Firstly, so that she could appreciate the breath-taking view. Their house was situated high up in the mountains of Antibes, in between Nice and

Cannes and the view of the twinkling Med was phenomenal, one of the best in the region. She also liked the windows open so she could hear her children's squeals from the infinity pool down below where they all played for hours every day under the supervision of Annie and Elisa and a life guard. The grounds were so vast there was enough distance to render their screams of excitement and all the splashing into a soothing, happy sound. A great improvement to being poolside with them, when their racket was boisterous, raucous and at times completely obliterated any sense of peace.

'Do I look alright?' asked Tim, bored of waiting for his wife to give him a straight answer.

'Yes,' she replied distractedly, not giving him so much as a glance to at least pretend she was interested. If she had, she would have thought he looked smart, Sloaney, older than his years and conspicuously wealthy. She would have found a t-shirt, shorts and a pair of flip flops far more appealing. She'd bet her life on the fact Joe would never wear such a stuffy outfit.

Joe.

Would there ever be a minute, a whole sixty seconds when he didn't pop into her brain? He consumed her thoughts. She was so in love it was ridiculous and for the first time in her life she finally understood why people spoke of being 'crazily' or 'madly' in love. What she was experiencing felt like a kind of madness.

She couldn't get him out of her head and would risk and do anything just to be with him and often felt like she would die if she couldn't be. She was aware this was totally over dramatic, but it was also a true measure of her feelings.

As Jennifer continued to ponder the intensity of her love for Joe, what she didn't pick up on was that if had she given Tim just a second or two of her attention it would have appeased him greatly and made her getaway far easier. As it was it was totally obvious his wife's mind was elsewhere. Tim's eyes narrowed as he wondered if he should cancel his trip to Monaco that afternoon.

'What are you doing this evening?' he asked, determined not to let things lie.

'This evening?' she repeated, going to the closet to find socks.

'Yes, this evening. What are you doing? Are you eating here? Do you have dinner plans with anyone?'

'No,' she said, sounding slightly irritated. 'Course not. I'm going to be here. I want to spend some time with the children before I leave. And besides, I've had enough dinners out recently to last me a lifetime.'

'Right,' said Tim 'I didn't realise it had all been such a chore for you.'

Jennifer rolled her eyes.

'It's just I thought you might have arranged to see Gail and James or something.'

'God no! Why would I want to do that?' she replied, perhaps a little too vehemently. Gail and James were supposedly two of their oldest and dearest friends but actually this holiday Jennifer had had her fill of Gail who had become increasingly materialistic and superficial as the years had rolled by. These days she wouldn't contemplate eating at a restaurant unless she thought it was one worth being seen in, which frankly made the holiday not feel like a holiday at all. Gail had also really overdone it on the fillers and cosmetic surgery front so now looked permanently like she was trapped in a wind tunnel. Jennifer increasingly felt like she had nothing in common with so many of their social circle.

'Are you going out this evening?' she asked, realising too late how shirty her tone had been and changing the subject in order to avoid a row which would only delay his departure further. Tim loved Gail and James.

'Not sure,' said Tim 'Pierre's having something on his boat tonight so I may go to that. It depends on these viewings and how long they go on for.'

'You don't really want to live there do you?' enquired Jennifer, wondering idly which jeans she looked best in from the pile she'd selected.

'I wouldn't be looking if I didn't want to,' said Tim, sounding irritated. 'Why would I waste my time?'

'I just didn't realise you were totally serious about it,' said Jennifer 'And it might have been nice to have had a discussion about it.'

A fortnight ago Tim had suddenly announced that he was going to look into making Monaco their primary country of residence.

'Well when *you're* earning billions of pounds and the government want to fleece you for half of it despite the fact you've done more for their economy than the majority of the population put together, plus contributed to endless charities, then you can have your say can't you.'

Jennifer clenched her fists so tightly, her nails made indentations on her palms. She said nothing, despite the fact her stomach felt full of rage.

If Tim had bothered to ask her if she wanted to uproot the children in order to live in Monaco she would have told him she had no desire to live there whatsoever. Furthermore, she would have added that she found the whole idea repugnant. After all, the move was being considered purely for tax evasion purposes and would put Tim on a par with businessmen such as Philip Green. That is to say millionaires who were desperate to avoid half their cash being pumped back into the country which had educated them and which had made them who they were today. Personally she found it abhorrent given that they had so much wealth they could easily give far more than fifty percent away and still never have to work another day in their lives.

'Anyway Monaco aside, which we can discuss when you're back, I have to say, I still don't understand why you're going to Karen. Or why you're avoiding giving me an answer. I mean, if she's prepared to take days off work just to hang out with you then surely she'd rather do that here in the sunshine than there in the pissing rain?'

Jennifer glanced at the clock on her dressing table. His helicopter was due at four. It was ten to. By this point she was so tense she would have done anything to make those ten minutes pass more quickly. Only once Tim had gone would she relax.

She sighed heavily, hoping that would be enough to shut Tim up. Apart from anything else she wasn't getting very far with her packing at all. This was another perfect example of where less would be more. She had such a stupid amount of clothes to choose from that trying to condense what she'd laid out on the bed as possibilities was more of a stress than it would have been if she only owned a few pairs of jeans in the first place. Next month she was going to have a huge clear-out and give loads away to charity.

Right, she needed to stop faffing about. Joe wouldn't care what she was wearing, as long as her knickers were nice of course, and she should be ruthless because ideally she'd just take hand luggage, a luxury she could never enjoy when travelling with four children plus staff.

She glanced up. Tim was still staring at her and not in a soppy way. He was watching her like a hawk. The clock said five minutes to. She suddenly felt horribly uneasy.

'So, Karen calls and you just go running. Again, it just seems a bit odd to me that she would expect you to leave your children in the middle of your family holiday just to go and listen to her problems.'

'Oh for goodness sake,' she huffed, realising she had to say something. She continued to avoid his eye though by going to search for some ankle boots in the walk in closet 'I've told you thousands of times now. She's got a lot of stuff going on in her personal life and she's asked me to come and see her so we can talk stuff through and spend a bit of time with one another. That's it. She wants me to go there and I don't want to insist that she comes here. Why should she?'

'Because it's a damn sight nicer here than it is in shitty Wandsworth,' he said, gesturing outside to the stunning panoramic view that lay before them.

'Look,' said Jennifer, feeling unbelievably claustrophobic despite the never ending vista. 'I'm not saying it again. *Me* leaving the children is easy. They're happy here and have endless people to look after them. You're not even going to be around for the next week so it's not like we'd be spending any time together whereas Karen simply hasn't got the funds to uproot herself and Suzy in order to fly over here just because I've told her to. So I'm going to her and that's final.'

'But I could pay for...'

'I know you could pay,' said Jennifer, starting to get angry now. God, if she had really been just going to see her friend he wasn't half being awkward about it. Pretty hypocritical given that he'd been known on occasion to casually announce in the morning that he was off to another continent for a few days, having failed to remember to tell his PA to tell her. 'But I don't *want* you to pay for her and Karen doesn't want you to either. So that's that. Come on Tim. How often do I ever go away and do anything for myself? Once a year with the girls and that's it. Other than that I'm at your beck and call or with the kids but I really want to do this. I want to be there for my friend when she needs me and it might help build a few bridges at the same time.'

'So what exactly is going on with her anyway,' said Tim, who *still* didn't look totally convinced. He was irritatingly sharp.

'Maritals,' said Jennifer a tad too quickly.

Tim pondered this for a while before saying eventually 'Well that doesn't surprise me, I suppose. If I were Pete I'd have left her years ago.'

'Ha bloody ha,' retorted Jennifer unenthusiastically 'Now, does that mean you're going to stop nagging me and let me go with your blessing?'

Fine,' said Tim and internally Jennifer breathed a sigh of relief. Only, the feeling that she'd got away with it may have been hasty because just as she was about to head for the en-suite bathroom to sort out her toiletries, Tim came up behind her and grabbed her arm. As she spun round to face him his expression made her gulp. It was flinty and cold, his smile had faded away and his eyes had a warning in them as he said 'But if I ever find out you've lied to me, I'll kill you.'

Jennifer felt petrified and regarded him for a while as she tried to work out the best way to respond. She decided to go on the offensive. How dare he threaten her like that? She hated him. The sooner she got away the better.

'And if you ever speak to me like that again I'll divorce you,' she replied icily at which point Tim looked thoroughly thrown.

'I was only joking,' he said lamely.
'Well don't. Because it's not funny and what you've just said is a pretty disgusting thing to say to your wife,' she said, blinking away angry tears. She shoved Tim away. He was blocking her path and she didn't want to be near him a second longer.

'Well, I apologise then,' he said flatly, still unsmiling 'And I'll leave you to pack now. My chopper's coming in a minute so I might as well say goodbye anyway.'

'I'll see you in eight days,' said Jennifer grimly.

'You will, oh, and Jennifer?'

'Yes.'

'Make sure you don't forget to pack these. They're vital for a trip to see Karen I'm sure,' he said and with her heart in her mouth Jennifer turned around slowly only to see Tim clutching a very sexy, very flimsy pair of knickers. She felt sick.

'Oh,' she said lightly, snatching them away from him and stuffing them back into a drawer 'I won't be needing those, that's for sure.'

'Right,' he said. His face was impossible to read. 'I'll be off then, I'll just go and say goodbye to the children.'

'Bye, have a great week in Monaco.'

'Thanks,' he said, and without so much as a peck on the cheek he left.

29 TUNNEL NUMBER TWO

Tim: what could have been

Joe had been dozing on and off for an hour now, his face a picture of pure contentment, his huge body heavy with sleep. All Jennifer had done during this time was stare at him, for his was a face she could quite happily gaze at continuously for hours on end. In fact, she reckoned she could probably do at least a month without getting bored.

She'd felt the same way when each of her new-borns had first arrived in the world. She'd spent hours examining their faces too, drinking them in, marvelling at their very presence and at how miraculous it felt to have them in her life. But she'd never felt anything remotely similar for an adult before. For someone who had facial hair and size twelve feet. And yet the comparisons between her feelings for Joe and the unconditional love she felt as a parent didn't end there. It was only the other day, during one of her long, angst- filled telephone discussions with Karen, (who she'd come to rely on increasingly as she tried to work out how to untangle the extraordinary mess her life was in), she'd told her friend that Joe was the only person alive, other than her kids, whom she could say with any certainty she'd take a bullet for. Not needlessly of course. She wouldn't do it just to prove a point or anything. That would be ridiculous. Yet, if it was a case of saving either herself or him, she'd sacrifice herself every time, just as she would with each of her offspring. However, if the choice were between saving herself or Tim, she'd scarper out of the line of fire quicker than you could say 'Sorry love needs must.'

Karen had laughed heartily at this, (perhaps with slightly too much relish), before adding 'If you think about it, it would probably be worth shoving Tim in front of a bullet. You'd get the life insurance for starters. Plus that way everyone would feel sorry for you for being widowed, so when you 'suddenly' took up with Joe they'd all be happy for you. Perfect.'

At that point Jennifer had checked herself. Reaching the point where you started fantasising about the untimely death of your husband wasn't healthy, even if her best friend had clearly been doing it for years.

Joe's eyes slowly opened. A leisurely grin sprawled across his face. 'Hello you, have I been asleep?'

'Yeah,' said Jennifer, laughing.

'What you laughing at?' he said, still half asleep.

'You've had an hour.'

'An hour? Have I heck?' he said, yawning and stretching out his huge arms before pulling her in for a hug. Jennifer had noticed that his Yorkshire accent had become more pronounced as soon as he'd arrived back in his home county.

'And what have you been up to while I've been resting my eyeballs?'

'Staring at you,' she admitted, totally unashamed. They were far too smitten with one another to bother trying to be cool. There was no point.

'Stalker,' said Joe.

'Creepy,' agreed Jennifer, nuzzling herself right into him.

'Aah this is such heaven,' he said, his eyes still squinting while he slowly continued to wake up properly. 'You realise we've done nothing for forty-eight hours now,' he added, one hand squeezing her bum appreciatively. 'God, I love this bottom you know.'

'I wouldn't say we've done nothing,' said Jennifer, thoroughly enjoying the sensation of having her bum stroked and stretching out one smooth, brown leg from beneath the sheets in order to wrap it round one of his large, hairy ones.

'We've hardly left this one room since we got here,' laughed Joe.

'Yes we have. You even made a roast yesterday. And we went to the pub.'

'For about half an hour,' he said, turning round in the bed but pulling her arms round with him so that she was hugging him from behind.

Jennifer loved the way Joe was in bed. Not just when they were having sex (they'd both agreed that the phrase 'making love' was repellent. Just one of the hundreds of silly yet important things they were in total agreement on) but when they weren't too. He was unbelievably affectionate and often she'd wake up briefly in the middle of the night to find that they were completely entwined with one another.

She nestled into his broad back, inhaling his smell and feeling more secure and happy than she had for ages. The prospect of being able to spend one entire night together was stupidly exciting, so the fact that they were spending seven whole nights in a row together was almost too much to comprehend. It was ridiculous but two days in and they'd already discussed how depressed they were about their little slice of heaven coming to an end.

'Well, are you complaining? Are you wishing we were

sightseeing?'

'No, I could happily stay like this for a year,' he said. 'I'm not joking either. Being with you is bloody bliss. I don't need anything else. Not even a telly.'

'Wow, now that is love. A proper declaration if ever I heard one.'

'It is. Now could you give my back a scratch please my little angel? I've got an itch.'

Happy to oblige Jennifer removed one hand from his and scratched his back.

'Ooh that's better. Thank you.'

'Pleasure, now how about anywhere else? Have you got an itch round the front?' she teased, sliding her hand around him, reaching for his cock which when she found it was already at half- mast.

'Ooh, that's a surprise.'

'You can't blame me, I'm lying next to you,' he said, turning round again so their faces were only centimetres apart.

'I love you,' she said for the five hundredth time that day.

'I love you too,' he replied sincerely, his eyes searching her face. 'So, so much. Never leave me will you?'
She shook her head, her eyes filling with tears.

He stroked her cheek 'Hey little squidger. Don't cry. It'll all be ok.'

She nodded but the tears kept on coming. She was so stressed all the time and no matter how hard she tried to keep it at bay, her anxiety about their situation was never far from the surface.
'You only get one life you know,' he said, eyes sad and full of concern.

'Do you want to go for a walk?' she sniffed, wiping her face with the back of her hand. She didn't want these precious few days together to be marred by her constant angst and worry. She wanted to relish every second they had together and to try to enjoy the present. 'The sun's come out.'

He shook his head and grinned 'I want to kiss you.'

A lazy, passion filled, self-indulgent hour later, Joe emerged from the bathroom, still wet from the shower 'Come on you,' he said, drying himself vigorously and despite the fact Jennifer was completely sated she still experienced a lurch of potent desire just from looking at him.

'Let's get amongst it, let's get some fresh air so at least we can say we've done something today. Time to leave our pit of passion.'

Jennifer loved every minute of their walk through the Yorkshire dales. The country side was gorgeous. Rugged and hilly and strewn with purple heathers and patch-worked with green velvety fields. It was a lovely warm day but not boiling hot like it had been in France. There was a strong wind and the clouds scudded across the sky as if in a race.

'It's so beautiful here,' she exclaimed as they came to the crest of a hill which they'd been climbing for a while. She was completely breathless as was Joe who flung himself down onto the grass.

'Come here you, come and share this view with me.'
She let him pull her towards him until she was sat between his legs, his arms wrapped tightly around her. Joe was a large man. Six foot five with the stature to match. She loved this about him. It made her feel small, feminine, protected.

'It's amazing,' she said, drinking in the scenery.
'I'm so happy to be here with you,' said Joe, nuzzling her neck with his nose. 'I've dreamed of this and here we are.'

They both stared at the majestic countryside that was spread out before them. It was seven thirty, the sun was starting to sink in the sky and the light was incredible. Suddenly Jennifer wondered why anyone in their right mind would want to inhabit a city. 'Do you hate living in town sometimes?' she asked, half terrified of what his reply would be.

'Erm...,' he thought about this for a while. 'I'm definitely a country boy at heart,' he said eventually 'always will be, but there are things about living in London I really appreciate. It's a very beautiful city I think and obviously I love the restaurant scene and the fact you can eat a different type of cuisine every night of the week. I mean, when I was a lad there wasn't one black face in my school so it's been an eye opener working in kitchens in London I can tell you. I've learned so much from living in London, about other cultures and stuff. Having said all that, I do prefer the pace out here and I do crave this feeling of space at times. I think ultimately, when I'm older, I'd be more than happy to move back out again, even if it meant just working in a nice pub that served really excellent food. Nice hearty stuff that was done properly and imaginatively.'

Jennifer digested this. Could she picture herself living out of town? She couldn't see Tim letting her take the children out of the schools they were in.

'But listen, what have we always said the meaning of life is?' Jennifer smiled 'Sofa.'

'Sofa,' he repeated. 'Home is wherever the person you want to be sat next to on the sofa is, and for me, that person is you. So, if that means I have to live out my days in the most overpriced part of London, surrounded by snobby arseholes where I can't afford to buy a beer, let alone a flat, then that is what I'll do so that your kids can keep going to those disgusting schools where they're forced to wear boaters and speak Latin for no sane reason.'
His tone was far less harsh than the words he was saying. Jennifer loved it when he told her how it was. He was so much more 'her' than her own husband was.

'Sofa,' she repeated laughing, her heart lurching with its usual mix of love, fear and dread of what she was facing.

'Now, let's take a picture on my phone of you and me with our view behind us.'

They both wriggled round and Jennifer snuggled right in as Joe extended his arm around them both, the lens of his phone pointing toward them. She smiled into the camera, desperate to milk every second of the time she had with him. Would there ever be a time when they could just be together without constantly pondering life without each other and the situation they were in?

'Look at that little face,' said Joe, his deep Yorkshire voice laden with affection as he regarded the snap he'd just taken. 'You are a beauty Jennifer you know. Look at those eyes.'

'Don't be silly,' she said. She thought she looked a state in the photo if she were being honest, what with hardly any make up on and her hair a mess.

'You've got no idea have you? Hey, what's up with you now? Do we need to have a chat?'

Jennifer blinked, loving him for being so intuitive 'Well, if you could bear it,' she said finally.

'Come on then misery features,' said Joe amiably. 'Let's be having it squidger, what's on that mind of yours?'

'It's just..........I just.....'

'What?'

Jennifer struggled to find the words to convey what had been gnawing away at her for a while now. 'I know it's difficult because we've not had the chance to experience being with each other under normal circumstances but....and again, I know it's a bit wet.......but, what I'm trying to say is, if I leave him then we *have* to work out Joe. I want us to make it. You see, I don't think I could bear to have two failed relationships behind me and, being really honest, I don't want to go through all the pain and upheaval and nastiness of a divorce only to find that when I'm out the other side you've……. changed your mind.'

She looked tentatively at Joe to gauge his reaction and was dismayed to see that she'd done exactly what she'd worried she might do by displaying a lack of faith. She'd pissed him off. The thing with Joe was that he loved her so passionately and was so loving to her the whole time, and yet when he was made to feel cross or annoyed about something, he had a habit of reacting in a way she found hard to handle. His entire body language and face would change as he withdrew from her in order to process what he was feeling. It had happened a couple of times so far, and when it did, there tended not to be much warning. Jennifer hated it because suddenly the person who loved her so much essentially disappeared and was replaced by someone who could barely look in her direction. On the few occasions it had happened so far, it always felt as if a light had gone out.

'Please don't be cross,' she pleaded now, desperate to avoid a row. 'I'm just being honest. You know all I want is to be with you but…. well, the whole thing is just so…….it's so bloody big, that I'd be lying if I said it didn't scare me and I suppose I just need to be reassured that you really feel the same way as me and that this isn't just about the chase of someone who's not available.'

Joe looked deeply offended.

'Not that I think you'd ever do that consciously,' she rattled on, knowing now that whatever she said was probably only going to make matters worse but unable to help herself. 'Only Karen did ask me once if perhaps the depth of feeling we have for one another might be heightened by the situation we're in, and perhaps it is?'

Joe lay back on the earthy ground and stared at the sky.

'Talk to me,' urged Jennifer.

'I don't know what you want me to say,' he mumbled, unable it seemed, even to look at her. Her stomach flipped as she realised quite how fed up he was.

'Well, just say what's in your head.'

Joe's face darkened and when he still didn't say anything her heart sank. She could also feel herself getting annoyed. Shutting down like this was a waste of time. She knew she was being needy and no doubt annoying but she couldn't help what she felt so what was the point of punishing her? She was on the brink of leaving her husband. It didn't get much bigger than that and she didn't mind admitting she was beyond terrified. Why couldn't he just humour her and give her the reassurance she obviously so needed?

'Please Joe, just talk to me.'

'I've got nothing to say,' he mumbled, almost incoherently.

At a loss to know what to do next she lay next to him for a while in silence, wishing she'd kept quiet and that she'd ignored her own pathetic insecurity. She prayed this wasn't going to ruin an entire night or more. What a waste that would be.
However, to her surprise, in the next minute, as they lay side by side she felt a hand reach for hers at which point her stomach instantly flipped back to normal for this was Joe's way of telling her it was alright.

'I'm sorry' she said, tears racing down her face. She briefly acknowledged that she really did have to address how much she was crying all the time.

He pulled her towards him so she was lying on his chest.
'You're such an idiot,' he said quietly, his voice full of nothing but despair and love.

'I know,' she blubbed.

Joe turned to face her. Then he held her face in his strong warm hands and said 'Right now, after some of the things you've just said I don't think there's anyone else on the planet I would do this for, but as it's you I'm going to say it again. And again. And then I'll say it again after that if I have to. I love you Jennifer. I love you more than any other human being in this world. I want to be with you. And that's that. And I'm not him so please don't act as if I'd ever be as complacent or thoughtless as him. Don't compare us or our relationships because it makes me feel like a pile of shit.'

'I'm so sorry,' she said truthfully.

'And also, accusing me of only being interested in 'the chase' is just about one of the most insulting things you've ever said to me. I hate the fact you're married. I hate the fact that in order to be with me you've got to break up your family unit. In fact the only thing that enables me to cope with it is that I can see how unhappy he makes you. You once said to me that the two issues were almost separate. That you'd probably have left him anyway. So why now make me feel like a piece of shit by making out you wouldn't?'

Jennifer felt wretched. How could she explain that in all truthfulness if it wasn't for Joe there was probably no way she'd leave, despite the awful state of the marriage. She simply wouldn't have the guts. Staying would just be easier.

'I'm sorry,' she muttered.

Joe shook his head despairingly 'Look, I know you'll be sacrificing a huge amount if you leave Tim but are they really the things that matter? I can't offer you five- star luxury and a designer wardrobe, but fuck me Jen, you wouldn't be the woman I loved if that was all you were interested in. I will always look after you though and I am here to support you as much as I can in every way. I will take on those kiddies as my own and am prepared to sacrifice having ones of my own if it means being with you.'

Jennifer began to laugh, knowing that her tear stained face was a state. It really must be love if he could still say things like that while she looked like this.

'But I am not going to sit here and beg you to leave. That has to be your decision. And if ultimately it comes to it and you tell me you don't want to, or that you can't, then I will understand. And I won't hate you. I will still love you but I'll let you get on with it. I'll move back here and spend the rest of my days trying and failing to forget about you. But I will say this and it's not a threat Jen, it's not, but I can't do this forever.'

'Do what forever?' she asked, her heart pounding with fear.

'Be in this state of limbo,' he replied simply. 'Because it's not easy not knowing if you're going to lose your world from one day to the next. I know it's hard for you and I don't want to rush you but at the same time I'm not sure how much more I can take.'

Jennifer gulped and nodded to show she'd understood what he was saying. She had to make a decision soon for all their sakes. They couldn't carry on like this.

A couple of hours later they were back at the cottage. Joe had opened a bottle of red wine which they were getting through nicely and he'd also cooked a delicious risotto with mushrooms and chicken and tonnes of parmesan cheese. Ensconced together, away from the rest of the world they couldn't have been any happier than they were then, just being.

They decided to eat in front of the telly, so that they could keep half an eye on an episode of 'Don't Tell the Bride.' It was a particularly funny one because the groom was managing to get everything slightly wrong. By the time they'd got to the bit where the bride was about to discover what dress had been chosen for her, which they both suspected she'd hate, Jennifer and Joe had tears of mirth rolling down their faces. The two of them had been making a stream of sarcastic running commentary throughout the show and now, snorting with laughter, Jennifer managed to say 'Ok, let's play 'you look like a princess bingo'. Bet you any money someone's about to say it.'

Literally the second the words were out of her mouth, the mother of the bride, started welling up on screen at the sight of her daughter in a cloud of tulle and net (which the bride did indeed detest having wanted something slim fitting) and uttered the inevitable words 'Ooh you don't half look like a princess' at which point Joe laughed so violently he practically choked.

'Ha ha,' Jennifer wailed, doubled up almost in pain. 'You've got to switch over;' she panted 'I almost can't handle this anymore. Look at her face. She wants to kill her.'

'Aaah,' groaned Joe, thumping his leg and trying to recover so he could swallow the mouthful of risotto he was otherwise in danger of choking on 'Bloody hell that was funny Jen. You are so funny. You don't half make me laugh.'

Jennifer swelled with pleasure at the compliment, loving how the simplest night in with Joe was such a joy. This wasn't the first time they'd both worked themselves up into a state of hysteria over something so silly.

'Hey, if we were on this show, what kind of dress would you pick for me?'

Joe gave her a very strange sidelong glance gathering the last bits of risotto onto his fork 'What do you mean?'

'What kind of dress would you go for?'

'I'm not marrying you,' he said, not unkindly but firmly, certainly as though he'd given the matter some thought. It wasn't exactly the light hearted response she'd been expecting.

Jennifer felt quite thrown. She'd only been joking. She wasn't proposing or anything. She was married for crissakes; getting married again was hardly something she was thinking about at this stage.

'Ok,' she said, trying not to look offended. She was surprised by how disappointed she felt that he didn't want to marry her.

Joe regarded her for a while, clearly weighing up whether or not to say anything else to go along with his very bald statement. 'It's just you've done it all before,' he explained. 'With him, so I just wouldn't see the point of spending all that money.'

Jennifer could be pretty astute when she wanted to be. Sat on the sofa, feet curled under her, she nodded but purposefully dropped the subject. Instead she turned her attentions back to the TV. Then, a little later, once what he'd said had melted away into the atmosphere a bit, she got up and went to give him a cuddle which he was more than happy to receive. Inevitably that cuddle turned into kissing, which turned into groping and eventually resulted in full blown sex on the floor.

And all the while they were having sex, Jennifer's mind was consumed by thoughts. When Joe had told her he wouldn't marry her, strangely it had perhaps been the most revealing sign of how much he truly loved her. She would never forget how sad his face had looked and although on the surface his words didn't seem that romantic, knowing him as she did, she had found them meaningful and heart-breakingly beautiful. For what it actually demonstrated was that he had thought about having her as his wife, despite the fact she was still married to someone else. He'd thought about it at length and it clearly pained him that she'd done it before with someone that wasn't him. Of course, what he didn't know was that first time round it had been more of a stressful experience than anything else. The wedding had been so huge it had totally swamped the reasons behind doing it. She'd not really enjoyed it, had felt hugely pressured throughout and had had tiny doubts even as she'd walked down the aisle which she'd valiantly dismissed as jitters.

But, like she said, he didn't know that and who could tell what ran through that head of his when he thought about stuff like that. It must be incredibly difficult and she didn't give him enough credit.

Joe loved her.

Finally she really understood that. He really, truly loved her and it was that moment that marked a change for Jennifer, because whereas *he* might not be sure about whether he wanted to marry her, she was. She could hardly believe she was thinking like this. She should be anti- marriage altogether. She'd broken her vows. She'd failed at the whole thing miserably, but she'd married the wrong person and yet here was the right person, inside her now, loving her to within an inch of her life and there was no way she was going to lose him. So that was that. And as for Joe, she was confident she could bring him round to her way of thinking one day. It dawned on her then that her decision had finally been made.

'What?' he panted now, breathless after an enormous orgasm. He rolled off her and lay flat on his back. 'Why are you grinning?'

'No reason,' she said. 'I just love you and also, I've made my decision. I'm in.'

30 TUNNEL NUMBER TWO

Tim: what could have been

The day Jennifer chose as the one she would finally tell her husband she was leaving him began pleasantly.

Tim had originally been due back from Monaco the day before but had rung to say he'd been delayed. On the one hand Jennifer was delighted to have had another day's grace from seeing him. On the other she could hardly bare the suspense. Still, she'd decided to make the most of her rare time alone with the kids. Aware of how hard they'd been working lately what with her having been away, she'd instructed the nannies to have the day off. It was *so* rare that she was in sole charge of her own children it was practically a novelty and at lunchtime she thoroughly enjoyed the simple tasks of cutting up the younger one's food, pouring their drinks, fetching the food out of the fridge and laying the table. Thanks to one of her many discussions with Joe she insisted that the children help her with all of this. Joe had pointed out in Yorkshire that if they didn't start helping out with normal domestic tasks they'd leave home pampered to the point where they wouldn't be equipped to look after themselves on any level. Jennifer totally agreed.

Unused to seeing their mother whirling around the kitchen, enthused and for once not looking distracted and worried, the children were responding eagerly and enthusiastically. It was fun to be involved and for the umpteenth time Jennifer resolved to be a better parent and to ensure that from now on she took more control of their upbringing. It wasn't too late for them to benefit from more of her influence and less of Tim's. It wasn't too late for her to be the woman she knew she could be. She had been weak and become someone she despised.

At one-point Tilly started singing a One Direction song so despite the fact they were still eating, Jennifer went to get her Mac so they could all listen to it and have a bit of a dance, something their father would never approve of and that therefore would never happen when the nannies were on duty. As a result, Jennifer and the children were all so busy singing at the top of their lungs (even Edward was entering into it instead of worrying about looking uncool for once) that none of them heard the distant sound of the helicopter landing in the grounds. So they had no idea that Tim had arrived back at the house, meaning that when he entered the kitchen he found them all dancing around screaming '*You don't know you're beautiful,*' at the top of their lungs, while using various kitchen implements as microphones.

It was only when Hattie yelled 'Daddy' that Jennifer realised he was there, at which point she immediately switched off the music.

'What on earth are you all doing?' Tim said, and his look chilled her to the very bone. The happy atmosphere in the kitchen vanished.

Tim looked disproportionately pissed off and Jennifer's heart lurched with dread. Did he know? He looked so angry.

'Oh come on, we were only having a harmless muck about,' said Jennifer, motioning to the children to sit down at the table which they did with no fuss. They never challenged Tim, although recently she got the distinct feeling that Edward, their eldest, wanted to and probably would in the not too distant future. Right now, still out of breath, he was watching his father from beneath his fringe. His expression was so pained it made Jennifer despair.

'Hmm, well I suggest you sit down when you eat in future or you'll get indigestion. Where are Annie and Elisa?'

'Gone into town. They needed some time off.' Jennifer's tone was defiant.

Tim didn't say anything for so long that eventually Jennifer felt like she needed to fill the gap.

'How was your trip?'

'Enlightening,' was all he would say and again her heart somersaulted with what could only be described as terror. The vibe she was getting from him was not good at all.

However, he suddenly turned everything on its head once again, making Jennifer wonder if perhaps she was just paranoid.
'I got you a present,' he said, reaching into his pocket and pulling out a small jewellery box.

'You shouldn't have done that,' his wife replied. She noticed that Jasper was looking anxious, obviously having picked up on the tension in the room. She went to ruffle his head reassuringly.
Meanwhile Tilly was staring down at her bread and cheese and almost seemed to have turned to stone. A stark contrast to the happy little girl who had been bounding about only minutes before, acting her age in the most carefree way. Only Hattie seemed completely oblivious to the strained atmosphere. But then that was Hattie. She was the most robust out of all of them. Jennifer's heart ached with love and guilt on behalf of her children. Living like this wasn't good for any of them.

'I probably shouldn't have,' said Tim, a crooked smile on his face 'But I have, so open it.'

Jennifer was left with no choice other than to cross the kitchen and take the box from his hand.

'Open it,' he insisted again when she hesitated.

Finally she opened the box only to find an exquisite pair of emerald and diamond earrings nestled on navy silk. They probably cost thousands. They also would have required precisely no thought on Tim's part. She didn't want them.

'Thank you,' she said robotically 'They're beautiful.'

'Good,' said Tim 'Right, I'm off to have a shower. Feel free to pick up where you all left off if you really want. I don't want to be a spoilsport. If you will insist on leaping around like chimps it's probably best you do it when we don't have any houseguests.'

'Can we put it on again please Mummy?' begged Hattie instantly.

'Um, I don't think so,' muttered Jennifer and all four children instantly knew that the window during which their mother had been liberated enough to have some fun had shut. They didn't even bother protesting and just picked at their lunch until they were allowed to get back to the pool.

From that moment on Jennifer felt like she was treading on eggshells and for the rest of the day she tried to avoid Tim as much as possible. For much of it she sat on a lounger, under an umbrella, her youngest boy Jasper cuddled into her, wrapped in a towel because he'd suddenly developed an earache and required some serious tlc. As she'd stroked his hair and watched the others splashing about in the pool, she'd suddenly felt overwhelmed with conviction that bringing Joe into their lives would be a positive thing for her children too. Of course it would. He would be an amazing step-dad. After all, she'd seen him interact with them on countless occasions and while it would obviously take some time for them to adapt to the fact their parents had separated and that their old chef was now her partner, they'd get there eventually.

She was desperate to speak to Joe but it was ages before she got an opportunity to ring him. Finally, once the kids had come in from swimming and had showered and been fed, and the nannies were back from town and on duty, she managed to sneak away. Checking first that Tim was safely ensconced in his study she went upstairs, figuring that the safest place to phone from was her walk- in wardrobe. When the phone went straight to answer machine it was a terrible anti-climax and she tried a further three times before eventually admitting defeat and leaving a brief but urgent message for him to call her.

She put the phone back in her pocket willing it to vibrate and sighed. She hadn't spoken to Joe since first thing this morning.

It felt like an age. Since she'd arrived back in France he hadn't asked her when she was planning on telling Tim once, even though she could sense he was desperate to. And for her part she hadn't been able to find the required words to explain that she was psyching herself up to do it and that she hoped the moment would present itself as soon as Tim returned from his trip. Probably due to a certain amount of nerves on both sides the conversation had ended up rather tense, which only made the fact she couldn't get hold of him now all the more frustrating. At the same time she knew it was unfair to expect him to hold her hand throughout this. It wasn't the easiest of times for either of them.

In Yorkshire, when she'd informed Joe of her decision to leave Tim, she'd expected him to be jubilant and ecstatic that at last she'd finally made her mind up.

However, whilst he'd clearly been pleased, he'd also been extremely cautious. 'You can still change your mind you know,' he'd even said at one point.

'But I don't want to,' she'd retorted indignantly 'I'm telling you I've decided and I know it's taken me a while to get here but I know myself and now I've got here, that's it. I thought you'd be pleased. I thought it was what you wanted.'

'Oh it is,' said Joe sincerely 'It's everything I've ever wanted but I'm just worried for you. I know what this means and the shit you're going to have to go through now. It might be what I want but it doesn't feel like cause for celebration right now. I'll reserve that for when everything's sorted out and for when we can be happy and start the rest of our lives together. But god Jen, please don't think I'm not happy about this because of course I bloody am. I love you so much.'

She thought about this exchange now, and needed no convincing she'd made the right decision.

A few hours later, once all the children were fast asleep, Jennifer regarded herself in the floor to ceiling mirrors which covered an entire wall of her dressing room. She looked fine. In fact she looked good. She was tanned and had gained a few pounds during her time in Yorkshire with Joe, which probably wasn't a bad thing at all. She'd lost a lot of weight lately due to all the stress and had been in danger of looking gaunt. Now she just looked enviably, as opposed to worryingly slim again. She smoothed down her Marc Jacobs sundress and applied a quick slick of lip-gloss before promptly wiping it off again. What was she doing? What precisely did she need to look good for anyway? She supposed it was her version of putting on armour.

Right.

She was ready, or at least as ready as she was ever going to be. She was also ridiculously scared and nervous and there were a million things she'd prefer to be doing at that precise moment. Like eating cat food, prising off her fingernails with a rusty screw, or running a marathon in nothing but a pair of clown shoes, in the rain. Only none of these things were on the agenda. Telling her husband she was leaving him was.

Since that pivotal moment in Yorkshire she'd known what she had to do. Leaving Joe behind in the UK had been such a wrench it had practically left her winded. She missed him so much it hurt. Yet whereas normally she'd be crying into her pillow about it, now she was experiencing a new sense of stoicism. Her feelings for Joe had become an unstoppable force. She simply had to be with him, no matter what the consequences. No matter how sad it made everybody short term, long term she fully believed they would all be better off.

Right, it was time. Jennifer took a deep breath, left the sanctuary that was her dressing room and went downstairs to find Tim who was outside, on the terrace, looking at some papers.

It was past eleven. Jennifer had wanted to make totally sure all the children were fast asleep when she told him.

'You ok,' said Jennifer, taking a seat opposite Tim. The moonlight was bouncing off the pool. Everything looked so beautiful. Would she miss it she wondered?

'What do you want?' said Tim, looking up briefly.

The look in his eyes made her recoil. These days she felt like they hardly knew one another.

'Um, I just wondered if we could have a chat?'

Tim picked up the crystal tumbler next to him and took a slow, deliberate sip of his gin and tonic. 'Go for it.'

'Right, well I don't think I need to tell you that we haven't been getting on well lately.'

'No, you're right. You don't. You're not even wearing the earrings I bought you which is pretty ungrateful.'

Jennifer immediately felt on the back foot. She'd always known Tim was her superior intellectually. Whenever they argued he always came out on top of the war of words, even when he was in the wrong. He could spar verbally with the best of them and would always have an answer, a riposte, or a quick witted put-down. Only today she wasn't looking for a discussion. She was telling him something and that was what she had to keep reminding herself of.

'Look, Tim, I know you don't want to hear this but I have to say it anyway.'

He continued to read his papers. So rude. In a way it helped.

Jennifer cleared her throat and ran her palms down her dress again. She was sweating. 'I think it might be time we went our separate ways Tim. I've not been happy for a long time now and I doubt you are either. So, while we're still both young enough to rebuild our lives I think we should call it a day and try to do so as amicably as possible for the sake of the children.'

Tim swirled the ice round in his glass which made a chinking sound. For a second Jennifer wondered if he'd heard what she'd just said. She took a deep breath. She felt nauseous and wished Joe was with her. Wished he wasn't so far away. Suddenly she felt a flash of real frustration that he hadn't been on the other end of the phone earlier. What was he doing?

She opened her mouth to reiterate what she'd just said but Tim cut her off.

'So, you have the audacity to sit there and calmly tell me that you've decided we should 'call it a day.' As if ending our marriage is as important an issue as changing your mind about what dress to wear or what colour paint you're going to decorate a room with.'

'No, of course not,' began Jennifer 'It's not like that at all. In fact, for what it's worth, it's taken months of turmoil for me to arrive at this conclusion. There is absolutely nothing about this decision that has been light or easy and I am so bloody sorry Tim.'

'So, how many months exactly have you been thinking about this then?'

Jennifer gulped, steeling herself for the onslaught she knew was around the corner. Her mind whirred as she tried to second guess why he was asking that. 'Look, you can't pretend you haven't noticed,' she said, trying to avoid answering. 'We've barely been speaking for months. We've been in separate bedrooms the vast majority of the time for years now and I can't remember when we last had sex. This isn't a marriage Tim and I know I'm the one saying it out loud but come on, you've never got anything good to say about me, you're always putting me down and acting as if I irritate you, so to be honest I'm surprised you're not pleased.'

'Pleased,' repeated Tim 'Mm, interesting choice of vocabulary there. You're surprised I'm not pleased that you've taken it upon yourself to be such a selfish bitch that you would actually consider breaking up this family, destroying the children's lives and everything I've been working hard to build up for the last, god knows how many years, with zero consultation or regard for my reputation.'

Jennifer blinked. Was that all he cared about? Suddenly she was amazed she'd lasted as long as she had in this sham of a relationship.

'But that's just it,' she said 'your reputation has nothing to do with our marriage. A marriage is a relationship between two people. Everything else just surrounds it. But our connection has died a death Tim. You don't love me, you don't even like me.'

'Ah finally you're speaking some sense, because you're right there,' he said coolly, putting down his papers and drink and leaning in to fix her with a stare that turned her stomach. 'I loathe you and do you know why I loathe you?'

She shook her head; sure he was going to fill her in anyway.

'I loathe you because without me you'd be absolutely nothing. I have carried you since university and you know it. You're a spineless, directionless, useless individual but for some reason I took pity on you and have let you ride on my coat tails for all these years.'

'I've given you four beautiful children,' Jennifer said quietly, her eyes pricked with tears. What he was saying was so hurtful. So cruel. So disgusting.

'Yes, you've *had* four children. Well done you for being fertile. But you haven't given me anything. You're not even a good mother.'

'That's not fair,' she said. He may as well just have slapped her. It would have hurt less.

'Maybe not but it's true. You do the bare minimum.'

'Only because you've always controlled me so much that that's all I've been allowed to do. My only crime is that I've been weak. I've let you steal all my confidence to the point where I've lost control of my own kids.' Even as Jennifer said it, the truth in what she was saying finally completely caught up with her and she vowed then and there that she would change, starting by playing a proper part in how her children were going to turn out. She wasn't going to be dictated to any longer.

Tim stood up and paced the terrace for a while.

Suddenly Jennifer felt incredibly vulnerable. Perhaps this had been a mistake? Perhaps she should have waited till they were back in London.

'You're a lying whore,' said Tim icily, almost from nowhere.

'I beg your pardon,' said Jennifer who was shaking.

'When were you going to tell me about your revolting little secret eh? Or were you not going to bother? Because we both know what this is really about don't we?'

He knows thought Jennifer. Of course he does. How could she ever have thought she could have kept anything secret from the omnipotent Tim?

She analysed how she felt. Numb really, but underneath there was also a sense of relief. She didn't want to lie anymore. She was sick of living like this. To hell with it.

'I love him,' she said calmly.

Tim threw his head back and only then did Jennifer see for the first time a glimpse of how he wasn't just angry but also hurt. She had damaged him with what she'd done. Of course she had and what could she ever have expected his reaction to be?

No matter how unpleasant he'd been to her in the past he still had the moral high ground. She was the one who had been unfaithful. She'd broken her vows and would always have to live with that knowledge.

'You stupid, stupid bitch,' he said, the cool tone having disappeared altogether. He was livid now. 'And how long's it been going on then? Because naively I had hoped you'd only decided to be a disgusting whore a short time ago, only now you've told me you've been debating whether to leave me for months I start to wonder? You see, I'm not stupid Jennifer so it doesn't take a great deal to figure out that this is all about your selfishness and desire to fuck someone.'

Jennifer swallowed. Of course, she still had no idea what he knew exactly. She needed to tread extremely carefully.

'It's not. They're two separate issues. That never would have happened if I wasn't deeply unhappy. I'm not justifying anything but you have to know that wanting to split up with you is because I honestly can't see a way to make our marriage work.'

'I had you followed when you went to 'Karen's',' he said, using his fingers to make inverted commas round her friend's name. 'A love nest in Yorkshire with my now-ex chef. I've never known anything so pathetic in all my life. But I tell you what; if that's what you think you want, you're very welcome. Only I'll tell you this for nothing my dear….'

His use of the words 'my dear' made her feel faintly sick.

'You've chosen the wrong person to pick a fight with because I am going to make sure you end up with nothing. And when I say nothing, I mean no money, nowhere to live, no friends and no children.'

'You can't take my children away. You're being ridiculous,' said Jennifer, and though her tone was designed to sound throwaway she couldn't disguise the very real sense of panic rising up inside her. He was insane. Surely no court in the land would stop her from having custody of her children and yet with

Tim she'd never known him to set his mind to something and fail. 'I'm their mother. The law would never allow you to take them from me,' she said more confidently than she felt.

'We'll see about that,' threatened Tim. He took a step towards her; eyes blazing with fury and contempt.

She swallowed. 'Well there's probably not much point in talking further tonight so why don't we sleep on it and try and have another chat in the morning.'

'There's nothing to discuss,' said Tim, stepping back again and picking up the sheaf of papers he'd been looking at. He sat down and returned his attentions to them.

She'd been dismissed.

Happy to get away from him she turned to enter the house, desperate to get hold of Joe and tell him what had happened. Surely he'd be answering his phone by now?

'No doubt you're off to phone lover-boy to fill him in on the latest.'

'Don't be ridiculous,' she answered immediately, un-nerved by his accuracy. She literally stopped in her tracks. Shit, maybe she should wait until tomorrow to contact him? Tim might come and listen at the door and there could be the most horrific scene.

'Still, if you really want to speak to him maybe you should try him. After all, it's been hours since you spoke to one another, hasn't it?'

How could he possibly know that? Jennifer's eyes widened.

Suddenly she was terrified. The situation had just changed to one beyond her control. Was Tim toying with her or did he really know something?

She turned. 'What are you doing?' she said, no longer bothering to try and sound nonchalant. She didn't care if he knew she was scared. She just needed to know what was going on. Now.

'Me? Oh I'm not doing anything. It's our ex-chef who's been very busy. And on that note, I want to make it very clear that he is not to come within an inch of any of my properties ever again. He also won't ever be working anywhere in London again either, which is a shame for you.'

'What are you talking about?' said Jennifer, her entire body trembling as she tried to digest what was happening. She'd lost control of the situation completely. How could she ever have imagined she could take Tim on?

'Well think about it,' he said, tapping his temple. 'If he can't work in London then he can hardly stay in the city where your children will be remaining which means you'll have some decisions to make. And in case you still don't get it,' he said patronisingly 'it means you'll have to choose between your children or an out of work, out of shape chef. So, how are you going to negotiate that one eh wifey?'

'Where's Joe,' she said flatly, heart pounding.

'Oh don't you worry about him,' smirked Tim.

'Tell me what you've done,' screamed Jennifer who had now officially lost it. She hated him with every bit of her being. He was a cruel bastard. 'If you've done anything to hurt him I will call the police.'

'Oh will you now,' said Tim mildly 'Interesting that even after all these years you still insist on thinking I'm stupid. Ironic really. Jennifer, do you really think I'd get my hands dirty over this?'

By now Jennifer was in floods of tears. He clearly knew where Joe was and she didn't and the sense of helplessness was so intense she could hardly remain standing up.

'I beg you, please tell me where he is?' she wept.

Tim regarded his sobbing wife with contempt. 'Why should I?'

'Because no matter what I've done to you, you can't do this. It's not right and you will damage your reputation if you do something stupid.'

'But I've already explained, *I'm* not doing anything. Look at you, you're a snivelling wreck, it's pathetic.'

Hearing this, Jennifer forced herself to stop crying. Her tears were only aggravating him further and for Joe's sake she had to play this right. The situation was too serious for her to fuck it up by letting her emotions get the better of her.

'Ok listen,' she said changing gear completely. 'I promise that if you just tell me what you know, because I can tell there's something, then we can work things out and make sure that no one ever knows about any of it. If you've done something stupid the last thing you want is for your reputation, which you've worked so hard to achieve to be tarnished in any way. So come on Tim, tell me what's going on.' Her tone was calm and measured and a bit like she was talking to somebody who was standing on the edge of a cliff about to throw themselves off. But it seemed to work. The madness which Jennifer had recognised in Tim's eyes seemed to be abating slightly.

'Joe's not far from here.'

'What do you mean?' said Jennifer, who was now wondering if he had actually lost it.

'He's in France.'

'Here? In France?'

'That's what I said.'

Jennifer paused. She was confused. What the hell would Joe be doing in France? Could he really be only kilometres away from here?

'Why? Who's he with?'

Tim regarded her coolly before replying 'One of my men.'

'What do you mean one of your men, Tim?' Jennifer demanded to know. Once again fear had got the better of her and had turned her tone shrill and hysterical.

'I'm not going to talk to you while you're in this state,' said Tim, marching brusquely past her.

But there was no way Jennifer was standing for that. Not if he really did know anything about where Joe was. Without considering what she was doing, fuelled by rage and frustration she launched at him like a woman possessed 'No you don't,' she screeched, grabbing at the back of his pale pink shirt. It was an attack Tim hadn't been expecting and his loafers slipped on the terrace tiles, causing him to stagger sideways before falling to the ground at which point his wife leapt on him and stared pounding his chest with her fist.

'Tell me what you know or I'm calling the police,' she screamed.

'Get off, you're mad,' yelled Tim, trying to protect his face from the punches which were raining down on him.

'Where's Joe,' she repeated, as Tim finally found the wherewithal to fight back. Grabbing her wrists he heaved her away from him.

'You're insane,' he yelled, flinging her to one side with considerable force. 'Get off me you fucking lunatic.'

Finally Jennifer's adrenaline started to subside. Panting she reached over to pick up one of her sandals which had come off and slid it back onto her foot. She got up from where she was sprawled on the ground.

'Just tell me,' she repeated, trembling with rage.

Tim regarded her for what felt like an age, clearly deciding what to tell her. For the first time Jennifer sensed that he was floundering a bit.

'There's nothing to tell,' he admitted finally, his tone weary.

'What?'

'I just wanted to spook you, make you feel as dire as I do. I have been having him watched though and I wasn't lying about one thing, he caught a plane this afternoon.'

'Why?'

'Why what?'

'Are you having him followed?'

'Why do you think?' Tim spat 'Because the minute he started sleeping with my wife, what he was 'up to' very much became my business. And besides, at some stage I might pay the arsehole a visit and explain that shagging your boss' wife doesn't exactly bode well when it comes to getting a reference.'

'You'll do no such thing.'

Tim shrugged, his demeanour almost that of a sulky teenager's.

'And you haven't done anything else?'

'What do you take me for?'

'Ok then,' said Jennifer, whose breathing was just about returning to normal. 'Ok,' she repeated, walking away.

'Where are you going?'

Jennifer turned round and was hit by a fresh, overwhelming sense of guilt and betrayal. Now she knew Joe was safe her focus returned to the fact that she'd just imparted the hugest of body blows to her husband 'To find Joe. I'm so sorry,' she said.

'You will be,' he replied, his face sour with regret and contempt, but this time Jennifer could tell his heart wasn't in it. It was over. Without another word she entered the house.

The second she was out of earshot she pulled her phone out of her pocket and dialled Joe's number. To her immense relief this time it was ringing and sure enough the ringtone was foreign. She was desperate to find out what on earth he was doing in France. She hoped he was ok.

And then he answered 'Hello, babe, is that you?'

'Joe,' she exclaimed, flooded with relief 'Where are you?'

'France. I've come to be near you. I've literally just got through passport control and was about to ring you but you beat me to it.'

'And you're ok?'

'Fine yeah course, are you? I was worried you might be mad with me for flying over but I couldn't sit around at home wondering what was going on. I've been a wreck. I know there's not a lot I can do but at least I'll be nearby if you need me.'

'Oh my god I love you so much,' gulped Jennifer 'Listen, I've got loads to tell you. I'll come and meet you. Give me forty minutes or so and I'll be there. You're at Nice airport right?'

'Yeah, but listen if it's tricky to get away…?'

'It's not, I'm on my way. Just stay put till I get there. Promise?'

'Promise,' he said.

And with that Jennifer grabbed a set of car keys, the ones for the jeep, and without looking back, slammed the front door behind her and raced across the gravel driveway to where the vehicle was parked. Once in the car she turned on the ignition and sped toward the electric gates, the only barrier now that lay between her and freedom. Winding down the window she punched in the code. The wait for them to open was agonising but finally they did and once there was enough space to squeeze the jeep through she took off at such a pace that the tyres screeched underneath her.

She'd been coming to France for years now so she knew the mountain roads like the back of her hand. Joe. She and Joe were going to be together. She couldn't believe it and though it had been horrific having to tell Tim, it was done. She put her foot down a little harder. Now she just needed to get to Joe. Heart racing and adrenaline pumping through her system Jennifer didn't take a moment to gather herself. If only she'd stopped for a second and taken a long deep breath. If only she'd realised that once she reached Joe, that they would have the rest of their lives together and that getting to him minutes earlier wouldn't make any difference. The physical desire to be with him was so immense though, common sense simply took a back seat. The relief of telling Tim after the most painful year of her life was so enormous it propelled her down the twisty mountain roads in a reckless fashion that normally she wouldn't even contemplate.

She flew round the corners and bends perfectly; driving with accurate precision, but what she couldn't have known was that around the next bend a moped was approaching. A young man was coming back from the bars of Nice. Earlier on that day he'd found out he'd got a promotion so had stopped after work for a beer or two. Now he was veering unwisely into the middle of the road.

As Jennifer turned the corner she saw him far too late, and was by now travelling at such a speed that she didn't have enough time to react. The shock of seeing his headlight in her line of vision was so great that she lost control of the wheel altogether and the jeep hurtled towards the edge of the cliff. Meanwhile, the brakes which she'd slammed on so hard simply didn't have time to bring the vehicle to a stop. The man on the moped had managed to steer himself to safety. He watched in horror as Jennifer's jeep smashed through the low metal barrier at the side of the cliff top and although her death would be instant once she made contact with the rocks at the bottom of the mountain, the drop down toward them wasn't. That fall took five long seconds and the thoughts that flashed through Jennifer's mind and the feelings she experienced in those last few terrifying moments were even darker than the ones Joe would have to live with for the rest of his life.

31 | Present Day

That evening Max left the hospital, and headed home to spend a much-needed night in his own bed, fretting in case the one night he didn't keep vigil would be when her condition would change. Still, his own health had taken a battering due to stress and lack of sleep and he was starting to feel like he might be going a bit crazy.

And so it was that Karen came to take over. She couldn't have been more pleased to relieve Max. Taking one look at him as she arrived at Jennifer's room she could tell he was on the brink of collapse from the way he couldn't be bothered to put up any resistance to her offer to stay as he'd been doing for weeks. Instead he just waved goodbye sadly and ambled away.

Once he'd gone Karen went to sit next to the woman who'd been her best friend since school, whom she'd shared a quarter of a century of friendship with. A friendship she simply couldn't comprehend not having as part of her life going forward. Karen chose not to think like that though. As far as she was concerned Jennifer was going to get better and that was that.

'Hello you,' said Karen, who unlike Max didn't feel at all self-conscious talking to someone who was in a coma. If anything it was a similar experience to talking to Pete when he was watching West Ham play. 'Do me a favour and get yourself sorted out will you. I miss you, you big lummox.

Max had been right of course. The one night he wasn't at the hospital something was bound to happen. It's simply the law of the sod.

It happened at around two thirty am. Karen was asleep on the visitor bed which was next to Jennifer's hospital bed. She didn't know how Max had suffered it for all these weeks and now fully understood why he'd been complaining of a sore back. The bed was profoundly uncomfortable, the spring's having given up the ghost years ago, and it took Karen ages to drop off. However, she was sound asleep when the machines around Jennifer suddenly started to beep urgently.

At first Karen wondered if an alarm had gone off. Was it time to get up for work? It was only when a nurse suddenly burst into the room that she remembered where she was, at which point she sprung up, eyes wide with fear.

'Oh my god, what's happening?' she asked frantically.

'Just a second please,' said the nurse as two other nurses also joined her in the room.

The sound of the machines was so distressing but not as distressing as what Karen saw next which was that Jennifer's face was contorted into the most frighteningly strange expression while her body was jerking in a disturbingly unnatural way.
'Is she in pain?' screamed Karen, wondering what the hell she should do. 'Why does she look like that? Is she waking up?'
But no one would answer her. The room was filling up with more and more medical staff all of whom were far too busy tending to the patient to give any clue as to what might be happening to her friend. They were all shouting at one another, mainly medical jargon which Karen had no chance of understanding. They administered something into Jennifer's arm by injection, they checked her pulses, changed her drip, there was more frantic shouting and then finally, finally the machines seemed to calm down, meaning whatever was happening to Jennifer was hopefully subsiding.

Karen was completely traumatised by what had just happened. She'd honestly thought Jennifer was dying.

'What happened?' she begged to know, tears rolling down her frightened face.

'Don't worry, she's stabilised now,' said one of the remaining nurses. 'She was having some sort of seizure. She seemed very distressed but this might be a good sign. It may indicate that she'll be emerging from the coma at some point. But why don't you try and get some sleep and we'll get the specialist to come and talk to you more tomorrow.'

'Ok,' said Karen and her voice came out as a whisper.

Once everyone had left the room, Karen went to sit next to Jennifer. She took her limp hand 'Hey you. You gave us a bit of a shock there lovely….'

Karen stopped in her tracks.

Then she blinked and went to switch on the bedside lamp to make sure she was definitely seeing what she thought she was seeing.

When the light from the lamp illuminated Jennifer's face she could see that she wasn't hallucinating. There was indeed one very real tear rolling down her now still friend's face. It was quite possibly the saddest thing Karen had ever witnessed. What was going on in that brain of hers? And how could she have missed quite how unhappy she was? If she pulled through this (and after what had just happened, finally Karen was admitting to herself that it was if as opposed to when), she vowed to do everything in her power to make her friend happy again.

The next morning a vaguely refreshed Max arrived back at the hospital only to be told that his wife had suffered some kind of inexplicable seizure during the night.

As Karen filled him in on what had happened any benefit he'd been feeling from the short break from the hospital he'd had was erased totally.

'Max look, I don't know whether I should be telling you this because it's a bit upsetting but at the same time the doctors thought it was a very encouraging sign.'

'Tell me now,' said Max.

'Ok,' said Karen, who knew she had to fill him in but was wondering how on earth to broach the second half of her news. 'Well the first thing is that she cried. Or at least I saw one tear roll down her face.'

'Really?' said Max, the mix of emotions he was experiencing at that moment unsteadying him.

'Yes, which is pretty amazing. After all it shows more or less that there's no way she's brain dead. I mean, she can't be.'

'What's the other thing?'

'She said a word Max.'

'What? When?' he couldn't believe he'd missed it. His wife had done nothing but lie there for weeks and the one night he chose to be away she'd practically put on a show. It was so typical. 'What? What word did she say? And when?' he demanded to know.

'At about three in the morning, just after I noticed the tear rolling down her face.'

'And what was it?' Max practically yelled.

Karen gulped and then she made a decision, for sometimes she decided, there was such a thing in life as a good lie. A necessary lie.

'The word she said was.....Max.'

'Was it?' said Max, his whole face lighting up and tears springing into his eyes. 'I can't believe it. Oh Jen,' he said, rushing over to the bed and taking his wife's limp hand and rubbing it with his. 'Oh Jen, I love you so much and I know you're thinking about me. Thank you so much. I needed a sign I really did and now you've given me one.'

Karen watched nervously, a weak smile on her face. She simply hadn't had the heart to tell him what her friend had really said.

More than ever she prayed that Jennifer would wake up soon for she was now desperate to ask her 'who on earth was Joe?'

32 FRIDAY MORNING
The day of the accident

'You haven't been for a while. It's good to see you.'

'Good to see you too,' said Jennifer, though she wasn't entirely sure it was. She'd definitely needed a break and the chance to reflect on whether therapy was actually working for her or not. On balance she'd decided that it was. She just wasn't a very patient person. She never had been, and yet it had become clear that achieving anything from her sessions would take time.

There were no overnight answers. Instead, she tended to go away after a session and ponder what had been discussed and from time to time perhaps understand *why* she felt the way she did about stuff but not necessarily what to do about it.

She was also wary of the constant need to analyse her childhood. It just felt a bit pointless. Her parents had done their best. They were good people. The past was done. What she was after was some help with the present. Still, she'd decided to persevere.

'So, what brings you back today Jennifer?' said Susan, a petite woman in her sixties with a disarmingly deep voice. She had a short cropped hairstyle and insisted Jennifer took her shoes off when entering her house which was where she held her sessions in the smallest of her three bedrooms. Her gravelly voice wasn't the only clue to her voracious smoking habit. Susan's face was considerably lined for her age and there were deep grooves running down toward her top lip.

'It's been a bit of a mad week I suppose,' admitted Jennifer. 'Last Friday, Max and I had the house to ourselves and I'd been hoping we might have a lovely night in together, only it never really happened and I think since then I've been harbouring all sorts of resentment. Then yesterday, Eadie, my eldest, broke her arm which was horrific.'

'Oh, my goodness, how terrible. Is she ok?'

'Yes, she's fine,' said Jennifer.

'And are you ok?'

Jennifer paused. Why was it the minute she got in this room she always wanted to blub like a baby?

'Um.......' She blinked rapidly. Thankfully Susan realised she needed helping out.

'Why don't we go back to last week then, which is obviously significant? Tell me about you and Max. Last time I saw you, you were worried that things weren't great between the two of you and today you've mentioned feeling resentful. How are things now?'

'They're ok,' said Jennifer dolefully. 'I don't know really. I mean, in a weird way, what happened yesterday with Eadie brought us closer than we have been in ages, but I do still feel like there's a big gulf between us at the moment. I think we've forgotten why we're together as a couple. We seem to have just become functioning adults who take the bins out, remember to pay the bills or argue about who should be more tired. It's like we exist but we don't live. Even our social life seems to happen for the sake of it.'

Susan nodded very slowly, her gaze never leaving Jennifer's face.

'Have you told Max any of this? Have you discussed your fears about your relationship?'

'I've tried to but weird as it may sound there never seems to be any proper time together and half the time he doesn't listen anyway.'

'And how does that make you feel?'

Jennifer sighed heavily. It occurred to her then how odd it was that she was sitting in someone's box room, on a sun-lounger which had been covered in a throw in order to disguise it, pouring her heart out to a stranger. A stranger who she occasionally spotted doing her shopping in Sainsbury's, no doubt spending the money she'd earned listening to people like her moaning about their lives, at which point she'd always hide from her in the aisles.

'It makes me feel old. Frumpy. Unattractive. Pissed off.'

Susan's expression didn't change. It never did which provoked Jennifer into wanting to say something purely for shock value. If she'd said 'it makes me feel like smashing his face in with a mallet', would her expression change then?

She waited for her therapist's response. Finally it came 'Jennifer, do you think there's any chance at all that you're having a mid-life crisis?'

Jennifer couldn't help it. She rolled her eyes.

'What?'

'Sorry, it's just you're not the first person to suggest that that's what all this is about.'

Susan continued to gaze steadily at her, still waiting for an answer. 'And, are you?'

'No.'

'No you aren't having one?'

'No, I mean yes I am. I mean… what I mean is, there's not a chance I'm having one because I'm definitely having one.'
For once Susan looked mildly taken aback. This was pleasing to Jennifer.

'Ok, so do you want to tell me about that?'

'Well, I think what I'm trying to say is that I just know that I am definitely, without a shadow of a doubt, having the hugest mid-life crisis ever.'

'Ok.'

'Only I don't think that should be taken lightly.'

'Right.'

'Look, I really hope you don't think I'm being rude now, it's just that even when you asked me that question it was almost as if you were dismissing having a mid-life crisis as something I should be able to face up to and get over.'

Jennifer paused in order to give Susan a chance to defend herself but her total silence appeared to indicate that she'd prefer
Jennifer to continue instead. So she did.

'Admittedly, I used to hear the phrase myself and think it was a tired old cliché which applied purely to people who were desperate to regain their youth and who were a bit pathetic or just wanted an excuse to wear leather trousers. Only now I'm having one myself I realise it's a far more complex stage. It's an actual genuine crisis, which is why people should focus more on that word. You know Susan...' Jennifer paused for a moment, trying to find the right words. 'I don't think what I'm feeling is as straight forward as simply wanting to be young. Instead I think what I'm going through at the moment is a proper, full blown *crisis* which I really need help with. And I suspect it's the same for everyone who goes through this stage. I know for some people it may manifest itself in dressing like an idiot, or having sex with someone just to validate the fact they're still vaguely desirable but that's just a symptom which will have stemmed from suddenly wondering what the hell has happened to you. A mid-life crisis is actually about waking up one morning and wondering how on earth you've ended up doing what you're doing. It's the sudden awful realisation that so much of your life is behind you, yet you haven't achieved what you wanted to, in which case it's likely you never will. It's about mourning your hopes and dreams and that sort of fizzy sense of confidence you have in your youth when it feels like anything's still possible. Then, once all that's caught up with you, you start to examine other areas in your life at which point if you realise anything is lacking, the crisis just gets worse. If I'm being totally honest Susan, which I know is the whole point of coming here, I suppose at the moment I'm slightly wondering if I can stand to be with my husband for the rest of my life because I'm not sure he really loves me anymore. It's also dawned on me that I'm probably never going to fall in love again with anyone else which somehow feels like a monumental disaster. Yet is it wrong of me to want to experience feeling giddy with love again before I die? Because despite not being young anymore, I'm also a long way from dead, and with a bit of luck I've still got a lot of life to live. Only now I'm finally wise enough to understand how quickly it's all going to fly by.'

Susan nodded.

'Sometimes I lie awake at night, listening to Max snore, and I start to feel panic rising. I start wondering if I should be grabbing my life with two hands and giving it an almighty shake. You see I can't think of anything worse than looking in the mirror in another ten years' time and thinking, well, you've had it now, you've lost the opportunity to make yourself truly happy. I don't want to die wondering what could have been.'

Jennifer swallowed. Susan looked terribly sympathetic but still said nothing.

'And I think people should have sympathy for others who are going through this because I know I'm not the only one. It's a stage that shouldn't be mocked because it's actually terribly hard and I can't bear what I'm turning into. I've spent most of this week day dreaming about my past, wondering what life might have been like if I'd made different decisions, or perhaps if I'd stayed with other men I've loved. And it's terrifying. I *should* be happy but I'm not and that makes me feel selfish and guilty which is even more depressing. I can't even eat at the moment. I've lost a stone in a year but I just want to be happy Susan. I want to get out of this state. I want to know that I've led my life in a positive way and that I haven't missed out and most of all, when I ask the question 'Is this it?' I want to feel like, if it is, then that's ok.'

Speech over, the room fell completely silent, apart from the ticking of Susan's clock on the wall. The clock was in the shape of a cow which had always struck Jennifer as slightly absurd. What did cows have to do with time? It's not like they needed to be anywhere.

Now she'd finished, Jennifer wasn't entirely sure where her outburst had come from but actually she felt better for it, if a little embarrassed. Jennifer watched the dust motes swirling in the shaft of light that was pouring through the window.

Thirty more seconds of silence passed and Jennifer could feel her face going red. She sat on her hands, stared out of the window and tried not to cry.

As she waited for Susan's response, she hoped it wasn't one which would belittle everything she'd just expressed. She hoped Susan had been listening properly. If she had been, then she'd know she wouldn't want to be patronised with something along the lines of 'well how does that all make you feel'.

It took an age but finally Susan's response did come and when it did it couldn't have been more unpredictable.

'Well...,' she said eventually 'I want you to know that I for one respect everything you're feeling. This is a really tough chapter in your life. I also want you to have a think this week about what you think the root cause of your unhappiness might be. I can tell that your soul is yearning for some change at the moment, but have you ever considered that by changing what you've already got that you might simply be swapping one set of problems for another?'

Jennifer cocked her head to one side as she thought about this. This was more like it. This was what she came to therapy and paid forty pounds a time for. What Susan had just said was actually very interesting.

'And, do you not think that rather than this being all about Max, this is actually about you. It's about you working out what you want, about figuring out who Jennifer is and what makes you happy. Until you can be happy in yourself I don't think anybody else can fill that gap for you.'

'Susan?'

'Yes?'

'Do you ever think that perhaps life is very transient?'

'What do you mean exactly?'

'Well, do you think perhaps we're supposed to be with different people for certain periods of our lives and that as we change and develop our needs, that the person we should be with changes too?'

Susan pondered this for a while. 'Are you trying to tell me there's someone specific you're considering a change with?'

'No,' said Jennifer hurriedly 'I'm not. There isn't anyone in my life except Max. In fact, lately I've spent more time harking back to the past as opposed to thinking about anyone in the present.'

'Give me an example.'

'Well, there was this one boyfriend I had, Steve. I went out with him before Max and I've been thinking about him a lot recently. When I met Max I was still going out with him. In fact I met Max at a party which I was actually at with Steve. Max and I instantly connected and I gave him my number, which of course was pretty terrible given that I was already going out with someone. Anyway, at the time I was convinced that Max and I were far more suited, and yet I'm pretty sure that Max has never loved me as much as Steve did. Steve absolutely loved me to pieces. Perhaps if I'd stayed with him I wouldn't be feeling like this right now? Perhaps if I hadn't given Max my number I would be with Steve and living very happily?'

'Or perhaps you'd be with Steve and wondering if you should have gone off with Max while you had the chance? It's impossible to say,' mused Susan 'and it's also very difficult to reflect on the past and remember how we truly felt at the time when our perception is so coloured by the present.'

'Mm,' agreed Jennifer, who was pretty sure this would be one of those comments she'd need to go away and think about before making up her mind.

'I think, for what it's worth, that projecting back and feelings of regret are very much linked to depression, just as worrying about the future is a huge cause of anxiety. It's when we're most rooted to the present that we tend to be at our healthiest mentally. So, for now, my advice would be to concentrate on trying to reconnect with Max again. Try telling him how you're feeling. I think you could be surprised by the results.'

'Really?'

'Really,' said Susan kindly and it occurred to Jennifer that she hadn't wanted to flee the room all session. Progress.

'Why do you say that?'

'Well, whenever you've come to see me in the past you've spoken very fondly of your husband and, at the moment, I think you're sad for lots of reasons, many of which aren't to do with him. As I said earlier, he's clearly not the only reason you're unhappy.'

'I tried to seduce him last week but it failed miserably,' admitted Jennifer for no other reason than the memory had just popped into her head.

'How do you mean failed? Could he not perform?'

Jennifer wrinkled up her nose, embarrassed 'No, nothing like that. I just got all dressed up in a bid to make an effort but he didn't even come upstairs to see me when he got home from work so I gave up.'

'Ok,' said Susan 'So Max wasn't actually aware you were trying to seduce him?'

'No.'

'So what you were really upset about wasn't being rejected, but the fact that when he got home from work he didn't seek you out?'

'I suppose so,' sighed Jennifer.

'Well, perhaps you need to tell him what your needs are. He may be totally unaware of how you're feeling and he at least deserves the chance to put things right. No?'

Jennifer shrugged. She almost preferred it when Susan remained impartial.

'How are the anti- depressants going?'

'I've stopped taking them,' admitted Jennifer.

'Why?'

Another shrug.

'Ok, well it's not for me to tell what you do but I strongly recommend that you go back to your doctor and discuss that with him. If you are suffering from depression then you need to give them a chance to work.'

'I don't think I need them,' said Jennifer.

'What do you think you need?' Susan asked softly.

'I think, after having talked to you today that I need to talk to Max properly and to try and set aside some time for us to perhaps go away and attempt to sort things out.'

'That sounds like a positive idea.'

A while later Jennifer left Susan's house feeling considerably better than she had when she'd first arrived. There was clearly not going to be an overnight solution to how she was feeling. She still had a lot of thinking to do and it would take time, but one thing she could take control of was her part in her relationship So tonight, she'd decided, was the night Max was going to be reminded of just some of the things he loved about his wife, whether he liked it or not. It felt like a step in the right direction.

33 | Present Day

Jennifer's brain had begun to slowly recover a little from the accident. Most of the time she was still existing in her otherworldly state. However, these periods were now interspersed with short spells during which her consciousness allowed her to connect properly with the here and now.

After tunnel number two had shut behind her for the last time Jennifer had been beside herself with distress and when that depth of emotion had coincided with reality it had been too much to cope with and caused her to suffer a seizure. The point where all the machines she was plugged into had started bleeping had signified the second when her brain had truly engaged with the enormity of what would have happened in France had she chosen that path in life.

She'd experienced love on a level she hadn't previously known was possible and then she'd died. It was incredibly painful. Ever since, she'd felt like a wounded animal and had regressed a fair bit. Her body was getting stronger though and refused to give up its battle for recovery. This, coupled with some willpower and emotional resilience she never previously would have given herself credit for, meant that eventually Jennifer was ready to consider her next move. It was that or give up, but her instinct to survive was stronger. So she'd decided that she had to hold onto the fact that the painful outcome in France hadn't been her true fate, or the one she'd really chosen. It was utterly tragic but thank god none of it had come to pass. Those children didn't lose a mother because they didn't exist. Joe didn't lose the love of his life, only when it occurred to her that he might actually exist in the real world…the idea was too mind boggling to even contemplate.

She turned her attention to the fact that there was still another tunnel to explore. Tunnel number three was beckoning. Its' light entranced her, beguiled her and promised something completely different to the experience she'd just had. This would be her life with Steve. Sweet, good looking, gentle Steve. Surely this life would have been untroubled, straight- forward and easier?

Perhaps discovering it would ease the pain of tunnel number two.

At the same time, she hoped her third life wasn't too perfect. She wasn't sure she could handle the regret. She'd been through enough already.

Joe.

Another wave of pain. She determinedly cast the image of him away. She couldn't handle thinking of him anymore. Instead, she made the drop toward the tunnels. Her descent took a while but by now the extraordinary sensation she felt every time was something she'd grown used to. As she landed she looked around.

It was eerily silent. The first two tunnels were completely sealed off. The third was waiting and shining brighter than ever.

34 TUNNEL NUMBER THREE
Steve: what could have been

Steve whistled appreciatively 'You look stunning babe. Absolutely stunning. Doesn't she mum?'

'Ooh she does,' agreed June who was frantically busy dusting and arranging her commemorative plates in one of her glass fronted cabinets. She'd bought the entire set a fortnight ago and had been beside herself with excitement when they'd arrived earlier. There were eight plates in total and each one depicted a different member of the Royal family at various events. Jennifer wasn't keen for many reasons but the one which featured Princess Beatrice grinning inanely had become a secret favourite in an '*it's so bad it's good*' sort of way.

'Lovely colour. I like you in brights.'

'Thanks,' said Jennifer, who was pleased with her new dress. She felt sexy in it. It was bright pink, quite fitted and showed off her figure. Being with Steve these last couple of years had given her a newfound confidence in her body and what she could get away with wearing. He complimented her every day and always seemed to mean it sincerely so at a certain point the compliments started to sink in and these days she positively revelled in them. He always noticed when she'd had her hair done, or when she was wearing something new and had an opinion on what he liked her in which she found very sexy. It was important to dress for yourself, but it was an added bonus if how you looked made your boyfriend want to take your clothes off. He hadn't asked her yet but one day Jennifer suspected it might make shopping for a wedding dress far easier too because he was even able to verbalise his idea of a beautiful looking bride (hair up, dress which wasn't too big). Though having said that, recently, whenever he'd alluded to their future together a few doubts had started to creep in. The trouble was that for a long time now Steve had just assumed they'd stay together forever but seemed to have forgotten along the way to ask her what she felt about this.

'Right, Mum, I'll see you soon. I'll be staying at Jen's for the next few nights or so,' said Steve, grabbing his jacket.

'Oh really? Alright then love,' said June, looking downcast.

'What?'

'No, no it's nothing,' said June, rearranging Prince Andrew into a more prominent position and relegating Princess Anne firmly to the back. You could tell she had a most definite pecking order.

Jennifer tried to ignore the nugget of irritation which was building in her stomach. She hated it when people said 'nothing' when clearly there was 'something.' Besides, with June there was always 'something'.

'Come on,' cajoled Steve, his voice laden with patience as if he was talking to a small child. 'Let's be having it. There's obviously something on your mind and we're not leaving for this party till you've spat it out.'

Jennifer didn't necessarily agree with this last statement. If June took too long she for one would definitely be off.

'Honestly, it's nothing.'

'Mum.....'

'No, it's silly really,' said June 'it's just I assumed you were coming back here so I went and got everything in for a roast tomorrow.

Steve looked stricken. 'Oh no, did you?'

Eager to leave, Jennifer quickly assessed the situation. 'I tell you what,' she chimed in 'Why don't we just crash at mine tonight as planned. That way we don't have to spend a fortune on a taxi or leave the party early, but then we could always come back here tomorrow for lunch couldn't we?'

'But what about you getting to work on Monday babe?'

Damn. To be fair Jennifer hadn't totally thought that one through but she could hardly backtrack now. 'Hmm, well… I guess I'll either have to go back home tomorrow night or I could just leave here very, very early on Monday morning.'

She was rewarded for her peacekeeping efforts with a ridiculously grateful smile from Steve whom she knew hated upsetting his mum. The two of them were extremely close and it was just another aspect of Steve's comparative warmth she'd always appreciated and had been surprised by when they'd first got together. Tim had barely given his mum the time of day. He'd never been able to get her off the phone quick enough, always answering her questions with bullet points and hardly ever bothering to enquire after her. But Steve checked in with June daily and told her everything. They had an amazing relationship really, although lately Jennifer had found herself wishing he'd stick up for himself a bit more when she was being bossy. Sometimes it seemed like she had her son wrapped around her fake nailed little finger.

'Really?' said June 'You'd come back tomorrow? It's just since Derek and I split up Sunday's can be very lonely. But only if it's not a pain.'

It would be a pain. A massive pain. Jennifer had been desperately excited about spending a whole rare day in bed doing nothing. Now they'd be trekking across town with hangovers, but to hell with it, at least she wouldn't have to cope with Steve feeling guilty and fretting about his mum all day. Plus they'd get fed.

'Course it isn't a pain,' said Steve 'How could it be a pain when it involves having one of your roasts.'

Jennifer cringed.

'What roast is it anyway?'

'Your favourite,' said June 'Beef.'

Steve pulled a face similar to the one he made during orgasm, sort of cross- eyed with bliss. He rubbed his hands together. 'Nice one Mum. Can't wait. Right my gorgeous, shall we go?'

***

On the tube, Steve thanked Jennifer profusely 'I'm so sorry babe, I know you were really looking forward to lying in all day. It's so kind what you did and so typical of you to be so unselfish.'

'That's alright,' said Jennifer 'As long as you promise me that next time you'll make it totally clear, days in advance, that we're definitely not coming back. So she doesn't get all that bloody food in.'

'Hmm,' said Steve, looking torn, clearly debating whether or not he should be divulging what he was about to tell her next.

'Actually, I kind of did to be honest, but I think she just loves having us around so much she chose to forget.'

Jennifer fervently wished Steve hadn't told her this. If June had in fact manipulated them into coming back to Leytonstone tomorrow it was actually rather irritating, especially since she was now facing a horrible trek to work on Monday. Suddenly she felt far less inclined to be doing June the favour. Dammit. Steve picked up her hand and gave it a little squeeze 'I'll make it up to you babe.'

Jennifer took a deep breath, and tried not to let anything ruin the night. She'd been looking forward to this party for ages. It was Esther's boyfriend Toby's best mate's party and promised to be a really good night. According to Esther there was going to be an amazing DJ, loads of booze, plus all her best friends would be there. Toby was a good laugh too so his mates were bound to be up for it. Bloody June. The more she tried not to think about it, the more she wished she hadn't said anything. Her enjoyment of the party was going to be marred now by the fact that if she got too pissed, the long journey back East tomorrow would be horrendous.

'You know what my mum's like,' persevered Steve. He could tell Jennifer was fed up. 'Like I said she just loves our company and she gets lonely.'

'I know,' said Jennifer, only she couldn't quite leave it at that. Usually she never dared criticize the mother-ship but today it felt warranted. 'Only perhaps, just occasionally, you could try putting me first? After all, we spend a lot of time bending over backwards to make sure she's happy and now my lovely planned day of doing nothing is going to be totally ruined, which I didn't mind until you informed me that she's basically conned us. If I'd known she was being sneaky I would have put my foot down and would never have offered to go back tomorrow. You always go on about how she wants to see both of us, but it's kind of annoying because she doesn't really. She wants to see you.'

'That's not true babe,' said Steve looking genuinely aghast 'She loves you. Only the other day she was asking when she's going to be a grandma.'

'And what did you say?' asked Jennifer slightly frostily.

'I said as soon as I could persuade you to have my babies.'

'Well, you're going to have to wait a bit longer I'm afraid.'

'I know,' said Steve 'one more year.'

As the tube rattled through the tunnels, Jennifer despaired. Steve insisted on hanging on to that 'one more year' for dear life. She'd only said it to shut him up. She definitely wanted to start a family at some point but they weren't even engaged yet and she hated the pressure. She loved Steve very much but his constant nagging to have a baby was starting to get on her non lactating tits.

'And again, her becoming a grandma has got nothing to do with me. It's the baby she's after,' she added through gritted teeth, her mood worsening by the second.

'Alright,' warned Steve. He was a softie alright but not when it came to his mother and Jennifer knew she was treading a fine line before he got annoyed, although given the mood she was in she wasn't sure she cared.

'Look, I'm sorry ok, and I know it's going to be a bit of a ball-ache tomorrow but we can laze around until at least ten thirty and it's not *that* much of a big deal going back. At least we'll be getting mum's roasties.'

Jennifer battled with the urge to tell him she'd always found his mum's 'roasties' a bit oily and that what she really fancied tomorrow was a nice Chinese takeaway.

'Oh shit, I forgot to tell you babe,' said Steve, manfully and wisely changing the subject 'You know mum entered me in for that competition.'

'Ye-es.'

'They've only gone and been in touch. They want to get me in for a meeting or something. Or maybe even a, hang on, what did they call it? Oh yeah, a screen-test.'

Steve had chosen his timing well. This was an instant distraction.
'I can't believe you didn't tell me. That's hilarious!'

'I know, although I reckon they probably only looked at her entry because no doubt she keeps the entire company afloat with her spending habits.'

Jennifer laughed. This was golden gossip. She couldn't believe Steve was only just telling her now and it certainly helped improve her mood.

'So are you going to go? When is it?'

'Nah,' said Steve dismissively 'Can you imagine me fumbling my way through a 'screen test'? I get embarrassed enough as it is just having my photo taken, let alone talking on camera.'

'Still,' said Jennifer 'Can you imagine what a housewives favourite you'd be?

Steve frowned, assuming she was taking the piss.

'I'm not joking. They mainly sell to women and they would love you.'

Steve rolled his eyes and shook his head.

'Seriously babe, plus there's nothing you don't know about DIY so it's not like you wouldn't be in your comfort zone.' Jennifer laughed, mainly at herself 'I can't believe I'm encouraging you, but you never know. You might find you're good and I bet they'd pay well too.'

'Well, you're very sweet baby but somehow being Price Smash's DIY expert isn't exactly a dream I'm up for pursuing. No matter how much Mum insists.'

Jennifer felt a definite sense of satisfaction that for once it looked like he was going to defy mummy dearest. Steve was right, if he were to work on one of her beloved shopping channels she'd be the happiest woman ever. Still, in this instance she was kind of on June's side. She couldn't see what he had to lose. He was a great plumber but in terms of broadening his horizons, prospects and earning power this could be his big opportunity.

Jennifer tried another tactic. 'She'll be devastated if you don't go. She'd never forgive you. I heard her telling Janice about it only the other day. She was so pleased with what she'd sent in and to be fair I was very cynical about it. I reckoned so many people would enter that you wouldn't stand a chance, so she's done well. I bet hundreds entered.'

'Hm,' said Steve, still not looking wholly convinced 'Price Smash is hardly QVC though is it?'

'Oh I don't know, I'd say it's definitely up there. It's certainly on a par with 'Ideal World'.' At that point Jennifer started chuckling 'Oh my god listen to me. What have I become? I'd never so much as glimpsed a shopping channel before I met you. Now I'm a bloody connoisseur.'

'I know,' laughed Steve 'It sort of seeps in though doesn't it? Even I nearly got sucked in the other day. Mum was asleep on the sofa when I got in from work, Tuesday it must have been, that night you were out with your workmates. Anyway, I sat down to have a beer, fully meaning to switch over and watch something proper. Next thing I knew I'd watched ten minutes of someone talking about an air fryer and was on the verge of buying one.'

Jennifer cackled whole-heartedly before eventually spluttering 'How much do you reckon she spent last month alone on stuff from those channels?'

'I dread to think,' said Steve drily 'but I caught her buying a steam mop from Price Drop the other day, the new sound bar is from QVC, thought to be fair I told her to get that, it was such a bargain, and that necklace she gave Sue for her birthday, I know for a fact was bought from one or other of them.'

The topic succeeded in diffusing what otherwise could have become a row and for much of the remainder of the journey they sat together in comfortable silence. As the train finally pulled into Hammersmith however, Steve leaned in and whispered 'One day you're going to be the best mum in the world you know babe. Even better than mine.'

Jennifer laughed.

'What?' said Steve, looking a bit miffed that his stab at being romantic was being giggled at.

'Bloody hell Steve,' she exclaimed 'until the day I give birth you really are not going to let it lie are you? You've got to change the record! You make me feel like a walking womb sometimes.'

Steve shot her back a rueful grin. Then he shrugged and made a renewed vow not to bug her too much about getting pregnant. He didn't want to put her off.

'Honestly,' said Jennifer shaking her head 'You're a nightmare and I need you to give it a rest for a bit. I've already told you I don't know how many times that at the moment I need to concentrate on getting this promotion at work. After that we'll see in a year or so.'

'Good,' said Steve, grinning to the point of stupidity.

As frustrated as she was, his expression was so sweet, Jennifer forced herself to be enveloped by the knowledge of how much he loved her and wanted to be with her, even if he did bug the living shit out of her sometimes.

35 | Present Day

Jennifer was confused. So far, what she was experiencing down tunnel number three wasn't what *could* have been. It was what *did* happen. What she'd remembered and reflected on so many times over the years was there to be relived, perfectly vivid and in full Technicolor. It was so bizarre to recall how she'd felt that day. To be reminded how in love with Steve she'd been and yet how much he'd aggravated her at the same time.

Only now did she remember how strong an influence June had been on him, how much she had dominated her son which in turn had affected their relationship.

Just then Jennifer was overwhelmed by another memory only this time it was far more recent. She couldn't pinpoint exactly when it was, everything was still very foggy. Yes, it was something her therapist Susan had said. She'd said how sometimes remembering things as they really had been was difficult because the past was so coloured by what was happening in the present. Surely this was a perfect example of that? She'd often recalled how Steve had showered her with affection, compliments and demonstrations of how much she'd meant to him, but the truth was he'd also frustrated her greatly at times. She'd forgotten that.

36 TUNNEL NUMBER THREE
Steve: what could have been

The party was in full swing by the time they arrived. There were loads of familiar faces and as soon as they'd set foot in the hallway, they were both engulfed by friends. As a result, within minutes of arriving Jennifer and Steve ended up going their separate ways. Drawn towards the music, and being pulled enthusiastically along by Lucy, Jennifer had headed straight to the makeshift dance floor in the lounge, her free arm in the air, moving in time to the strains of the funk which was being played. Meanwhile, Steve had bumped into Pete and had gone off to replace the warm beers he'd bought with him, for cold ones which were sitting in an empty bin surrounded by bags of ice. Pete had seemed genuinely pleased to see Steve so Jennifer knew he'd be alright. All Jennifer's friends really liked Steve but then he was easy to get along with so becoming part of their group had been an easy transition.

'There she is,' said Lucy, literally shoving Jennifer in Karen's direction 'She's been pining for you.'

'Yeah,' screamed Karen, upon realising her friend had finally arrived and barrelling over to Jennifer. She'd clearly been dancing energetically for a while now if the sweat patches under her arms were anything to go by. 'It's too loud for me here,' yelled Lucy at the top of her lungs 'I'm going outside for a fag.'

She left them to it, right by the speakers where the mixer was set up. She was right. The music was indeed loud enough to make your ears bleed.

'You're here, you alright?' yelled Karen.

Jennifer took a deep breath in preparation to scream back her answer.

'Yeah good,' she shouted 'just glad to be here. It took ages.'

'Oh well, you've done your stint at June towers for the week. Now you can chill babe.'

Jennifer was about to fill her in and explain that actually she couldn't and that she'd be trekking back there tomorrow but decided it would only inflame her annoyance which she was doing well to keep a lid on at the moment. Plus, it would be too much effort to make herself understood over this racket.

'I haven't seen Esther,' she yelled directly into Karen's inner ear instead, which was the only hope either of them had of hearing each other. The music was so loud. The police would be round soon no doubt.

'She's upstairs I think,' said Karen, pulling a face 'Her and Toby were having a massive barney about something when Pete and I arrived.'

'What about?'

'What?'

'I said what about?'

'Oh I don't know, I think he was eyeing up Rochelle. You know Rochelle? That silly cow with the massive tits. The one Esther hates.'

Jennifer couldn't make out what she'd said so she just nodded and smiled enthusiastically.

'How's Steve?'

'Good.'

'No ring yet?' teased Karen.

'What?'

Karen tapped her ring finger.

'No thank god,' laughed Jennifer, only half joking. 'Although he'd rather get me up the duff first anyway I reckon.' It had become a standing joke within the group that out of the two of them it was Steve who was eager to settle down and have babies while Jennifer was doing her best to cling onto her last vestiges of freedom.

Just then the music changed and someone saw sense to reduce the volume to a less painful threshold. The funk came off and suddenly one of Jennifer's favourite house tracks came pouring out of the speakers, causing her to squeal with delight.

'Wooooh,' yelled Karen, hands aloft.

Jennifer turned round to show her appreciation to the DJ only to find that he'd gone and that someone else had taken his place. Someone who perhaps wasn't deaf? The guy behind the CD mixer had dark hair, an attractive lopsided grin and was only wearing a scruffy t shirt yet managed to look really good. Just then he caught Jennifer's eye. She didn't need any more encouragement than that to go and tell him how much she appreciated his choice of track. 'Oh my god this is such a tune,' she squealed, scuttling over.

He nodded his head, smiling at her girlish enthusiasm 'Better get dancing then,' he said, shooting her a grin.

Jennifer did as she was told and for the next couple of minutes danced with gusto to the tune that sent shivers down her spine whenever the chorus kicked in. At one point she and Karen clutched onto one another and just jumped around together. By now a far larger group had been attracted to the dance floor.

'Who's the DJ?' panted Jennifer, after the fifth brilliant track in a row.

'Max Wright,' said Karen 'He's cute isn't he? He's a mate of Drifter's.'

Jennifer looked blank.

'You know Drifter don't you? Toby's cousin's ex.'

Jennifer shook her head.

'Well anyway, he's called Max. Why?'

'No reason, I just love the music he's playing. It's brilliant.'

'Do you want a drink?' asked Karen. 'I'm going to see if I can hunt down some vodka. If I can't I'll probably go to the off licence. Do you want to come?'

'Do you mind if I stay here for now? I want to dance a bit more.'

Karen nodded and disappeared off into the crowd.

Jennifer turned to see if anyone else she knew was about. As she did her eyes met with the DJ's again. She'd sensed him watching her a few times when she'd been dancing and now he was looking directly at her. He gave a small nod of his head. Jennifer smiled back and acknowledged to herself that if she wasn't attached she'd probably be making a beeline for him right this second.

Right, it was definitely time to find Steve.

It took her a while to find him. By this point the party had crossed the line from being pleasantly heaving to unpleasantly packed. The stairs were three people deep and not one inch of carpet could be seen now. After a pretty unpleasant ten minutes of barging her way through small groups of people who were so engrossed in what they were doing they were reluctant to move, she finally found him in one of the bedrooms. Even then it took her a while to detect him because the room was so full of smoke she could hardly see into it. There were about eight lads in there doing shots of limoncello. Pete was one of them. In fact, it was obvious he was the main instigator and had provided the bottle. When it came to the acrid yet sweet smelling smoke which hung thick in the air someone else was the culprit. A guy she didn't know had an enormous joint hanging from his lips and Jennifer watched amazed as he offered it over to Steve and he accepted. Steve didn't even drink alcohol very much and certainly never normally smoked pot or went anywhere near drugs, which was probably why he was looking a bit green.

'Hey gorgeous,' he said, looking up, finally realising she was there. Oh god he was wasted.

'Hey, you alright?' she enquired gently, aware that he wouldn't want her to make him look like a loser in front of the other guys by exposing how out of it he was.

'Yeah good,' said Steve, beckoning to her to come and sit next to him on the bed. His hand was all floppy and limp. She perched on the end of the bed, very conscious of the fact that she was the only female in what felt like a male dorm. Steve tried to sit up more so he could give her a kiss. He missed her mouth a bit and ended up smooching her cheek after which she had to resist the urge to wipe her face with her hand. The kiss was sloppy and wet and it had felt a bit like being kissed by a Labrador.

Then he reached over to her and rubbed her leg which was fine. But then he sat up and started kissing her neck and stroking her hair which felt ok, only it was also a bit weird given that there were seven other people in the room. She tried to pull away without drawing too much attention to them but clearly failed.

'Oi oi,' said one lairy looking bloke.

'Get a room you two,' said Pete and Jennifer felt her face redden.

'If I want to kiss my beautiful girlfriend then why shouldn't I?' proclaimed Steve.

Pete pretended to stick his fingers down his throat and replied 'Because you show us all up mate and I'll have Karen moaning at me later saying 'you don't show me as much affection as Steve shows Jen' blah blah blah.'

'Er, I am in the room you know,' said Jennifer, firmly pulling away from Steve's hands now which were still trying to stroke her. He was getting on her nerves. How had he got so out of it so quickly?

While Pete turned round to concentrate on the serious business of doling out another round of shots to everybody, she took the opportunity to turn to face Steve properly. He looked stoned. His eyes were bloodshot and his expression was positively dopey.

'Babe, I hate to say it but it's still pretty early, so don't get any more fucked because we've got to get all the way back to Leytonstone tomorrow remember?'

Steve's face instantly clouded over 'urgh, you're not still going on about that are you? I wish you'd give it a rest. Honestly, I really thought you were being so kind offering to go back but you're making such a big deal out of it,' he slurred.

Jennifer was outraged. 'Oh my god,' she fumed, in a seething whisper she hoped no one else could hear 'As if! I was hardly having a go. The opposite in fact. I was trying to look out for you and was only saying that if you get too wrecked you'll pay for it tomorrow. But if you want to be like that, then do what you want.'

Steve sighed heavily and she could tell he was trying to come up with a good defence but it was never going to happen. He looked really peaky now. Pale and a bit sweaty. She gave up. She didn't care what he had to say anyway. She was incensed. He was being an idiot.

'I'm going back downstairs,' she said, shaking off his right hand which was trying to paw at her again.

As she left the room, she heard Steve calling out 'Oh babe come on, come back a minute, I didn't mean it.'

She cringed. Great. Well done Steve. Now they'd all know they were arguing.

Back downstairs, the party was starting to lose its appeal. There were simply too many people and by now it was obvious that lots of them hadn't been invited. No one dared go up to the unknown group loitering in the hall, to ask what the hell they were doing there, but their presence leant an uneasy atmosphere. She searched for Karen for ages but failed to find her anywhere so assumed she must still be at the off licence. She did bump into Esther and Lucy though. 'Hey,' she said delighted to see them until she realised Esther's face was tear stained and that Lucy was leading her by the elbow like an old lady. Her mascara had clumped and she had rings of black eyeliner half way down her face.

'Oh my god what's happened?'

'It's ok,' said Lucy, on Esther's behalf. 'She's just split up with Toby. He's been a total prick.'

'Oh no why?' asked Jennifer, but Lucy shook her head and pulled a warning face, telling her not to enquire further. 'Ok, so what are you both doing now then?'

'I'm going to take Esther outside and make sure she gets in a cab. I'll either come back or I might just get in with her,' replied Lucy.

'Ok,' said Jennifer, feeling really sorry for Esther who was clearly so drunk and upset she couldn't even talk. Jennifer watched as she shuffled off, Lucy keeping a firm grip on her.

'You ok?' said a voice.

Jennifer turned round and was pleasantly surprised to see the man she already knew was called Max standing there 'Oh hello. It's the DJ who isn't deaf.'

Max grinned 'It was a bit painful before wasn't it? No doubt it will be again. Drifter's on again now for his next set. Do you fancy a drink?'

'What you got?'

'Rum,' said Max, pulling a bottle out of the back pocket of his jeans.

'Don't mind if I do.'

Max gestured to a small two-seater sofa which had been dragged up against the wall, which had miraculously just become free.

'Quick,' he instructed.

'Ah, bloody brilliant. I've been dying to sit down for ages,' said Max once they'd successfully nabbed the seats. Jennifer had to admit it felt very good to sit. Her heels were starting to kill her. So, how come I've not met you before then?' asked Max.

'Don't know,' shrugged Jennifer, taking the bottle which he was handing to her now and taking an enormous swig. Man alive that was strong.

'Because I've met Karen and Pete a few times now but you've never been around.'

'International woman of mystery me.'

'It's Jennifer isn't it?'

'Yes, and you're Max?'

He nodded 'So Jennifer, international woman of mystery, have you got a boyfriend?'

'Yes,' she said, turning to look him straight in the eye. Her tone almost defiant.

'And who is he?'

'Steve.'

'Steve. Hmm. And what's Steve like?'

'He's lovely. Obviously. Or I wouldn't go out with him.'

'Fair enough,' said Max, grinning and taking the rum back off her.

'What about you? Are you single?'

'Yup.'

Jennifer looked around the room. One couple were snogging up against the opposite wall. They were both so drunk it was pretty off-putting and rather grim to watch. You could see their tongues from here.

'Nice eh?' said Max.

Jennifer pulled a face. 'I hate public displays of affection like that.'

'I'm not even sure if that counts as affection,' Max laughed 'More like desperation.'

They sat in silence for a while, Jennifer wondering if perhaps she shouldn't be going to find Steve. Only she knew he was fine and actually they had found a pretty good spot here and she was reluctant to give it up and return to stalking round the house looking for something to do or someone to talk to.

'Great set earlier by the way?'

'Oh good. Glad you liked it. To be honest I haven't DJ'd since my university days but Drifter was desperate for me to help him out so he didn't have to do it all night.'

'Ah, well that answers the next question I was going to ask then, which was do you do it for a living? Only, there's a girl at my work who's looking for someone good for her thirtieth.'

Max regarded her in a way that she liked. He was very sexy. She knew if she wasn't attached he'd be flirting with her. She turned away. She didn't want to encourage him or give him the wrong impression.

'Well, you never know, if it was for a friend of yours perhaps I could come out of retirement,' said Max, which only confirmed what she'd just thought.

She didn't reply, instead her gaze drifted back to the couple who were now really going at it. His hands were everywhere, up her skirt, down her top. It was horrible.

'So where's Steve now then?' enquired Max.

'Upstairs. He's a bit wrecked to be honest.'

'Ooh, upchucking is he? Last of the great romantics.'

'Oi you,' said Jennifer, giving him a bit of a nudge 'I'll have you know Steve is ridiculously romantic.'

'Is he now? In what way? What's the most romantic thing he's done for you then?'

She toyed with telling him to mind his own bloody business but in the end decided he was only having a bit of fun so went with it. 'Ok, well he's always telling me I'm beautiful.'

Max nodded 'Well, he's got a point there. He's a lucky guy your Steve and I hope you know I'm only being like this because I'm disgustingly jealous of him and totally unable to get a lovely girlfriend like you myself.'

Jennifer laughed 'You're terrible.'

'Why? It's true. Anyway, come on, I'm intrigued, what else does he do? You've got to tell me because maybe I can learn. Does he compile playlists of music which remind him of you?'

'No,' admitted Jennifer, thinking that actually that would be quite nice. Steve had never massively been into music, certainly not as much as she was.

'Really?' said Max 'I'm surprised, I would have thought that would have been a dead cert. But the two of you have a song obviously?'

Jennifer wrinkled her nose up 'Um, not really.'

'Oh ok, maybe I'm thinking too inside the box,' admitted Max 'It's just when I saw you dancing earlier I assumed you loved music and that you'd be the sort of person who would always have a song for everything. You're a good dancer by the way.'

'Thanks,' said Jennifer blushing.

'So, out of interest what is your favourite tune?'

'Impossible to answer,' she shot back. 'Totally absurd question if you don't mind me saying because it depends on the mood doesn't it?'

'Alright Miss Pedantic, then how about if you could only ever hear one song for the rest of your life and you *had* to choose one or have your tits burnt off with a soldering iron. What would it be?'

'Bittersweet Symphony by The Verve maybe?'

'Interesting,' mused Max 'Rum?'

She took the bottle and swigged from it greedily. 'We're like pirates,' she said, gasping as the strong liquor trickled down her oesophagus.

'Not really,' said Max in a way that really made her giggle. 'I've got all my teeth for starters, I haven't got scurvy and I'm not wearing an earring. You look a bit like an addled old sea dog admittedly, but only a bit. Anyway, back to your romantic boyfriend I want more details'

'Why are you so interested?'

Max shrugged 'Well, my options are to sit here and chat to you about life and the universe or get forced to DJ for another hour and a half which I really can't be bothered to do. Besides, I've played all my best tunes already, trying and failing to impress you.'

By now Jennifer was thoroughly enjoying herself. She was enjoying Max's brand of banter a lot. 'Right. Well let's just sit and talk rubbish then because the last thing this party needs is the scrapings of your DJ barrel.'

'Pirate barrel,' added Max 'Right, let's continue the interrogation then. What else does Steve do for you that's romantic?'

Ok then,' she began 'He cooks for me a lot.'

'Nice. And of course he does. I can tell we're dealing with a proper twenty first century perfect specimen of manhood here. What kind of thing does he cook?'

'All sorts,' lied Jennifer. The fact was Steve did cook for her regularly but only ever a variation on one thing. Breakfast, which always comprised of four of the following – sausage, bacon, beans, egg, grilled tomatoes, mushrooms and toast. She'd probably had every possible combination and frankly she loved his breakfasts, though did sometimes wonder if he'd ever experiment with anything else. When questioned he always said there was no point learning when his mum was so good.

'I've heard this before you know,' said Max 'That being a dab hand in the kitchen makes girls go weak at the knees. I'll have to brush up. I can pretty much only do roasts and curries.'

'Well that sounds pretty impressive,' said Jennifer truthfully.

'Chuck in a mean spaghetti bolognaise and I reckon any girl would be very happy with that.'

'So what else?' persisted Max 'He cooks, he tells you you're beautiful but what else? Has he ever whisked you away to Paris in the spring, bought you flowers for no reason, showered you with thoughtful gifts, written you poetry or are these sorts of gestures all too trite and cliché for perfect Steve.'

'Aha,' said Jennifer triumphantly, glad to have finally come up with something. She'd been starting to panic 'I tell you what he did do that was very romantic. He bought me a piece of the moon for my birthday.'

The expression on Max's face was not what she'd anticipated at all though. Rather than looking impressed he looked thoroughly offended.

'What?' said Jennifer, feeling herself get embarrassed and faintly wishing she'd never mentioned it.

'You are kidding me?' said Max 'You're not telling me you're the kind of girl that thinks that sort of thing is actually cool. You've suddenly gone right down in my estimation.'

'Why?' she squealed, blushing furiously.

'So you're telling me that your boyfriend handed over good money for some bullshit piece of paper that says you own however many square feet of the moon?'

Jennifer didn't say anything, but gave him a look which was designed to warn him not to take the piss too much.

He didn't take any notice.

Max laughed, holding his sides as the concept really took hold. 'Let me guess, did it come with a revolting teddy bear to go with it?'

'No it did not,' lied Jennifer, hating Max for being so spot on but hating herself more for having given Steve's lunar purchase as an example of something romantic when at the time she herself had thought it a truly senseless gift.

'But who did he think he was buying it off?' gasped Max, who was really enjoying himself now. 'No one owns the bloody moon so no one has the right to sell it. I tell you what if I go and make a nice certificate on the computer that says you own some of the sun will you buy it off me for fifty quid?'

'Shut up you,' said Jennifer, though she couldn't help but smile a bit. It was pretty funny when you thought about it.

'Is that really romantic or just gullible?' laughed Max.

'Well, if anyone was to colonise the moon then at least I could claim my piece of it,' she said lamely, remembering what Steve had tried to tell her as she'd looked blankly at her pointless 'certificate' wishing it was a voucher.

'Yeah, cos that's bloody likely isn't it?' wheezed Max 'That's really likely to happen in our lifetime. Mm, let's inhabit a freezing cold oxygen-less satellite we can't breathe on.'

'You're very sarcastic aren't you,' said Jennifer, turning away so he couldn't see how much she was starting to laugh.

'And, of course, if anyone did decide to inhabit the moon and managed to find a way to do that without dying, surely traditionally it would be the people who colonised it who'd be the ones staking their claim? Not numb-nuts like you, all the way down here, waving your meaningless certificate around and berating them via your teddy bear.'

Jennifer narrowed her eyes but Max was laughing so hard now it was becoming increasingly infectious and eventually she was laughing as much as he was. The truth was deep down she completely agreed. At the time she'd told her friends how sweet and meaningful she'd found Steve's present but deep down had wondered how anybody over the age of nineteen could have fallen for such a load of garbage.

Still, he could tone it down a bit. He was being rude.

'Screw you,' she said to Max, elbowing him in the stomach as he bent double laughing.

A few hours later and it was most definitely time to leave. The police had been round to warn them to turn the music down or get fined, people were starting to look like they needed to be horizontal and Jennifer was concerned that Steve was going to be sick everywhere if she didn't get him back to hers soon. 'Come on,' she urged, trying to heave him up from where he was slumped on the bottom stair, his head leaning against the wall for support.

'Coming,' he slurred, finally staggering to his feet.

'Where's your jumper?' barked Jennifer who'd really had enough by now.

'Shit. My jumper. It's upstairs, let me go and get it.'

'For god's sake,' she tutted.

'I know,' said Karen, who was also in the hall, shivering with tiredness, waiting for Pete to stop male bonding with someone so they could go.

'I'm starting to feel like a bloody sheepdog,' despaired Jennifer.

'Exactly and I am gagging to get this bra off too. It's really digging in now.'

Rather than wait in the hall any longer, Jennifer decided to pop back into the lounge to say goodbye to Max. They'd been keeping each other entertained most of the night and she'd found him great company. Steve had been unable to leave the bedroom where he'd originally got so stoned and although she'd sat with him for a while, stroking his brow and reassuring him he'd feel better tomorrow, his 'whitey' had started to bore her after a while. As a result she'd ended up hanging out with Max for the majority of the party. He was really bright and funny and challenged her more than Steve ever would. It was refreshing.

'Hey you,' she said, giving the back of his arm a little tap.

'Alright? You off then?'

'Yeah, so I just thought I'd come and say bye.'

'Bye,' he said.

It was sharp and to the point. Jennifer rolled her eyes at him as she had been all evening but inside felt a sharp little stab of disappointment at his lacklustre farewell. However, just as she was about to walk out the door of the lounge and back into the hall the unmistakeable sound of the sweeping strings from the beginning of 'Bittersweet Symphony' filled the room.
Her automatic response was to turn and walk back in. She was so happy to hear it. Back in the room she pointed at Max to acknowledge his gesture and, touched that he'd remembered, blew him a kiss.

In return Max did something that was the singularly most romantic gesture she'd ever experienced. It was probably even more romantic than all the compliments she'd ever received from Steve, and definitely beat all the extravagant gifts she used to get from Tim. As she watched, Max raised his right hand up, made a little fist and patted his chest right where his heart was and gave her a look that told her all she needed to know.

Her stomach whooped with real delight and with that fluttery feeling of butterflies. Oh god what was happening here?

Having managed to stay in control all evening, convincing herself they were just getting on well as friends, suddenly she didn't know what to do. She should go.

Sensing her quandary Max came over. 'Can I give you my number?' he asked over the sound of the tune's beautiful violin chorus. 'Actually, scrap that because you'll never ring and I'll spend the rest of my life staring at my phone, or getting all excited when it does ring only to discover it's my mum, so can I have yours?'

Jennifer honestly did not know what to do.

She had a boyfriend. A boyfriend who wanted to have her babies.

A boyfriend who was sweet and lovely to her. A boyfriend who was currently upstairs, staggering around, trying to find his jumper.

But she was attracted to Max on so many levels and they'd connected in a way that seemed quite rare.

'I don't think I can,' she said eventually 'I'm sorry.'

She turned to go but giving it one last shot Max said 'Well, at least let me take it so I can talk to you about DJing at your friend's birthday. In other words let me take it in a professional capacity.'
Jennifer smiled, her mind racing, knowing that what he'd just done was to provide her with an excuse. Bittersweet Symphony was still playing. She was feeling quite tipsy and was annoyed enough with Steve to reason that just giving out her number hardly equated to being unfaithful. It would be rude not to if all he wanted to do was talk about playing at Jackie's birthday party.

And then, everything in the tunnel froze for a second, like a film which had been paused. In that moment the past collided with the present and Jennifer found herself circling her twenty-five-year-old self. And it was the strangest thing because of course she knew precisely what was supposed to happen next. She knew that she simply hadn't been able to resist the pull of Max. That she'd had a feeling deep within her gut that she would be insane to let him slip through her fingers. Furthermore, she knew that any second now she would get her lipstick out of her pocket and write her number down Max's arm, thus ruining her favourite lippy in the process.

But, as everything started moving again, none of the above was what she saw and Jennifer now understood that this was the point where 'what could have been' was about to become apparent for the first time since she'd entered this world. She could feel her younger self's indecision, could see her conflicted mind swirling and knew it was the exact point when things could have very easily gone the other way.

And in this version she said 'I can't. I just can't give you my number and it's unfair of you to ask. I'm really sorry.' Then she tore out of the room and into the hall where she hauled Steve to his feet from where he was slumped at the bottom of the stairs and left before anything else could happen.

As for Max he went home alone and lay in bed thinking about the girl in the pink dress and how he hadn't met anybody remotely as pretty and funny in years and what a lucky, lucky bloke that Steve was. His last thought before he fell into a deep, dreamless sleep was that he hoped that one day Steve would give her a song that could be theirs. That seemed to be the least she deserved as opposed to what he suspected might be a life sentence of cuddly toys.

37 | Present Day

As far as the doctors were concerned, Jennifer was doing really well. Outwardly it seemed like she was making progress and her condition had now been stable for the last week. What they had no way of knowing of course was that inside she felt so desperately sad.

Meeting Max again had been the most surreal of her experiences so far. She'd been flooded with memories as she recalled how good they'd been together back in the early days of their relationship. The nostalgia had been overwhelming and she couldn't believe either of them had ever forgotten what had first pulled them together in the first place. He was her Max. Her funny, sweet, good looking, bright, laid back, clever Max. How had they managed, over the years, to forget what they had together? How had they let becoming parents change them into different people? It made her feel so angry. It was ridiculous. They were the same people they'd always been, just with less time for themselves and more responsibility. Along the way they'd also managed to lose their shared sense of humour.

Suddenly she had more reason than ever to get back. She wanted to get back. She needed to get back so she could have the chance to make everything alright. She needed to tell him.

But her body hadn't caught up with her mind yet, so she was powerless to do anything but wait. Her physical self still needed longer to heal. What should she do?

She didn't have much choice. She had to see this through and so she headed down tunnel number three again, having resolved to find out once and for all what life with Steve would have brought with it.

38 TUNNEL NUMBER THREE
Steve: what could have been

Jennifer and Steve sat in the car, gazing fixedly ahead at the windscreen. The weather matched their mood. It was a grey, bleak, miserable day.

She was the one to break the protracted silence first by suddenly sniffing loudly before rummaging in her handbag for a tissue.

'We'd better get going hadn't we?' she suggested, her voice tight

'You don't want to be late.'

Steve sighed heavily and by way of reply simply turned the key in the ignition.

While he was putting his seatbelt on Jennifer asked 'Is there really no way you can get out of going in? Surely if you said you'd been violently sick they'd have to cope without you somehow, wouldn't they?'

Steve shook his head, his face despairing. 'I'm not lying. No point letting them down.'

'Ok.'

'What about you? Where do you want dropping?'

'Um.....' Jennifer's brain felt utterly blank. She decided then there was no way she personally could put herself through going into work when she was feeling like this. 'If you've got time to, just drop me home. I'll phone and say I'm going to work from there for the rest of the day.'

'Fine.'

Twenty minutes later Jennifer waved goodbye to Steve and shut the door behind her. She had thought she'd prefer to be with him but it turned out it was a relief to be alone.

There was so much to say, but not yet. They needed time to absorb. Time to digest. Besides, Steve was a big boy and if he thought going into work was the best thing to do she wasn't going to stop him. Perhaps he needed the distraction.

Unsure quite what she should be doing herself she pottered aimlessly about the kitchen. It was already pretty tidy but she wiped all the surfaces and unloaded the dishwasher, drawing comfort from these mundane tasks. Once there was nothing left to tidy she made herself a huge doorstep sandwich, stuffed with cheese, ham and mayonnaise which she chewed morosely at the table.

Once she'd finished she felt stuffed but decided to have a piece of cake as well. It would be total comfort eating, but frankly it was comfort she was after. She was dealing with so many different emotions at the moment; relief, horror, grief, pity and above all a huge sense of injustice. Her stomach churned at the mere thought of how they were going to cope.

'Cooeee,' came the familiar voice of her mother in law. She heard the front door slam. Her solitude was destroyed. She felt like screaming.

'You home Jen?'

'In here,' she called back, glancing at the clock. Damn. Just for once, she'd thought she'd have the house to herself for a change. She could have sworn June had said she wouldn't be back till gone six.

'What are you doing back so early?' she said, trying but failing not to sound accusatory. Not that June noticed.

'Janice had to leave. We were at the Marks and Spencer's café having a nice éclair and a cup of tea when she got a text. There was an emergency,' she said, bustling in, arms laden with shopping bags. 'Her daughter in law needed her to pick up the little one from nursery. Something had come up at work so she couldn't get away early enough. Janice was obviously only too happy to help. That little girl is the love of her life.'

Jennifer smiled a rueful smile, used to these kinds of veiled digs.

'Anyway, have you set the Sky plus? Stevie boy's on in a minute isn't he?'

'He is indeed,' said Jennifer 'I was going to watch him with a piece of cake and a cup of tea.'

'Good idea, get the kettle on then love. Though I'm not sure you want to be having any cake. You'll lose your figure before you've even got preggy,' the older woman cackled.

Jennifer's jaw literally dropped. What a bitch. How she hated living with her mother in law sometimes. She could still hardly believe she'd allowed it to happen, even if it did make perfect financial sense. She and Steve were saving a fortune between the two of them each month and had already built up a pretty impressive nest egg. Their wedding had been stupidly expensive and if they wanted a chance of buying a place of their own this was the only way. Still, at moments like this she'd sooner rent for the rest of her life.

As Jennifer and June sunk into the settee, Jennifer felt a dull ache in her lower abdomen.

'I'm just going to the loo,' she said dully to her mother in law.

'Well hurry up,' June flapped 'He'll be on in a minute.'

Jennifer thought she would probably get over it if she missed a few minutes but didn't say anything. In the privacy of the bathroom however, once she'd seen the inevitable tell-tale sign that once again there would be no baby that month, she wept.

She may have been far cooler about getting pregnant when she hadn't wanted to be, but the minute she'd decided it was time to go for it, it had become her be all and end all. She and Steve had been mutually upset each month when their attempts kept failing. In fact, recently, it had probably been her who'd been most despondent as every period had arrived with sickening punctuality.

Right, she needed to be strong. Firstly, because she was not ready to discuss anything with June yet, and secondly, for Steve. She fumbled under the sink for a tampax, splashed her face with cold water, washed her hands and went to join June in the lounge just as the title music for the Price Smash DIY bonanza was about to begin.

'Good afternoon and welcome,' said the heavily made up blonde who Jennifer had met a few times and actually quite liked. Her off screen persona wasn't nearly as brassy as her on screen one.

'You're watching Price Smash with myself Debbie Pierman, and Steve Barrett, our resident DIY expert. Hiya Steve.'

'Hiya Debbie.'

'Now, over the next two hours, we're going to be bringing you some incredible deals on big name brands from the world of home improvement aren't we Steve?'

'Yeah that's right Debbie. Not only have I got a leaf blower coming up for you but also a power drill from Black and Decker and a pressure washer from Karcher which we're selling at the lowest price it's ever been.'

'He's so slick,' said June.

Jennifer nodded and was relieved to see that on screen at least Steve appeared to be ok.

Later that night, Jennifer lay in bed half watching a box set of Sex and the City on the DVD combi at the foot of their bed which they'd purchased with 30% off from Price Smash, passing the time as she waited for Steve to come in.

It was gone midnight when the door finally opened, and Steve tentatively peered round it, trying to detect whether or not his wife was asleep.

'Hey you,' said Jennifer.

'Hey,' said Steve, coming in properly now he knew she was awake and going to hang his suit jacket up.

'How are you, babe? Are you ok? How was work?'

Steve took off his tie then sunk heavily down on to the end of the bed, narrowly missing Jennifer's foot under the duvet. He hung his head and massaged his temples with his thumb and finger for a while but didn't say anything.

Jennifer crawled across the bed to where he was and stroked his back at which point her husband turned around. Her heart ached as she realised he was crying. Clearly the ordeal of having to go to work and then not only having to appear normal but having to talk about power tools for two hours straight, while looking as if he actually gave a shit, had caught up with him. As the sobs racked through his tired, stressed body his shoulders began to shudder. It was so sad. Jennifer's heart actually hurt.

'Oh Steve,' she soothed, her own tears finally catching up with her properly.

A while later, having let it all out, they lay in bed, facing one another. Eventually Jennifer decided to ask the question which had been on her mind all day.

'So, what are we going to do? Do we adopt?
Steve sniffed and raised a hand to stroke her hair 'I don't know. I don't think I want to. I just don't think it would be the same.'

'But you're not ruling it out?' whispered Jennifer, who also had no idea at this stage how she really felt about anything.

'No, I'm not ruling it out,' said Steve.

Jennifer leaned in to kiss him on the mouth but Steve pulled away. 'I'm sorry. I can't. Not tonight.'

'I'm not trying to have sex,' she said 'Just a kiss.'

He pulled her in close and kissed her on the top of her head. It would do. It was closeness Jennifer was after.

'Everyone's going to laugh,' he mumbled into her hair.

'What?' asked Jennifer, bemused and by this point utterly exhausted too.

'When it's this way round. Blokes get the piss ripped out of them.'

Jennifer was moved to half sit up 'I'm sorry,' she said softly, resting on one elbow 'but if anybody thought this was an appropriate thing to take the piss out of someone for, then frankly they're not worth knowing.'

Steve shrugged and gave her a strange look which took her a while to decipher.

'Oh my god. You want to say it's me don't you?'

Unable to say it Steve shut his eyes and turned over. Jennifer started to cry. It was all so shit and so bloody unfair. Why them? Eighteen months they'd been trying for a baby. Eighteen months of shagging on cue, not drinking, peeing on sticks and taking supplements, interspersed with bitter disappointment every four weeks or so. All of that time, money, energy and effort had been used up, only for Jennifer to find out that her fit, seemingly virile husband who had desperately wanted to be a dad ever since she could remember was firing blanks and had as much hope of conceiving as he did of becoming President of the United States.

Steve turned round again, face full of despair. 'I completely understand if you want to leave me. I'm expecting it.'

'Oh you silly sod,' she sniffed 'No, I'm just a bit flabbergasted that you care so much about what other people are going to think. Personally I think we don't tell them anything. It's none of their business, and I for one will just say that we've had trouble and that it's not going to happen. End of story. I don't think either of us need to go around filling people in on the details.'

'Ok,' said Steve, looking sheepish. 'But also..... if you do want to leave me and find someone who can give you children I'd understand.'

'Are you kidding me?'

'Kidding me,' said Steve, his eyes full of bitter disappointment and despair 'Good choice of word.'

Jennifer laughed through her tears 'Oh come here you.'

She held him tight and slowly could feel some of the tension starting to seep out of his body. They clung on to one another in this manner for hours, united in their grief for the family they'd never have.

'I love you so much,' said Steve at one point 'I can't believe you're not going to leave me.'

'If you even suggest that once more I'll be livid,' said Jennifer firmly.

It was three am by this point. The digital clock by their bed displayed it in green. Sleep for either of them seemed unlikely now.

'But....'

'But what?' said Steve, his expression one of pure panic.

'Please don't totally rule out adoption. There are lots of children out there with nobody to love them.'

'I know,' said Steve. 'I know. I love you Jen.'

'I love you too. And Steve?

'What?'

'I'm so so sorry.'

39 | Present Day

Jennifer was getting used to finding out things she never could have predicted. Poor Steve. Of all the people to be infertile. Sometimes life didn't half play cruel tricks on people.

For a while Jennifer pondered over the lives she could have had and the children she'd have borne in each of them. If she'd been with Aidan she'd have had endearing, sweet Nathan who she knew she would have loved fiercely with every inch of her being. Then there were the four children she'd shared with Tim, each one lovely but very much a product of their upbringing and ultimately all to be damaged by losing their mother at such tender ages. Then she thought of Polly and Eadie and with a stab of potent, maternal love, her insides lurched with urgency, another sign that slowly, reality was taking hold. She needed to return to them. Her little girls. Her real, living, breathing girls who thrilled and drained her every day in equal measure. Jennifer could sense her experience was drawing to a close. Something was either going to change or end soon. But first she had one more journey to make. She hoped, really hoped, that everything was going to be ok. Not perfect. She would probably never expect that ever again because she no longer believed it even existed, but ok would be just fine. Ok would be nice.

40 TUNNEL NUMBER THREE
Steve: what could have been

Jennifer got out of the shower and wrapped herself in a towel before removing her shower cap. She'd been to the hairdressers earlier and hadn't wanted to ruin her hair before the party. She was very pleased when it tumbled out and didn't look frizzy.

'You alright gorgeous?' called Steve from the bedroom where he was also getting ready. 'You excited?'

'Very' replied Jennifer, applying a nice generous portion of Lancôme moisturiser to her face. As the steam started to clear from the mirror she regarded her reflection. Her hairdresser had done a great job. All the grey was covered and recently she'd started having a few low lights which helped soften everything up a bit. She was confident that once she had her make up on and was wearing her nice new Phase Eight dress, she'd look elegant and 'good for her age'. Although when your age was sixty you were never going to look how you'd like to look ideally. Never again would she exude either a youthful bloom or the kind of sex appeal she'd had in her thirties and to an extent her forties and fifties. Still, one of the few advantages of getting older was that you tended to care less about things that weren't really important in the grand scheme of things. Walking past a building site and not being whistled at wasn't the end of the world. These days Jennifer was happy blending into the background and being a spectator rather than the main event. As time marched on she had an increasing amount of life to look back on and less future to worry about which enabled her to enjoy the present more. Sometimes Jennifer could almost feel herself starting to slow down and taking the time to stop and look around at the world a bit more.

Her patience levels had definitely improved too. Take the arrangements for today for instance. The person she'd been in her twenties would have spent the last few weeks panicking that it wouldn't be perfect, that people would be bored/not come/hate the food and then she would have probably had insomnia last night just to make totally sure she wouldn't one hundred percent enjoy herself today. But now she'd taken all the planning in her stride, knowing that of course her guests would have a lovely time and that if the caterers she'd hired to do a barbecue weren't very good, it wouldn't be the end of the world. Perhaps people should put off getting married till they were in their sixties she mused idly? If she had her time again she certainly wouldn't have wasted all that energy fretting about what colour napkins to have or about the weather which of course she had had precisely no control over.

'Who's dressing your mother?' she asked, poking her head out of the en-suite as the thought suddenly occurred to her.

'I'll do her,' replied Steve, bending down from where he was sitting on the edge of the bed, levering his shoes on with a shoe horn. When it had come to what suit he was going to wear he'd been spoilt for choice. As one of Price Smash's highest sellers he was provided with a new suit every quarter. Over the years he'd accrued so many that he regularly sold them on eBay.

'Thanks love,' said Jennifer, glad he was happy to do it. She wanted to put some polish on her nails and getting June dressed would have meant she couldn't.

Three hours later, glass of champagne in hand Steve stood under the gazebo which they'd had erected on the patio the day before. He tinged his glass.

'Hi everyone, can I have your attention please? And don't worry, I'm not going to try and sell you anything.'

The forty or so assembled guests laughed with varying degrees of gusto determined largely by how much they'd had to drink. Jennifer experienced a huge pang of thankfulness as she surveyed the scene. So far the day had been blissful. The garden and house looked fantastic, the weather had held, the food was delicious and everyone seemed to be enjoying themselves. To be surrounded by all their friends and family was a wonderful thing and so rare too. She loved the mix of generations present and it was great watching her parents, who despite their age were still in rude health, catching up with some of her friends. She could tell they were having a wonderful time, as was June, who despite driving Jennifer mad on a daily basis had earned her respect. She may have been in a wheelchair for the last five years but today she was sitting upright in it, surveying proceedings almost regally. Of course she loved the fact that so many of Price Smash's presenters were currently standing in her back garden. At the last tot up, Jennifer and Karen had counted six of them.

'Come on you rowdy lot, listen up now,' bellowed Steve, a huge grin on his face.

Jennifer felt a swell of pride. Steve had aged very well and was still incredibly good looking. He hadn't let himself develop a paunch unlike so many of her friends' husbands. She glanced at Pete who was still tucking into the remains of the buffet. That must be at least his third plate and his shirt was straining to contain his belly. He was a big bear these days. Some people mocked Steve for being groomed and taking care of his personal appearance, which he did because of his job, but she had no complaints and knew his fitness levels contributed to his still healthy libido.

As Steve waited for quiet, some people persisted in carrying on chattering, forcing others in the crowd to eventually do some very loud ssshhing until those who weren't listening finally shut up.

'Thank you. Right,' began Steve 'So, as you know we're all here because, as hard as it is to believe, Jennifer, my beautiful wife, has turned sixty years old today.'

A few people cheered and someone at the back did a wolf whistle which made everyone laugh.

'Jen, I don't want you to go anywhere near that man,' joked Steve, pointing at the culprit 'He simply can't be trusted. Take it from me I know,' he added, winking at his work colleague to show he was joking. 'Jen, actually where are you babe?' he said scouting the crowd, one hand up to shield his eyes from the sun 'I want you up here next to me where we can all see you.'

'I'm here,' she waved, from where she'd been attempting to keep a low profile by the buffet table.

Lucy who was stood next to her gave her an encouraging shove.

'Well get up here,' Steve insisted.

There was another loud cheer at which point Jennifer realised she definitely should have served the food earlier. They were all three sheets to the wind. Grinning madly, she went up to join her husband.

'Come here beautiful,' said Steve, loving the whole thing and waiting for the cheers to subside. 'Now, I just want to say in front of all our friends and family that I honestly feel like I owe you my life, for you Jennifer are the kindest most unselfish, gorgeous woman ever to have walked this earth.'

Jennifer could feel herself welling up. Steve had never been anything but kind or generous to her. Sometimes he drove her mad, like when he insisted on watching his Price Smash shows back when he got in, or when he refused to go to the theatre or watch anything that wasn't certified a 'blockbuster' but over the years he'd almost been over the top with his love due to the guilt he felt over not being able to give her a child. Still, she'd always tried to reassure him that she was happy with her lot. Having their own family simply hadn't meant to be. It had taken a while for true acceptance to arrive but she'd got there in the end. Strangely she'd been experiencing fresh pangs of grief recently as she'd contemplated not just never being a mother but never being a grandmother, although she refused to dwell on it for too long, knowing that in so many other ways her life was very blessed. There had been some massive advantages to not having children, ones which they reminded one another of regularly. For instance, they'd always had plenty of time to devote to each other which had kept their relationship strong, loving and totally intact.

Over the years she'd witnessed how the very tiring years when children first arrived had damaged some of her friend's relationships, had turned marriages stale and left people with no energy for anything until they resembled empty, tired husks for a few years. Without anyone else to focus their time, energy and indeed money on, she and Steve had been able to concentrate on themselves and what they wanted to do. There had been periods when unlimited time to devote to one another had felt like a luxury they didn't want, but she simply had to look at the upside or die bitter and full of sadness which would never do.

Determined never to lead a life which felt even remotely empty she and Steve had made an inordinate effort to achieve the opposite. As a result, they were one of the most well- travelled couples she knew having toured round the continents of India, Africa and America. They'd climbed the Himalayas, raised £110,000 for their charity and, thanks to Steve's ever-increasing salary at Price Smash and not having to shell out on dependents, had never had to worry about finding money to fund all these ventures. They entertained constantly, played golf, did yoga and took classes. Their lives were full to the brim. Different to the one they would have had given the choice but a perfect example of making the most of your lot.

'Not only does she look after me,' continued Steve now 'but she's always helped take care of my old mum, the duchess,

June. Alright Mum! In fact, we should all raise a glass to my mum because without her, shopping channels would probably go bankrupt. In fact, if you don't believe me, take a look at how many figurines are crammed into our cabinets. And in case you were wondering, four combination ovens for a three-person household is three too many but there's no telling her is there Jen?'

Laughing, Jennifer shook her head in agreement and gave June a little wink who in turn cackled away, adoring being the centre of attention.

'So here's to June,' instructed Steve and there was a long pause as everyone drunk from their glass and then raised them 'To June.'
'And watch out Kevin Jameson. She's got her eye on you,' he quipped which again got a raucous laugh from the Price Smash crowd. 'Right, lastly I'd like to thank Jen's parents as well, Lesley and Nigel, you've been a constant support to us both over the years. Nigel, we still can't believe you ran a half marathon only fifteen years ago for our charity. I'm not sure we'd want to see you attempt it now but what an achievement that was mate. I'll never forget it. And also, Jennifer's gang of friends, where are you girls? That's Esther, Karen and Lucy who between them have given the two of us five godchildren in total. So where we haven't been blessed enough to have our own they've made sure that we've had lots of wonderful little people to spoil at Christmas. Of course they're all grown up now

and it's so lovely that three out of the five could be here today. We really do love you as our own don't we Jen?'

She nodded and could feel a lump in her throat.

'You've honestly all enriched our lives, well, apart from the time Suzy stayed over and wet the bed…sorry Suzy! You were only four, it's alright we know you wouldn't do it now. Although the way I'm drinking today… I might.'

Another huge laugh.

'Anyway, on a serious note you've really all meant the world to us.'

By now Jennifer had properly gone and she was frantically trying to stem her happy tears with a hanky.

Steve leant in and gave his wife a kiss on the forehead. 'My darling Jen, you're one in a million and if we could please now all raise our glasses to my wonderful wife. To Jennifer. Happy birthday babe.'

'To Jennifer. Happy Birthday,' said everyone pretty much in unison.

Much later Jennifer was slumped on the sofa with her oldest friend. The rest of the guests had left, been seen into cabs or in a couple of cases had arguments about who'd drunk less and swerved off into the night. Jennifer had begged Karen not to leave though so she and Pete and their daughter Suzy were going to stay over. Suzy, Pete and June had all hit the sack leaving Jennifer and Karen to have a good gossip and to laugh at Steve's snoring. He was passed out in the armchair.

'Oh bless him,' said Karen 'He's wiped out.'

'I know,' said Jen.'

'You're a lucky girl you know,' said Karen, patting her friend's wrist.

'I know,' said Jennifer and it was the greatest feeling in the world to actually mean it.

'Not many people can say their husband adores them like he adores you.'

'Pete adores you,' said Jennifer.

Karen gave her an arch look and raised one eyebrow 'I'd say adores is a bit strong' she countered. 'Tolerates more like.'

'No. Don't be silly.'

'Oh we're alright,' said Karen 'We're fine and I'm very fond of him even though I do wish he'd take a leaf out of Steve's book and do a bit of bloody exercise. He's got massive lately.'

Jennifer snorted.

'He is, when he rolls on top for a quickie I feel like I'm getting crushed,' she complained.

'Yeah well I think you two are great and you've got lovely Suzy,' said Jennifer, the drink making her sound more wistful than she would ordinarily allow herself to be.

'I know love,' said Karen, although you know she sees you as her second mum. You are her second mum.'

Jennifer squeezed her hand 'Right you, come on. Time for bed. Now we're old crones and eligible for our bus passes we need all the sleep we can get.'

'We do,' said Karen, heaving herself reluctantly from the sofa.

'Love you Jen.'

'Love you too,' said Jennifer, going over to attempt to wake up Steve so she could get him up to bed where they would both sleep very soundly.

41 Friday Evening

The day of the accident

Jennifer was ready. She was also shattered. It had taken a huge effort in order to *be* ready. Having taken the day off in order to help with the kids, Max had managed somehow to mess up the entire house. The girl's bedrooms were a state, every toy had been pulled out in the lounge and then left out and nothing had been cleared up from lunch. When she'd returned from her therapy session she'd managed not to say anything though. The kids were having a lovely time playing with their dad and despite her broken arm and how uncomfortable her cast was, Eadie was in good spirits.

However, the minute Max had gone out this evening to a boot-camp fitness session in the park, Jennifer had decided she would get everything ready for a night of seduction during the small window of time he would be out. In order to have the children fed, bathed and in bed, the house tidy, the dinner on, herself looking attractive, with sexy underwear underneath her clothes she'd had to run around like a woman possessed.

She was very nearly ready now but was slightly concerned she'd be too exhausted for the sex she was making all this effort for.

Nevertheless, as she crept out of her bedroom, she felt a flush of excitement as her satin G-string rode up her bum. How anyone could wear these for non-sexual pursuits she had no idea but she was happy to suffer it for tonight. She went to check on the girls. By some miracle it seemed they were both actually asleep. Yes!

Then, just at that second, Eadie, who on the contrary was still obviously very much awake rather ruined the moment by calling from her bed 'Muuuumy.'

Damn. Jennifer cursed inwardly. She should have known it was too good to be true. Polly usually fell asleep pretty much as soon as her head hit the pillow but Eadie was the kind of child who often took ages to get to sleep.

She tip toed into her bedroom 'What is it?' she asked, slightly impatiently. She and Max so desperately needed to have a good night together she'd worked herself up into a bit of a state about it. 'Come on now,' she said to her daughter 'It's time to go to sleep.'

'I'm not tired though.'

'Yes you are,' insisted Jennifer, already halfway out the door again. She wanted to make a nice mushroom sauce to pour over the steak.

'What time is it?' said Eadie, refusing to play ball though and sitting up and looking around as perky as a meerkat, waving her plaster-cast about.

'Ten o clock,' lied Jennifer.

'Ten o clock?'

'Yes, it's very, very late.'

Eadie didn't look convinced. She wasn't stupid. Apart from anything else it didn't feel like ten o clock, probably because it was only quarter to eight.

Just then they both heard Max's key in the door.

'Daddy!'

'Ok, that is Dad and I'm sure he'll come up quickly to say night night, but then we're going to have some grown up time, so I want you to go to bed like a good girl. Then, if you go to sleep nice and quickly I'll buy you some sweets tomorrow.'

'Can I have a magazine too?' said Eadie, spotting an opportunity.

'Eadie,' hissed Jennifer, her patience starting to wear thin. 'That's enough now. I'm getting cross. Just *go to bed*.'

Jennifer left the room and went downstairs to see Max. 'Hello,' she said 'how are you?'

'Good, that was full on today. Legs are going to kill tomorrow. I need a shower. Are the girls already in bed?'

'Yes, well Polly is. Eadie's still awake. In fact, can you quickly say goodnight to her, then with a bit of luck we can have our dinner in peace.'

'Mm smells lovely, what are we having?'

'Steak, salad, jacket potatoes with sour cream, and corn on the cob.'

'Oh wow,' said Max 'Fantastic, I could eat a horse.'

'Well you'll need to leave some room for me,' said Jennifer, in an attempt to get the whole sex thing rolling. Her comment got rather lost however because Max was looking straight past her.

'Hello Eadie Beadie,' he said, managing to ignore what Jennifer had said quite magnificently and gazing up at his daughter who had just appeared at the top of the stairs, arm aloft. She looked like a mini angel of the North.

'What are you doing?' spluttered Jennifer 'You promised Mummy you'd stay in bed.'

'Alright,' said Max 'Calm down, she's not doing anything. It's not even eight yet anyway.'

'See,' said Eadie triumphantly.
Jennifer gave up. Leaving them to it she took a deep breath and headed to the kitchen to make her sauce.

By the time Max finally appeared, showered and wearing a t-shirt and checked, pyjama bottoms, dinner was on the table.

'Ooh this looks amazing,' said Max appreciatively 'A bit of red meat's just what I fancy.'

'Me too,' joked Jennifer, injecting tonnes of innuendo into her voice and wondering if she should flash Max a bit of stocking so he'd get the hint. 'Is Eadie asleep by the way?'

'What do you think?'

Jennifer groaned 'Do you think she wants us never to have sex again for the rest of our lives or something. It's like she knows.'

'It doesn't matter,' said Max tucking in 'She'll be asleep soon enough so let's just enjoy our dinner, take our time, savour it and by the time we're done and maybe have had another glass of wine she'll be out like a light and we can go upstairs and have sex.'

'Ok,' said Jennifer, feeling calmer already. Honestly, once they'd got tonight out of the way she was going to ensure they got back into a routine of having sex far more regularly. Leaving it this long meant she was a bit nervous. Not in an exciting, butterflies in the stomach type of way either. Instead it had reached the point where having sex with her husband felt like some sort of barrier she had to cross. She knew this was a slippery slope and was terrified of starting to view Max as her best friend or housemate. She needed him to want to be physically intimate with her and vice versa. Occasionally having your husband's penis inserted into you was what marked your relationship out as special and different to the one you had with other males in your life surely? She picked up her wine glass and pretty much drained it.

'So anyway, how was therapy?' enquired Max, slathering his steak with mustard 'Helpful?'

Jennifer appreciated him making the effort to ask. She was well aware that really he thought it was a load of old hokum.

'It was fine,' she said 'In fact, it was good.'

'Good,' said Max, as if that was all sorted then.

'I mean there's a long way to go but…. you know……I felt like I really got something out of it today.'

'Eadie what are you doing down here sweetheart?' asked Max as their daughter suddenly appeared at the door.

Jennifer glared at her.

'I can't sleep, my arm's itchy.'

Jennifer stopped glaring, felt guilty and rearranged her face into one of concern instead. 'Hang on, I'll go and find the Calpol.'

One hour later and Eadie was finally asleep, Jennifer and Max were both stuffed with food and had polished off a bottle and a half of red between them. Jennifer's face was hot and she could feel her tongue furring up from the tannin already.

None of this was particularly conducive to sex but she didn't care.

'Right, shall we go upstairs then?' she suggested, almost briskly. If she could have done, at this point she'd have just herded him up the stairs if that was what it took. Anything to just get the deed done.

'Yes,' said Max 'let me just check in with Judith first though. Make sure everything was ok today, what with me being out of the office.'

'Why don't you do that after?' asked Jennifer, trying not to sound intensely irritated.

'Because I'd rather get it out of the way,' said Max 'And also because I don't want to disturb her too late.'

Jennifer was definitely quite drunk because she felt like sticking her tongue out and giving that whole notion the finger. Still, she found some restraint from somewhere.

'Ok well be quick won't you,' she said, walking as sexily as she could out of the room 'And I'll be waiting upstairs for you....although, actually hang on, I need to take some water up. That wine's made my mouth so dry.'

Oh Christ, when did life get so unspontaneous she thought, returning to the tap.

Twenty minutes later Jennifer was starting to get deeply pissed off. She'd been lying wantonly on the bed in her slutty underwear waiting for Max for ages now. As soon as she'd got upstairs, the first thing she'd done was to check that the girls were definitely asleep. Upon finding out they were she'd stripped off, only leaving on her new Basque, stockings, suspenders and the G-string (cheesewire). She'd also put on her highest pair of stilettoes, glugged down half a pint of water, brushed her teeth and then arranged herself on the bed and waited, all the while contemplating how she was pretty sure that there had once been a time when she and Max had barely been able to make it up the stairs so eager were they to have sex with one another. Making her wait like this was so depressing and hardly made her feel very attractive. It was almost like he'd be doing her a favour or something. As if having intercourse would be his final chore of the day. I mean, why of all times did he have to pick now to phone bloody Judith? He'd had all day to do it. If he'd been truly looking forward to a night of passion like she had, wouldn't he have called her earlier and got it out of the way?

From downstairs the sound of Max's phone conversation floated upwards to the landing. It was like pouring petrol on the flames of her suspicion. He sounded so jovial, so alive, and like he was making every effort to be charming and engaging. This wasn't helping her mood at all, and if he laughed that nauseating laugh again she'd be tempted to take off one of her shoes and stab him in the eye with the heel.

Another ten minutes later and Jennifer felt stupid. She also felt unloved, unbelievably jealous, rejected and because she was trying so hard not to cry and be sad, her emotions were steadily transforming into crystallised fury. How could he do this to her?

By now Jennifer had given up sprawling on the bed and had decamped out on to the landing, so that she could hear exactly what was being said. Their conversation was all fairly innocuous and largely unrelated to work. They were gossiping and sharing private jokes, which only confirmed that this was a chat they definitely didn't need to be having now. The rawness of what she was feeling, combined with how much wine she'd drunk meant that by the time he did finally terminate the call she was ready for a fight.

'How could you?' she said to a surprised Max as he finally rounded the top of the stairs only to find her squatting on the landing dressed like a prostitute.

'What are you doing? What are you wearing?'

'I'm wearing what I thought you might possibly find sexy enough to want to fuck me in but clearly I was wrong. Why did you have to talk to that stupid cow for so long? You knew I was waiting for you up here. It's so rude,' she cried, hot jealousy welling up inside her, like a volcano about to erupt.

'Calm down,' said Max, only fuelling the fire further 'I told you I had to phone her because I took the day off today to help *you*. I'm sorry it went on for a bit but you know what Judith's like once she gets going.'

'Oh, and I suppose you were physically unable to say something like *'I need to keep this quick because I'm in the middle of something'*. Or, *'I'm sorry Judith I've got to go because I haven't had sex with my wife for so long she doesn't know if I even love her anymore'*. Or' *I must dash, my wife's dressed like a slut, only I've got to the point in life where I don't care because I'd rather talk to you*." Jennifer was so upset by now she knew she was looking deranged but was unable to stop herself. She just needed him to say sorry.

'You're being ridiculous.'

Jennifer recoiled because of course she *felt* ridiculous. There was no part of her that wanted this to be happening. This was supposed to be their evening for a bit of love and romance. Instead, she was dressed in this 'get up' which she'd hoped he'd find really sexy but which was now making her feel like a cheap hooker, and she felt totally embarrassed. Worse still, Judith had impinged on their lives once again. She couldn't stand it.

'I hate you,' she cried.

'Oh for fuck's sake, you're being so dramatic. Just because you've had a couple of glasses of wine you act like an idiot.'

'Fuck you,' screamed Jennifer.

'Ssh, keep your voice down you'll wake the girls.'

Jennifer was trembling with rage and hurt. She took a sharp inhalation of breath in an attempt to calm herself. She could sense it was crucial that she did. Max had never taken kindly to histrionics. Plus, she really didn't want to wake the children.

'Look, I'm sorry I've got myself into this state,' she said, happy to acknowledge that she was acting like a crazy woman but also determined to make him understand why. 'I just want you to try and get how I feel. I've made loads of effort for tonight and I had really hoped that you might like what I was wearing. I wanted you to fancy me and for us to feel like we used to when we had sex. I wanted us to be close.'

'You look great,' said Max unconvincingly.

'But instead,' Jennifer said, smearing mascara across her face 'it's just another time which has been dominated by Judith, who you know I feel insecure about as it is.'

Max traipsed wearily from the landing into their room where he sunk onto their bed, shook his head and rubbed his face with his hands. 'I'm too tired for this Jen. I just want to go to bed now.'

Following him in, she felt sick. His lack of effort to make things better made her stomach turn. She was so upset, yet intuition told her to keep digging. Why should she let him get away with this shitty treatment? Why was she constantly apologising all the time? It wasn't *all* her fault and she was fed up with being made to feel like it was, like she was mad.

'Do you have feelings for her?'

Suddenly Jennifer was convinced that this was the crux of the matter and probably had been for weeks.

'Oh Christ,' said Max, sounding angry now.

'I mean it Max. I want to know. Do you have feelings for Judith? Because I think you do. I think that's why you hardly look at me these days. I know you think I'm a mad, crazy cow but you're the one who keeps making me feel like that. You used to make me feel beautiful and loved and happy and now I'm just miserable all the time and feel like I'm constantly waiting for you to announce something.'

Max looked pained and refused to even glance in her direction, staring into the middle distance instead.

'I don't have feelings for her,' he said quietly.

'Swear on the girl's lives,' said Jennifer so menacingly that Max actually gulped.

And then he did something that practically cracked her heart in two. He looked at her briefly and then looked away again and sighed. A heavy, sad, terrible sigh that felt like such a huge sign of betrayal that Jennifer thought she might actually be about to have a panic attack. Her whole body went cold and clammy. She wondered if she was going to be sick or faint.

'You'd better tell me everything,' she said 'and I mean everything.'

Even as she was saying this she was wondering if this was it. It was so surreal. Could this be the end of her marriage, of life as she knew it? She willed Max with every cell in her body to make it all go away. To look at her in such a way that she would know he was playing with her, trying to be funny. Only that could make things OK. But he didn't.

Instead he said, looking truly wretched 'Jen, I swear there's nothing to tell. Nothing has happened and that's the god's honest truth...'

'But...'

'But nothing,' he repeated, getting up and coming over to her.

'Don't lie to me,' she warned him and as he reached over to touch her arm her entire body flinched, a totally reflex action. It was as if sub consciously she was scared he would harm her. This was harming her. The pain she was experiencing was on a physical level. Again she wished fervently she wasn't dressed as she was and yet it hardly mattered.

'Tell me.'

'Nothing's happened.'

'Max, the truth, please?'

Max gazed at her, his expression bleak, his eyes searching hers as if he hoped to find an answer through her. And then he shrugged, almost imperceptibly, and that was all she needed to know.

Jennifer froze and for a fraction of a second time seemed to stand still. The house fell silent, and then she ran. Stopping only to discard her heels, she hurtled out of the room and practically threw herself down the stairs in a bid to flee. Downstairs in the hall she desperately searched for something to put on her feet that didn't come with a six-inch heel. These would do. An old pair of disgusting gardening Crocs her mother had left the last time she'd been round. They were far too big but Jennifer didn't care, she just needed to be away. To escape from what was happening. She'd go to Karen's. That's what she'd do. She wouldn't stop to think until she'd got there. Wouldn't stop to contemplate what this all meant until she was safe with her friend. Karen was only ten minutes away. That's where she'd go.

When Max came thundering down the stairs after her she only increased her efforts to get away but he tried to block her exit by standing in front of the door.

'What are you doing? You can't go out of the house dressed like that,' he said, his face frantic 'Jen, just stay so we can talk. You've got it all wrong anyway.'

'Oh I don't think so,' she cried 'In fact, the only thing I've got wrong is putting up with your bullshit for this long. Now get out of my way.'

'Look, calm down,' tried Max again, using the same tone he often used on the kids 'You simply can't go out dressed like that.'

'Fuck off,' she spat, grabbing a coat from the hooks in the hall and shoving it on. She grabbed her phone from the hall stand so she could ring Karen and then, with every bit of strength in her body, shoved Max out of the way so that she could wrench open the door. Once free she sprinted down the road as fast as her oversized shoes would allow.

Max didn't know what to do. He suspected she'd be going to Karen's, or to start a new job as a pole dancer. Either or. Part of him thought it was probably for the best that she took some time out to calm down. Another part of him wanted to run after her, to grab her, hold her and tell her it was all going to be ok. Suddenly he was hit by a monumental urge to simply say sorry. How had they got here? How had he let things get to this point? She was right of course. Over the last few months she'd picked up on his absence. Not a physical absence but his mind had been elsewhere and rather than admit it he'd let her think she was the one to blame. It was ridiculous and in that second Max regretted what had happened and wished he'd been able to tell her it had only been a fumble. They hadn't had sex…. yet.

Thank god.

Tonight, he'd seen the hurt and grief it would cause. It had been the sharp reminder he'd needed that he didn't want to lose his wife. He loved his wife. He wanted to throttle her sometimes and Judith's attentions had been desperately flattering but he needed to sort his life out.

He felt totally drained. Making sure the door was on the latch he walked out and stood at the gate where he called down the road 'Jen, what the hell do you think you're doing? Come back. For goodness sake, you've made your point.'

She didn't so much as look back though and eventually she was a pin prick at the bottom of the road. The boring bloke from number forty-two who'd witnessed everything and been rubbernecking quite spectacularly, gave him a judgemental look as he passed the house. Max returned it with a glowering frown. Right, there was nothing he could do. He'd leave it for a bit, let her cool off and then send her a text telling her he loved her and that he was the biggest idiot on the planet. With that last thought, Max was just about to head back indoors, when he heard the ungodly sound of screeching tyres, a sickening crunch and a scream. From what he could make out the sound had come from the end of the street. His heart skipped a beat and the fear Max experienced in that second was white and petrifying. And then he prayed.

42 | Present Day

One of Jennifer's eyes, her left one, slowly opened. She couldn't focus on anything specific. As light flooded in it took a while for her pupils to adjust. They'd become so accustomed to a vista of black. Everything was blurry and before her vision had had a chance to fine-tune itself, the eye snapped shut again.

Half an hour later the same eye opened once more and then the second one fluttered open as well. This time Max was in the room having just returned from the canteen where he'd bought himself a packet of Highland shortbread and a cup of tea.

'Jen,' he cried. The sound of his voice penetrated through to Jennifer. Max was there. Where was *there* though? That bit was foggy and she was pretty sure that although she'd like to ask him, she wouldn't be able to. Articulating anything felt impossible. She didn't know how to.

An hour or two later and Jennifer's brain and body were making huge leaps back into the real world. The doctors had swarmed around her as soon as Max had raised the alarm. Blood had been taken to check for levels of serum glucose, calcium, sodium, potassium, magnesium, phosphate, urea, and creatinine. Then, as Max had known they would, they wheeled his wife off to perform yet another MRI brain scan on her.

A while later and the results were in. As far as they could tell, her brain was showing no signs of permanent damage, although it would be a long time before they could completely confirm it. After five long weeks Jennifer was officially coming out of her coma.

Max couldn't believe it. What he'd prayed for each day was happening. It felt as close to a miracle as anything he'd ever experienced.

For the next couple of days Jennifer would wake up for short bursts, and sometimes be profoundly confused, at other times relatively lucid. For the time being she was suffering from dysarthria, the inability to articulate any speech, although she didn't appear to have any other disabilities.

The moment when she recognised her husband and was finally able to speak was the best of all.

'Hey you,' he said, stroking her hand gently with one finger. She was looking right at him and not as though he was a stranger as she had been previously.

'What's happened?'

'You were in an accident Jen. You got hit by a car. You've been asleep for weeks. We didn't know.....' Max stopped, took a gulp and composed himself.

'Eadie and Polly?'

At this Max was overwhelmed by relief and happiness and it took every bit of his willpower not to break down. 'They're fine Jen. They're absolutely fine. I don't think either of them ever doubted they'd be seeing you again. I think they reckon you're Sleeping Beauty.'

That was more than enough for her first proper conversation though and as the doctor urged Max to let his wife rest again, Jennifer fell into a deep sleep.

'Is she ok?' asked Max as he tended to every time she did this. 'She hasn't gone into a coma again has she?'

'No,' said the doctor, who happened to have been making his rounds 'Don't worry Mr Wright. Your wife is doing phenomenally well. Recovery usually occurs very gradually and Jennifer will take a while to acquire the ability to respond for any decent length of time. However, like I said, she is doing fantastically well at this stage and I really think her outlook is extremely positive. But, you must be prepared for your wife to still appear confused at times and try not to worry if she does. It's totally normal after somebody has been in such a deep coma.'

It was a good thing the doctor had warned him about this because later on that night in the early hours Jennifer started muttering in her sleep. Max who had been sleeping fitfully on the camp bed (which by this point in time he officially hated and viewed as an actual instrument of torture) sat bolt upright. 'Jen?' he whispered, but when it became clear that she was only sleep talking he got up and went over to see what she was saying. Although then he sort of wished he hadn't….

The next day, Karen brought the girls into hospital in the afternoon during visiting hours. They'd all decided that with so much less machinery around her it was time for them to finally see their Mummy again.

It couldn't have gone better. The timing was great. Jennifer was awake and aware of their presence. Tears poured down her face, she was so happy to see them. Just the fact she recognised them was another incredibly encouraging sign that she was on the road to a full recovery. Eadie and Polly had been lectured at length about not wearing their mother out and were rising to the occasion beautifully, being quiet and good as gold.

Until at one point they asked if they could sing a song to her. 'What song?' asked Karen.

'I'm sexy and I know it?' suggested Eadie.

'No, that's probably not the best idea,' her godmother vetoed 'Why don't you sing Mummy a lovely lullaby instead. Rock a bye baby or something?'

The girls obeyed and as they started to sing, Karen took the opportunity to take Max to one side and ask 'How are you bearing up?'

'Good,' said Max, an emotional wreck 'I just can't believe she's going to be OK.'

'I know. Thank god.'

'Karen?'

'Yes?'

'I'm so sorry you know. I never ever wanted this to happen and I can tell you now that I will spend the rest of my life making sure she's happy.'

'I know you will,' said Karen sadly 'And it's fine, you really don't need to apologise to me. Besides, now you can apologise to Jen herself.'

Max suddenly looked sheepish. It was obvious Jennifer had confided in her friend pre accident that things weren't great but she wouldn't know everything.

'Listen,' reassured Karen 'I understand and I don't judge anyone else's relationships. After all, you get to our stage and learn that life isn't black and white like you think it is when you're young. It's bloody grey.'

'Fifty shades?'

'Ha ha,' said Karen 'And no, more like one thousand shades of grey, but it'll all work itself out now that Jen's on the mend. I know it will. I've seen how much you love her and I know for a fact she adores you.'

'Thanks,' said Max 'For everything. For all your help with the girls, everything.'

'You're very welcome,' said Karen.

'Oh, and by the way,' said Max 'I'm making a donation to the hospital.'

'Oh, nice idea.'

'Mm, I'm buying them a single bed with a really comfortable mattress so that the next poor bastard who ends up kipping in here might actually get some sleep.'

'Good one. Now, Max, do you think we should stop Eadie and Polly singing? Otherwise I'm worried Jennifer might wish she was back in a coma.'

'Oh god yes, yes,' agreed Max, jolting back to the here and now and realising how right she was. The caterwauling was pretty terrible and Jennifer was looking glassy eyed, dazed and a bit exhausted. 'Excellent sick joke by the way. Jen would approve.'

'Thanks,' said Karen.

EPILOGUE | 6 Months Later

Jennifer and Max were getting ready to have Karen, Pete, their daughter Suzy and Jen's parents over for Sunday lunch. It was December and the kind of day you wouldn't go out in unless you absolutely had to, or unless someone else was cooking you a lovely roast chicken and an apple crumble. The house smelt of cooking, the girls were playing peacefully with their play-dough and Max was working out what sort of wine they should have and laying the table. Jennifer's iPod was on shuffle, selecting great tune after great tune. The atmosphere was harmonious, cosy. She felt genuinely content. Domestic bloody bliss.

It had taken a while to get here. After the accident, she and Max hadn't exactly clicked into happy mode straight away. The marital bed had repelled her for months as she tried to digest what had or hadn't gone on between her husband and Judith. For a long time, the slightest thing would remind her of his betrayal. There were many tears, remonstrations and moments where she wasn't sure they'd make it.

Max had done the right thing by showing tremendous patience. He had understood why at times she needed endless reassuring, to cry, or to be furious with him. He'd bent over backwards to prove how sorry he was and to demonstrate how much he regretted the 'almost affair.' He was horrified by how much he'd hurt his wife. Eventually, his anguish and regret were so clear to see her pain began to ease. Then, when he sat down and wrote an email to Judith, in front of her, declaring that their contact had to be minimal and work related only from that day forward, she felt a great deal better. The fact he hadn't had full sex with Judith helped. The fact he'd considered it made her feel violently sick. But time heals and Jennifer was finding it easier to remember what had brought them together in the first place and was working hard to cauterise her feelings whenever Judith infiltrated her brain.

And now, months later, they were doing OK and if someone was to ask her 'Is this it?' she'd reply 'I hope so.'

As she added some ground cinnamon to the apples which were stewing in the pan, Max slid up behind her and kissed her neck 'Hello beautiful.'

'Hi.'

'Are you ok?'

'Yeah, you?'

'I literally couldn't be happier than I am right now,' Max said sincerely. 'I just had such a big pang for you and for what we've got. Never leave me, will you?'

'Given that I haven't left by now,' said Jennifer 'at this point it looks like you're stuck with me. Unless you do anything stupid ever again.'

'I won't,' said Max, looking like he really meant it. This experience had put him off for life.

Jennifer laughed 'Oh, by the way, I've been meaning to tell you….' she wrinkled up her nose and paused while she debated if this was the right moment to broach the subject or not.

'Go on.'

'Well, it's just that Lee from the office - you know lovely Lee? Anyway, I always go on about how much I miss dancing and music, so he's said that if I want to go clubbing with him and his mates, I can. I said I might. He specifically said there's one place where loads of older people go, it's very eclectic apparently. What do you reckon? Do you think that's tragic?'

'I reckon you should go,' said Max at once 'As long as you don't snog 'lovely' Lee or any of his mates.'

'Really?'

'Yeah, why not? If you want to go why shouldn't you? I won't come with you because I'd rather stick needles in my eyes but if you want to go out and let your hair down, I'm not going to stop you. No snogging's the only proviso.'

'Er, obviously I won't snog anyone,' tutted Jennifer indignantly as an acute flash of anger reminded her that he'd done exactly that. Still, if she was going to forgive him, she couldn't just say she did or they'd never recover.

'You'd better not,' said Max 'because you're only ever allowed to snog me. Speaking of which, I hope you'll be in with me again tonight?'

'I'm sure I will.'

As he got back to laying the table, Jennifer found herself grinning into her apples. Things with Max were finally back on track in that department and whilst their relationship still had that sense of familiarity and comfort, which stemmed from years of togetherness, it wasn't breeding contempt. There was still hard work ahead but they were getting there......

Jennifer was taking responsibility for her own feelings too and was less restless as a result. The grass probably wasn't greener after all and even if it was, she no longer cared as much. She knew Max and she would have rough patches again, that was a given. No one ever warns you that marriage is a meal which starts with the pudding and then works backwards, but she was far less confused than she'd been and was determined to stick at it.

Lunch was a raucous, chaotic, but lovely affair. Jennifer was quieter than usual. There was something about having her parents there, along with her best friend that was making her feel pathetically grateful and emotional. Polly had sat on her lap for much of lunch. She'd been quite physically clingy ever since the accident which was completely understandable. If anything, Jennifer felt the same.

After lunch though the children slipped away from the table so they could escape to play, leaving the adults to chat.

'So, Jen's off clubbing with 'lovely' Lee from work soon,' said Max.

'With who?' asked Jennifer's mum, Lesley.

'Thanks Max,' said Jennifer, feeling about fifteen years old 'He's just a friend from work Mum.'

'A young, handsome friend,' said Max, winding her up.

'Ooh you're going clubbing? Are you? I can't remember the last time I went clubbing, can I come?' said Karen 'When are you going?'

'When I'm totally up to it,' said Jennifer 'and of course you can come. In fact *please* come. I'd be so much happier with you there. It sounds amazing and he's promised me the crowd are very mixed; lots of thirty somethings.'

'You can't go clubbing,' said Pete, looking horrified.

'Why the bloody hell not?' said Karen.

'You'll get laughed at,' said Pete, which annoyed Jennifer.

'Oh, I don't know,' said Max, who was definitely three sheets to the wind 'I reckon they'll be a right couple of 'milfs'.'

'What's a 'milf'?' asked Lesley.

'Oh god,' despaired Jennifer.

'Nothing,' said Max hastily 'Just……. mums you'd like to… fancy.'

'Ooh,' said Lesley, striking a pose at her husband 'Am I a milf then Nigel?'

'Oh wow,' said Jennifer, trying not to laugh and frowning at Max.

Pete was snorting into his napkin.

'Aaaanyway,' said Max, changing the subject 'The point is, I think it's great you're going. Although I've put in a caveat haven't I, Jen, which is that she's not allowed to snog anyone. Oh, and I hope no one called Joe's going to be there?'

'What?' said Jennifer, her smile instantly fading.

'I said I hope no one called Joe's going to be there.'

Karen looked visibly perturbed by this comment but not as much as Jennifer did. She'd gone very pale.

'Why would you say that?' asked Jennifer.

'I forgot to tell you,' said Max, still laughing 'When you were in hospital it was the oddest thing. You'd not long been out of the coma and you were sleep talking one night. Anyway, I was desperate to work out what you were saying. Think I was hoping for something along the lines of 'oh Max I love you so much' only instead, you kept muttering the name Joe. It was very weird.'

Karen studied her friend's expression and couldn't wait to get her on her own.

An hour or so later and she was able to. Everyone had gone through to the lounge to entertain the kids with some board games and have a look at the football. Only Jennifer and Karen had stayed in the kitchen.

'Jen, you know what Max said earlier about you sleep talking?' began Karen tentatively, seizing her opportunity.

'I know. How strange was that?'

'It's just, I don't know how much Max has filled you in about when you were in the coma.'

'A fair bit,' said Jennifer, grabbing a clean tea towel from the drawer. 'Although I don't think I did a lot when I was in it, wasn't the most scintillating I've ever been. He's mainly filled me in a lot about how uncomfortable his bed was.'

'Ok, well, there was one night when you had a seizure. I was there.'

'Oh god,' gasped Jennifer 'I don't think I did know that. That must have been horrific for you.'

'It wasn't the best night of my life,' admitted Karen drily 'But anyway, the point is, that night you said one word out loud.'

'Did I? What was it, help?'

'No,' snorted Karen, laughing.

'Vodka?'

'No, you arse. You said Joe.'

Jennifer immediately stopped grinning 'Are you serious?'

'Yes,' nodded Karen 'Which is why I didn't say anything over lunch. Jen, have you met someone? Who do you know who's called Joe because there must be someone?'

'I genuinely don't know,' said Jennifer, shaking her head, confused beyond belief. 'Wait here. I need to show you something.'

'Jen, what the hell is going on? Where are you going?'

A minute or so later Jennifer returned with her laptop. Making sure the kitchen door was firmly shut, she placed it on the island.

'If I show you this, I need to know you won't say anything.'

Karen nodded.

'Here,' said Jen.

It was a page from *ReUNIon*. Staring back at her was a picture of a man she didn't recognize. A man called Joe. His name was listed alongside his photo in the usual *ReUNIon* format and at the top of the page it said he was a 'friend' of Tim Purcell's.

'Since when are you friends with Tim Purcell on *ReUNIon*?' asked Karen, astounded.

'Since the other week when I sent him a request. I wanted to look at his contacts. I sent requests to all my exes as it goes. I just had this…. compulsion to look at their friends, even though I wasn't entirely sure what I was looking for. Anyway, look at the name.'

'I know,' she replied. 'Joe. But who is he?'

Jennifer shrugged. 'I don't know.'

Karen was so confused.

'Look, I know this sounds mad but when he came up, I felt like I knew him, or that I'm supposed to. I don't know. Maybe I'm even supposed to find him? I just had this sense, and now you've both confirmed that someone called Joe has obviously cropped up somewhere along the line and maybe I just can't remember him because of the accident? It's driving me mad and, in a way, it's a relief hearing that I probably do know him somehow.'

As far as Karen was concerned this train of thought was madness. She decided to nip it in the bud as quickly as she could.

'Jen, listen to me, you've had a terrible, terrible time of it but I'm not going to patronize you by pretending any of this makes sense. It's crazy talk. No doubt brought on by the extreme bump to the head you suffered. You said the name Joe? Big deal. That doesn't mean to say that just because someone you once knew knows a Joe that he's got anything to do with you.'

Jennifer wasn't convinced. Why had she felt such a strong urge to reach out to people from her past in order to search for someone or something? And, if this man was nothing to her, then why did her whole body react so strongly every time she looked at that picture? It was a face she didn't know, yet it felt so familiar. Of course, she was totally aware that none of this made any sense. It was why she'd avoided telling anyone. Maybe she *was* going mad? If she didn't understand what was happening to her, how could she expect anyone else to?

'Jen, Max is desperate to make everything ok and if you want to save your marriage you need to be concentrating on him. Not some man you've never even met.'

'I know, and I am, only I feel like I *do* have some kind of connection to this man and every time anyone's said the name Joe today, I've honestly wanted to burst into tears. But I can't think why. It's so frustrating. I feel like my brain knows but can't tell me. It's the oddest thing. But then I've had it a bit since the accident with other things.'

'Had what?'

Jennifer struggled to put it into words 'I'm not sure really. Just this feeling that I'm really lucky to have you in my life for instance, and that things could be different, I guess. Also…..'

'What?' Karen could see she was really rattled.

'I don't know, I feel like I've lost things too. Like when I hear that name or sometimes when I look at the kids, I get this huge pang of emotion. I don't know. I probably am just going a bit mad or something.'

'But you're definitely not *seeing* someone called Joe?'

'No,' she said adamantly.

'Ok, that's fine then, only if you are, I hope you'd feel able to tell me. I wouldn't judge.'

'You're my oldest friend. I'd tell you, but I'm not.'

'Ok good.'

Jennifer looked so unsettled Karen went over to give her a hug. 'Come here you.'

'I don't know what's up with me today,' sniffed Jennifer into her friend's shoulder.

'You've been through a lot. It's bound to catch up now and then.'

'I know,' said Jennifer, pulling away so she could ask her something. 'Karen, do you believe in fate? Do you believe our lives are mapped out for us? That Max and I were supposed to be together?'

Karen pondered for a moment 'Not sure really. Am I supposed to be with Pete? Were we drawn together by fate, mistake, circumstances or completely randomly? I don't know. Though I'm enough of a realist to know that if I'd been born somewhere completely different, New Zealand for example, no doubt I would now be in a relationship with a New Zealander.'

'I guess so.'

'Oh, I don't know. I suppose, Jen, my answer to your question is that deep down I don't believe Pete's the *only* man in the whole wide world I could be compatible with. But I'm glad I've ended up with him and can see the romance in simply sticking with one other. Even if sometimes I'm tempted to kill him. I guess life's a mixture of fate and how you choose to steer the fate you've been handed. It all comes down to the choices that we make doesn't it? Like, if you'd buggered off with Aidan for instance. Weren't we saying only the other day that you'd probably be living the life of riley on the beach?'

Jennifer shrugged. She honestly wasn't so sure.

'Or if you'd stayed with Tim or Steve, perhaps you'd be better off, happier, frustrated or who knows? But for what it's worth, I reckon you're one of the lucky ones Jen. I reckon, despite everything that's happened, you're with a good man.

'I know,' said Jennifer and as the two friends embraced, she knew that certain things in life would always remain a mystery and that perhaps they should. When it came to relationships, there were always so many factors involved such as timing and fate, that our decisions weren't necessarily right or wrong, but simply what needed to happen in that moment. And sometimes the easiest decisions weren't the right ones and vice versa.

Just then the sound of sweeping strings filled the room.

Breaking away from Karen, she looked round to discover that Max had come back into the kitchen and selected a track on her iPod. It was Bittersweet Symphony. Their song. Catching her eye he looked adoringly at her and then did something which made her feel young again and utterly loved. He made his hand into a fist and patted it over where his heart was.

'Love you,' he mouthed at her.

'Love you too,' she said tearfully.

And with that her husband blew her a kiss and wandered off, happy and content. And Jennifer knew, it was time to enjoy the present, to stop wondering about the past and projecting into the future. It was time to just be. She'd made her decision, there was no room for regret and that was a wonderful thing.

Jemma Forte grew up wanting to write for glossy magazines, be a famous actress or work in Clarks shoe shop (she loved the foot measuring device). Her parents didn't want her to go to stage school because, according to them, she was 'precocious enough already.' However, they actively encouraged her obsession with reading and writing and she wrote her first book, 'Mizzy the Germ,' when she was eight. She even sent it to a publisher (unwittingly backing up the precocious theory).

In 1998 she became a Disney Channel presenter and after five years leaping about there, went on to present shows for ITV, BBC1 and BBC2 and Channel 4.

These days she can be found on C5's Jeremy Vine Show where she is a regular panellist, on QVC where she guests for *Molton Brown*, as a contributor on shows such as GMB, and on the radio. She lives in London with her children, Lily and Freddie.

Mad Wife Crisis is Jemma's third novel.

Reading Group Discussion Points

1. Is there such a thing in life as 'The One?' Or is it more likely that we could have a great connection with thousands of people. We just won't ever meet them all.

2. In the book, Jennifer is able to see how life could have been had she made different decisions. In reality, would this be a gift, or a terrible burden?

3. We meet three men from Jennifer's past. She split up with each of them for good enough reasons at the time but perhaps she also wasn't ready to settle down. Are you more likely to marry someone partly because you have met them at the right time in your life?

4. Jennifer is suffering from a mid- life crisis. This is a stage which the book takes very seriously and chooses not to laugh at. But what do you think a mid- life crisis is by definition? What causes it? And is it an inevitable phase which most of us will go through, or have gone through, upon hitting the half- way point of our lives?

5. Jennifer's therapist suggests during their session that if she were to change her life partner she may only be 'exchanging one set of problems for another.' Does this resonate?

6. Max was unfaithful to Jennifer emotionally and physically. However, he didn't go as far as to have actual sex with Judith. Should this make his behaviour easier to forgive?

7. Mad Wife Crisis explores how the partner we choose to share our lives with affects our circumstances greatly. It governs who our in- laws are, where we live, what we do, even our finances. Is this something you ever stop to think

about and would any of the above criteria prevent you from being with someone? For instance, if you had a mother in law you despised how much would this affect your relationship and govern whether you stayed or not? Or are all external factors irrelevant in terms of how happy someone makes you?

8. All Jennifer's men are very different. Does what we look for in a life partner change as we get older, or do we just learn from experience what we need from a partner?

9. When we first meet Jennifer, she is thinking a lot about her life and about her past. Is there one person you think of from time to time and wonder how life would be if you'd stayed with them? Or do you prefer to never look back?

10. When Jennifer is going out with Tim her friendship with Karen suffers greatly. In tunnel two it becomes clear that had she stayed with Tim their relationship would have deteriorated further. Are friendships often affected by who their friend is married to or going out with? If so, is this right?

11. Divorce is very common. Do people give up too easily? Or are we just benefiting from living in a time when people aren't condemned if a marriage fails?

Printed in Great Britain
by Amazon

43897975R00262